# OUTRIDER

# OUTRIDER

## A NOVEL

## STEVEN JOHN

NIGHT SHADE BOOKS
NEW YORK

Night Shade books may be purchased in bulk at special discounts for sales promotion, corporate gifts, fund-raising, or educational purposes. Special editions can also be created to specifications. For details, contact the Special Sales Department, Night Shade Books, 307 West 36th Street, 11th Floor, New York, NY 10018 or info@skyhorsepublishing.com.

Night Shade Books™ is a trademark of Skyhorse Publishing, Inc.®, a Delaware corporation.

Visit our website at www.nightshadebooks.com.

10 9 8 7 6 5 4 3 2 1

Library of Congress Cataloging-in-Publication Data is available on file.

Cover design by Danielle Ceccolini
Cover illustration by Yip Lee

Print ISBN: 978-1-59780-533-9
Ebook ISBN: 978-1-59780-556-8
Printed in the United States of America

**For my brother. A finer man I've yet to meet.**

"These men were so akin, so near each other, that the slightest gesture, the tone of voice, told both more than could be said in words."
—Leo Tolstoy, Anna Karenina

# 1

"We got a leech."

"Hm," Scofield muttered, shifting in his saddle. "I don't see him."

"You will," Kretch whispered back, nodding slowly. His voice was dry, grating. "He's down the line."

The sun was nearly overhead, flattening the few features that marked the beige expanse of loam. Scofield pulled the brim of his hat lower on his forehead and cupped his hands around his eyes to block the glare. He began a steady scan along the row of towering QV pillars, letting his eyes lose focus. There it was, that thin trail, almost invisible but unmistakable to the trained eye: a buried tap line. Scofield let his eyes drift along the line and sure enough not five seconds later he spotted a telltale depression in the sandy soil.

"Oh yeah. I got him."

"Looks like it's just one all by his lonesome," Kretch said, leaning off to one side of his slate gray colt to spit.

"Follow the line or grab 'im?"

"Let's just get him now."

"Suits me fine," said Scofield, drawing his long-barreled revolver. "Cover me, then. I could use a stretch anyway."

Kretch drew a rifle from his saddle bag and checked the chamber as Scofield slid off his brown mare. His boots crunched loudly on the dry earth, and he paused to look for any movement from the leech. When none came he took a few slow, cautious steps towards the concave patch of sand, then broke into a run and closed the thirty yards in seconds.

Scofield leapt through the air and landed with both boots right in the center of the shallow depression. The tarp, held up by and loosely covered with sand, collapsed beneath his weight and from the newly revealed hole came a cry of pain and surprise. Scofield scrambled out of the ditch and threw the canvas sheet aside, training his pistol on the leech.

He was an old fellow. Bald with a wispy, five-day beard. His flesh was red and craggy and his eyes yellow. They were filled with fear.

"I . . . I—please don't shoot!" he stammered.

"Get up," Scofield said, his voice low. The man rose to his feet and then climbed out of the hole, his joints popping and cracking. He wore a dirty gray button-down and old jeans and his boots were scuffed and shabby. His stooped shoulders rose and fell quickly as he sucked in shallow breaths, eyes averted.

Wilton Kretch came up from behind, still mounted and leading Scofield's horse. He dropped both sets of reins and rested his repeater across his lap, the barrel aiming toward the leech.

"All alone out here, old timer?"

"Yes." The man replied barely above a whisper.

"Well, that oughtta make things easier," Kretch sneered. The leech's eyes snapped up, wide with fear, and Scofield shot Kretch a quick look. Not quite one of disapproval—just a look.

"Wilton here don't mean to threaten you, mister," Scofield said with false brightness. "He just means for you to know your options. Which ain't many." He turned and looked out across the barren plains as if to punctuate his point. It was hot for October. Easily ninety out. The faintest breeze sighed across the land now and then but it was not enough to soothe, merely to be felt.

"See, thing is, we got a job to do out here. We gotta protect them sun stacks." Scofield said, approaching the trembling man and laying a hand on his shoulder. He turned the leech and swept his hand along the miles and miles of quantum voltaic pillars. "But you know that, dontcha? Know all about it, I'm sure. Let's check your hookup." Scofield knelt and dug in the soil until he found the buried tap line. He wrapped a fist around the thick, insulated cord and gave it a solid shake. The cord popped up from the sand, revealing a clear trail to one of the QV pillars. Scofield straightened up and pushed the man toward the array, calling over his shoulder. "Wilton, why dontcha check out that hole."

Kretch dismounted and made his way over to the leech's burrow. Scofield guided the man toward the nearest QV pillar, keeping his revolver vaguely trained. Beads of sweat streamed down the old man's neck and he wrung his hands constantly. For a moment Scofield thought to whisper something reassuring, but let the notion go and squared his jaw. The man was a thief, after all, even if he were old and frightened. They stopped in the shade of the massive panels above.

"Oh yeah. Pretty."

"I didn't mean to . . . to do wrong. Just ain't got nothin' else."

Scofield ignored the man, turning his back on him, and studied the power tap he'd set up. It was a simple, standard design: two big magnets and some copper spooling held together by a wooden frame. This contraption was slid over one of the steel braces of the pillar. It would draw off enough power to run a life free from governmental regulation or to trade or sell for a few bucks, but never enough to be noticed.

"Set your spool a bit close to the steel, didn't ya?" Scofield asked over his shoulder, running a palm across his unshaven face.

"It's perfectly safe." The man replied, his voice steady for the first time.

"Yer an expert then, hmm?"

"I didn't mean that. I just—"

"Yeah, listening to you talk ain't what I got on my mind right now. Why don't you be a good little leech and dismantle this thing here and then maybe all three of us will chat a moment."

Scofield brushed past the old man and walked back to Kretch and the horses. He ran a hand along his mare's flanks, whispering "Old one, huh Reese?" The horse turned her head at the sound of her name and Scofield pulled a canteen from the saddle bag. He took a long pull of water himself, then cupped his hand and let Reese use it as a bowl as he slowly trickled the tepid liquid into his palm.

"Nothing to write home about." Kretch said as he climbed out of the hole. He coughed and shook sand from his long gray jacket, stamping his boots to kick dust off them. "A bit of food and drink and a worn out book. Blankets. Some tools. Not even a change of clothes."

"What book is it?"

"Didn't check."

"No matter. What d'you think?"

"Long enough way back to camp just us two." Kretch said quietly, looking over at the old man who was busily breaking apart his tap.

"That's true." Scofield nodded. "Other hand, I don't see this old fellah causing much more trouble. Think we oughtta bring him in."

"Hell, fine by me," Kretch shrugged. He raised his voice loud enough that the old man could surely hear and went on saying: "But those ancient legs give out, it's Reese that drags him, not Shady."

"Fine by me."

"I'll follow the line and find his collector. Any trouble, squeeze two quick shots."

Scofield tossed back his head and laughed. "You be sure to rush back'n help with this one. Got a killer's eye!" Kretch let out a rasping cackle of his own and turned to look at the old leech. The laughter frightened the man even more than had the harsh words. He was hobbling back toward the outriders, a jumble of parts in his arms.

Kretch went to where a part of the tap line was exposed and took a C-clamp off his belt. He fastened it around the line and then walked to his horse. He drew a thin cable from his pack and looped it over the saddle horn. Once the other end was secured to the clamp, Kretch hopped up onto the colt.

"Less go, Shady." The colt wheeled and began trotting away. "See you down the way," he called back.

"Yup. Down the way." Scofield turned to the leech, who stood there like a frightened child, his meager possessions cradled between frail arms. "Dump it all in the hole and bury it. Time for you to find a new line of work."

Sunlight poured through the windows lining Mayor Franklin Dreg's office. Two walls of the large room were almost entirely glass. The light reflected off myriad treasures. A large brass ship's compass, cut crystal glasses, a half dozen paintings hung in heavy frames, a milk white steer's skull; countless objects the man had gathered about him as his wealth and power grew. Most of the art and objects were from centuries past and clashed with the sleek steel walls and numerous panels of LED lights and data screens. The Mayor had commissioned a console that kept a running ticker of all the electricity use in every grid of New Las Vegas. It was over four feet tall and ten feet wide and dominated the wall opposite the longest row of floor-to-ceiling windows.

Mayor Dreg sat behind his massive mahogany desk staring to the right, watching the numbers rise and fall on the console's many screens. His desk sat near the back wall of the long rectangular office, across from the thick double doors that led to the even larger outer chamber. He loved the effect this room had on those who entered it: the tableau of his ample carriage framed by a wall of glass and perched behind the imposing desk unnerved even the most confident of visitors.

The Mayor looked all of his fifty years. Not so much because he had aged poorly, but rather because for so long had he lived a life of privilege that his body was in general atrophy from disuse. His face was neither wrinkled nor well defined. He was a large man, but neither obese nor stout, caught somewhere in between. His eyes were sharp and piercing, his gaze more that of an appraiser than of an intellectual. He was constantly calculating, with his own gain firmly rooted at the right side of every equation.

All was steady today. The megawatts rose and fell with the comforting rhythm of the city. Traffic patterns shifted, people flipped on screens as they arrived home from work, trains moved from grid to grid, and air conditioners dropped a setting as the sun crept toward the horizon—the system plodded along smoothly. Dreg nodded to himself, briefly turning to look out the windows at the sprawling city below him.

"Mr. Hale," The Mayor said, touching a button on his desktop.

"Mayor," came his right hand's reply through a speaker.

"Step in when you have a moment." Dreg released the com button and rose slowly from his leather-bound chair, straightening his vest and tie as he stood. He grabbed his dark gray suit jacket from its spot on a coat tree and worked the blazer on as he heard the heavy outer doors open. A moment later, Mr. Hale let himself into Dreg's office and approached.

"This collar straight, Tim?" The Mayor asked, turning away.

"Mhmm." Timothy Hale was a man of medium height with wide shoulders. He could have been handsome had his forty year old face not already assumed the lines of one who never smiled. He was always clean shaven and his blond hair was full and close cropped—a stark comparison to Dreg's thinning black mane and thick mustache.

"The water commission from San Diego is still waiting to hear back about a rate shift, just to remind you," Hale said as Mayor Dreg turned around again.

"When did they first start pissing and moaning about this?"

"A month and a half back, maybe two. August sometime."

"Well . . . it can wait. I have a feeling they'll get the picture. Or they can try running their little town without power, ey? Always an option!" Dreg winked, then summarily brushed the matter aside. "I think I might make some unannounced visits around town. Care to come along?"

"Of course, sir," Hale replied.

"So boring when everything runs this smoothly." The two men walked toward the doors, Hale pausing to key in a few codes on a wall panel.

"I'll take it over the alternatives," Hale said. He punched in a final few digits and heavy steel shutters slid down over the glass windows, plunging the office into a dim, artificial yellow glow.

"So will I, Tim."

As the men passed through The Mayor's opulent outer chamber, a room double the size and twice as heavily decorated as his office proper, Mayor Dreg put a hand on Hale's shoulder to stop him for a moment. As usual, something in this self-dedicated museum had caught his eye. He walked to a shelf wrought of glass and iron and picked up a small, intricately carved wooden cane. It was two feet long and had a deep notch cut into one end.

"Any idea what this is for, Mr. Hale?"

"None, Frank."

The Mayor snorted. "Neither have I. I just liked how it looked."

Mayor Dreg and Timothy Hale walked through the marble-floored lobby of the executive building past the twenty foot long reception desk. Hale nodded to the various security personnel and receptionists who sat attentively at their stations; The Mayor's eyes stayed forward. There were four guards, each dressed in black fatigues, and three women, each beautiful and wearing a low-cut blouse under a scarlet blazer. The women smiled back; the men nodded. Near the pneumatic doors, which sat in a wall of solid glass, a female custodian dragged a mop across a small section of stone. She was an elderly woman with yellowed, wispy gray hair. She trailed an IV stand behind her. Hale distinctly went out of his way not to look in this woman's direction, despite her pausing to grin at him and The Mayor.

The tall doors slid silently open before Hale and Dreg and the men stepped out onto the streets of New Las Vegas. It was still mid-afternoon and blindingly bright out and The Mayor paused to retrieve a pair of dark, circular sunglasses from his breast pocket. Hale squinted in the sunlight and let his eyes slowly adjust, following Dreg toward the nearest pod stop.

Several waiting commuters stepped aside as The Mayor approached, a few sidling off and leaving altogether. If Dreg noted this, he made no sign of it. The Mayor could, of course, have used his private pod, which disrupted any traffic patterns as needed, but more often than not he chose to travel the city among "his people."

A strong gust of hot air blew down the street momentarily turning the cool air dry and dusty. As soon as it had come, the wind subsided and the temperature returned to a pleasant stasis, cooled by the air conditioning and misting systems that were placed atop poles all around the city's affluent grids. Hale looked around, his pupils now shrunk to accommodate the afternoon glare. The tall buildings that flanked the wide boulevard reached proudly up to the cerulean sky, each a differing shade of pale gray or alabaster white. From every corner of the city came the sounds of steady urban life. The four rails of the traffic lines hummed; two with the gentle drone of cross-town consistency, the others with the higher-pitched whine of frequent local pod stops.

It was onto one of these pods that Hale and Dreg stepped after it arrived. Three or four other citizens boarded the black, cigar-shaped tube behind them. Dreg settled down onto a bench and Hale sat behind him on a single seat. Advertisements and bulletins flickered across the many screens around the pod. There were about a dozen other passengers already aboard—business men and city workers and casually dressed commuters. Eyes flitted to and then away from The Mayor. He was known to all; loved by some, feared by others, but universally respected. Timothy Hale always felt a touch of pride to be seen with Mayor Dreg; to be counted as part of his aura. The golden chevron on Hale's smartly pressed lapel identified him as a man of some regard and his regular propinquity to Dreg elevated his status to that of one with clout.

Hale had been a nervous child and an awkward teenager, but his preternatural intelligence and adaptability had served him well once he had grown into an adult's body. Years of service at the highest levels of city government taught him to act the part of a confident and assertive man. Still, a twinge of unease often crept down his spine when he felt eyes upon him, and he habitually went so far as to remove his executive pin when not accompanying Dreg. Fortunately, in a city of nearly ten million residents, it was easy enough to achieve comfortable anonymity.

The pod gathered speed without so much as a tremor felt by its riders, zipping along for several blocks until its next scheduled stop. The Mayor turned to Hale, saying "Should we pay a visit to Central Bank, or press on to Grid 3's power station?"

Hale cocked his head to one side, thinking for a moment. "Let's stop by the power station, if it's all the same to you. There were a few surges last week and I think it may do them good to see your face."

Dreg's jowls rose into a smile. "And it may do you good to see that lady who works in operations."

"I think seeing her does us all good."

Dreg laughed. "What's her name again?"

"Maria something. I keep forgetting."

"Why haven't you just asked her out, Tim?"

"Ah, there're plenty of women out there."

"She won't say no. You know that, right?" The Mayor leaned in, a conspiratorial gleam in his eye.

"Not with you around, sir," Hale smiled back. Inwardly, he thought that if Maria Rodrigues had no reason to say 'yes' other than fear of upsetting Dreg, he would just as soon leave her be. Timothy had been infatuated with her for months, and despite his best efforts to conceal it, Franklin Dreg was not a man who missed these things, nor the opportunity to give a ribbing about them. "Maybe I will. But not when you're there." He looked away from The Mayor, hastily adding "I wouldn't want to waste your time chasing tail."

Dreg nodded, looking around the pod at the various commuters. As he often did, he picked one at random and rose. Even at nearly fifty miles an hour, the commuter pod barely trembled, and Dreg walked over to a young man wearing blue jeans and a t-shirt. He sat down beside the fellow and smiled widely.

"What's your name, son?"

"Tom Bowman," the youth answered, holding The Mayor's gaze.

"And what do you do?"

"Nothing much. Or not yet, sir. I'm a student."

"Oh? That's plenty! What do you study?"

"Um . . . well mathematics. I guess. I might switch to economics." The young man's poise faded as Dreg looked him up and down.

"Well, Mr. Bowman, a word of advice. Drop them both! Women want engineers or artists!"

"Yes sir. I'll . . . try to incorporate that too. Them too, I mean."

"You do that, Mr. Bowsen. Find your calling then stay in your post!" Dreg rose and clapped the student on the shoulder. He returned to his bench by Hale, a satisfied look on his large face. Despite his propensity for reading people, Dreg regularly mistook uneasiness for respect. While the gulf between inspiring those two sentiments was not vast, it was definite. After the brief exchange between the young man and the swaggering Mayor, the other commuters worked all the harder to act preoccupied. Hale realized this; Dreg did not.

The pod came to rest at the first stop in Grid 3 and Hale rose, waiting for Dreg to do the same, then the two men stepped out into the bright, cool streets. The buildings here looked much the as they did in Executive Center, just a few stories shorter.

# 2

Scofield's thoughts were wandering when the old leech spoke up.

"Sir?" The man's voice was timid and small.

"Hmm," Scofield grunted in reply.

"I know I've no right to even ask . . . but may I have some water?"

From atop Reese, the outrider looked down at the elderly man, stumbling along with his sunburned scalp and creaking joints. Scofield had not bothered tying him to the horse—there was no chance he'd put up a fight or make a breakaway across the desert. He had been plodding unevenly beside the trotting mare for miles now and was visibly failing. A mixture of compassion and pragmatism worked their way through Scofield's thinking and after a minute or two more he drew back on the reins and slid off Reese. He pulled the canteen from her saddle bag and first took a pull himself, then offered water to the horse. She lapped up only a few drops from his palm before tossing her mane and looking away.

Scofield handed the canteen to the leech, saying "Don't touch your lips to that. And don't take much."

The man gratefully accepted the canteen and tilted his head back, letting the warm liquid pour into his gaping mouth. He swished the water about behind his cracked lips and then, with a rueful sigh, handed the canteen back. Scofield looked the old man up and down, then shook his head.

"Mount up," he barked, looking away. The leech made no move. When Scofield finally looked over at him, the man's face was a portrait of bewilderment. "Get on the damn horse, old man."

The leech took a halting step, paused, and then walked to Reese. His hands trembled as he grasped her saddle and his knee buckled as he tried to lift his weight in the stirrup. Scofield thrust his large, calloused hands under the man's shoulders and roughly lifted him up onto the mare. Reese sidestepped and let out a whinny at the feeling of the foreign rider.

"S'alright girl," Scofield whispered to her, taking her soft muzzle in one hand. He pulled the reins from where they were looped about the saddle horn and set off walking, following the faint trace of the leech's tap line.

The sun was at their backs, maybe an hour from dipping below the horizon. The land was just beginning to lose its features while still maintaining what little color the desert palate had to offer: soft beige under foot, coffee brown mountains in the distance, and the charcoal grays of occasional rocky outcroppings. The sky had eased from azure blue to a powdery yellow above a thin layer of late afternoon haze. It was still warm out.

Scofield's boots crunched methodically, two falls to every four from Reese's hooves. Again his thoughts had begun to drift when the old timer spoke.

"Thank you."

Scofield made no reply. Not even a sidelong glance or a shrug. A few minutes passed before the wizened fellow spoke again.

"You're a good man, Scofield." The outrider looked up and the leech hastily added: "Mr. Scofield. You're a good man. Thank you."

"No, I ain't. Don't get that thinking into your head." He looked away again, pulling off his hat and wiping the back of one sleeve across his sweaty brow. "I'm just not a bad man. That's all. Ain't too big a distinction. Remember that."

The leech drew in a rasping breath as if to say more but let it go silently. They walked on. Scofield found himself ruminating on what he had just said. Was there much of a distinction? Had he really meant it one way or the other regardless? He could count on one hand the times he'd done things he knew to be categorically wrong. But the times his deeds had fallen into a gray area were as measureless as the desert sands. He always sought to do right but didn't let some ambiguous nod to morality play counsel to his day-to-day living.

Given more to aimless brooding than active reflection, Scofield let the notion drift. He wondered how far inside the glowline the leech's collector was. They'd been following the tap wire for easily an hour and would surely be catching up to Kretch soon. He just hoped it was before darkness fell. It had been slow going with the aged man on foot and he had lost track of time. Scofield dreaded a night spent bunked with this old wretch. He'd heard their tales of hard-luck misfortune and their pleas for clemency all too many times. His only desire was for a night alone bedded down in silence. Scofield drew a cigarette from within his long black coat and dug about in another pocket for his lighter.

As he took his first drag he looked up at the leech. The old man bounced along uneasily in the saddle and cast furtive glances at the outrider, clearly hoping to be offered a smoke of his own. Scofield turned his head away, facing the darkening sands before them. He hadn't brought enough tobacco to consider sharing.

Timothy Hale sighed as he crossed the threshold into his large but spartan apartment. He had again failed to summon the courage to talk to Maria. Or really talk to her, anyway: they had exchanged the usual pleasantries as he and The Mayor toured Grid 3's power station, but the discourse had been professional, sterile. Hale let himself imagine that her demure glances and soft tone had been anything other than the awkward discomfort they had seemed, but he knew well that his attraction to her was one-sided.

He carefully removed his suit jacket and tie, hanging them each in their respective places in his walk-in closet. Before leaving the closet, Hale took the golden government insignia from his jacket's lapel and laid the pin on a bare section of shelf. He pulled off his slacks with less care, tossing the pants into a hamper in the hallway, and donned soft linen trousers and leather slippers lined with sable. Hale entered his immaculate kitchen and flicked on a light switch.

White light filled the room, shining off the polished marble countertops and smooth steel appliances. Timothy never paid a penny for electricity, a perk of his job title; poorer denizens of New Las Vegas lived switch-to-switch, saving power whenever and wherever possible. Currently, Mayor Dreg was keeping local rates affordably low, in fact; but that could all change overnight, based on demand from other markets, a dip in supply caused by inclement weather or technical issues out in the sunfield, or merely based off a capricious whim. Numerous were the times when millions had quite literally paid for the foul mood of Franklin Dreg, keeper of the power, as it were.

Hale opened the refrigerator and selected from the several half-empty bottles of wine an '87 chardonnay. There were less than two glasses worth of wine left in the bottle and Timothy allowed himself a private moment of impropriety, swishing back a mouthful of the cool liquid right from the bottle before filling a glass. He threw out the wine bottle and then, as he did most every night, began to stroll slowly through the rooms of his home, replaying the day's events in his head.

Overall, it had been an unremarkable Wednesday. Save for the underwhelming visit to Grid 3, his waking hours had been consumed with paperwork and numbers, all the mundane actual work required to run the city's executive office and for which his boss had not the slightest concern. No meetings or visitors had been scheduled for the day, so his interaction with others up until the late afternoon had consisted of two or three minutes talking to Dreg and countless phone calls diverted from The Mayor. Dreg hated talking to people who called him, preferring only to speak to whom he chose, when he chose. Hale was in effect a glorified buffer between The Mayor and the world at large. In fact, if he wanted to, he likely could have taken much of the control of the city into his own hands simply by not telling The Mayor what was happening at any given time.

But Hale had little interest in power. Not in any direct, definite way, at least. He preferred the comfort of stability that came from being near the top but with his neck underexposed. It rarely bothered him to act as a considerable portion of the brain while letting Dreg's face alone occupy the minds of the millions of citizens of NLV. Hale had achieved most of his life's goals—save any meaningful romance—before the age of forty-one. This thought brought him less satisfaction than he would have expected, and he quickly tried to clear the notion from his head as he leaned against a window frame in his living room. Only a few lamps shone in this room, their soft yellow light diffused through ornate stained-glass shades.

Fifty stories below, New Las Vegas sparkled in the clear night. On an evening such as this the city would consume approximately two-hundred eighteen million, four-hundred thousand kilowatt hours of energy between sunset and sunrise. A shift in temperature could drive the figure up or down, depending on the season.

While Hale had no direct authority to regulate power consumption, his status as Dreg's right hand put him in a position to, at any given moment, say the word and darken any (or all) of the twenty-one grids that made up the sprawling city. As he let his eyes drift across the glowing metropolis and then out to the dark stretch of desert beyond, a faint smile crept across his lips. Not that he would ever abuse his role, but the knowledge that he could brought him an inner warmth—something akin to a sense of manliness.

On certain nights, when Hale indulged in more than his usual one glass of wine, he found himself muttering three words over and over: "I'll show them." He had no clue who "they" were or exactly what he would show them, but they were out there and he was up here. (Though sometimes "they" took on the visage of a large, mustachioed man as sleep overcame Timothy.) When Hale lay down to sleep on this night, he was sober and his thoughts drifted to more reasonable matters of breakfast and scheduling and business.

Fifteen years ago Hale had been a graduate student and an aspiring social activist. New Las Vegas in the seventies was a different place than today's city. The city government sparred with the statehouse for influence; the power company was still private; the traffic patterns were erratic and the streets were often choked with tens of thousands of angry commuters. No one had known for years who was really in control. Then Dreg had come into office on a platform of ostensible reform. This turned quickly to consolidation of power—both literal and figurative. By taking total control of NLV's electricity production and distribution, Dreg had also established New Las Vegas as something closer to a city-state than a city within a state; these days, the governor asked The Mayor's permission, rather than the other way around.

Hale had seen government from the outside and mistrusted it. Then he had been offered a low-level bureaucratic job. Over-educated and under-employed, he took it, meaning only to accept the work—a clerical position with the transportation bureau—for a short time. Hale was surprised to find himself fabulously adroit at maneuvering through the arcane channels of government and within two years was overseeing a staff of some fifty workers. Soon he was managing three times that, heading up a department charged with integrating the latest breakthrough in battery technology, the massive molten salt facilities that could store enough heat to generate power for days when rare instances of inclement weather came to sunny New Las Vegas. It was thanks to the success of Timothy Hale's department that the city had finally achieved a reliable enough surplus of energy to begin selling it to other regionals; arguably, it was thanks to Hale and his team that New Las Vegas had become such a mighty power center, and of the political stripe, at that: with electricity to spare, the city could leverage deals on grain and livestock from the Midwest, produce from California's Central Valley, and desalinated water from myriad coastal cities.

It was only a matter of time before he came to Dreg's attention. The Mayor had extended an offer Hale could hardly turn down, and Hale's keen intellect, attention to detail and excellent memory had rapidly moved him into Dreg's confidence and good graces. Thus the man who had once planned to stand up to and petition against the government became its enforcer, the acting right hand of its ruthless head.

Given his memory and his propensity for detail, it was surprising that it would take nearly a week for Timothy Hale to catch onto a pattern that began to emerge that night. Somehow, between the time the sun set and the day broke, power consumption in New Las Vegas rose by over forty-million kilowatt hours. That spike in usage would require nearly half of the city's ten million residents to dry their hair, make toast, vacuum, and do laundry all at once. Which was unlikely in the dead of night.

It was well after nightfall when Scofield and the leech crossed the glowline. The cord of blue filament pulsed against the dark sands and not a hundred yards beyond it lay the trappings of everyday life: the charge station with its crackling insect lamps, the nearly derelict motel, the grocery store and the rows of huts outriders called home for months out of the year. A score of shadows flitted about in the artificial light; several employees leaving the grocers, a few women of less-than-fine repute, and an outrider or two. Kretch was nowhere to be found.

The same mild sense of distaste that always washed over Scofield when he returned to society after days out on the land settled over him now, heightened by the fact that he had to deal with the leech. He had found the man's collection rig about a mile back. The leech had placed it inside the glowline, about a mile west of the Outpost but well safe of the power field's potent reach. Wilton had clearly taken care of the rig without so much as dismounting. The storage box/generator was riddled with bullet holes; its molten salts had leaked out onto the sands and long ago cooled into a gray pile. The rig was ruined if not properly disposed of and, too tired to much care, Scofield had severed the tap line and traded places with the leech, mounting Reese for the last leg of their trek.

He had paused to slice and re-bury the tap line three times during their ten or eleven mile journey, but doubted that this old timer would ever again return to the power field. What was next for the leech was none of his concern; the fifth of bourbon and shower awaiting him in his hut were what counted.

As the lights of society had come into view on the twilight horizon, the leech had begun wringing his hands and making a soft, high pitched whimper. The sound seemed to squeak out of the back of his throat, becoming more and more frequent the nearer they drew to the glowline. He had sounded like an animal scenting a predator's approach. On a different night, that analogy might have been apt—Scofield had decided what to do with this old fellow hours ago, though, and his fate was to be fabulously mild.

The outrider and leech entered the omnipresent pool of halogen light bathing the Outpost and Scofield quietly sighed to himself. He led the man a few hundred yards down the thin stretch of asphalt that began not ten feet from the glowline. The only sounds were the stirring of a faint breeze and the click of Reese's hooves on the paved road. Scofield reined the horse to a stop beneath a streetlight. He slid down from atop the mare and stretched his neck from side to side, kneading one shoulder between his palm and fingers.

"I'm guessin' you ain't got a penny, hm?"

"No," the old man replied, his hands knit together across his belly. Scofield nodded, then turned to face his horse. He dug in a saddle bag and retrieved the satchel where he kept a few coins and crumpled bills. Scofield counted out eleven dollars and fifty cents then turned to face the leech.

"There's a commuter pod station a half mile down this road. This here's exact change to get you from there to Vegas Central." He extended his arm but kept the cash held firmly in a fist. "Listen real good, old man," Scofield whispered, his voice cold. "I ever see you out in the sunfield again, you're dead. Simple as that. Don't you say a goddamn word, either. Take this cash and get the fuck out of here. Stay out of my power fields. I was you, I'd head east. Way east." With that he pressed the money into the old man's gnarled hands and turned back to his mount, once more spitting over his shoulder: "Not a goddamn word."

Scofield took hold of the saddle horn and hefted himself up onto his horse. Reese wheeled at the gentle tug on her reins and set off at a trot due north. She knew the way and Scofield didn't so much as cluck his tongue for the next ten minutes as he rode toward the shack he called home a few nights out of each month. He never once looked back at the leech. Had he done so, he would have seen that the old man had scarcely moved a muscle as the outrider faded into the artificial twilight haze. The leech watched until the horse and rider were mere shadows, then were gone, before finally nodding his ancient head and beginning a slow shuffle to the pod station. The half mile walk took him almost twenty minutes.

Scofield poured feed into Reese's trough and turned on the tap above her water basin. Dropping his hat, he splashed some of the cold liquid across his face and hair and stretched, shivering in the cold night air. He tied the long lead to the horse's bridle and unhooked his saddle and bags, tossing them into the storage locker beside his hut. He kicked shut the heavy iron door, not bothering to fiddle with the digital deadbolt. Scofield had requested the most remote post possible and had been rewarded, such as it was, with a hovel nearly a mile from the center of the Outpost proper.

The lights of the saloon and stores and charge station shimmered in the distance, a little pocket of light diminished by the undulating glow of New Las Vegas some twenty miles away across the sands.

He keyed in a code and the door to the ten-by-twelve foot building clicked open. Scofield tossed his hat and jacket inside and pulled two heavy horse blankets from the floor where they rested just inside the hut. These he spread next to his horse as she ate. Then he sat on the step outside his modest home to remove his boots and socks. Finally stepping inside, Scofield flipped on the lights for just long enough to find his kerosene lamp and a book of matches. Once he had the lamp and a few candles lit, the outrider turned the lights down to their lowest setting and stripped naked. All of his clothing he shoved into the washer/dryer unit. He had not changed in two weeks and despite his rugged nature, Scofield was thrilled to be finally free of the musty garments and mere minutes from bathing.

Stretching his arms to the ceiling then twisting from side to side, he looked about his little home. There was a simple cot, perfectly turned down as he had left it, his little kitchenette, a shelf laden with canned food and an eclectic mix of books, and the armoire where he kept his few items of clothing. The things that mattered were in a steel trunk under his cot. Sealed away behind an old-fashioned padlock were a .44 magnum, hundreds of rounds for both of his pistols and rifle, a few random personal items, and Scofield's store of tobacco and whiskey. The last two items were all that interested him now. When out riding the sunfield Scofield rarely if ever took a drop of liquor, but once off assignment he partook gladly of his bourbon, if sometimes only for the first night back in the everyday world. Overall, he was a sober man.

An ordered, settled existence had never sat well with Scofield. He had become an outrider to escape the poisonous monotony of "civilized" life. Others—Kretch among them—made a beeline for New Las Vegas just as soon as their tours of the sunfield were up, throwing dollars and cares to the wind. For Scofield, one good dose of bourbon or rye was all that made coming back into the light (as he and a few others called it) remotely tolerable. He could count on his hands the days he'd spent in the city over the last three years. Many a night—even when he was off duty—he spent bedded down under the stars beside his horse. Reese was better company than any man or woman Scofield had ever met. If it had not been for the occasional need for the latter, the outrider might never have made his way into the light. But there were no women on the plains and he was a man. Scofield had no qualms about picking up a hooker when need be, but his preference was to find some female of the same disposition as him: ready to go and, afterward, ready to leave.

He stepped into the tiny bathroom of his unit and keyed on the fluorescent lights. In the harsh glow of the pale bulbs his skin was a mix of ruddy brown and milky white where the sun always and never touched, respectively. Scofield took a piss while eyeing his hairy face in the mirror. A few more lines; a few more grays. No matter. He brushed his teeth with meticulous precision, as he did every night, then stepped into the shower. He bathed cold, using the same bar of lye soap on his body, face, and shaggy hair.

Later Scofield lay naked atop the covers, a tepid glass of whiskey resting in one hand and a cigarette smoking in the other. The ash on its tip had grown to nearly an inch in length, so still was the man. He was not lost in thought; rather his mind was a total, near meditative blank. Eventually gravity bested the ashes and their hot sting on his fingers jolted Scofield back into the present. He sat up in bed, threw back the rye in one large swallow and then dropped the cigarette butt into the glass.

Scofield rose and slipped on a pair of worn blue jeans and a wool sweater and let himself out into the chill night air. The sand hissed gently beneath his bare feet. He found Reese sleeping soundly and lay down against the horse, easing himself under a part of her blanket. The mare whinnied softly, then was still. Soon Scofield's thinking was again all but empty, occupied only by his savoring the familiar musty-sweet odor of his horse. Before long he drifted off, his conscious mind melting away into the night.

Above a thin layer of clouds a new moon lurked in darkness. A few stars snuck through the silken layer of gray but the land was all formless shadow. A gentle breeze crept along the sands, drifting among the pillars of the sunfield and curling about the dunes at its northern border. It was cold out, scarcely forty degrees and, not yet midnight, the temperature was dropping still.

The QV arrays hung limply in the night air, still and lifeless. The cloud bank thickened as the evening wore on and, at this rate, it was possible that for only the sixth day that year no direct sunlight would find its way down to the hungry quantum voltaic panels the next day.

What little life persisted in the late fall desert was burrowed away in the near-frozen sands. Save for the gentle rustling of sage brush in the breeze, not a sound stirred the air. Miles away, New Las Vegas glowed on the horizon—a stark contrast to the bleak landscape. Three perfectly still figures crouched atop the tallest dune for miles. Each wore a long black jacket and cowl. From a distance they appeared to be nothing more than a trio of dark stones. Certainly they moved no more than had this been true.

For a long time the three men knelt in the frigid air. As the night wore on and grew ever darker, their hooded faces were lost even to one another. Just enough diffuse starlight fell across the landscape to make it visible. Three pairs of eyes watched the hills and the sands and the towering arrays before them. Dark cloth fluttered silently in the breeze. Finally, one of the three rose slowly to his full height. After a pause the other two joined him and for several minutes they remained still, now like black monoliths in the night.

The first to rise turned his back to his compatriots and gently shook his hooded head. "Not yet," he whispered, "go back down."

The New Las Vegas sunfield was comprised of three thousand two hundred and twenty-nine individual QV pillars. It was roughly fifty miles east to west and, at any given point, an average of two miles wide. Certain geological features broke up its mostly straight shape: here and there the line was diverted by hills too large to level or canyons too wide to fill. Atop each pillar sat an array of four massive quantum photovoltaic panels. Throughout the course of the day, a series of motors guided the light-absorbing panels to follow the sun across the sky. In summer, there were more megawatts than New Las Vegas and the dozen smaller cities on its grid could ever use, thus the city's ability to sell and trade its abundant power. During the winter, energy was still plentiful, but on cloudy days during the season of long nights the grid often dipped deeply into its massive reserve of power stored in cavernous vaults of molten salt.

Each night as the sun set, the grid began to draw off the stores of energy waiting in its daily reserve chambers. In mid-October, this superheated mixture routinely produced more than enough steam to turn generators through the night without a chance of tapping into the surplus stores. In fact, the salt caverns could likely have kept the turbines churning for weeks. Power had become an endless commodity; no more a concern than air to breathe. Few knew of the immense infrastructure and constant maintenance behind the light switch or microwave; few grasped the fragility of the stability they had come to take for granted. Mayor Dreg knew about it. Timothy Hale understood far better than most. And Scofield was aware at least that he was a part of something much greater and more complex than he fully comprehended. The first man took comfort in knowing he was in control of the balance; the second man lost sleep thinking about each and every transmission wire and transistor. The third didn't much give a damn about any of it—Scofield's job was to keep it all running and his job description kept him far from the rest of it; kept him out on the land where not a single electrical circuit could be closed without the risk of a catastrophe. It was a beautiful trade, for it kept him away from the great All of It.

# 3

A week and a day later found Wilton Kretch back out in the field doing what he did best: tracking down leeches. He had a preternatural knack for finding them. His eyes were fantastically sharp, the rods and cones aligned so perfectly that he saw subtle contrasts, colors, and details where others saw only sand. Many times each year an outrider would trot past a stretch of QV pillars only to have Kretch patrol the same area later and come up with tap lines or the leeches themselves.

For his skills, Kretch was respected; for his demeanor he was almost universally, if privately, despised. He sensed this and often opted to work alone. It didn't much bother Kretch to be disliked—he assumed the others were jealous of him. This may have been true with some of his comrades, but it was only one factor of his reputation, and far from the decisive one at that. Wilton Kretch had an itch on his right index finger that no trigger could amply scratch. He had killed three men that year, the same number as had been shot by all the other fifty-odd outriders combined. And he had put lead into two other leeches as well. Both had survived, but one would never walk again.

Wilton Kretch was a heavy drinker and his inclination for violence grew with inverse proportion to his shortening temper when he was full of whiskey. Many a man and even a handful of women bore scars on their cheeks or crooked noses from a perceived slight against him. Deep down Wilton was and always had been a coward, but his assumed persona had so obscured this fact from the exterior world that even internally his fears had withdrawn from his consciousness, residing only in the shadows of the id. Perhaps Kretch's propensity to shoot first or start punching at the smallest infraction came from his deep-seated terror of injury or embarrassment. It was far simpler to be feared and loathed than to be perceived as even a bit vulnerable.

The sun had set not long ago, and true night was taking over. For years Kretch had feared riding through the desert alone at night. But time and self-denial had tempered this sensation, and now he traversed the darkened plains with confidence if not with ease. He kept a monologue running constantly in his head: *Alright you sonsabitches . . . you fuckin' shitkickers . . . ol' Kretch is here . . . c'mon on out and make it easy . . . . Goddamn cold tonight . . . goddamn dark and cold . . . just me n' Shady and all these motherfuckers . . . fine by me . . . just fine by me . . .* and so on it went. Hour upon hour Kretch muttered to himself as if another person were listening. Effectively enough another person was listening: a sickly child abandoned long ago by a mother who called her boy Willy.

His keen eyes did little for him at night, and Kretch seldom dismounted to scout around the base of the pillars as outriders were instructed to do. He preferred to maintain a leisurely trot at a good distance from the arrays and let himself believe he was doing his job. Three times on this penultimate night of October the outrider crossed buried tap lines. Two had been set by a leech that had bunked down atop a nearby dune and who, soundly sleeping, was unaware that he was ever in danger. The third tap line led to a freshly planted hook up.

Even in the gloaming, Kretch easily would have seen the large, bright eyes watching him had he so much as glanced toward the sunfield at the right time. Wilton rode slowly, eyes on Shady's mane, as he passed within thirty feet of the terrified young man. As the light faded the leech had worked feverishly securing his rig to a pillar, and he had just begun scooping sand over it when Shady let out a random whinny.

Too terrified even to crawl behind the QV pillar, the youth was lying prone on the cold sand, eyes foolishly locked onto Kretch. Foolishly, for on this night with only thin clouds between the stars and waxing crescent moon, the whites of his eyes shone clearly in the dark. He was perfectly still for a solid ten minutes after the crunch of the horse's hooves had faded. Then, with trembling hands, he finished covering his hookup, carefully smoothed the sand over the tap line, and then padded off toward the dune where his father slept.

Soon Kretch reached the end of his route. Every third mile, a thin filament was suspended between the pillars, pulsing with the same chemical blue as the glowline. On a given assignment, each outrider was sent to one of the three-mile-long by two-mile-deep grids marked by these softly glowing cords. The standard time in the field was two weeks, the schedule altered only by Round Up or by rare extenuating circumstances such as illness or a shooting incident. Whenever an outrider used his weapon—or, more accurately, when his lead found its mark—he was obliged to head back to an outpost and debrief. Kretch had debriefed about a shooting three times that year, and only one of those had been about a fatality. Everyone knew about the other two leeches he had killed, but no one gave much of a damn. It was so much simpler just not to ask.

The young leech, now scrambling up a dune to his camp, had no idea that the outrider who had so nearly seen him was the same man who had put a bullet through his slumbering father's lung two years ago. Kretch hadn't so much as dismounted; he'd come upon a middle-aged man tinkering with a hook-up in the shade of a QV array, quietly slid his rifle from the saddle bag, aimed, and fired.

When Wilton had approached the man, who was writhing in agony on the ground, he had every intention of finishing the job. But the poor bastard's tears of suffering and his pitiful stammering—about a son and all the usual bullshit—had been enough to stay the outrider's hand. He had spat on the sand next to the leech and told him that if he ever returned to the sunfield, his death would be summary. The growing patch of crimson on the man's chest and his gasping breaths had suggested it was rhetorical anyway.

Kretch stared at the glowing blue filament for a moment longer, and then gave a gentle tug on Shady's reins, turning the horse ninety degrees to the right. The pair set off across the interior of the sunfield. Every now and then Wilton looked around random pillars and scanned the ground for tap lines or hideouts, but mostly he kept his eyes forward and down, muttering to himself. *Cold tonight, Shady. Ain't gonna be much warmer tomorrow, neither. Gotta watch these fuckers, y'know? Gotta run 'em hard and fast all day. Just you'n me . . .*

It was the first Monday of November. Mayor Franklin Dreg was in a fine mood as he sauntered through the lobby of the executive building wearing a beige suit with impossibly wide lapels and a smile to match. Without glancing at a single person's face Franklin called out boisterous greetings: "Hello! Good morning to all, hello! Monday again! Hello all!"

The receptionists and security personnel murmured replies; the old janitor, trailing her IV tower and shuffling about in orthopedic shoes, was the only one to respond in a full voice, saying "Good morning, Mayor!" Her bright smile was lost on Dreg, who was already boarding an elevator and jabbering into his phone. The elderly woman's smile faded back into the innumerable lines of her face. She cast her eyes downward and got back to work on the scuff marks marring the marble floor.

The elevator's doors closed behind Dreg and it began its race up fifty floors. Whenever he or Timothy Hale was aboard, the lifts would go directly to whatever floor was requested, overriding all other stops. The gold chevron pin Hale kept on his lapel and Dreg usually had loose in some pocket did more than display status: their small transistors literally opened doors—or, in this case, kept them closed.

The Mayor tossed wide the doors to Timothy Hale's office—a decently large room in its own right, but sparsely decorated at Hale's request—and warmly greeted his secretary and confidant. "Morning, Timothy! How's my city today?"

It was just before eleven o'clock and Hale had been in the office for more than four hours already. His face showed the strain of a sleepless night and stress-filled morning. Hale rose to greet Dreg and attempted a bright and energetic reply, but even as he opened his mouth to speak The Mayor raised a hand to silence him.

"Don't bother with the pleasantries, Mr. Hale. Something's wrong here, isn't it?" Dreg stripped off his suit jacket while continuing. "Very wrong, based on how shitty you look. It never gets easier, hmm?" Hale sank back down into his chair and wheeled to face the wall, glancing out the window behind him at the cloudy day.

"I figured it had to be the math. My math somehow . . . I've run the numbers a dozen times. Frank, we're losing power. Have been for a week. Lots of power."

Dreg settled into one of the two chairs across from Hale and unbuttoned his vest, letting his paunch out into the room. He put his hands on his knees and leaned forward.

"Just shoot me straight."

"For the past week, the grid has been bleeding between thirty-five and forty-five million kilowatts every night." Hale turned back to face The Mayor. "One night we almost hit fifty."

"Christ, that's a lot of juice!" Dreg slammed a fist down on one thigh, his other palm pressed to his forehead. "Fifty million! How is that even possible?"

"Either a major malfunction . . ." Hale trailed off as Dreg lowered his hand and looked up at him. Timothy raised his palms as if to indicate he was just the messenger.

"Have you talked to anyone else?"

"Of course. I've talked to everyone—don't worry, all I did was listen, no one knows anything. That's what kept me up all night . . . none of the grids have reported anything but the standard fluctuations. As far as everyone knows it was a boring, stable week."

Dreg furrowed his brow. "So the problem is somewhere in supply."

Hale nodded slowly, intertwining his fingers and resting the nails of both thumbs against his lips. "Somewhere in the salt caverns or else in the field."

"What's your gut, Tim?"

"My gut says it's in the field. We've been dipping into the reserves every night so it seems to me that the standard stores are under-heated."

Dreg rose and began pacing, his slacks swishing noisily as each thick leg rubbed against the other. His expression was dark; brows furrowed. The two men were silent for more than a minute, Hale lost in reverie while Dreg grew angrier by the second. When The Mayor next spoke it was in a loud bark. Hale jumped a bit and was relieved Dreg's back was to him.

"And not one of the damn engineers or the computers or the fucking line jockeys caught this until now! How many millions of my dollars were wasted? Goddamn them all!" Both of Dreg's hands curled into large, meaty fists and he trembled with rage. His wormy lips curled into a sneer, spittle collecting at the corners of his mouth. As it usually did, the fit passed quickly and The Mayor took in a long, slow breath.

"What would I do without you, Mr. Hale?"

The secretary shrugged and forced a smile, then looked away. "Worry less, I sometimes think. It seems I'm always the one to stumble onto the bad news."

"Stumble? Hell! You're a keen son of a bitch. You're my tiger out there prowling! You're my boots on the ground. My man! Without you I'd have to wipe every ass in this city, no less worry about the power and all the rest of it."

Hale mumbled, "Well, thank you, sir," but was internally insulted by his boss's words. His tiger? His boots? *His* man? He, for all intents and purposes, was the executor of the whole of New Las Vegas! Dreg merely waltzed into the office when he felt like doing so and shuffled documents around for a few hours. It was Hale who found the problems; Hale who fixed them. And this, the secretary general was sure, would be no exception. He made up his mind to put The Mayor at ease then deal with the issue on his own time, in his own way.

"Listen, Frank—I've got this. The worst case scenario is that we have a few pillars down or one of the main transmission beacons failed. You have a speech to give at the Chamber of Commerce this afternoon, gotta make them feel like we listened to their proposal for decentralizing some of the programs we . . ." Hale trailed off as Dreg smiled and pumped his fist above his crotch. He started up again, saying: "Fine, I'll handle drafting that speech, but *you* need to prepare to head to Boston in the morning."

"Boston! Christ, that's right! When do I leave?"

"In the morning," Hale said flatly, quickly adding: "Tomorrow, sir, at eleven."

"Tomorrow! That's right . . . . Right, Tuesday . . . ." Already Dreg was focused on other affairs. The gravity of the power loss situation at hand had totally escaped the portly man as he turned to a mirror and brushed one of his eyebrows into shape. Hale sighed. Had damage to the system been the culprit of so massive a loss of electricity, it would surely have been reported by now, regardless of the standard IQ of the minimum wage workers who tended to the city's infrastructure. If it was a problem in any individual grid he'd have heard about it long before his three dozen outgoing phone calls that morning.

Thus the problem had to be in the fields. And that was the worst kind of problem to have: on this scale it meant a disastrous equipment failure, an act of sabotage, or worse. Timothy Hale didn't allow that last possibility to fully take root in his mind. He rose and followed Mayor Dreg to the inner office, resolved to deal with the more mundane affairs of the day before returning to the mess at hand in private.

The old woman tossed and turned on her threadbare cot. The thin mattress scratched at her papery skin through gaping holes in the worn cotton sheets. The pains had just begun in her fingertips and toes and she knew a searing headache was not far off. In vain she tried to fall back to sleep. Late afternoon sun streamed through the solitary window of her one room home, painting the insides of her eyelids red. Coughing, she curled into fetal position, her head with its straggly white hair hanging over the side of the metal bed frame.

Extra blood coursed into her head but it was no use—the pulsing pain was already beginning as her brain thirsted for hydration. Relenting, she cursed and began the laborious process of getting out of bed. Every joint creaked in protest; every muscle groaned with reproach. It took the septuagenarian more than a full minute to go from curled to extended to shakily sitting up with her feet on the cold linoleum. Finally she stood, one hand pressed against the cracked plaster wall, the other reaching towards the bag of diluted saline mixture suspended from a wheeled stand.

Her hand trembling, the old woman slid the case off easily the three thousandth needle of her life and affixed its backside to the tube hanging from the saline bag. She slid the needle's tip into the permanent port just below her left elbow and turned a small valve on the IV tree. It would be approximately three minutes before she felt any relief from her chronic dehydration, and while motion—any motion, even a slow, pathetic shuffling walk back and forth around the tiny room—would speed this relief, the old woman couldn't muster the effort, and she sat back down on the cot to wait.

The only other furnishings in her little cell were a large armoire, a wooden chair, a dirty sink, and a mirror she tried to avoid. The commode and shower were in a separate room, barely large enough to turn around in. Her home was a half hour's commute from the buildings of Government Center which she cleaned daily, and a whole world apart from the life she envisioned living.

After a while, the throbbing in her fingers subsided and the ancient janitor began to fidget with the knot holding up her dark blue trousers. When the pain left her feet, she rose again and stepped in front of the mirror. Tired, broken eyes stared back at a woman who had once been pretty—almost striking—and vigorous. She sighed as she took note of every liver spot, every wrinkle . . . her gnarled hands . . . the sallow skin. The old woman's interior matched her exterior to a tee: her arteries were lined with plaque, her stomach was an ulcerous mess, and her kidneys had shrunk into knotted lumps, thus the IV and the drainage bag she would need within the half hour. Her eyes drifted away from the mirror and she let out a very long sigh.

# 4

Scofield took a long pull of cool water from his canteen. He refilled it up to the brim from the spigot on the side of his hut, and then screwed the cap tight and set the canteen down beside the two water sacks. Reese's feed bags were full. He'd oiled the saddle and bridle and stirrups and even all the straps for good measure; he'd be out for over three weeks this time. While satellite outposts were never more than an hour's ride from any point in the sunfield, Scofield preferred to spend some time preparing alone at his home before each assignment to help minimize visits to posts; minimize contact with others.

He'd be meeting Kretch in six days to patrol the farthest perimeters and he figured he could haul enough chow and water to remain entirely alone until they linked up. The outrider had only been in town—as much as one could fairly call the place that—for four days, but already he felt stifled by society, worn down by it. He'd gone to the saloon the first two nights of his time off. The first night he'd spent nursing a warm beer and turning a cold shoulder. Scofield had merely wanted a couple hot meals prepared by someone else, and during the first evening he'd been left blissfully alone. The second night had been different.

That second night there were whores out in force, and his total indifference to their overtures had only made him more of a target. During the hour he'd spent hunched over a corner of the bar no fewer than four women had approached him. Their solicitations always began saccharine sweet, soon turned to direct appeals for guiltless sex, and ended with a mix of mockery and confusion. It was strange, Scofield thought, as he shook the sand from his wool socks before sliding on his boots, that a hooker could be so affected by rejection. Take any good, chaste woman and all she wanted was to be either left alone or approached with the most patient, delicate courtship. But with these whores here in the post, anything less than an immediate fuck or a drunken slap was seen as some sort of breach in etiquette.

Scofield wasn't sure what was worse: the confused contempt of the women or the silent eyes of the other outriders. Scofield was well respected by those who knew him, mildly disdained by those who didn't, and something of a mystery to both. The respect and mystery were both well founded: he was damn good at his work, he hardly ever talked, and he certainly never opened up when he did. The disdain was borne of misunderstanding—others perceived the man as constantly judging them, whereas in reality he just didn't give a good goddamn about most people. It was neither like nor dislike, he just didn't care to know. Scofield had spent his second evening "in the light" drinking much more than suited him just to pass the time as he waited for and then ate a hot meal.

And then there had been last night. Scofield had awoken the day before with a hangover owing to far too much bourbon at the bar followed by a good deal more back in his hut. He had spent the morning wallowing atop his disheveled sheets, disgusted with himself at wasting so many hours, but not so disgusted as to rise and face his headache full on first thing.

By early afternoon he had been back to right, and he spent time straightening up his already tidy shack. He refolded his few articles of clothing, wiped down the diminutive bathroom, and generally killed time with pointless pursuits—well aware of that fact—waiting for the night to come and a few hours of sleep to bring around the time for him to ride back into the field.

It had been around eight o'clock in the evening when the knocking rattled the door. Scofield was not actually alarmed, only mildly confused, but he grabbed his pistol and tucked it into the back of his pants before opening the door without bothering to ask who was entreating.

In the weak glow cast from within the shack, Scofield was met with the stern face of Tripp Hernandez. Beyond Tripp, he could see Eric Bay, ever squinting regardless of the light and, behind him in the shadows, a large man, who from the square shape of his head and the width of his shoulders, had to be Noah Fischer.

"Evening, Scofy," Tripp said quietly.

"What's this, Hernandez? Some kinda hangin' mob?"

"Much worse." Tripp Hernandez looked back over his shoulder and nodded to Eric Bay, who stepped forward. "It's a drinkin' mob."

Hernandez turned back to Scofield and smiled widely, taking the bottle Bay had just handed him and extending it to Scofield, who leaned against the doorframe with a sigh. Tripp's face broke into a wide, lopsided grin. His big teeth were yellow but even behind his light brown skin.

"And you're coming with us."

"Gotta ride early tomorrow, boys."

"Tripp thought you'd say that," the big fellow said, stepping into the light and, sure enough, revealing himself as Noah Fischer. Fischer tried to keep his face hard as he continued. "That's why they brought me. I figure a bastard my size can convince a man to take a drink or two. Or ten."

Scofield shook his head ruefully, smiling despite himself as he straightened up again. "I guess there ain't gonna be any chasing off of you assholes, huh?"

"Not until we're good n' drunk and you are too. Mr. Matteson told us you was out at his bar last night and us three boys decided if you was good enough to drink alone, you were good enough to drink with us." Hernandez was still holding the whiskey bottle out to Scofield, who finally grabbed it and pulled the cork out. He took a decent swallow, then turned and stepped back into his hut.

"Come on in then, dammit."

"Ain't hardly enough room in there for you, Scof. We'll never fit with ol' Dumptruck Fischer here!" Eric Bay said with a laugh. "Come on. There's gonna be a fire lit up over near my brother's n' my places."

Eric Bay had a half-brother named Joseph who was ten years older and every bit as taciturn and silent as Eric was not. The Bay Boys were an odd pair—they were nothing alike in any way and yet had never once been known to have an argument or even a mild disagreement. Rather they seemed to have the same take on everything, from what constituted a moral imperative to what whiskey went down the quickest served neat to which rifle performed best with sand in the breech. The Bay Brothers were constant companions.

The light caught the polished silver cross Eric Bay wore around his neck as Scofield turned around to look out at the boys again (Joe Bay wore an identical cross at all times, a point Scofield noted for the hundredth time).

"Christ," Scofield said, perhaps cued by the necklace, "can't a man forced to drink at least do it in his own home?"

Hernandez looked over his shoulder at Bay and then at Fischer, sighing as he caught the second man's eye, and then he turned back to Scofield. Before Tripp Hernandez could speak, Noah Fisher jumped in, rumbling:

"Just get your boots on, you whiny bastard. We're gonna drink, boy!"

Less than ten minutes later, the group spotted the camp fire Joseph Bay had kindled between the two huts he and his brother called home. They were by far the closest two shacks of any outrider dwelling, separated by a mere forty feet. The fire circle between them saw use most every night the brothers were not out riding the field. The Bay brothers had sat with crackling flames between them time and time again, discussing the mother they shared, or the fathers they didn't, the leeches they'd dealt with together over the years, women, and all the other disasters.

Joe Bay rose as his comrades drew near. He stood, backlit by the fire, with his hands on his hips and his hatless head cast back. His eyes were on the stars. Joe looked down as the men reached him.

"How do, gentlemen? Looks like you managed to wrangle him OK."

"How deep does this conspiracy go?" Scofield asked, smiling as he looked askance at Tripp Hernandez. He had taken several large swigs of liquor on the short walk over—his hangover from the morning already an ancient memory—and was feeling more affection for the other outriders than he had in months.

"Deep enough to lead back to the Bay Brother who keeps a case of bourbon in his footlocker, I'll tell ya that much!" Noah Fischer clapped Joseph on the shoulder as he walked past him, easing his hefty carriage down onto one of the wooden crates beside the soot-blackened circle of stones Eric Bay had set two years prior.

"Y'know, your little brother and these boys are some real keen negotiators," Scofield said as he handed Joseph the bottle and dug in his jacket for a pack of cigarettes.

"Oh yeah? What'd they say?" Joe turned and made a loose gesture toward another of the crates that doubled as seats, shivering in the cold night air.

"Uh, what was it . . . oh, right. Drink!"

All five men shared a laugh as they settled themselves on their makeshift seats. Joseph had laid the fire in stages, starting with a loose pile of twigs and paper shreds beneath stacked lengths of slender branches on which was piled a jumble of boards and thicker logs. This top layer was just now catching and the fire's warmth and glow grew quickly.

In the bright light, Scofield looked around at his friends. Hernandez had pulled off his wide brimmed hat and repeatedly ran his hands through his shaggy mop of black hair, a habit of his. Noah Fisher had a faint smile on his large face and his eyes were fixed on the flames. Scofield could barely see the younger Bay brother across the fire, but Eric was nodding as Joseph said something to him.

*It's good not to be such a damn hermit all the time*, Scofield thought to himself. He realized he had nodded and grunted in the affirmative to his own thought and, embarrassed that one of the men might have heard him, he voiced his thinking.

"I'm glad you boys drug me out. Good to spend some time not, uh . . . not sitting around alone thinking so much."

"What'd'ya spend yer time thinkin' about?" Tripp asked, reaching out for the whiskey bottle.

Scofield handed over the whiskey, then hesitated before saying "Well what do you think, Tripp? I think about your Mexican ass all day."

Fischer let out a howling laugh. "We ought to get you some tequila, actually, and you hand me that bottle of bourbon! Ain't that right Trippy?"

"Hey, my ass is Mexican-American-French, OK? I can drink whiskey, tequila, and wine, if I want."

"French? Fuckin' French!" Eric exclaimed.

"One eighth is one eighth, Mr. Bay."

"All I see is the Mexican," Noah added, still laughing. "Speaking of whiskey, how we doin' on that front, Joe?"

Joseph Bay rose without a word, tipping his cap and turning to walk toward his shack. No one noticed him sway and almost stumble. The bottle made the rounds and each man had a small swallow before it was gone. Eric unsuccessfully tried to light a cigarette off the fire several times. He kept singing the hairs of his hand and having to pull back when the searing heat grew too intense.

"Y'know we all got matches and lighters, young buck," Scofield said.

"Yeah, but it's better this way if you can do it. More caveman."

"Everything caveman is better, sure. That's why we moved outta caves and started cookin' things, and wearing clothes, and having medicine, right?" Hernandez asked sarcastically.

"Sir, what works, works," Bay responded with mocking severity. He jerked his hand back from the fire for a fifth time. "Gimme some fuckin' matches!"

Fischer handed Eric a lighter as the elder Bay brother rejoined the group. Joe Bay sat and placed a full bottle of bourbon on the sand between him and Noah as he took a seat. Scofield leaned to one side to take a look at Joe—he had seen him listing as he walked back to the fire.

"How you doin', Joe B?"

"Doin' . . . real drunk. Doing fine."

The two men were about the same age and had been riding the sunfield for about the same length of time, but it bothered Scofield to realize just how little he really knew his brother-at-arms. He studied Bay's face for a few seconds more before resting his elbows on his knees and staring into the crackling fire. It was warm on his face and hands. He wondered if his own wrinkles looked so deep and black in the firelight; if his own eyes were so dark beneath their brows. He heard Fischer slurp at the whiskey bottle and then cough. Eric chuckled and reached out for it.

Perhaps it was the liquor settling in or the long days adding up, but all of the men seemed to fall into silent reverie at the same time. Silence reigned but for the crackling, whistling fire for a good long time before Hernandez spoke.

"So, what do you spend your time thinking about, Scofield?"

Scofield took in a breath to crack another joke about Tripp's "Mexican ass," but exhaled again as he actually pondered the meaningful question.

"Be straight honest with you, I don't know. There's not a singular thing I find myself thinking about, like a . . . like the one that got away or the good ol' times I this or that, y'know? I think about riding and about my horse and the job. That's sure. I wonder about other people. What the fuck is some guy doing right now in Europe or Russia or wherever it's daylight? Sittin' at a desk or riding along on a train or . . . or waiting in line. I wonder how it is that we few wound up out here. That we ended up in this day and age knowing the smell of horseflesh and what silence can sound like. I . . ." he paused, searching for the right word. Four sets of ears waited patiently for him to find it.

"I marvel at it. At this," his hand described a wide arc across the desert night. "And I can't imagine life being like anything else. But I know if I'd been born a different day, a town over, whatever, y'know, it all probably woulda been different. It's impossible to know what's coming, but just . . . fuck, boys, it's amazing to trace the trail you've already walked. Just amazing."

Thoughts formed in his head—complete thoughts; meaningful thoughts with poignant memories attached—but he knew it would be no use to try and voice them through his whiskey-thick lips. Scofield had no idea if he had made his point or not, or even if he had really had a point to make, but at least internally he felt good for having spoken a little bit of the monologue he kept running in his mind day in, day out.

Noah Fisher of all people, not a man known for profundity, broke the silence. "If my dad hadn't died I bet ma woulda stayed back in Philadelphia and I'd be punchin' controls working a drill press, just like pops. Probably drunk by noon right there on the job, just like pops."

"What did him in?" Eric Bay asked. His older brother shot him a look that no one, including Eric, happened to see.

"The bottle and a weak heart, I guess. I dunno. After we got to Vegas I never much asked my ma about him. She hated him every bit as much when he was dead as she did when he was alive, y'know? Stayed real angry. It made me not want to be around people much."

"That's why I'm out here. People? The fewer the better. Present assholes excluded, of course." Scofield said quietly.

Hernandez chuckled. Then, suddenly, he was laughing out loud. He fought to get his breath as his comrades demanded he share, and, finally,

Tripp managed to gasp out: "I was just remembering that time Hutton and Greg White come into the bar."

Joe Bay and Scofield, who had both been present for the incident Hernandez was surely relating, both began to laugh as well. Eric looked from face to face, smiling in confusion, infected by the other's laughter.

"Hutton comes walking in and he's pissed and he's got something to say to all of us, right?" Tripp addressed himself mostly to Eric Bay. "And he looks and sees there's a bunch of hookers in there, so he turns to Greg and tells him to clear the women out, right? And so White takes one step forward, takes in a breath and just goes . . ." Tripp took a breath of his own, as did Scofield.

In unison, the outriders shouted: "Whores! Get the fuck out!"

All five men laughed good and long. Eventually Tripp added: "And Hut says: 'You ain't much of a diplomat Greg, but that got it done,' and then we was all laughing so much Boss Hutton started crackin' up too and he never even remembered he was supposed to chew us out over something!"

Again laughter lifted into the night, rising like the smoke and embers that swirled off the fire, just now burning past its brightest, hottest point and beginning to slowly die out.

Tripp Hernandez swayed back and forth unsteadily, unable even to simply stand still. Between his side steps back and forth and Scofield's blurred vision, it took over half a minute for the cigarette hanging from Tripp's mouth to link up with the flame dancing from Scofield's lighter.

Finally, his smoke lit, Hernandez reached out and managed to clap his friend on the shoulder.

"OK . . . Scofy . . . thanks fer the smoke. Good talks."

"Why dontcha cool your jets here a while, man? Yer more drunk n' me an' I can't see straight with both eyes open."

Hernandez shook his head, smiling widely and turning away. "Nah 'm fine. Gotta shit n' shower. You don't wanna be 'round for either of those."

Scofield watched Tripp leave from the doorway of his shack. He thought to call out a goodbye, but let the notion drop. Hernandez faded into the haze beyond the glow spilling from within the hut, his steps quick but his stride short and uneven. Scofield laughed under his breath and turned to enter his tidy little home. On the floor, all of his provisions and gear were neatly packed and stacked, ready to go for the ride ahead of him.

"See, ain't you glad you're a retentive little prick?" Scofield said aloud. "Now all you gotta do is pass the fuck out."

Which he did a matter of seconds after he hit the bunk, still wearing his clothes and one of his boots.

* * *

When Scofield awoke, he was utterly shocked to find his hangover mild. His head ached but he knew it would soon be gone with a good dose of water. His stomach ached from hunger but he felt overall healthy and was acutely alert and even restless to start the day, despite the dull pain behind his eyes and at the base of his skull. He rose and stripped naked, then stood still for a minute or two, pressing the fingers on one hand into his closed eyelids, the fingers of the other on either side of the back of his neck.

Then he stepped into his little bathroom and slurped water from the sink as he let the shower warm.

The outrider was bathed and dressed, his thirst slaked, and his hunger curbed within fifteen minutes. Outside in the predawn air he found Reese on her feet. *Good girl. You're as ready as me, ain't ya?* He fed and watered the horse.

As he made a few trips carrying the saddle, saddle bags, and feed sacks from his shack and began to prepare his horse for the ride, Scofield reflected on the night he had shared with his boys. It was first a sense of melancholy that took him when he realized he had not had such an evening in longer than he could remember, but this line of thinking was immediately replaced when it occurred to him that *hell, you had a fine night just last night. Why dwell on the rest?*

He was glad the men had drawn him out last night. Out of his home and out of himself. But he was equally anxious to get back to the field. He had been away for only ninety-eight hours but in his mind it felt like forever. Scofield had no pride or sense of grandeur about him that made him feel the sunfield was unsafe when he was not present; he was simply aware that he was one of the top hands and that his place was out there and not back here.

Still, he found himself grinning thinking about the stories the group had swapped and about the ribbing and bullshitting and all of it. It was good to spend time with good people. But the bad folks were calling.

Even though it had been just four days off the field it had been three and a half days too long and one night well spent. As Scofield locked up his little shack and adjusted his belt and revolver to mount Reese, he looked back at the scattered buildings that made up the town. Dawn light flattened the dimensions of the scattered outrider huts and distant general shop and charge station, rendering the Outpost a blue-gray cut-out against a pale beige expanse of loam. At this time in the morning the sunlight was just strong enough to overpower the glare of New Las Vegas but not yet full enough to expose the many hues of the land. For a little while each morning one could imagine a West that had faded into memory some two centuries ago. For the thousandth time, Scofield lamented his having been born those two centuries too late.

Then the outrider cleared his mind, took hold of the saddle and vaulted up onto his mare's back. Reese tossed her mane and whinnied softly, glad to be returning to the itinerant life the both of them relished. Through the cold morning air came the low whine of the day's first commuter train arriving at the Outpost. Soon the hum of the charge station would begin and not long after that voices and neighing horses and all the rest of it would make up the din of another day. Not for Reese and Scofield, though. For them there would be nothing but the breeze and crunch of sand under hoof for days.

The horse and rider crossed the glowline at a steady canter. Reese was a powerful, reliable horse. She seemed almost indefatigable with enough water and feed. Scofield would ride her at this clip until they were well into the field, slowing only to begin his patrol at the pillars.

The ten mile ride to the sector where Scofield would begin his assignment usually took half an hour. But ever wary of the poor job done by others, he'd decided to make straight for the sunfield and ride to his area of patrol among the pillars. The detour would add nearly an hour to the trek. But it turned up something remarkably peculiar.

Scofield rode along in the shade of the quantum photovoltaic arrays overhead, his mind drifting but his eyes sharp. It was still early in the morning and the wind was up, stirred by the sun's warmth shining down through the cool air. A thousand veins of sand crisscrossed the land like miniature mountain chains as the desert took shape once again. It always amazed Scofield how such a seemingly barren place could change from hour to hour. The colors of the land traveled through a rich palate in the course of any day. The land grew from flat, dead loam into a sea of sandy waves and drifts that settled into low dunes before softening out again in the evening breeze.

He would have missed it had Reese not changed her stride. The horse bucked under him, hopping as she would have done to avoid a prairie dog hole or snake. Scofield snapped back into the moment and looked over his shoulder to see what had spooked the horse. Hauling back on the reins (he never ignored a signal from Reese), at first the outrider saw nothing but the usual patches of light and shade. As his horse came to a full stop and he could let his vision settle, the rider's eyes immediately locked onto something else. Some sort of cord.

Scofield dismounted, staying Reese with a pat on the flanks, and walked back to the cord, cocking his head to one side. It was like nothing he'd ever seen in the sunfield: a thick tube, easily the circumference of his bicep, covered in a canvas sleeve almost the exact shade of the desert floor. Scofield knelt and held his forearm near the cord. The hairs on the back of his arm didn't rise so he slipped his fingers into the sand and raised a length of the tube. It was dense and surprisingly heavy. The covering was painted cloth with a thick rubber sleeve underneath.

He rose and gave the cord as solid a shake as he could, stumbling under its weight. Only about a fifteen foot length shook clear of the ground. Scofield hooked an arm under the cable and began to follow it toward the nearest QV pillar. After twenty yards, he found one end of the cord. It was capped with a steel disc fitted over a threaded iron pipe. After a good struggle, Scofield managed to unscrew the disc, revealing six individual cords within. Each of these cords ended in a standard four prong tap—the kind one would use in an everyday appliance.

The outrider stood, holding the iron housing in one hand and examining the taps with the other. He'd never seen anything like it. But his first thought was that it must be legitimate; some sort of refuse left over from construction. No leech would ever use a cable like this. It would take three men to carry just the section he'd unearthed. He trailed the cable sixty yards before its other tip popped free of the soil. This end consisted of the same heavy disc and casing, but when the outrider worked the steel cap off, he found only one large tap. It was tri-pronged and bigger than anything he'd ever seen out in the field. After a minute spent crouched studying the tap, he reattached the steel disc and dropped the line back onto the desert floor.

Scofield kneaded his neck with both palms, pressing his eyes shut tightly. After a moment, he made up his mind to disregard the strange cord. His gut told him there was nothing much he could do about it and therefore not much call to worry about it. *Probably some sort of old transmission line,* he reasoned. The grid had run on hard wires for years before switching to transmission beacons. It was uncommon but far from unheard of to find detritus from the older technologies strewn about the miles of open land; the engineers were thorough but certainly not perfect. And at any rate, Scofield was late to start his route. He waved Reese toward him and hitched his trousers up an inch to mount.

Mayor Franklin Dreg hardly noticed the rivulets of sweat streaming down his neck. Here beneath the spotlights and before countless pairs of eyes he was in his element. The Boston Metropolitan Convention Center held over twelve thousand people in its auditorium at capacity and the attendance was well over half of that muster today. Dreg was not the keynote speaker at the Annual National Civic Planning Summit, but even though he had already sailed past his allotted ten minutes, the crowd was held rapt by his presence and he could feel their focus upon him. It penetrated and energized him; it empowered him.

The handful of other mayors who had spoken before him were stodgy and sterile or nervous and mumbling, prattling on about power shortages or water issues or trade concessions—Dreg on the other hand relished the sound of his booming laugh echoing from the dozens of speakers around the large hall, and *his* city had plenty of power to offer . . . for a price. He paced about the stage, pointing and gesticulating at random faces he could hardly see through the garish glow of the lights.

Dreg had already dispensed with all pleasantries about his host city and its governance and virtues and the like and was well into a shameless lauding of New Las Vegas. While he never directly took credit for the city's extreme efficiency, his generous use of the word "we" was clearly meant in the Royal sense.

"We love the charm and the history of cities like Boston and Charlotte and Pittsburgh," he grinned, nodding as if to representatives of each of these places, "but in New Las Vegas, we take pride in having added that word up front. New. *New!* In a metropolis of some ten million citizens, in our minds, the people come first. If that means rezoning certain acres for electrical infrastructure or for a government center, we don't worry about the cost or the effort, we worry about how the end result will help us, we the people. Now I know that our gracious hosts here in Boston have been presenting to you the benefits of heliostat and central tower projection for power production, and I certainly respect that in New England land is at a premium, but I urge you to look at my proposal for quantum photovoltaic installations offshore. Pound for pound and inch for inch, you can't beat QV if you ask Mayor Dreg. And our municipally owned and operated production facilities are ready to churn out QV panels at a moment's notice, it just takes some inspired thinking from a few government types." Dreg winked, adding: "As you all know, of course, cloudy days cut heliostat production up to eighty percent more than they do with QV arrays, and as I've noticed today, the clouds seem to like it here in old New England."

Timothy Hale had, of course, written every word of Dreg's speech. And while he careened on and off message, The Mayor was making his point: our systems work better than yours. And as the government of New Las Vegas had long ago assumed control of and consolidated its power companies into one apparatus, if he could convince any of the assembled players of this, it would be funds directly into his coffers. Never mind that appointed topic of this session was transit—Dreg was here to sell electrons. And sell them his way.

As he rambled on well past twenty minutes, The Mayor had no idea that at just the same time his closest advisor was beginning to connect a series of dots that would render much of his rhetoric about the stability and advantages of a system run via quantum photovoltaic power arrays inaccurate.

Timothy Hale sat some two thousand seven hundred and fifty miles away with his head in his hands. "Not here," he mumbled, sitting alone in The Mayor's opulent receiving chamber. "Fucking hell . . . not here . . . please . . .."

It was his fourth day in the field and Scofield had been tracking the snaking path of a freshly removed tapline for over twenty minutes. The leech had been reckless, not even bothering to scuff up the trail traced in the afternoon sand. The outrider had spotted a patch of disturbed earth by a QV pillar and immediately zeroed in on footprints leading out into the desert. After a mere hundred yards the leech seemed to have grown weary of looping his power cord and had let it drag behind him. Scofield could hardly believe when he spotted a man hunched over a generator a mere two miles from the sunfield.

The sun hung directly above and the wind was at the outrider's back, so the leech heard and then spotted the horse and rider when he was still a good distance off. The man rose and began to sprint away before apparently realizing he was in the middle of the desert. He came to a stumbling halt. Scofield drew his rifle from the saddle bag and chambered a round. The leech seemed to be fidgeting with something in his coat so the rider slowed Reese to a trot and fired a shot near enough to the man that he'd hear it crackle through the air.

"Raise 'em up!" Scofield shouted, further slowing Reese until he could draw an even bead on the man. He unbuttoned his black vest to more easily twist into firing position, holding the walnut stock of the rifle tight against his shoulder. Scofield's finger rested on the trigger.

The leech put his hands out, palms forward, but kept them closer to his body than Scofield liked. As Reese slowed to a trot—she knew the drill and needed no more commands—Scofield shook his head in disbelief.

"Just what the fuck are you thinking?"

The leech was maybe thirty-five; older if he'd lived well, younger if he'd lived hard. He wore a long tan duster over a slate gray workman's uniform and boots. His face was covered by a thin beard the same coffee brown as his close cropped hair. Beneath the beard his lips were turned up into a faint sneer.

Scofield reined Reese to a halt within spitting distance of the smug bastard and reached across his torso to draw the revolver with his left hand, his right keeping the rifle barrel trained. Then he slung the rifle and leapt off his horse. The outrider switched his pistol into his shooting hand and slowly approached the leech.

"Real slow, OK . . . real slow I want you to shed that jacket." At first the man just stared back, eyes squinting in the sunlight but unblinking. Scofield didn't move a muscle as he waited. Eventually the man nodded in mocking deference and slid both arms from his duster, letting the coat fall to the sand.

"Now roll up that right sleeve and take two steps this way." The leech complied, breaking eye contact. Scofield didn't even have to ask: the fellow finished sliding the heavy cotton sleeve back and then presented his forearm. Sure enough, there was a ragged L-shaped scar carved into the flesh just below his elbow.

"Fuck's sake," spat Scofield. "You stupid shit! A goddamn two-timer and . . .." His arm trembling with a surge of anger, the outrider stepped even closer to the leech, the gun barrel a mere foot from the man's chest. "Were you actually gonna power that goddamn jenny on?"

"Wanted to listen to some radio." The man said. His voice was calm and confident, arrogant.

"Unless you went'n cut an L into your arm for fun, I'm gonna guess you kind of understand a thing or two about what's out here, hm? What them big pillars and panels you were fuckin' with back there do, yeah?"

The leech was silent, his sneer returning.

"Smilin' at me, huh? Think it's funny, hm? You know what woulda happened if you'd powered that thing up here?" Scofield snarled, pointing at the old, rusting generator the man had been crouched over. The leech was silent, his face melting back into an expressionless mask. "You'd be real fuckin' dead, mister. And hell if I care about that, but me and my girl here woulda probably been scorched too."

"I've heard the lecture, Mr. Cowboy, sir." He crooned back, his voice dripping with disdain as he tapped at his scar.

Scofield's face grew hot; his vision swam red. "Well," his whispered inching closer, "perhaps you need to pay closer attention . . . in class!" He shouted these last words as he slammed a boot heel into the leech's right knee. The man crumpled with a yelp. Scofield was on him in an instant, his left hand at the man's throat, the pistol's tip pressed to his forehead.

"Now," the outrider continued, his voice calm, "as much as I like your attitude, let's us change our tone a bit, OK?"

The leech groaned, cupping his injured knee.

"O . . . Kaaay?" Scofield repeated.

"Sure. Why not."

"We're more'n five miles from the glowline. You think that thing's for fun? Huh? If you'd gotten that old piece'a shit to fire up we'd both be charred nothing. Are you stupid or you got a deathwish or what?"

"I saw you coming. I figured it'd give me a bargaining chip."

"Bullshit. You didn't drag a generator five miles north of safety for a chip. Why the fuck are you out this far into the field with a generator?"

"Just a living, man. Take it easy with the six gun."

"We'll see about that." Scofield rose, keeping his pistol trained on the leech's chest. "Arms and legs out straight and don't you even breathe." The man complied, and Scofield searched him thoroughly; he removed the leech's boots, checked every pocket and gave him the business, smiling ruefully as the man coughed and sputtered. The outrider rolled the thief over and ran a hand over every inch of his back, relishing the sound of the leech spitting sand. Finally, satisfied the fellow was unarmed, Scofield rose.

"Stay just like that." He searched through the pockets of the long coat and found some scraps of food, a large folding knife and a dog-eared novel. A small leather satchel lay near the ancient generator and loosely coiled tapline. In the bag Scofield found more rations, random tools—pliers, a wire cutter, and screwdrivers—and a worn pair of binoculars. The last item he pulled from the sack was wrapped in an oily rag. It was an old two-way radio, jury-rigged back to life. Copper wires stuck out from its rusted tin casing here and there and the mesh of the tiny speaker was ripped to shreds. Gingerly, Scofield eased open the slot on its back and exhaled in relief to find the battery housing empty. He tucked the radio under one arm.

The outrider walked in a slow circle around the leech and his meager possessions. Something wasn't right. As if to echo his thoughts, Reese tossed her mane and whinnied. Scofield raised a hand to calm the horse. "Wait a sec . . ." he muttered under his breath. Then aloud he asked: "Where's your hook-up?"

The leech raised his head from the sand and turned to look at Scofield but said nothing. "Where's your tap rig, boy? And water . . . you ain't got a drop of water on you. Fuckin' speak up, leech!"

"Just traveling light," the man said, slowly rising from the sand. Scofield brandished his pistol but the leech continued to move, easing himself up to sit Indian style.

"More like traveling short," the outrider whispered. "You were actually gonna use this damn thing?" He indicated the radio. "You, a two-timer out here with a goddamn generator and radio? You *must* got a death wish, boy." Scofield knelt near the man. "Can you think of any reason in particular why I ride a fuckin' horse? Hm? See this here area around us? It don't much care for sudden electrical charges, y'know?"

With that Scofield tossed the radio aside and fired three rounds into it. The little device splintered apart across the desert.

"That's better." The outrider rose and inclined his head to make the leech follow suit. The two men stood at about the same height and now for the first time Scofield studied his adversary's face carefully. Lurid details that had earlier escaped him now stood out. The man's forehead was covered with a spider web of fine veins. He had several hairless patches in his beard and his lips were pale and cracked. There were tight wrinkles framing gray, intensely staring eyes. When the leech did not look away, eventually Scofield broke the gaze and almost shuddered. There was something deeply disturbing in those eyes. Or behind them.

Scofield took a few steps backward and then half turned to Reese. He pulled the coiled rope off her saddle and secured one end to the bridle. Then he made a slipknot on the other end of the rope. Turning to the leech, he quietly said "You try anything, this goes around your neck. Simple as that."

Without being asked, the leech pressed his wrists together. Scofield wrenched the slip knot shut and then looped several lengths of the coil around the man's wrists, tying these off in a tight knot. Last, he fished a book of matches from his hip pocket and struck several at the same time. When he had melted the knot into a mass of fibers, he lit one more match and fished a cigarette from his vest.

"Let's take a walk." The outrider mounted up and slid his boots into the stirrups. "Don't come too close to my horse and don't talk." Scofield tapped Reese and the trio set out at a fast walk towards the nearest station, some twelve miles east.

# 5

Timothy Hale's soles clicked loudly on the lobby's marble floor. His shoes were polished and his shirt was smartly pressed and starched. He had resolved himself to remain calm today; to be analytical and objective, but his heart was racing and his flesh was pale and damp. The fabric of his stiff collar chafed against his neck. Hale checked his pulse three times while waiting for the elevator. It was shortly after 10 a.m. and already he had been to the power stations in Grids One and Two. He half hoped Maria Rodrigues would not be at her desk when he got here to Grid Three. Without Mayor Dreg, Hale felt less sure of himself and had less reason for diversion, so his normal air of confidence was gone. That coupled with his growing sense of dread and now Maria smiling at his approach rendered the usually cool and collected man near the point of hysteria.

"Hi, Timothy." Maria said as he stopped before her desk. "Flying solo today?" She asked. Her tone was warmer and more casual than he had ever heard it when accompanying Dreg, with a tone so unlike her usual professional voice it almost sounded like a different accent.

"Yes, but still all business." He replied, his voice oddly quiet. "Much to my chagrin, of course," Hale added quickly. *Smoothly done, idiot. Perfect,* he thought to himself.

"Isn't it always?" She looked down at her monitor and pretended to be typing something, her voice reverting to its standard tenor. Hale drew in a breath, resolved to conduct his mission efficiently while not making a fool of himself.

"Listen, Maria ... I know whenever I come through here we always chat ever so briefly and I wish I had time now to be less ... well, businessy, I guess ... not that that's a word, but you know what I mean."

She looked back up and Hale continued.

"But something is up and I have nineteen more grids to visit, so I'll just be my usual businessy self. Can you please run a scan on your usage fluctuations between midnight and dawn over the past week?"

"Sure, Tim." She put on a pair of reading glasses and clicked away at her console for a minute, then spoke without looking up. "Can't you do that from your office? I mean I don't mind at all, but I just figured you could save time."

"We can run diagnostics on everything, yeah. But only on the macro level. If there were any, eh, problems within the station itself it would just show up as a grid issue, not as a station issue . . . you see . . ."

Maria nodded, watching a slew of orange and green numbers scroll past on the screen. A few strands of her coffee brown hair had slipped away from their silken cascade, dancing in the air-conditioned breeze. The scan finished and a detailed bar graph popped up on the monitor showing the peaks and valleys of power use over the last week. "It's totally standard for the season."

"OK . . . OK well that's good, then. And no one has reported anything unusual?"

"Not to my knowledge. And I manage regulation so, y'know, if it's not to my knowledge then no. Or someone needs to be fired." She pulled her glasses off and smiled. Timothy forced a big grin in return, but quickly dropped it as she reflexively blinked and leaned ever so slightly away from him.

"Anything I should be watching out for?"

"Um, no . . . not really. Just some screwed up software someplace I'm sure. Just . . . just keep an eye out for irregularities and please report any if you see them."

"That's pretty much my job description." She replied, nodding.

"That's true—I don't know why I . . . yes, that's true." Hale took a step back from her desk, feeling foolish. "OK, well, have good one, Maria."

"You too." Hale began to turn when she added, "you know you can always just call." He faced her again. "I mean it's not that I mind you coming by, of course, I just meant to save yourself time," Maria said, glancing up and then away again.

"I don't mind. I like to see you," he paused for half a breath. "And everyone, face to face. To keep in touch."

"Sure. Well . . . I'll be here watching the juice."

Hale pressed the heels of his palms into his eyes as he rode the elevator back down. *Why don't you ever grow out of that schoolboy bullshit?* he asked himself, unsure whether the "you" in question was rhetorical or personal. He allowed himself the elevator ride and the walk back out into the sunshine to think of all the things he could have said to Maria, and then he reverted to focusing on the issue at hand.

The massive dips in power supply had grown routine which, obviously, ruled out irregularities. There was still the outside chance that some software or machinery was running out of synchronization with the grids, but that was unlikely. The watt usage had begun spiking both day and night, and entirely different systems ran the current beacons used for sun power transmitted by daytime and the salt cavern heat stores used at night. Added to the issue was the fact that every bit of the grid was backed up by redundant mechanisms except for the actual sunfield itself and the molten salt caverns themselves. Hale loathed dealing with the outriders, but if he had no further clues by that evening, he would have to call Boss Hutton.

Franklin Dreg stood in the middle of the Boston Common smiling like a schoolboy. Thick, luscious snowflakes drifted around him. The gauzy-white sky hung low above the city and the air was an indistinguishable mix of cloud, haze, and falling snow. The Mayor had not experienced true winter weather in years and he was held rapt by it—all of it: the white flakes, the biting cold . . . even the smell of the damp, frigid air and the hard packed soil beneath his polished wingtips.

"You know, I could get used to this," Dreg said, barely above a whisper, to no particular member of the entourage that stood waiting patiently around him. A committee of ten city officials, along with Dreg's usual retinue of assistants and porters and security detail, exhaled thick plumes of breath into the afternoon. It had been Franklin's idea to eschew the highly efficient—and heated—subterranean network of pods that crisscrossed the city to walk the three miles from Government Center to his grand hotel.

The Mayor was positively smitten with the centuries old city. Its ancient brick buildings and real, working gas lamps (fueled by a small methane reserve dedicated solely to these archaic icons) and plural parks and trees were all so diametrically opposed to the parallel lines and right angles that made up New Las Vegas. It was a mix of acquired nostalgia and smug condescension that colored Dreg's impression of this, America's oldest megalopolis. Boston was charming, yes, but woefully inefficient, in his estimation.

The Mayor wrapped a gloved fist around the lapels of his heavy black greatcoat and turned to face the waiting group. "Amazing, isn't it, to think of the hundreds of years . . . the thousands of people who have stood here in this space . . ."

Dreg trailed off and the chairman of the Greater Boston Commerce Department, a tall man with a birdlike face and an impossibly thin neck said: "Right here in the Common three hundred years ago there would have been cattle and sheep grazing where we stand."

"American history, gentlemen," Dreg continued, utterly disregarding both the man who had just spoken and the fact that the group contained several women, "is the richest asset of our nation. Centuries of progress. Not once in this great land's years have we had a single violent transfer of power. Not once have our citizens had to lie in their beds at night and wonder who was in control—who was looking out for them; wonder if in the morning there might not be a current behind the light switch or water in the tap."

The Mayor nodded at his own profundity while the Commerce chairman seethed beneath his heavy fur cap. The snow had begun two hours earlier and several inches blanketed the land, muffling the sounds of the city. An occasional rumble under foot or the moan of a ship's horn drifting from the distant harbor melted into the soft whisper of the breeze and falling flakes.

Mayor Dreg suddenly decided he wanted to be alone. He grunted out a summary "Good day all, I must go," and began walking at a clip toward his hotel in Copley Square. He planned to go to his suite, don heavier shoes, and then set out incognito; he did not want to be seen as he met with the two men he had contacted earlier that afternoon, men who seemed very interested in a contract for well-priced power. It never crossed Dreg's mind that no one here would recognize him anyway.

It was late afternoon and the temperature had begun dropping. Wilton Kretch had long ago learned to trust both his eyes and his gut, but the two were at odds just now. On the distant horizon he could clearly see, or so he thought, a rippling mirage. But it was far too cold out for that to be the case. He blinked and rubbed his eyelids repeatedly, straining to make sense of the undulating vision.

Shady whinnied in protest as the outrider stood in his stirrups, stretching to get a better view. The sun was setting behind the swirling air and only when Kretch looked indirectly west could he be sure there was indeed something there. But it was fading now, and as the shimmering patch of air grew ever fainter it seemed to be drifting south. The wind was gentle but steady and was decidedly blowing northeast. None of it added up, and reluctantly Kretch let himself assume his eyes had been playing tricks on him. He knew somewhere in his subconscious, though the notion never formed itself into a true thought, that eyes don't play tricks—only the mind does.

It could have been a dust devil caught in the shifting breeze. Or even just speck of dust on one cornea. He had never seen a mirage on a November evening, but thought to himself *hell, I ain't no weatherman.* Kretch wheeled his mount and turned to face the sunfield. Here, at the westernmost tip of the miles and miles of arrays, he always felt the most isolated and, though he never allowed himself to call it such, afraid. There was nothing but open desert for the next hundred-plus miles to the west, and for a good part of that distance in any other direction. At any given time, the closest human being could be up to ten miles distant and riding farther away at that.

At least, anyone who was supposed to be out here. Most leeches didn't much frighten Kretch once he had eyes on them. But the unknown was a different story. The thought of being watched without knowing it chilled him to the bone. And not just by human eyes. There were countless other eyes out here. Late at night they became ever-present and even mythical. Glowing eyes perched unblinking above yellow fangs set in hungry jaws. Grasping hands and creeping feet. There was no solace to be found out here; not where electronics were forbidden and fires discouraged.

Sometimes his fear would come to a head and Kretch would begin blind firing in the night, hoping to frighten off whatever was coming for him. Often the loud crack of the pistol was comforting—sometimes it was jarring and made things all the worse. After all, a shot in the dark could ward off evil but could also show evil exactly where you were.

It was barely dusk and the land was still aglow beneath a pale sky. The night fear had not yet taken Wilton and in his mind he was still the force to be reckoned with. The badass to be feared. *You and me, baby. Shady and K. We got 'em all right where we want em, huh?* He thought. Then out loud Kretch continued. "Ain't a fuckin' thing out here to be feared 'cept for us, ain't that right Shady? Ain't that right Shady boy?"

Kretch hummed softly to himself as he wheeled the colt to begin his rounds of the sunfield's western perimeter. Far away the city of New Las Vegas and its surrounding towns were switching from solar energy to molten salt power. Wilton fell silent for a moment, thinking he had heard something. There came no sound save the horse's plodding hooves and the rising wind, beginning to swirl as the evening air cooled. Then the mechanical drone of hundreds of QV arrays swiveling back toward the eastern horizon drowned out all noise. The slow, familiar grinding of gears lasted for nearly two minutes and then, after a series of clicks, the desert was perfectly still. Kretch must have imagined the distant, baleful moan. It must have been just the night's fear setting in. He drew his six shooter and rested the pistol across his saddle as he began to whistle softly.

The janitor wheezed and coughed as she leaned against the large terracotta planter. She had slipped on the marble floor she herself had just mopped and it had taken her nearly three minutes to regain her feet. Her left knee throbbed and both wrists ached where she had caught herself. She feared something was broken. A slow trickle of blood stained the sleeve of her cobalt blue uniform where the IV needle had been ripped from its port.

The old woman sighed wistfully, looking at the two hundred plus square feet she had yet to clean. The swirling veins of the dark stone floor leered back at her. This was the lobby outside Dreg's office—a room she rarely entered and one in which she was loathe to be caught doing a poor job. She knew The Mayor was out of town but at any moment the elevators were sure to open with one of his secretaries or guards or even just a courier; even the latter had security clearances here in the executive building and thus were of a higher station than the janitor. In the eyes of most everyone, she was the lowest of them all—a virtual untouchable.

Her heart leapt each time she heard the drone of an elevator rising in the shafts below; her one wish at that moment was not to be seen by anyone, to merely finish what she had to do without drawing any attention. Slowly she rolled up her sleeve and re-inserted the IV line, wincing at the sharp pain from her damaged forearm.

Then the worst happened. Finally one of the elevators rose all the way to The Mayoral penthouse and the doors slid open. Out stepped none other than Timothy Hale. The executive secretary's face was dour even for him. His eyes were glued to the ground and his steps quick and angry as he surged off the lift. The ancient janitor tried to melt against the wall, pressing herself between the dark panels of mahogany and the large potted fern. Hale had taken only six steps when his leather-soled loafers slipped on the wet marble and he stumbled, breaking his fall with one hand on the stone floor and the other against the wall.

"Jesus fucking—dammit! Fuck!" Hale spat, livid, as he stood and straightened out his suit jacket. He cracked his neck from side to side, letting out a series of angry grunts before he realized he was not alone. The city's de facto second in command locked eyes with one of its lowliest peons: a cold, steely gaze met watery, frightened eyes. The two stood unblinking for a pregnant moment before Hale unleashed his rage on the poor woman.

"Goddamn simpleton! What the fuck do you think you're doing?" The old woman trembled and was silent as Hale marched toward her, one foot slipping again. "Shit!" He shouted, stopping on the other side of the planter and peering between the fronds. "What's your name?"

"I'm sorry, sir." The old woman stammered.

"What . . . is . . . your . . . name." Hale paused between each word, his eyes seething.

"Candice, sir."

"Candice . . . what?"

"Wilbee. Candice Wilbee, Mr. Hale. I'm sorry I—"

Hale held up a finger and the janitor snapped her mouth shut. "Who is your supervisor, Wilbee?"

"Mr. Tansingco. Sir—Ronald Tansingco. Services unit twenty three."

"Don't move a muscle, Wilbee." Hale took a few careful steps until he was on a dry patch of floor. Then he pulled his slender, silver-plated mobile phone from a pocket and pressed the small circular button at its bottom.

"This is Hale, executive eight-two-one. Give me City Services immediately." Hale glared at the old janitor as he waited. "Services? Exec eight-two-one. Give me unit twenty three, supervisor Tansingco."

"Sir . . ." the janitor implored.

"Silence!" shouted Hale. Then into his phone he continued, "Is this Tansingco? What? Well where the hell is he? Excuse me? This is Timothy Hale, who the fuck is this? What's your name? Number? Well when your boss gets back from lunch, you have him call me immediately and I will remember your number, five-one-six." Hale ended the call and slowly, pointedly, slid the phone back into his jacket pocket.

"Come here." He beckoned the janitor without so much as looking over. From behind him came shuffling footsteps and an odd creaking. Hale turned to see the old woman trailing a mop in one hand, an IV tower in the other. He was struck by the pathetic sight before him. But he kept his jaw firm and his shoulders pulled back. "Listen, Wilbee . . .." Hale thought of all the things he could say but the moment had passed; his anger had all but melted away. "When you mop the floor up here . . . dry it."

The janitor nodded emphatically, her neck popping and crackling.

"Now just . . . go away. Go clean somewhere else." Hale jabbed a finger into the down button on the nearest elevator to summon a lift for the woman and then hurried from the lobby. He drew his phone as he opened the door leading to the inner offices and feigned a conversation as he passed the two secretaries seated in the outer waiting room without looking up.

Once in his own chamber, Hale sighed and dropped his mobile onto a chair. He leaned against his desk, hating himself for how he had just acted. The strain of the afternoon had come to a head when he slipped in the lobby and the wizened janitor had borne the brunt of his anger and stress. Hale had personally called or visited all twenty-one grids in New Las Vegas and had spoken to all the major transmission stations as well. Power usage was spiking hourly now and there was no other explanation left . . ..

# 6

Scofield watched the leech's every move from the corner of his eye. *You actually think I don't see you, you dumb bastard?* he thought to himself. The man had been slowly closing the gap between himself and the horse and rider over the past ten minutes. He'd been patient, gathering slack in the line tied to his hands as he drew ever closer. Scofield had slid the revolver from its holster minutes ago. His hand gripped the weapon tightly while his shoulders and neck remained loose, his head bouncing casually as he rode. From behind, he was the picture of relaxation. But his teeth were clenched and his breaths shallow. The outrider could easily track the leech's long shadow on the sand, which was painted lavender by the setting sun. The move would come any second.

The leech made his attack with impressive speed. In one motion, he tossed the rope over Scofield's head and lunged for the rifle protruding from Reese's saddle bag. This, however, was exactly what the outrider expected, and despite the man's surprising quickness, Scofield was faster still. His left hand parried the tightening rope and with his right he cracked the grip of his pistol down on the man's head. The rider spurred his horse and Reese took off into a full gallop.

From behind came a shriek of agony as the rope went taught and the leech flew into the air, his shoulders wrenched by the initial shock and the wind knocked from him as he landed on the ground and was dragged. Scofield let Reese keep up the pace for a few hundred yards and then reined her back into a fast trot. He twisted around in his saddle to see the leech bouncing along on his back, his legs kicking helplessly at the loam.

"Enjoyin' yourself, asshole?" Scofield shouted angrily. He turned around again and spurred Reese up to a canter. The leech coughed and moaned behind him.

"Please! Please stop!"

The outrider clucked his tongue and the mare came to an abrupt halt.

Scofield leapt down from the horse and pulled the rifle from the saddle bag.

"Well sure, since you asked so nice," he said, chambering a round as he approached the crumpled figure. The leech had curled into fetal position, his chin tucked against his dusty gray shirt. The rider stopped with his boots inches from the man's face. "Stand up." Scofield waited, silently counting to five. Then he took up the rope and leapt back, wrenching the man prone, before grabbing the thick knot around the leech's hands and hauling the whimpering wretch to his feet. The leech gritted his teeth; his eyes were tearing.

"Popped a shoulder, huh? Both, even? That's what usually happens. Y'see buddy," Scofield dropped the rope and sized up his wounded rival, rocking back onto his boot heels, "you're not exactly the first fellah I've brought in. And you wouldn't be the first one I haven't brought in, read me?"

Mucous dripped from one of the man's nostrils. His face was cut in a dozen places and sand stuck in his brown hair and five day beard. His knees buckled constantly. It was not to be underestimated what even a short dragging could do. The fight seemed to have gone out of him, both in body and spirit.

"I want you to give me a good reason why I shouldn't end you here and now," Scofield hissed through clenched teeth. "And I'm serious, mister. I'm fuckin' dead serious. Give me one reason."

"Paperwork," the leech whispered back.

At first the outrider was perfectly still, his face an inscrutable mask. Then, slowly, he cracked a savage smile. "Well . . . I guess you really do know how it is out here." Scofield gripped the hard wood of the rifle stock firmly, taking a slow step toward the bloodied man.

It was nearing midnight when Reese and Scofield crossed the glowline. The leech was still unconscious from the rifle butt cracked across his jaw. A squat cinderblock field station sat some fifty yards off, bathed in a pool of halogen light. It was garish and ugly in the black night; an insult to the crisp stars above. This far out on the southern line even the glow of the city was diminished to almost nothing. The sky was truly dark.

Scofield had looped his drag line around the man's feet and wrapped him in a tarp. It was more than the bastard deserved but there was something unique about this one. Unique and unsettling. The outrider wanted him compos mentis when they arrived at the station.

When the trio reached the light of the little compound Scofield dismounted and first made sure the leech was still out cold. Some taps to the face and a gun barrel to the cheek accompanied by a few choice words confirmed that the man wasn't playing possum, so Scofield cut away the excess rope and then tended to his horse. He'd not planned to make a stop at a post for days so the water sacks were still mostly full, but after testing the station's water tap for purity, the outrider emptied and refilled his stores with "fresh" water (it tasted just like what it was, after all: desalinated ocean water piped across hundreds of miles and stored in a zinc-lined basin).

Scofield filled the trough beside the water tap and then led Reese to it, letting the mare drink her fill. As she did so, the outrider untied the rope from her bridle, then removed the saddle and gear from his mount. Scofield keyed the November code—three-six-one-nine—into the station's door, and tossed Reese's harness and saddle and all the bags and provisions inside. He entered the building and switched on the lights and water heater; no reason to skip a hot shower and a night in a clean cot as long as he was already here. Then he searched for the cell key.

Scofield stepped back outside and, glancing over at the leech, walked around behind the station, key in hand. Scofield worked the key into the heavy, rusted lock of the door to the iron cage—so many of the criminals who took to the field were engineers and technical professionals that the outriders had come to revere a good old deadbolt over anything electronic—and after a brief struggle it swung open, creaking in protest. The cell was a five by eight rectangle of metal beams with a concrete floor and ceiling. There was a water tap set into the wall above a steel grate—this was sink, shower and commode. A few of the stations had an old surplus cot. This one had a pile of burlap sacks.

His standard mix of pragmatism and compassion led Scofield to pull a few horse blankets from the shed beside the cell. These he tossed into the cage. No good to let a man freeze to death—corpses don't talk much. The water from the cell's tap came out putrid and tinted orange with rust, so Scofield filled a bucket in the horse trough and set it inside the cage. Walking back to the trough, he topped off his canteen after taking a long pull of water. Finally, he approached the leech.

"Wake up, asshole," the outrider barked. The man stirred and muttered something. "Already awake, huh? Then get up, asshole." The leech fell still again. Scofield waited a moment, and then roughly unzipped his fly, making the action as loud as he could. He held out his canteen and let a thin stream of water pour onto the man's head.

"Fuck's sake, mister!" The leech bellowed, contorting into a ball and then trying to rise. As the leech fell back to the sand, his feet still bound, Scofield let out a howling laugh.

"Easy boy. Just water. Now get up."

"My feet are tied together."

"Well then you're gonna do some hopping."

Groaning and swearing under his breath, the leech slowly got to his feet. The myriad cuts on his face and hands were caked with dried blood and sand. His body sagged from the trauma of being dragged. But his eyes were sharp and defiant. He somehow managed to look dignified as he stood there despite his constant shivering and bound hands and feet.

"Hop." Scofield said without venom, turning his back and walking toward the cell. He paused after a moment and waited, without looking over his shoulder, until he heard the leech awkwardly following him, alternately jumping and shuffling across the dusty soil.

When the pair reached the cell, Scofield stood back and the man entered without protest. The outrider slammed home the iron-barred door and clicked the heavy lock shut.

"OK, now go ahead and put your feet by the bars and don't try shit," Scofield said sternly, brandishing his polished, eight inch knife. The leech lowered himself to the cement floor and held his bound feet against the iron bars. Scofield reached into the cell, grabbed the rope, and with one smooth swipe severed the singed knot.

"You can work the rest of that off yourself."

"What about my hands?"

"Yeah. We'll get to them." Scofield sheathed his blade and walked back around the station. Reese was standing by the trough expectantly.

"I know girl. Don't you worry your pretty head." He pulled open the station door and dug through the largest saddle bag until he found her feed sack and an apple. This he cut in two, munching on half himself. Back outside, Scofield fed the other piece of fruit to Reese, then knelt and poured a generous mound of oats into a plastic tub lying beside the water trough.

Sighing, resigned to the unpleasant business at hand, Scofield returned to the clapboard shed and gathered a small armload of kindling and logs. The outrider fashioned a simple pyre and stuffed bark strips beneath it. He pulled a cigarette and lighter from a pocket and gathered the lapels of his long black jacket around his neck as he knelt.

Once Scofield had a few timid flames licking at the piled wood, he held his cigarette to the embers, rising once it was lit. He stepped back and smoked, taking long, slow drags as the fire grew. Orange-yellow sparks crackled and danced up into the black night. Standing still, the heat of the fire beginning to warm his hands and face, Scofield first realized just how cold the night was. The breeze, calm since its usual twilight surge, was now picking up again. Scofield shifted back and forth on his heels and then began to lightly stamp his feet, fighting back the chill that had crept into his boots.

The fire crackled as one of the thicker logs succumbed to the heat. As the flames licked and sang, Scofield thought for a second that he had heard a deep, distant moan drifting across the desert. He took a few hurried steps away from the fire and cocked his head to one side to listen. The only sounds that came were the crackling flames and swirling breeze. Scofield finished his cigarette, crushed the butt beneath a boot heel, and then drew his knife. He carefully slid the blade into the glowing embers and then stood back to let the metal heat. It was time for the leech to get another mark. Then they would talk.

Dreg panted for breath as he stumbled across the frozen street. The pavement was coated in a thick layer of ice beneath five inches of fresh snow. Already The Mayor had slipped and fallen several times. It was just after 3 a.m. east coast time, and Dreg had been on a bender since nine o'clock that evening. The day had consisted of so much mindless drivel: he'd sat with the mayor of Boston to discuss advanced diffuse photovoltaic arrays—panels that could extract usable electrons through rain and fog— he'd met with the ambassador of some godforsaken eastern European nation still holding out from continental federation over a natural gas dispute, and he'd suffered through a gala dinner where countless state and local yes-men had jockeyed for his elbow.

"Don't they fugging know I've better things . . . better time to spend . . ." Franklin muttered as he stopped under the awning of a men's apparel store. Dreg had put away several gin and tonics at the gala and, upon returning to his hotel, announced to his security detail and personal assistants that he was feeling ill and wished to be left alone. Like a debutante awaiting her father's snore, Dreg had stood by the door to his suite until he heard his head of security walk down the hall for a piss. Then The Mayor, wearing his most non-descript three-thousand dollar suit, sharkskin boots, a fedora, and a heavy wool overcoat, had run to the nearest staircase, lumbered down fifteen flights, and burst forth into the wintery New England evening.

The Mayor could, of course, have ordered his staff to leave him alone. Many were the times, usually when drinking, that Dreg had simply turned to his retinue and said: "Fuck off." Legally, they were obliged to do so; personally, they were thrilled to do so. But Timothy Hale had become such an integral part of his life, both personally and professionally, that "fuck off" no longer much applied to him. Even with his countless duties and responsibilities—in truth, Dreg understood less and less of Hale's activities as the years went on—Hale always seemed to be there, whether The Mayor was chairing a conference on public transit or was passed out in his own alabaster bathtub.

With Hale safely two-thousand-odd miles away, Dreg felt a thrilling sense of freedom. The Mayor loved the power and clout that came with his job but he hated the work. It was all bullshit to him until it came time to say "yes" or "no." Dreg didn't give a good goddamn how long someone had worked on this proposal or studied that phenomenon: give him a couple things he could decide between and he'd decide the matter with time for a toast left over. In truth it was Hale who usually made the decisions, presenting The Mayor with only the simplest of options after whittling away any confusing or conflicting aspects and then leading his boss to the conclusion he wanted; Dreg both saw through and rather preferred this arrangement. It left him free to talk big and think little.

Franklin Dreg had put in his time, as he reasoned it. "Son of a goddamn coal miner," as he always said. And birthed by a woman with terminal cancer. Never mind that his father had been a foreman and later manager of the mine, or that his mother's cancer had been in remission at his birth, only to return years later when the young Dreg was away at boarding school. And never mind that said school was one of the most prestigious and expensive in the country. Franklin had spent as much of his time on horseback or playing golf as he had actually studying.

But somewhere in his later teenage years, Dreg had slowly begun rejecting his pedigree. His distaste for the green lawns and white sweaters of his prep school grew steadily into disdain, and by the time of his graduation, Franklin had become Frank and would soon be introducing himself solely as Dreg. Frank had moved to Las Vegas (indeed at the time the city was known only informally as "New"—the official adjective was a part of Dreg's legacy) because it was far from home, was different from home, and there were jobs available. All that, and he'd heard that people in Vegas didn't ask too many questions. So the young man had reinvented himself, tougher, sharper, and colder.

The Mayor rarely thought of and never missed the days of his youth. He was better off without any of it. But his looks had gone. As he wobbled unsteadily, his knees buckling, Dreg stared at his reflection in the shop window. Where was the handsome, square-jawed face that had once captured the interest of women and commanded the respect of men? Heaving a sigh, Dreg pulled off his fedora. When had his thick head of dark hair grown so thin and . . . and greasy? And that mustache! Why the hell had he grown that? Somewhere from his cavernous vault of suppressed memories—unlocked by the gin and wine and whatever else he'd drank—Dreg recalled once studying a photo of Joseph Stalin with something near reverence.

It seemed foolish now as he began to lumber erratically down the street. It was all foolish: the mustache, the sneaking out to drink alone, Stalin, the many women come and gone. Dreg didn't even know if his father was still alive. Or his sister, for that matter. He couldn't remember the key code to his palatial apartment. He didn't know any of the maids', or cooks', names or why he had grown that damn mustache. He scratched at his hairy upper lip in disgust. The snow was falling ever faster; the flakes ever larger. It was freezing cold in the deserted streets. There were no taxis and The Mayor did not know Boston's transit system. Sighing, he fumbled about in several pockets before finding his phone.

The meeting he had conducted alone after leaving the hotel that evening had not gone as well as he had hoped when he conceived of it back in Vegas. He had already been slightly drunk when he met the two Federal men and they had talked over him, rather than listened to his plan. He had accomplished little, gaining only their tacit support, not their guaranteed business, and he left saying he would follow up with them once he was back west and better informed. He was now so drunk he could hardly even remember what it was he needed to know more about. New arrays of some sort—some systemic vulnerability they would prevent . . .?

Dreg collapsed onto a bench and managed to hold down the large gold key at the bottom of the phone. He was vaguely aware of the chief security officer's voice as his large, soft chin dropped forward onto his ample chest. Snow slowly piled up on and around the slumbering Mayor. Any passerby would have taken him for just another beaten-down drunk. Beneath the streets, trains ran here and there, humming along on magnetic rails. The streetlights dimmed as Boston shifted to a reduced usage pattern. The weather was not set to change for days, and power needed to be conserved.

"I don't like this part either, but it comes with the job description." Scofield glowered through the iron bars at the crouching leech. In the pale light of the station, the outrider's eyes were mere shadows. In his hand, the sinister, eight inch blade glowed orange. He could clearly see the leech, however, and the man's face registered not so much fear but sorrow, resignation.

Scofield was shocked when, without so much as a word of protest or even a sigh, the man stood and proffered his arm, sliding his bound hands between the iron bars.

"Make it a clean cut if you can." He whispered as Scofield took hold of his left forearm. The outrider nodded, and then quickly raked the smoking knifepoint along the man's flesh, carving and instantly cauterizing a hash mark beside the L-shaped scar.

The leech winced and pulled his arms back into the cell, hurrying to the tap on the wall and fumbling with both hands to get the water running.

"Don't use that shit!" Scofield barked loudly. "The water's full of rust. Dip in the bucket." The leech did so, glaring over his shoulder as he held his arms down into the tepid water. Scofield knelt and slid his knife into the sand to let it cool. "You smoke?" He asked, fishing for his pack of cigarettes.

"Sometimes," the man answered quietly, looking away.

"Well, seems a good time to me. Got a name you like being called?"

"My name is Sebastian. I like being called that." The leech rose and shook the dripping water from his arms.

"OK, Sebastian it is. You can call me Scofield. Don't worry, I ain't gonna chat you up all night. We'll make this short'n sweet." Scofield drew his blade from the cold soil and checked the metal. It was cool enough to touch so he waved Sebastian toward him and reached through the bars. The leech allowed him to cut away the knotted rope and then rubbed at the raw skin of his wrists. Beads of sweat had formed along his forehead despite the chill night air. His jaw was firm but the crows feet wrinkles by his eyes bunched more deeply as Sebastian fought the searing pain from his fresh wound.

Scofield put two cigarettes in his mouth, lit them, and then passed one through the iron cage. The leech accepted it and took several long, deep drags.

"You know three is the limit, right?" Scofield asked.

"Limit . . .?" Sebastian was confused, thinking the outrider referred to cigarettes.

"I'm gonna have to bring you in but if you're straight with me, I'll give you a clean report and leave out the little bits about you going for my rifle and trying to blow up a goddamn square mile with that generator of yours. They'll probably let you out in a few weeks. But three is the limit. You get caught one more time, you ain't gonna see the sunshine again, be that from the pen or the grave. So listen real close, Sebastian—don't fuck with me. I can make things very simple or very complicated for you."

Sebastian seemed to contemplate this for a moment, the cigarette hanging loosely from his chapped lips. Finally he nodded.

"How long have you been leeching?"

"Three years."

"When did you get that first cut?" Scofield pointed to the man's arm.

"About a year ago. It was in late ninety-four."

"What did you do before?"

"I was an accountant."

"No shit. You—no shit? What changed?"

"I got bored." He shrugged. "What did you do before you got up on that horse?"

Scofield blew smoke out through his nose and pulled off his hat. "We can keep this amiable or not, Sebastian. I don't much care. You decide to answer me straight or not."

"I did answer you straight. I got bored. And sick."

"Sick?"

"I have colon cancer. It keeps trying to take me and then giving up, coming back, going away. I'm dying and I was a fucking accountant. So I got bored. Came out here. Figured I'd leave a few extra bucks behind for some people."

"You're terminal, hm?"

"Yes."

"Well I feel for ya, man. But I ain't. And you were fixing to take me out with you. Why does a former pencil pusher with a death sentence want to kill a stranger?"

"I didn't want to kill you, Scofield. I just didn't want to get caught. I've got precious little time. I didn't want the end to come in a cell."

"That makes sense. But it don't change the facts from where I sit."

"It does for me."

"Noted. You work alone?"

"Yes."

"Always?"

"Yes."

Scofield had been crouched, continually flicking at the butt of his cigarette. Now he rose and dropped the smoke onto the sand, not bothering to stamp it out. He buttoned his long jacket closed against the breeze and put his hat back on, twisting it from side to side until it sat comfortably on his brow. It was near to 1 a.m., and Scofield planned to ride at first light. There was no doubt left that Sebastian was lying, so there was nothing more to be said. For now.

Without another word, Scofield walked around the corner of the cement building. He paused out of sight of the cage for a minute, then walked back and stood before the iron bars.

"So one sick man, working alone, dragged a three hundred pound generator five miles past the glowline? An accountant jury rigged an old radio to transmit shortwave? I don't think so. I do not think so, Sebastian, or whatever the fuck it really is. We'll talk again tomorrow before I bring you in to Corporal. You got one more shot at having a rest of your life, however short it may be."

# 7

Dreg answered on the fifth ring. Of the seventh call. Hale had been repeatedly dialing The Mayor for a half hour, alternating between the Boston hotel room and Dreg's personal cell phone. Hale had spoken to Colonel Ridley Strayer (the head of the Civil Defense Forces and thus the man in charge of the mayoral security detail whenever Dreg travelled) four times, but the man was adamant that he would not enter Dreg's chambers; Franklin had ordered him and his men to stand fast, interrupting him for nothing, and Strayer was about the only man in the entire bureaucracy of New Las Vegas that Hale could not overrule. And there was no love lost between the two, so despite Timothy's saber rattling—despite his use of the polite term "fucking emergency"—the secretary general had been reduced to dialing over and over again until finally he heard life at the other end of the phone line.

Or something similar to life. Dreg said nothing. Hale could hear him muttering and rolling about in bed. He moaned several times and may have even vomited during one coughing spell. Timothy waited patiently for a few moments until there was relative quiet on the other end of the phone line and then spoke in loud, clearly enunciated words.

"Frank. Can you hear me?"

More coughing.

"Mr. Mayor. It's Hale. If you can hear me, just say anything, alright?"

"Fuck man . . . what . . ." The Mayor slurred.

"Sir—we have a situation. A bad one. I need you to put the phone to your ear." Hale held his handset away from his head as Dreg shouted a series of curses and apparently knocked his mobile to the ground. Hale pressed the button for speaker phone and sat back in his chair as Dreg muttered something about: "Gotta piss . . . got to have a piss somewhere . . . ."

It was a full five minutes before Hale heard the distinct sound of a toilet flushing followed by what may have been a cork pulled from a bottle. Finally, after more swearing and crashing about, Dreg's voice came through the phone line loud and clear, though far from coherent.

"The fuck it is . . . is . . . Hale?"

"Sir . . . can you understand me? If you can't, I'll just deal with this for now and brief you later."

"Fucking talk man!" Dreg howled.

"Frank . . . we're being drained." Silence. Timothy heard the distinct sound of a bottle hitting the floor followed by a low whimper and then another clatter, as if Dreg had tried to retrieve the liquor or wine or whatever and immediately dropped it again.

"What?" The Mayor finally managed.

"We are being drained."

"Drainers?"

"Yes."

"Well . . ." Dreg must have dropped the phone down on the bed. When next he spoke his voice was muffled. "Must be a malfunction or error . . . mistake. Error somewhere."

"It's not, Frank!" Hale barked loudly, a finger pointing angrily toward the phone as if The Mayor would sense the urgency through the gesture.

"Gotta be a fuckup, Tim. Gotta be someone's fuckup. Don't call me for an hour. I just . . . gimme an hour. Two hours. Leave this alone. You don't know what yer talking about. Leave it all alone." The line went dead.

Hale leaped to his feet and grabbed the handset from his desk, slamming it home on the receiver. He pulled at his tie, loosening the knot, and stalked about his office looking for something to smash or upend. Then, quickly, Hale sat down and forced himself to count to ten. By number six he was already dialing Strayer again.

"Security," Strayer crooned into his phone. He knew damn well it was Hale.

"Strayer. When will you be getting Dreg back here?"

"Well, we were scheduled to travel at thirteen hundred, Hale, but with this weather I doubt we'll be leaving anytime today."

"What the fuck do you mean?" Hale spat, seething.

"What the fuck I mean, Timbo, is that there's a blizzard here, and no plane is flying anytime soon. Situation back home or not."

Hale thought of a thousand things he could say but opted instead to very slowly, deliberately, hang up the phone. He rose again and walked to the window, keeping his steps calm and measured. It was a few minutes before nine a.m. Pacific Time and the city was just coming to life. On the streets some seven hundred feet below, pods shot to and fro and pedestrians scurried about like so many ants. *So many blissfully ignorant ants*, Hale thought. He alone knew what was happening. Or rather not he alone, but only he on this side of the situation.

Timothy stood by the window for a long time debating his next move. Then he wheeled and made for the door, grabbing his suit coat off its hanger. As his hand grasped doorknob, the phone rang.

"Came to your senses, asshole?" Hale whispered aloud. He practically leaped to the phone. "This is Hale."

"Hale?" came an unfamiliar voice.

"Yes."

"Eight two one?"

"Yes, dammit, this is Tim Hale, exec eight-two-one. Who is this?"

"This is Supervisor Tansingco from Services twenty-three. You called to complain about one of my janitors?"

"Oh. Yes. Forget about that. It doesn't matter anymore—just cancel the report." Hale moved to hang up the phone but heard the man continue speaking. He put the phone back to his ear in time to hear:

" . . .all fine and good, but do you know where she went?"

"What?" Hale asked, only half paying attention.

"Do you know where my employee went?"

"No. She got on an elevator."

"OK, but that was a day ago now, and she hasn't reported in since."

Hale worked his arms and shoulders into his suit coat until it fit him comfortably. He was standing before the bank of elevators, poised to summon a lift. But as he had exited his chambers, an idea had flitted through his mind. Unresolved, he hesitated, standing alone in the lobby, weighing his options. There weren't many, with Dreg useless for the time being and his details still spotty. He'd been planning to travel across town to the Office of Security and mobilize an investigative team, but now the thought occurred to him that no one but he yet knew of the potentially dire straits facing . . . well, everyone.

Timothy was in the position to call all the resources of the metropolis to bear, or to take a bit more time and see if he couldn't work through some of this mess alone. He took a slow step back from the elevators, then turned on his heel. Hale let himself into The Mayor's opulent reception room. He walked with purpose across the plush carpet and past the assembled treasures. Keying in the code known only to himself, Strayer, and Mayor Dreg himself, Hale entered The Mayor's office. He pressed a few buttons and the exterior metal curtains slid up, letting morning sun bathe the room.

Removing his blazer, Hale went to drape it across one of the chairs facing Dreg's desk, but then turned and instead hung the jacket on the tree in the corner. Awkwardly self-aware, the secretary general slid The Mayor's chair away from the desk and eased himself down into it. The soft leather caressed his thighs and back. Timothy allowed himself to savor the sensation for a moment, and then sat forward abruptly. He slid open the top left drawer of the desk and produced a remote control. He knew this device like the back of his hand, and casually punched in a host of commands.

The panels along the interior wall of the office came to life. Their various monitors and displays and banks of lights pulsed and glowed with the rhythm of the city. Or cities, to be precise: Hale was not looking at the New Las Vegas grids alone, but rather he had pulled up an overview of the entire network, some five thousand square miles of Vegas County. There were twelve independent communities, a scattering of loosely incorporated villages, and then the city itself. Technically, all the numbers were correct for 9 a.m.: this many trains were running and that many blocks were being treated with warm air and this many citizens had reported to that many work stations. But sure enough the power consumption was running at a near perilous rate.

"So we're definitely being drained. No fucking question." Hale spoke aloud as if consulting someone else in the room. "Services are stable . . . no individual spikes . . .." He rose and approached the displays. Hale let his eyes track along each monitor, watching numbers and graphs rise and fall. *And it's in the fields.*

Hale sighed. In the bottom right drawer he knew Dreg kept a decanter of thirty-year-old brandy. It was time for a drink. He retrieved the fine cut crystal vessel and a tumbler and sat back down in The Mayor's chair. Pouring himself a finger of liquor, Hale reached for the phone.

"Can't you walk any faster, man?" Scofield practically sighed.

"What's the point?" Sebastian replied wearily. They'd been on the move since just after sunup. Scofield had woken when it was still dark and fed his horse and eaten a simple meal, then roused the leech at dawn. He'd let the man drink his fill, splash water on himself and then, when the prisoner refused food, they'd set out.

By brief agreement, Sebastian was walking a few yards in front of Reese and untethered. Scofield had the rifle tucked in the crook of his shoulder. Based on the conversation they'd had last night and the man's comportment the day before, he was hoping against hope he wouldn't have to use it, but with this fellow a length of rope wouldn't have changed anything—if Sebastian was going to make a move he would find a way to do it one way or the other. Somewhere in the back of his mind Scofield felt that if he was going have to shoot the bastard, the leech ought to at least have a chance. It would make the paperwork simpler, anyhow.

"The point is ambling for the next three goddamn miles ain't gonna change anything, Sebastian. I know you can make better time'n this. Let's just get it done with."

The leech picked up the pace for a hundred yards or so, then came to an abrupt halt, facing eastward, the sun in his eyes. The outrider pulled his mare to a stop and then gently tapped her twice with one heel. Reese backed up a few feet until Scofield let off the reins and patted her neck. Both men were silent.

Finally Sebastian turned to face the horse and rider. His pupils were mere dots from staring past the morning sun. His clothes were a mix of dusty and damp where breeze had stirred up the loam and where sweat had pooled around his collar and down his chest. Scofield had given him a battered old tin canteen from the outpost and this he now slowly unscrewed. The leech took a sip, and then held the canteen above his head, letting the tepid water flow over his hair and neck. As he poured the vessel out on himself, he never once broke eye contact with Scofield.

"I figure there's no way out of this."

"This?" The outrider replied.

"Yes. This."

"No. I guess not."

Sebastian nodded and turned back to face the east again. Scofield cocked his head to one side, regarding the man curiously. After a while, the leech slowly shed his long jacket. He held the duster at arm's length, studying the worn garment, before carefully folding it. Sebastian deliberately smoothed out each crease and seam, tucking the folds just so until the jacket was evenly worked into a tight square. Then he carelessly dropped the coat onto the sand.

"You ever had a cause?" The leech asked, his voice strong.

"A cause? You mean like . . ." Scofield trailed off, realizing he didn't know what the man meant.

"A cause, Scofield. Something you believed in."

The outrider ran a calming hand along Reese's flanks as he dismounted. He slid his rifle into the saddle bag and drew his long barreled six gun, but kept the pistol down against his thigh.

"You mean to say that riding the fields was your life's goal?" Sebastian continued, looking away across the miles.

"I don't mean to say that. I didn't say that." Half conscious of the action, Scofield buttoned his vest with one hand. He'd learned long ago how loose clothing could complicate a fight, and one seemed potentially imminent. "But it beats living in that goddamn city. Or any city. And it suits me. Maybe it is a cause, then."

"It beats living in the city . . ." Sebastian nodded, turning, a rueful smile lifting the corners of his thin lips. "It's better than that so it's good enough, huh? That's the exact kind of thinking that perpetuates this mess."

"I'm all for philosophy and debate and whatnot, Sebastian. But to be real blunt, I ain't so much for those things with you. I get that this is hard for you and I'm real sorry for your situation and all that . . . but if you don't turn the fuck around and start walking east again we're gonna have to drop the rhetoric."

"You think this is rhetorical?"

Scofield took a few steps toward the leech. Less than five feet separated the two. Again the outrider noticed the fine spider web of veins crisscrossing the man's forehead; his tiny pupils set in gray, watery eyes. The patchy spots of his beard. Somewhere in that face's past Scofield could imagine a handsome man—an everyday man sitting at a desk drinking coffee, even—but it was a hard face staring back at him. Sebastian wore the look of a man fully committed to something.

"Yeah. This is rhetorical. Turn around. Walk." Scofield said quietly. Sebastian shook his head. "I answered your question. There's no way out of this."

"You only answered my first question. And you answered it wrong. There is a way out." His eyes flitted down to the pistol.

"I'm not gonna kill you. Not because you ask me, anyway."

Sebastian sank to his knees. He tore at the buttons of his gray shirt, practically ripping it open and exposing a pale chest.

"Fucking hell man!" Scofield spat as the leech spread his arms.

"Do me the last favor I'll ever ask of anyone, Scofield. Just do it!"

The irony of the gesture not registering, Scofield trained his revolver on the man. "Get up!" He shouted, his voice cracking with a mix of rage and fear. "Get the fuck up!"

"Do it!"

Sebastian slumped back to sit on his heels, his hands dropping onto the sand. For a painful moment the two were still and silent, Scofield's pistol trembling in the air between them. The outrider saw it coming only a breath before it happened: Sebastian gathered a handful of sand and sprung forward, hurling the dusty earth at the outrider's face. Scofield wheeled and covered his eyes, firing a shot deliberately far to one side. He spun round again, lashing out with his left fist, and landed a textbook jab on the leech's nose. He slashed the gun barrel across Sebastian's temple and then sank a savage kick into the man's guts. Before he'd even fully gotten his feet under him, the leech staggered and then collapsed onto the soil.

"Stupid fuck! I didn't sign on for this shit! I give you respect! I give you water! And you keep trying to fucking take me out? You want to die so bad, just kill yourself! It ain't fucking hard! Kill yourself you want to die so bad!" Scofield panted for breath as he loomed over his fallen foe, weapon aimed.

Sebastian gasped for breath, coughing and wheezing. There were flecks of blood on his lips and a gash above his left eye. He held a hand skyward, palm out to ward off any more blows. It was clear that despite his fervor, his body was weak. Scofield backed up a few steps and holstered his pistol, too worked up to be holding a firearm at the ready. Despite everything, for some goddamn reason he had a grudging respect for this man. He wanted to understand him.

"Is this . . . this is really your cause, Scofield? Your calling?" the leech gasped.

"Jesus, man. Enough with that." Scofield reached down and grabbed Sebastian under the armpits, hauling him to his feet. He stepped back again, resting a palm on the pistol grip. "What's your fuckin' calling? Stealing electricity?"

"Taking power."

"Well cause or not, I got a route to patrol and a paycheck to think about, so let's just walk, goddamnit."

"Is Boss Hutton there?"

"What?" the voice on the other end of the line shouted. The background was a din of blaring music, rowdy voices, and glasses slammed against tables or clattering off one another. This was the third bar Hale had called. There was only one more place he knew to try if he couldn't locate Hutton here.

"Boss . . . Hutton!" Hale said loudly. "Is Hutton there?"

"Who'n the hell is this?" the man spat back.

"This is Timothy Hale from Mayor Dreg's office."

"From where?"

"Mayor Dreg! Jesus, man! Just tell me if Hutton is there!"

"Sit tight, cityboy." It sounded as if the phone had been unceremoniously dropped onto the floor. Hale pressed the button for the speaker-phone and leaned back in Dreg's chair, the clamor of the tavern filling the office. *It's fucking 11 a.m. . . . they have nothing to do but drink at eleven in the morning?* Hale shook his head in disgust, looking out the bank of windows to his left.

When nearly five minutes had passed the secretary was sure that once again his call had been forgotten and he'd need to re-dial, re-dial again, and get nowhere. By the afternoon he figured he'd be travelling to each of these dives in person. Hale sighed and reached for the handset to hang up and end the call when a different voice crackled into the room. Hale grabbed the phone and held it up, switching off the speaker.

"Who's this?" The voice was deep and gravelly, shaped by a life of shouting and smoking and too much inhaled dust. It was Hutton.

"Boss Hutton?"

"Who's this?" the man repeated.

"This is Timothy Hale. Executive General Secre—"

"I know who ya are Hale, you don't gotta get all fancy with me."

"Right."

Hutton must have held the phone away to cough. Or to have a coughing fit, more accurately. Over the background noise Hale heard him mutter "Jesus Christ" and hack once more. Then his voice came through again.

"Well?"

"I wanted to ask if you'd had any problems out there. Out in the field?"

"Any problems? Anything at all? Sure. We got all sorts of problems. Sick horses and sunstroke and shit for pay for my boys. Sure. Care to be a bit more specific, Hale?"

"Um . . . yes . . . have you noticed any . . . increased activity? Increased leeching activity?"

"No."

"Nothing unusual at all?"

"Hale if I gotta repeat every damn thing I say this call is gonna take a while."

Timothy nodded as if Hutton could see him and leaned forward, resting an elbow on the desk and pinching the bridge of his nose between his thumb and forefinger. He closed his eyes.

"Well, allow me to come to the point then: we're being drained."

There was a long pause. "Hold on," Hutton muttered. A loud clatter took Hale by surprise as the bar's phone was again dropped. He heard Hutton shouting: "Shut up! All of you shut the fuck up! Quiet! Don't make me start shootin', goddammit! Pipe down!" After a few seconds, relative calm set in on the other end of the phone line. Hutton came back on the line.

"What did you say, Hale?"

"We've got drainers."

Boss Hutton turned away from the open floor of the bar, facing the knotted wood of the back wall. He could feel the eyes of the dozen or so other outriders upon him and he didn't want his face to display any of the emotions beginning to seethe within him. He kept the phone pressed to his ear, though neither he nor Hale spoke for a long time. Finally, his voice a mere whisper, Hutton asked: "You're sure?"

"There's no doubt. None."

Hutton sighed. In all his sixty-seven years he had never felt the mix of anger, confusion, and abject fear now taking hold of him. When next he spoke, the gruff edge and even the twang were all but gone from his voice, drawl replaced with a measured, even timbre.

"OK. How bad is it?"

"We're at double usage. It started just at night—we were tapping into the reserve salt every few evenings. But for the past week it's been during production hours, too. And the numbers just keep rising."

Hutton sighed and pressed the palm of his left hand against the roughhewn wall. He could barely feel the grain and splinters of the wood through a thick layer of callous. "Has there been any system failure yet? Or any overloads?"

"No."

"So it's a pretty even drain, then."

"Is that good? I mean, is that less bad?"

"No. It's worse. It means whoever's fucking with us is spread out. Organized." Hutton's mind was racing. A slew of questions, theories, and doubts clattered off one another. His first concrete thought was that he needed to get the message out to his boys. If they could buy a few days, though . . .

"Hale, can we make it four more days without doing anything?"

"What!" the bureaucrat yelped, his voice jumping an octave.

"We got Round Up in four days. I'll have ninety percent of my riders in one place and I can brief 'em all. We can put together a plan and implement it uniformly. Otherwise . . . word gets out too early . . . my boys are gonna start turning up dead."

"We can't wait, Hutton!"

"I know the way these things run. If the drainers find out we're onto them, they'll either disappear or start shooting. We have to come at them in force. Organized."

There was a pause and Hutton could hear the secretary muttering something to himself. Then he asked quietly: "How do you know 'the way these things run?' We've never had an issue before. Ever."

"Not us and not here, no. But Lensk did. And the Australian Field. And Madrid. Ephesus."

"OK . . . I get it."

"Give me four days. If the city can keep running for that long, then give me that long. We'll be in touch; I'll be here same time tomorrow. Check in. Or actually . . . you know, don't do that, just be reachable."

"I take it you understand the gravity of—"

The business done, the outrider chief dropped all pleasantries, reverting to his old self. "I get it Hale! Not sure you do, but don't go and question me. I been riding these fields since before you were born. I was here before the fuckin' fields, alright? I get it."

"I just—"

"I'll call you back, Hale," Hutton interrupted. "What do I do, just call Main and ask for The Mayor?"

"Yes."

Without another word, Boss Hutton hung up, gently returning the phone to its receiver. He checked twice to make sure the handset was evenly placed in the cradle, awkwardly tapping it from side to side. He ran both hands through his coarse gray hair and then smoothed the front of his black vest. One of the cuffs of his checkered shirt was damp where he'd rested an arm on the bar. He sniffed at the fabric. Stale beer. Turning to face the bartender, Matteson, Hutton mustered as much calm and confidence as he could and said: "Pour me a bourbon and a water."

Matteson nodded and turned away to comply. Hutton walked out from behind the bar, limping ever so slightly—as he had since being thrown from a half-broken colt three decades back—and sat on a stool, facing the room. Every set of eyes in the bar was turned away or down, each man feigning focus on some unrelated thing. It was clear that they were waiting for him to talk.

"On me," Matteson mumbled for the two thousand and eighty first time. Hutton hadn't paid for his own drinks in this or any of the nearby bars in years. But he bought rounds for others like his money was on fire. He was at home here among his boys. And they were comfortable whenever he was present. Technically, Hutton had no more authority than any other outrider, be he an old hand or a young buck. They all reported to the Office of Civil Defense just the same on paper. But

Hutton had been tending the fields for a solid decade longer than the next most senior outrider. His authority was absolute, if only de facto. No one—him included—even remembered when he'd gone from Cliff Hutton to Boss Hutton, but the handle was accurate. He was The Boss.

With the title came respect. But with the respect came responsibility, and a damn good serving of it at the moment: Hutton knew full well that if word got out about the drainers his boys would go trigger-happy. Innocent leeches (or rather those siphoning power only for themselves or for petty profit—there were no real "innocents" in the fields) would end up shot by the outriders, and sure as sunrise the riders would be targeted as soon as whoever was draining knew their cover was blown. What chilled Hutton to the core was the sheer volume of power being sapped. Anyone savvy enough to suck half the juice out of Vegas was surely smart enough to know people would notice. The unafraid are to be feared.

Hutton took a long pull of his whiskey, easily putting away half the generous pour. His eyes scanned the room. Hell if he himself would make the trek into the city to meet with Hale and that shifty-eyed bastard from security, Strayer. But someone needed to head into town. And none of the half-drunk, whore-mongering men in the bar would do. In fact the only man Hutton trusted implicitly was at the farthest reach of the fields. The Boss briefly considered dispatching a rider to bring Scofield back in early, but then decided it would have to wait. Had Round Up not already been scheduled for the very next weekend he'd already be on the horn to send someone. But the information he'd gather at the meeting was crucial. New Las Vegas had never been drained before; a botched response would be far worse than a delayed one.

"Fuckin' hell," The Boss muttered, downing the bourbon. He slid the glass back across the bar without looking and heard Matteson grab a bottle and refill it. Hutton turned and nodded his thanks.

"Bad call?" Matteson asked so no one else could hear, gesturing toward the phone with a tilt of his head.

"Bad call."

# 8

Dreg had chewed the inside of his left cheek bloody. He was livid. Furious. The flesh of his face was literally red. Not just pink or flushed—red. He had been pacing a box of approximately fifteen by fifteen feet for more than half an hour now. His route was well trod into the snow on the tarmac. Seven paces then a ninety degree turn to the right; seven paces then another turn. And so on.

Twenty yards away his private jet was perched on the runway. Its batteries were at full charge and the engines were humming, just as they had been all day. It was nearing 3 p.m. on Wednesday, east coast time, and The Mayor had expected to take off hours ago. The snowstorm had lifted for a while during the night and in the dawn hours Colonel Strayer had awoken Dreg, saying that they could likely make it into the air if they moved fast.

By the time the executive retinue had reached the airport a few miles outside Boston, the weather had again turned grim. The forecast called for at least another twenty-four hours of constant snow, but Franklin had insisted on waiting with the plane in case there was a window. For the fifth time that afternoon he broke from his diminutive parade route and stalked over to the pilot, huddled near the jet.

"You're good and goddamn certain you can't just force this thing into the air?"

"Sir, with the thunder storms all the way up to forty thousand feet, we just can't risk it. A few thousand feet lower and we'd be able to suck enough air in with the water to edge above the system, but we're begging for trouble like this. If you can find an old plane that runs on jet fuel, hell, I'll fly it for you. But this plane with this much precipitation at these temperatures? Begging for a short-out." The pilot paused, blowing hot breath between his interwoven fingers. He looked down, adding: "It's begging for a disaster, Mayor. I won't fly in this."

"I oughtta find someone who fucking will," Dreg muttered as he turned away and stamped his feet. He caught Strayer staring at him. The colonel immediately looked away, pretending to check his phone. A dozen other pairs of eyes flitted to and from The Mayor in turn. It was clear that no one was going anywhere soon, but Dreg was indignant and determined to wait indefinitely. No matter that everyone else had to wait also, he had business to attend to.

If only he could recall what that business was—Hale hadn't answered his phone all day. *I could snap his fucking neck!* Dreg raged to himself. What the hell had Timothy said yesterday? What the hell was he now keeping to himself? The Mayor had slept until 7 p.m. the previous day and, upon awakening, immediately began drinking to quell his rampant hangover.

It hadn't been until early this morning when Dreg had erupted from his sleep sober and wide awake that he even realized there was a problem. Had Hale said there were drainers? That New Las Vegas was being drained? How could he have said something like that, the small-minded fool? The Mayor could swear it had been a dream, but there in his call log was a fifteen minute conversation with the secretary general.

Once again he dialed his right hand man. Two thousand three hundred and seventy-five miles away, Timothy Hale looked down at his cell phone. He lay draped across a couch in his apartment, half drunk at noon. With a long sigh, he tossed the phone aside.

"What do you want me to say, Mr. Mayor? We're fucked and I can't do a thing about it?" He had been checking the meteorological reports for New England every half hour all morning long. "Enjoy the snow, Frank. When you get back here it's all fun and games."

Reese had been at a full gallop for miles. It felt good to rise and fall in rhythm with the horse. Her sinuous body churned below him as the desert flew past. It felt good to be alone on the open sands. Scofield knew that at any moment he'd spot Kretch, but for now it was just him and his mare. He knew he'd likely sail past a tap line or two, but this was his last chance for a good solo ride for more than a week. He and Wilton were to patrol the western border together for three days and then it was time to head in for Round Up.

The sun shone above, brilliant but without fangs, bathing the land in light free of heat. The days had finally taken a turn toward winter. It always amazed Scofield how quickly a season could change. It could go from baking heat to nightly frost in a matter of a week and, what's more, it would stay that way for good. One season, at a given point, just stepped aside, making way for the next.

The outrider reined Reese down to a trot. "Good girl. Take it easy for a bit—you earned it." He leaned forward and vigorously scratched both sides of her neck the way she liked. Sitting back up with a final pat on the horse's withers, Scofield fished about in the pocket of his vest and found a cigarette and lighter. He lit the smoke and took several long, slow drags, letting the last drift out of his mouth without inhaling. The smoke trailed off slowly in a thin blue-gray tendril. The air was near perfectly still. Scofield clicked his tongue once, slowing Reese further to a plodding walk.

Turning his head until he couldn't see the sunfield, Scofield let his mind wander. For as far as he could see there was no trace that mankind had ever touched these lands. There was no sound but Reese's hooves and steady breathing. In the crate under his bed, lying among the ammunition and bottles of rye, was a dog-eared copy of *Walden* by Henry David Thoreau. Try as he might, Scofield had never been able to read the damn book cover to cover. But over the years he had read the whole thing piecemeal more times than he could count on his fingers and toes. The passage that always struck him was Thoreau describing his displeasure at hearing distant trains from his secluded pond. *If you'd lived today, old boy, hell if you wouldn't a shot yourself or started in on the rest of us*, Scofield thought. Walden Pond had likely been filled in, built over, bulldozed, and built up again a half dozen times by now. And he couldn't imagine a place like it left on earth or a man who could relive what it meant. What it was. Thoreau had captured lightning in a jar—or rather on paper—at its last flickering. There wasn't a soul alive who wasn't to some degree plugged in; connected. Scofield knew he'd read excerpts of the book as a schoolboy but couldn't for the life of him remember if its words had helped draw him out into the fields or if the fields had led him back to the book.

It didn't much matter. He spent eleven out of twelve months in one of the few places on the planet where one couldn't be plugged in to the rest of it even if he wanted. So maybe he'd found his Walden Pond, at least as best as one ever could again. But it was by definition an itinerant life the outriders led. Settling down was so much more in Scofield's nature, if only he could have found a place without so much goddamn noise. And without so many people. He wasn't sure if he'd ever been in love but he knew what it would mean to have that. If he could find a good woman and relative quiet he'd be happy enough. Barring the completion of that equation, only solitude and silence would serve. So for the moment, alone beneath the open skies, Scofield was happy. But he also had a job to do. He took one more drag off his cigarette and exhaled with a wistful sigh.

"OK girl. Let's ride." With two gentle boot taps, Reese lurched into a steady canter. The horse and rider headed west by north west, making their way toward the end of the sunfield.

"Sloooow out here, I tell ya!" Kretch bellowed when Scofield was finally in earshot. He was standing next to Shady, having dismounted to take a piss just as his compatriot came into view past a line of QV pillars.

"Yeah? Well, that's good for business!" Scofield called back over his mare's pounding hooves. He rode Reese hard to within five yards of Kretch before reining her to a quick stop. Scofield stretched his neck and kicked off the stirrups, then jumped down off his horse. "Howya doin', Wilton?" He asked, reaching out a hand.

"Not bad, Scofe, not bad. Been boring but easy," Kretch replied, taking Scofield's hand in a hearty shake. "You got any loose tobacco? I been dyin' for a stout smoke."

"Sure. Lemme dig it out," Scofield answered, turning to look through a saddle bag. He found a pouch of rolling tobacco and tossed it to Wilton. "Need papers?"

"Nah, got them," Wilton said, fishing about in a pocket of his long beige duster. "Just went and smoked all my shake leaf early. Been stuck with stogies for two days." He set about rolling a thick cigarette while leaning against Shady. Kretch had let his beard come in during the past few weeks. His face was half covered in coarse blonde hair and half ruddy where the wind, sand, and sun could find flesh. "How was your ridin'?"

"OK mostly. Got one, though. You?"

"Uneventful is the word." Kretch licked his cigarette closed, clutching the sack of tobacco between his elbow and side. He blew on the cigarette to dry it and then placed one end in his mouth. Wilton slid the sack of shake leaf into a pocket of his duster and drew out a book of matches.

"Save 'em," Scofield said as he walked toward the other rider, a lighter extended in one hand. "And remember your manners."

"Well, shit, right you are," Wilton grinned, pulling the bag of tobacco back out from his pocket and trading it for the lighter. "Thought you might not notice."

"I always notice."

"Tell me about yer leech."

"Strange one, Wil," the outrider said, taking back his lighter. His usual distaste for conversation temporarily suppressed by days spent in silence punctuated only by unpleasant talk with Sebastian, Scofield started right in chatting.

"Ugly son of a bitch. Maybe thirty five but he looked like hell. Said he had cancer and that was why he started leeching but I'd bet that was a goddamn line," Scofield spat, strangely aware that he did, in fact, believe every word Sebastian had said to him, save for the lie about working alone. The veins and tight wrinkles of the leech's face flickered briefly before his mind's eye, then Scofield shook his head and went on. "He was a two timer."

"You mark him?"

"Yup. Man, I hate that part. We had to spend the night at the station over by mile ten. Fun fucking night—the sumbitch tried to get the drop on me twice. I clocked him and dragged his ass the better part of an hour."

Kretch tossed back his head and let out a hearty, savage laugh. He found genuine delight in the image of a two-timing leech dragged unconscious across the sands. Scofield cast a sidelong glance at his compatriot. There was something deeply unsettling about the pleasure Wilton took from suffering; this was far from the first time Scofield had noted the trait.

"Laid him out, huh?"

"Yeah," Scofield replied, looking away. He had meant to tell Kretch all the rest of it—about the radio and generator, about Sebastian there on his knees, begging for death. He had even thought up a line of conversation the two men could share about the life of a desk-bound accountant; he had planned to raise the topic as soon as their conversation went flat. But now, not ten minutes after the reunion, all Scofield wanted was to be alone. Or at least not near Wilton Kretch.

"Well, what about you? Not a soul, huh?" Scofield asked, turning to straighten out a few straps and buckles on Reese' saddle.

"Nah. Cut a few tap lines. Saw an old broken down collector. It was all quiet on the western front, as they say. What day is this, even?"

"Thursday I think." Scofield slid one foot into a stirrup, grasped the saddle horn and vaulted atop his mare. "Yeah, Thursday. Definitely." He ran a hand across one side of his face. He had shaved that morning and his skin was smooth on the down stroke, like sand paper as he slid his palm back up the other cheek, wiping off a few grains of sand.

Unconsciously, Kretch mirrored Scofield's motions, scratching at his beard. He took a few more drags off the cigarette then stamped it out under a heel. Wilton turned to face Shady and grabbed the saddle, one hand on either side of it. He leaped up and hauled himself onto the colt—which sidestepped and shook its mane—then slung onto the saddle, leaving his boots free of the stirrups.

"Well, let's find us some trouble."

"That's why they pay us the big bucks." Scofield took the reins in both hands and wheeled Reese to face west. The two riders set out at a trot toward the end of the sunfield.

They rode in silence for a good while, each man occasionally coughing or spitting or muttering something to his horse. Kretch had his hat tied to the side of the bridle and his naked head bobbed along above Shady, his eyes squinting in the bright sun. Finally, he turned to Scofield.

"You hear anything strange the past few days? Last night, too?"

"Nah."

"Hm." Kretch looked away again. "Thought I heard something a couple times. Like a . . . I dunno, like kind of a moaning or something. Like the way the wind will blow through trees or between buildings. Ain't ever heard anything like it out here, though."

Standing beside the fire two nights ago Scofield had indeed thought he'd heard some odd noise drifting faintly across the land, but he had been unsure of himself then and was in no mood to speculate now. He tried in vain to remember what it had sounded like but by the time he'd moved away from the crackling logs it had already stopped. He could recall it now only as if from a fading dream.

"Don't think I heard anything. Got any theories?"

"Probably just my head playing with me."

"Probably was. Gets that way out here after days alone, y'know."

"Oh yeah!" Kretch snorted. "Man, you get to thinking some goddamn bent up things after that much time by your lonesome. Hearing things. Seeing shadows. Sometimes I'll just plan what I'm gonna say next time I find me a real asshole of a leech. Or what I'm gonna do to a lady next time I got a dollar and an hour. I tell you, Scofe, the night after Round Up 'ol Wilton here is gonna paint the town so fuckin' red they're gonna need some bastard with a can of primer and a brush to follow me 'round!" (Kretch had thought of this phrase a week ago.) "I been ridin' too many goddamn miles lately. Hutton gotta send some of the new blood out here and give us some R&R."

Scofield nodded one and a half times, looking away. Kretch continued talking about all the things he would do back in New Las Vegas but his partner was no longer paying any attention. The two men were riding just inside the western line of pillars, keeping in the shade of the PV arrays as much as possible. As Wilton droned on, something caught Scofield's eye. Far out across the desert—easily twenty miles distant, the land here was oppressively flat—he thought he could see a mirage. The air rippled and danced. Though it was bright out it was not hot; certainly not hot enough for heat waves. He squinted, straining to get a better look at the remote phenomenon, but when for a second he looked down from the shimmering sight to scratch the corner of one eye, it disappeared entirely.

Scofield scanned the horizon repeatedly, finding nothing but sand and stones and scrub brush.

"You listening, Scofield?"

"Yeah, yeah, I hear ya."

"Because she was a fuckin' ten. Or at least maybe a seven but I was ten beers deep, you get me?"

Scofield forced a convincing laugh, then turned his eyes back west. But there was nothing to see.

"Good evening, Maria."

"Ay—shit! You scared me!" Maria Rodrigues exclaimed, her voice taking on a strange aspect in her surprise. She did her best to collect herself, having just spilled the contents of her handbag on the sidewalk. It was 5:03 in the afternoon. She had packed her things, left her desk, and jogged down the stairs just the same as she did every day. Her routine had become so ingrained—reading glasses off as she rose, hair let down at the door to the stairs, phony smile dropped as she passed through the lobby—that Timothy Hale's quiet greeting had been enough to startle her as she stepped out onto the street.

He was leaning against the doorframe, dressed in blue jeans and a black t-shirt. Maria had never seen him in anything but a suit and tie. It had taken a second for his face to register perched above such casual attire.

"Didn't mean to frighten you."

"No, it's alright. I just ... um I ..." she trailed off, scooping up her phone and makeup case and wallet. Hale remained still against the door. As she shoved the last downed item—a brass lighter—into her purse, she noticed that in stark contrast to his clothes he was wearing polished wingtips. As she rose, Maria wondered, *do you not even own a pair of sneakers?*

Hale looked directly into Maria's eyes. She held his gaze for a moment then began to organize things in her handbag,

"How are you, Maria?"

"I'm fine. I'm doing well," she began to say "Mr. Hale" but quickly diverted to "Timothy. I'm fine." Maria fished about for her cigarettes and, finally finding the pack, drew one out and placed it between her lips, an embarrassing tremble in her hand. "How, uh, how are you?"

"Me? I'm fine too, Maria ... I'm fine. I'm just so ... I'm so *drained*. So tired."

"Good old nine to five, right?" She said, her voice fluttering up an octave, eyes on his with a sudden sharpness.

"Good ... old ..." Hale looked away and then dropped his chin against his chest, an awkward, nasal laugh sputtering out.

Maria wrapped her left hand around her right elbow and held the cigarette butt close to her lips, her head facing forward but her eyes still on Hale. She was nervous; confused.

"So you're OK? Really? You seem . . . rather . . ."

"Seem what?" he spat angrily, eyes darting up.

"No, I . . . Timothy, are you drunk?"

"Drunk? Am I—are you . . . drunk? Who's to decide that? You?"

"I didn't mean to—"

"No, not at all!" he interrupted. "You look very nice tonight, Ms. Rodrigues. Nice skirt and jacket and all." She was wearing her standard attire, but demurred with a quiet 'thank you' and then turned away, again digging about in her purse.

"Would you like to go have a, uh . . . to grab a drink?" Hale asked, finally pushing away from the wall and standing up. He swayed slightly.

"I don't really drink, usually."

"No? You don't drink? Well, you should come watch me then. I have some wine you could watch me drink."

"I really have to get home."

"For what?"

She opened her mouth to respond but couldn't think of anything to say.

"Aha!" Hale laughed much too loudly. "You're putting me on, Maria! Come on. Come with me. I'll show you The Mayor's office." He took a lunging step toward her and reached for her arm. Maria shrank back instinctively and Hale almost fell to the ground, his knees buckling as he grasped at the air where her shoulder had been.

"Mr. Hale—Tim. This is very inappropriate."

"So formal . . ." he muttered, dragging out the 'or' syllable.

"OK. You're making a fucking idiot of yourself. How's that?"

Hale took a few uneasy steps back to the doorframe and leaned against it, his head hanging like a scolded child. When he looked up, the drunken haze had cleared from his eyes. "Jesus. You're right. I'm an idiot. I'm sorry, Maria . . . this is fucking pathetic."

Maria sighed, letting out a bit of tension. She dropped her cigarette, even though it was not even halfway smoked, and came over to stand beside the secretary.

"What were you doing here, anyway?"

"Waiting for you," he said matter-of-factly. "I like you and I'm a coward so I got drunk and came to talk to you. And now I've blown it all. So if you'll forgive and excuse me, I'm gonna go home and finish off the bottle." Hale pushed himself away from the wall and began to shuffle off, his shoulders stooped, swaying beneath the artificial glow of the streets. Above the city lights the sky was darkening.

Maria shook her head, watching Timothy stumble and nearly fall twice in less than thirty feet. She took in a breath, hesitated, and then called aloud: "Are you OK, Tim? To get home, I mean?"

"Sure. Great." He waved without looking back. An elderly woman clutched her handbag more closely as Hale lurched toward her, then regained his footing.

"Well, I tried. Whatever." Maria turned on her heels and began to march quickly in the other direction. She had already missed the local 5:10 pod and would need to hurry to catch the cross-town line a few blocks south. Two things occurred to her as she reflected back on the awkward encounter. One was that, despite his dismal condition, Hale had looked rather handsome dressed in a fitted t-shirt and casual pants. Second was that, while she couldn't be sure, it looked as though he had recently been crying.

Dusk was just taking hold of the desert when Scofield broke the near hour long silence. "What the fuck is that?"

"Hm? Oh, shit. Right." Kretch was casually rolling a cigarette. He had forgotten that he told Scofield he was out of shake leaf. "Found me a bit of tobacco after all. Inside pocket, y'know."

Kretch had not looked up while talking, the rolling process requiring his full attention while on a moving horse and in twilight, no less. Finally happy with the cigarette, Wilton licked it shut and placed one tip in his mouth. His eyes rose at last to Scofield, a guilty grin on his lips. But his partner's eyes were staring straight ahead, intensely focused. Kretch followed his gaze down the line of QV pillars. His sharp vision immediately isolated the object of Scofield's concern.

About a hundred yards ahead of the men, a massive structure had been built around the base of a pillar. It was the size of a small building. Though it was hard to distinguish much detail in the gloaming, they could see various facets and components jutting from every angle of the object. Both riders reined their horses to a halt without a word. Kretch sat forward in his saddle, eyes squinting to take in as much visual information as possible. Scofield meanwhile let his gaze drift among the arrays and out over the desert, watching for any movement. Then he shut his eyes and listened to the night, silent but for the breath of two men and two horses.

Scofield opened his eyes. "Move slow or charge on in?"

"Gut says slow."

"Mine too. Let's leave the mounts here."

Kretch nodded and the outriders kicked free of their stirrups and slid to the ground in unison. Kretch grabbed a length of rope from Shady's saddle and passed one end through the bridle of each horse.

"I'll tie 'em off," Scofield whispered, taking the rope in his hands. "You keep watch, you got better eyes."

The horses secured, the pair set off toward the strange construction, each with rifle loaded and at the ready. It was almost true night by now, the western horizon minutes from relinquishing a final swath of light. Scofield waved Kretch over to him as they reached the last pillar between them and the structure.

"If anyone's been lookin' out they probably got a bead on us already."

"Woulda heard the horses if they was payin' attention."

Scofield nodded slowly, removing his hat to peer around the pillar exposing as slight a profile as possible. "Maybe we're being felt out. But good chance there ain't a soul for miles, too." He leaned back beside Wilton. "When was the last time you passed this stretch of field?"

"Rode through about noon, I guess. Maybe one." Kretch craned his neck from side to side, vertebrae popping loudly in the silent evening air. Without being asked, he added, "and no, that thing wasn't there."

Scofield slung the rifle over his shoulder and drew his pistol, easing the hammer back to full cock. The air was cold enough to see his breath for a fleeting second as it left his body. "Let's split up. You stay put for a count of two minutes, OK? I'm gonna head into the field a bit then jog east. When I've counted a minute fifty, I'll make for that thing at a full run."

"Sounds good. I'll stay put and cover."

"Nah, move in at two. It's a good hundred yards—I need you tighter if we got company."

"Fine by me. I'll move in two."

Scofield nodded and set out east by southeast. He moved as fast as he could without his boots crunching loudly on the sand. Counting the seconds in his head as he moved deeper into the sunfield, the outrider kept his eyes trained on the massive object around the QV pillar. He came parallel with the structure and turned north, slowing to a measured walk as he counted the seconds.

When by his reckoning just about a minute and fifty seconds had passed, Scofield broke into a run. He kept his pistol in front of him, gripped between both hands, and swept back and forth across the sand with the gun barrel and his eyes. Thirty yards out and nothing. Ten yards and closing at a sprint; still nothing.

Scofield was only feet from the pillar; the intricate wiring and gears on the huge object had just become visible in the starlight when the first shot rang out. Scofield dove to the sand and rolled over his left shoulder, coming up on one knee with his pistol ready. He took long, deep breaths to keep his arms steady. His heart raced. No sound. No movement. A second report rang out—the bullet tore through the air so close to Scofield he felt its rippling wake. He wheeled to face west, the direction of the shooter, and rose, sprinting to the foreign structure and flattening his back against it.

Scofield sucked in a deep breath and held it, keeping his body perfectly still. He listened for any sound; sniffed the faint breeze. Then he slowly removed his hat and eased along the structure. His vest caught on a protruding barb and the outrider swore breathlessly, trying to wriggle free. He popped clear of the snag with a loud rip, pain lancing through his shoulder blade then quickly forgotten. Closing his eyes and letting the air drift from his lungs, Scofield gripped his revolver tightly in his right hand. Then with his left he tossed the hat away from the pillar, leaping around it a second later. Nothing.

Scofield quickly circled the whole of the fifteen by fifteen foot object. There was not a soul to be found. As he began to relax his grip on the pistol, something occurred to him. His face grew hot, flushed; he stopped dead in his tracks. "Wilton!" He bellowed. "Is that you shooting goddammit!"

Silence.

"There's no one here, Kretch!" Scofield waited a beat before realizing that he may have made a fatal error. The images came in a rush: he pictured Kretch dead on the sand, a bullet in him, and a barrel trained this way; a finger tensing on the trigger. Just as Scofield spun to confront his imagined adversary, Wilton's voice finally called back.

"Scofe?"

"Jesus Christ," he muttered, then shouting: "Yeah, Wilton! It's just me." He strained to see through the gloom and let out an exasperated sigh upon realizing that Kretch had been hiding behind the same QV pillar the whole time. Only now did Wilton step clear of his hideout and approach, the rifle held down by his waist but still trained.

"Check your fire, Wil! What the fuck were you shooting at?"

"Just givin' you cover, bud."

"Cover! I heard the second goddamn shot whistle past my head, Kretch!" Scofield hissed as Wilton reached him.

"Thought I saw something heading toward you."

"You got keen eyes, Wil. You were blind firing."

"Hell if I was." Kretch spat back, his voice icy. In the pale starlight, Scofield could see Wilton glaring at him, his eyes unblinking. Several thoughts flitted through of Scofield's head, none fully realized and together forming more of a gut feeling than a reading of the situation. *Never broke cover . . . pretty accurate for shooting wild . . . but he'd finish it now if he'd meant . . .*

Scofield let the notion drop, allowing himself to believe that Kretch had indeed been cowering and fired without looking. He also decided to curb any further derision of his partner's lack of assistance.

"You got a torch?"

"Got a few back on Shady."

"Well, let's take a look at this sumbitch."

Kretch nodded, slinging his rifle as he turned to walk back toward the horses. Scofield holstered his pistol then searched about until he found his black hat. He beat the dust from it on a thigh, then set the hat back on his head. His hair was matted and sweaty despite the chill air. Only then, finally calm, did the outrider realize he had cut himself when snared on the structure. He put a hand to where his clothes were torn and felt warm blood on his fingertips. Nothing bad—just a scratch and some ripped cotton. He found his pack of cigarettes crushed but the few smokes in it were intact, if slightly battered. Scofield lit one and took a long, deep drag.

Finally he turned to face the QV pillar and its strange accessory. While he couldn't see much in the dark, it was clearly a complex construction, to say the least: easily ten feet high and studded with countless parts. From over his shoulder came the sound of the horses' hooves and Kretch quietly admonishing them to behave. Reese had never liked Wilton and whinnied when she caught sight of her rider.

"Hey girl," Scofield crooned as Kretch and the horses drew alongside him. He ran a hand along his mare's flank, then slid the lead rope from her bridle and tossed it to Wilton.

"What do you make of it?" Kretch asked, winding the rope around his forearm.

"Can't see much. I never seen anything like it, though—tell you that much right now."

"Here," Kretch said, handing a torch to Scofield before securing the coiled rope over his saddle horn.

Scofield peeled back a few inches of the thick paper wrapped around the magnesium stick, then flicked his lighter to life and held it to one tip of the torch. After a few seconds the magnesium caught, sparkling to life with a brilliant blue-white rush. Both men quickly averted their eyes, making sure to not stare directly at the searing flame.

By the light of the torch a swath of desert lurched out of the darkness. Scofield stepped forward.

"What the hell is this thing?" Kretch whispered, his tone near reverence.

The massive apparatus was made almost entirely of cables, piping, and tubes. Serpentine copper coils wrapped around thick bundles of wiring in a series of switchbacks all along the ten foot tall structure. Beneath this outer layer were more intricately threaded filaments strung from little knobs on the copper casing and branching out to five steel discs that encircled the QV pillar. On the central disc, glass spheres shaped like oversized light bulbs perched atop aluminum dowels. These spheres were evenly spaced two feet apart from one another.

Holding the torch above his head, Scofield began to walk around the machine. Three sides of it were identical; the fourth, the side against which he'd taken cover, was a sheet of solid iron. The metal wall was studded with protrusions: a dozen steel caps were screwed onto copper posts and two rows of metal brackets ran parallel to each other, one by the outrider's knee and the other at shoulder height. Scofield held the flaming torch near one of these brackets to get a better look. A thick L-shaped bar of iron stuck out above a square recess cut into the metal plate.

"C'mere Wil."

Kretch had been holding his lighter near one of the spheres to study it. The glass was thick and lightly yellowed as if with age, its surface riddled with imperfections. "Yeah. One sec," he called back. Wilton snapped his lighter shut and returned it to a jacket pocket, rubbing the bridge of his nose with a thumb and finger. His mind was reeling and he tasted bile at the back of his throat.

"These look like couplings. See here?" Scofield said, pointing to the brackets once Kretch had joined him.

"Yeah. Looks like it. Big fuckin' thing to move, huh?"

"Mm." Scofield grunted. "Explains why you didn't see it earlier today though."

"It don't explain how'n the hell someone got this thing here. Or who."

"Yeah. No. Doesn't explain that. You think it's anything legit? Official? Maybe some kind of test or measuring device or something?"

"Nah." Kretch shook his head, squinting against the bright blue-white flame of the magnesium torch. "Come look at these glass things."

The two walked back around the structure and Kretch bid Scofield inspect one of the spheres.

"Pretty shitty craftsmanship, hm?" Wilton said.

"And every one is fucked up in a different way," Scofield added, nodding in agreement as he moved along a side of the machine. When he got back to the iron wall, he noticed several threads torn from his vest hanging off one of the brackets. He gingerly removed the fabric, rolling it back and forth between his fingers. Then his eyes drifted past the scrap of cloth and he let it fall, fixated on one of the metal caps. He reached out and took hold of the disc. At first it wouldn't budge. After a considerable effort it began to twist, and with a grating whine, Scofield slowly unscrewed the cap. Beneath it were six plugs; receptors for the standardized four pronged cords used in everyday life. And surely designed to fit the strange cable he'd found days earlier and miles away. Scofield silently berated himself for disregarding the buried cord when he'd found it: *You know better'n that goddammit! Sloppy, man! Sloppy.* He shook his head. His thoughts raced, struggling to make some connection. Nothing added up, and he decided not to mention the other cord for now.

The outriders spent a few more minutes inspecting the peculiar device, then Scofield buried the torch in the sand to preserve what was left of it. He stood still for a while to let his eyes readjust to the darkness, then walked over to Kretch and the horses. Wilton was rolling a cigarette, swearing under his breath as he spilled tobacco in the dark. Finally getting the smoke into some semblance of a tube, he lit it and looked up at his partner. His eyes reflected the orange glow of the ember as he breathed in slowly. Then he exhaled through his nose and his face was hidden behind a swirl of smoke.

"This is bad, ain't it?"

"Safe bet," Scofield whispered.

"We ought to head back. Report in."

"I think we need to wait for morning."

"Why's that?"

"That thing didn't walk here on its own. And those couplings or brackets or whatever—that thing was moved here by a . . . I don't know. Wasn't man power or horses, though. Not something that big. Had to be a machine."

"How the fuck would that work out here, Scofe?"

"Your guess is as good as mine. But we should wait for the light and look for tracks. Maybe see if there's a trail to follow."

Kretch put the cigarette back in his mouth, gripping its soggy end between his teeth. He slid his hands into his jacket pockets, making fists to ward off the cold. Again his eyes shone above the smoldering cigarette tip.

"Good thinking." He spit the butt out and stamped on it. "But we should bunk down a fair distance off. Someone might be coming back."

# 9

"Frank, it's me. It's Hale. Mr. Mayor. My phone was dead all day . . . my phone was in the office—I left it in the office. Or at home . . . just say it was at home . . ." Hale wandered around the room aimlessly, now and then bumping into a sofa or shelf or table. He tripped over a plush carpet spread across the middle of Dreg's outer chamber and stumbled against the wall, knocking a painting askew.

Timothy straightened up and took a slow step backward, staring intently at the work of art. If he closed one eye, he could see it clearly: an oil wrought in thick, decisive jabs. The painter had used his palette knife for the whole piece—there was not a brushstroke to be found. Up close, the canvas was just a patchwork of color. Swaths of grays here, tan and beige near the center, and auburn mixed with deeper browns below. But from a distance of two feet one began to perceive a ship. Here was the prow, there the rigging and sails, below and all around the roiling sea.

At five paces the tableau was complete: a tri-masted ship-of-the-line cresting a giant wave. The sky and sea were rendered in a matching slate color, the only differentiation being a flat stillness in the air and a rough, thickly applied chop to the waters. A small patch of pale yellow in the top right corner of the painting suggested sunshine. It was unclear whether the ship was heading into the storm or had just weathered it. In the bottom left corner, the artist had signed the work in small, precise black lettering: "Marion–'21."

Hale took another step back and leaned against one of the couches set in the middle of the room. He didn't know to which century this "21" referred. *Doesn't matter*, he thought, closing his eyes. *Or does it? Dead and gone. No matter.* His glass of bourbon and ice had formed a thick ring of condensation on the mahogany table perched between the sofas. Hale craned his neck around, both hands gripping the back of the couch, and looked longingly at the liquor. But it was nearing midnight and if he didn't make the call to Dreg soon he would be derelict in his duty, having avoided The Mayor all day. He had left his mobile phone at home that morning—an intentional and absolute first—and upon returning to his apartment an hour ago found no fewer than seventeen missed calls from Dreg, not to mention several from Strayer and a few from unimportant city employees. Hale erased all of his messages unheard.

He had retrieved his phone, thrown a weathered, fraying suede jacket over his t-shirt, and grabbed a bottle of whiskey and a glass of ice, leaving home again without so much as turning on a light. He'd walked the twelve blocks from his apartment to the executive building while pouring himself fingers of bourbon. The day had started off bleak, taken a turn for the wretched after his embarrassing rendezvous with Maria, and now was spiraling toward bottom.

Hale awkwardly crawled over the fine silk couch and snatched his drink from the table, running a palm across the damp trail it left. He was vaguely aware of the fury he would have felt to see someone else dragging their shoes across the executive upholstery or setting down a glass without a coaster. But these notions were foolish when viewed through the lens of liquor. Propriety made no sense at the moment. It never made much sense, did it? This pedantic nod to civility, to manners—it was all aggrandizement of the insignificant; the unimportant made indispensable.

It was time—he had practiced enough: sitting down on the plush sofa, Timothy held down the number "1" on his phone and gritted his back teeth, staring off blankly into space. The phone rang five heart-stopping times before Hale's own voice greeted him, saying in a measured, sober cadence: "You've reached the executive office. Leave a concise, detailed message."

Then came the beep. "Mr. Mayor. It's Tim Hale." His tongue felt thick; his lips sluggish. "I see that you've been trying to reach me. My phone was disabled. Nothing to report. Carry on."

Hale lowered the phone, closing his right eye to be sure he had an index finger on the red "END" button, and terminated the call. He let out a long, heavy sigh of relief. Rising unsteadily, Hale tossed back the last few ounces of whiskey and dropped his phone and empty glass onto the cushions. He made his way to the door outside Dreg's office and keyed in the entry code.

The lock clicked open and Timothy turned the heavy brass knob, pushing the door inward. Light spilled from the receiving chamber into the office, mingling with the glow from the pulsing, multi-colored displays along the left wall. Hale entered the office slowly, cautiously, as if someone were sure to burst in and catch him at any moment. He usually walked into The Mayoral chamber with panache, but his mission on this night blunted any swagger. Illogical fear played at Hale's nerves. There was no way anyone could ever uncover what he was about to do, yet still his hands trembled as he approached the desk.

The secretary general pulled back Dreg's chair but did not sit. He slid open the oak panel covering The Mayor's keyboard and monitor, both built into the desk, and punched in the pass code known only to him and Franklin Dreg. After less than a minute of feverish typing, there was a new code and a new reality; one Hale had dreamt of for years. Now no one but he had full access to the near-omnipotent Mainframe Control System of New Las Vegas.

Across the country, snow was still falling on Boston, but the flakes were smaller and fewer in number as the night wore on. The storm was drifting west as the wind shifted and blew inland from the sea.

Scofield tossed and turned fitfully. He had kicked the blanket clear of his body and was shivering in his sleep, his dreams feverish and dark. Sebastian's face loomed before him, covered in strange tattoos. He sneered, baring teeth filed to sinister points. The leech stood in the middle of a landscape so barren not even a shadow marked the expanse of sand.

Scofield was on his knees, bare-chested. In his hands he clutched a book. Try as he might, he could not focus his eyes to make out its title. The leech was speaking, his arms slowly rising until they stuck straight out as if in crucifixion. He was wearing the same gray workman's clothes as in waking life, but the garments were pristine, pressed and creased to perfection.

Sebastian's speech was muddled; his words sounded like language but were unintelligible. He leaned forward slowly, arms still outstretched, and though Scofield could not understand him, he knew the leech was referring to the book he grasped between trembling hands.

Suddenly lucid, Sebastian whispered: "This and more," then wheeled to face away. The color began to fade from his clothing, gray becoming ever paler until his uniform was pure white.

Suddenly all was black and then, with a ragged gasp, Scofield was awake. The sky above was still dark and studded with stars, but on the eastern horizon the first hint of dawn had made its appearance. A thin strip of pale blue melted into gray and then into purple-black night sky. It would be the better part of an hour still until any of the desert was illuminated.

Scofield shuddered, a tremor working its way from his heels all the way to his neck. The fingers of his right hand were numb. His left, he realized slowly, was balled into a tight fist and stuck between his thighs. He lay on his side, curled into fetal position. Coughing, Scofield rose to his knees, massaging his cramped shoulders.

Reese was on her feet and in the haze of the coming dawn Scofield could see that she was watching him. Shady slept on the ground between him and Kretch, and slowly, stiffly, Scofield rose to peer over the colt. Wilton was out cold, his breathing steady beneath a thick blanket that covered him from head to toe.

Scofield got to his feet, his joints popping and creaking and every muscle aching in protest. He rolled up his bed mat and secured it to Reese's saddle, then threw the heavy wool blanket around his shoulders. His hat was lying where he had left it beside the laundry sack he used as a pillow. The canteen lay a few feet off, and Scofield wondered if he had kicked it in his sleep or if Reese had been nuzzling at it as she sometimes did. He jammed the laundry bag and canteen into a saddle bag, retightening the straps and buckles on his horse's bridle and saddle once his sundries were secure.

With a final stretch, Scofield slid a boot into Reese's left stirrup and mounted the mare, leaving his right foot dangling freely. He leaned down against her neck and wrapped both arms around her warm, firm flesh.

"Real quiet, OK girl? Let's roll." Scofield tapped the horse gently with one heel, giving a brief tug at her reins with his right hand. She set off at a plodding walk headed east by southeast. At Kretch's insistence, the outriders had bedded down a solid mile from the strange device. Scofield had wanted to stick nearby and stake out the scene but Wilton had been intractable, convinced that either nothing would happen and sticking close would be pointless or that all hell would break loose and staying nearby could be deadly.

Scofield hadn't bought either of these scenarios but the potential for the latter had been enough to convince him not to stay put alone. The two had agreed to sleep in shifts, but after catching Wilton dozing for the second time, Scofield had decided to scrap his worries and just nod off for the night.

When he had ridden a few hundred yards from Kretch, Scofield tapped Reese into a canter. They reached the sunfield after a few minutes and turned east, traveling just outside the line of pillars. Scofield peered through the gloom, counting the arrays they passed under. After the sixth had gone by, he reined his mare to a halt. By his count last night they should have found the foreign array on the fourth pillar of the sector. Scofield was certain he had neither miscounted the evening before nor just now, but still he turned his horse around and rode back west for the better part of ten minutes.

After another ride past every QV pillar in two sectors there was no question left: the strange array was gone. Dawn was fast approaching and the wind was beginning to stir, blowing the loose top layer of sand about. Scofield spurred Reese away from the field and out into the desert. He reined the horse west and slowed her to a trot, his eyes glued to the ground.

The slow ride back to Kretch took more than twenty minutes, but it let him be absolutely sure that he had not missed anything. There were no prints in the sand. No drag lines. No sign that anyone had been there in days, but for the phantom machine. Wilton was still fast asleep when the outrider drew near to their simple camp. Shady was on his feet, milling about, and whinnied at Reese's and Scofield's return.

Kretch rolled over, groaning and peeling back his blanket. He blinked several times, clearing the sleep from his eyes, and shivered in the frosty morning air. The sky above was pale, the land around them still largely formless.

Scofield jumped down from Reese as soon as they were alongside Kretch. He pulled the canteen from her saddle bag and took a sip, then cupped his hand and poured water for his horse. Without looking over his shoulder, he said: "It's gone."

"Come on, you son of a bitch!" Boss Hutton muttered, jamming his foot down on the gas pedal and twisting the key back and forth. The engine turned over and coughed at him, then went silent again. "Don't make me get under that hood, girl!" Hutton lifted his foot from the pedal and sat back, counting twenty seconds to let fuel drain from the engine. Then he gripped the wheel and stomped down on the clutch, turned the key and slowly eased his right foot back down on the accelerator.

The jeep rumbled to life. Hutton let out a victorious whoop and threw the gearshift into neutral. It was best to let the vehicle warm up for a good long while before driving it—Boss Hutton's jeep was eighty-three years old. It was the only gas-fueled vehicle within hundreds of miles and one of the last combustion engines in the whole of North America. Hutton had his gasoline shipped to him at enormous cost but the freedom afforded by a car that never needed to plug into the grid and wasn't stuck on a track was priceless.

The jeep was open on all sides with a thick roll bar across the top. Hutton had installed massive tires with three inch treads. Sand flew twenty feet in the air when he cruised across the desert at high speed. He touched up the forest green paint as often as it needed and kept the four jerry cans strapped above the rear bumper, each topped off with fuel at all times. The vehicle was his pride and joy.

On this cold, pale morning, the lasting surge of pleasure that usually accompanied the engine's rumble was conspicuously absent. As he pressed down the clutch, Hutton's mood was grim, his jaw set tight. He pulled off his wide brimmed hat and replaced it with a gray knit cap to ward off the cold, then threw the stick in gear and accelerated along the concrete heading west.

Hutton eased off the gas as the paved road ended and he crossed onto the desert loam. He turned to head southwest, looking back over his left shoulder. Miles away, the outline of New Las Vegas was just becoming visible in the dawn light. Hutton shook his head ruefully as he sped up to fifty miles an hour. He'd been a skilled horseman all his life, but as he aged and his joints grew ever creakier, his muscles stiffer, Hutton had come to prefer his jeep to a horse whenever possible.

The rule of thumb went that for outsiders, the glowline was the limit; for outriders it was known that you could bring an electric charge about a mile across the line; Hutton often risked a good mile after that. He'd be pushing it today, but decades out in the fields had taught him to sense when he was about to go too far. It was a combination of the hairs on the back on his neck, a taste he got on both sides of his tongue, and the never-unheeded feeling in his gut. Hutton could sense the field's power before even the most delicate measuring equipment. So maybe he'd be a bit south of safety, but time was of the essence. He had to get his boys together fast.

Hutton crossed the glowline still doing fifty, but quickly eased off the gas and slowed to just above twenty miles an hour. He pushed down the reset button for the trip meter—the plastic toggle was worn to less than half its original length—and then split his time between watching the desert and watching the numbers roll. He wondered for the thousandth time how many miles this jeep had driven. When he'd bought it thirty years ago it had already been fully rebuilt several times and he'd had it overhauled a handful more. He was sure it could have circled the globe dozens of times by now.

When the trip meter read one-point-six miles, Hutton dropped from third to second gear and turned west by southwest, slowing to under fifteen miles an hour. After another minute that definite but indescribable sensation began, and The Boss knew he was as close as he could get to the field. He steered the jeep to face true west and accelerated again. The day was coming on quickly, ever brighter. Hutton popped open the glove box and fished out a pair of sunglasses. The lenses were mottled where countless grains of sand had blown against them over the years, and through the glasses the world took on a soft, gray blur.

After another ten minutes of driving, Hutton spotted his destination. The squat cinderblock building perched low against the sand, a tall tower topped with three giant klaxons stuck into the air above it. This unit had sat above the San Francisco Bay in decades long gone, calling out to ships through the fog. Five other identical structures were placed around the perimeter of the sunfield. Two were from Boston, one from Newport News, one from Seattle and the last somewhere in Asia. Their baleful horns had sounded across the desert only two times in all the years since the field had been established; since the way the world worked changed, from another point of view.

The first sounding was after a powerful earthquake forty-two years ago. The second had been twenty-nine years ago when the alarm summoned the riders together to inform them that the country was at war. Despite the massive damage to much of Vegas and its surrounding communities, the sunfield had weathered the quake with ease in the first instance. And when diplomacy cut short the march to arms, the riders were ordered to stand down from their double shifts and turn in the extra ammunition they'd been rationed. Including Hutton, only five of the outriders still on active duty remembered either occasion. And he was the only man who had served through both.

Hutton drew alongside the sirenhouse and turned off his jeep, easing to a stop with the vehicle in neutral. He left his hands on the wheel, sighing. Those times, the threat had been external. Now, if Hale was right—and, based on the work Hutton had done the previous day, he was—the outriders would not be merely on alert, they would be in their own private war. Round Up would have to come a day early; there was no time left to spare. The grid was losing over a million kilowatts an hour. That would require enough build-up of infrastructure and manpower to where easily scores, if not hundreds of drainers were working together. The Boss had fifty-seven outriders on the roster. And two were out of commission: Fischer with a broken hip after his horse had bucked him and Moses Smith laid up with what everyone was calling pneumonia but knew damn well was the clap.

Hutton lit a long, slender cigar and puffed at it until the tip was glowing. He pulled off the knit cap and grabbed his gray hat from the shotgun seat. The door to the eight-by-eight building was secured by several deadbolts, but each opened by the same key. Hutton had one copy and the other was locked in a vault in the city. It was an ironic system: electronic locks worked better but weren't used this close to the sunfield despite the fact that the system within the building required an immense amount of electricity when operated. The klaxons were placed as close as safely possible to the field. There was a second irony to the situation: using the horns was not only the only way to call all the outriders back to the main Outpost so a unified plan could be enacted, but would also inform every leech for miles that it was open season on the pillars. Every leech . . . and every drainer.

The locks removed, Hutton set his shoulder against the iron door and heaved inward. The door gave way with a groan, and stale, musty air swirled from within the building. The outrider flipped a switch just inside the doorway and two of eight light bulbs came to life. The room contained nothing but a single panel on the far wall, this made up of a dial and a black button housed beneath a corroded plastic cover. Hutton wasn't even sure the system would still work.

Without a moment's hesitation, Boss Hutton twisted the dial clockwise as far as it would go. It stopped turning with a click and a deep bass hum began to fill the room. Slowly growing louder and higher pitched, the hum became a rumble. Dust drifted down from the ceiling and bits of concrete fell away from the walls. As the reverberating whine became nearly overwhelming, Hutton decided it was time, thinking: *Ain't gonna stand on fuckin' ceremony.*

He flipped up the plastic casing and rested his left palm on the large black button beneath it. Hutton took in a long breath and held it. Then he jammed the button down, his palms flying to his ears immediately after.

Across two-hundred square miles echoed the doleful moan of warning. In Vegas, amid the bustle of the morning commute, here and there people stopped walking or set down their coffee mugs to listen, most quickly deciding they had imagined the sound. Memories of salty air and sun dappled waves drifted briefly out of the subconscious of some. In the desert, many ears perked up at the seldom heard horns. Very many ears.

"Sweet Jesus Christ," Kretch stammered, his breath catching in his throat. His heart rate doubled, pounding in his chest. He glanced over at Scofield, who was looking all around them, his head spinning back and forth erratically. The horses were beginning to whinny and sidestep as the baleful tone rolled across the desert.

"Is that the horn?"

"Yeah," Scofield replied just loud enough to be heard. The deep, awful sound persisted for what felt like hours but was less than a full minute. The silence that followed was in its own way even more ominous. With one noise, everything had changed. The sun seemed brighter but colder; the sands more barren and endless . . . the very air harder to breathe.

"OK. Alright . . . let's drop our extra chow, feed, and water and get moving, double-time." Scofield was already dismounting. He began to rummage through his saddle bags the second his boots were on the ground. Kretch remained glued to his saddle for a long moment more, finally kicking free of the stirrups. He slowly climbed off Shady and began lightening the horse's load in a stupor. He was terrified.

A clean-shaven, sober, and conflicted Timothy Hale sat at his desk, racing to deal with all the work he had eschewed the day before. There were forms to be approved, calls to return, a schedule to establish. The secretary general was determined to have Mayor Dreg return to an executive office free of any issues—and to keep it that way for as long as he could.

A mix of contrition and frightened excitement coursed through Hale's veins. The first thing he had done that morning was to port control of the monitor wall in Franklin's office to his own computer. Then he had entered false information into the systems that tracked power consumption. Hale was going to deal with the drain himself and on his terms. For too long had he stayed in Mayor Dreg's shadow, watching the lumbering braggart make rash decisions, issue foolish orders, and generally muddle the handling of the city. If he could assume management of the problem from its outset, Hale reasoned that he could see it through to resolution. Why not finally take the reins when the biggest catastrophe yet had struck? Was not he the best man for the task? If The Mayor thought Timothy Hale would be forever content in his current post, would never seek to rise, well then Dreg had much to learn. Outside, the morning was brightening; inside, Hale's confidence was growing.

Then the phone rang.

"Hale."

"Secretary Hale? This is Major J. P. Engel. Security deputy."

"Oh, right. You work under Colonel Strayer."

"Correct."

"What can I do for you, Major?"

"Can you get outside fast? Or are you near a window that opens?"

"What?" Hale asked, almost laughing. "No. I mean . . . yes, I guess I can crack a window in my office, what the hell are you talking about, Engel?"

"Well please do it right now. As fast as you can. And listen."

Shaking his head incredulously, Hale pressed the key for speakerphone and rose, turning to face his window. He clicked open the lock and slid the heavy frame aside a few inches, holding his head near the open gap. At first he heard nothing but the standard din of a New Las Vegas morning: pods and trains cruising along their tracks, a chorus of voices, and the clang of construction. But then, a different sound, a foreign sound . . . a deep, echoing drone.

"What is that, Engel?" Hale asked loudly, his ear still held to the open window.

"It's the warning horns from the sunfield." The deputy officer's voice crackled through the speaker. "It means we have an emergency out there."

Hale's knees buckled. His face went cold. This was too fast. Too big. He slammed the window shut and returned to his chair. Picking up the handset, he took in a slow, steady breath. His voice was unnaturally calm when he spoke.

"We're already on it. Don't worry about this, Engel. No need to spread alarm. I'm in control here." Hale hung up immediately.

The men dozed in the morning sun, another night's work finished. From atop the dune—the highest in sight—the sentry could see miles of the sunfield and easily spot anyone approaching across the barren stretch of sand. It would take a galloping rider ten minutes to close the gap between the field and this outpost; more than enough time for the group to decide whether to fight or flee. None of the outriders ever bothered to stray more than a few hundred yards from the field anyway, and even bothering to post a guard was done merely out of routine.

The sentry was wearing a loose, beige robe over his jeans and flannel shirt. He glanced back at his sleeping comrades, only one of whom had bothered to switch from the black robes they wore at night when working. He snorted, then smoothed the thick whiskers of his brown beard flat, shaking his head with a smile. It was almost too easy.

The man turned back to face the sunfield. He had been lying prone and was just rising up on his elbows to fish a cigar from his jacket when the horns began to wail. He froze, his left hand in a pocket, his right unconsciously grabbing a fistful of sand. The sinister moan grew stronger, deeper.

"Guys!" He called out, not yet looking back. "Wake up, guys!"

"The fuck's that?" one of the others mumbled. The sentry got up on his knees and raised a pair of binoculars. He scanned the field but could see no one. Behind him the men began to stir. He glanced over his shoulder to find the group in varying degrees of wakefulness. Two men were already up and alert, one was still fast asleep, and the other three groggily coming to.

The sentry again raised his binoculars. He spotted a lone outrider, galloping at full speed. The rider was headed east, though, away from their dune and off toward New Las Vegas.

The first man who had awoken was on his feet. He rolled out his massive shoulders, then pulled the dark robe off, not bothering to don its beige replacement. He rubbed at the black stubble on his powerful jaw, his eyes clear, serene. "Gather your things. Fast. And one of you head down and make sure everyone's ready. We got work to do."

# 10

Dreg wrapped his thick fingers around the armrests, his yellow nails leaving crescent divots in the tan leather. His plane had just reached its cruising altitude of thirty-five thousand feet and was nearing transcontinental flight speed. In less than three hours, The Mayor would have his feet back on home turf. He ground his teeth together, his mustache quivering. His eyes were fixed on a bare spot of wall.

After ten minutes spent barely blinking, Dreg turned to look over the back of his seat at Strayer, who was leaning over a table spread with documents. "Any word from Hale?"

"Nothing," Strayer answered, his pale eyes briefly meeting Dreg's then glancing over at his computer screen.

The Mayor faced forward again, loosening his tie with slow, deliberate motions. He had resolved not to call his secretary; he was so infuriated by Hale's lack of communication that he felt trying him again would be in some way a personal failure. But he had to know. "Nothing to report," Hale had said in his one voicemail from the night before. "Carry on." *Fucking carry on! What the hell did that mean? Insubordinate bastard,* Dreg thought, his face flushing.

There was something to report. Dreg couldn't remember what, but there was something very large indeed to report. Something was wrong with the executive network, though, and he'd been unable to wire into the mainframe and check up on the city remotely. His eyes drifted back to the same patch of wood-paneled wall. His hands gripped the armrests again. The jet bounced through a rough pocket of turbulence. Dreg hardly noticed.

It was mid-morning but still the desert air was chilled. Winter was coming on fast. A cloud bank had filled much of the sky, blowing in from the eastern plains. It moved slowly, a mix of cottony splotches frozen into perfect forms high above and a muddled carpet of gray closer to the ground. Cold sweat dripped down Wilton's back as he clung to Shady with his knees.

The outriders had kept the horses at full gallop for miles that morning, easing to a canter only when either animal began to lose its rhythm, and once to give them water. Kretch could see spittle congealed into foamy clumps at the corner of Reese's mouth and knew his colt was likely worse off, being the weaker horse. Wilton too was exhausted from the hours of riding. His thighs burned and his elbows ached. His neck was sore from the constant bouncing and even his jaw throbbed from being clenched tight for so long. He looked askance at Scofield. Envy tinged the anger he felt upon finding his companion with a smile on his face.

Scofield was relishing the ride. Reese was going strong, her coat slick with sweat but her stride steady. The ten minutes the group had rested a while back was more than enough for the horse to recharge. She and her rider were in perfect harmony: Scofield's head dropped when her flanks rose and bobbed up again when her back legs hit the sand. Reese let out a short whinny of protest when Scofield hauled back on her reins.

"Kretch, let's slow up a sec!" Scofield hollered over the pounding of hooves. Wilton slowed Shady to a walk and looked over his shoulder.

"What's up?"

Scofield had brought his mare to a standstill. Wilton wheeled Shady about and trotted over to his partner.

"Let's give the mounts a sip."

"Only got a few miles till we cross the line, Scof. Oughta just finish the ride."

"They're *thirsty*," Scofield fixed Kretch in an unusually intense glare, then looked down and to his left.

Kretch nodded slowly. "Suppose we should give them a quick drink." He pulled the brim of his hat low over his eyes and tried to follow Scofield's suggested sightline. In the flat sunlight, diffused through the clouds, at first Wilton could see only the dusty sands. Then he caught it. About thirty yards back there was a wide, shallow depression in the sand. It was discernible only by its perfect flatness amid the parched, uneven soil. A big burrow, by the looks of it.

"Let's each give these fellahs a drink at the same time," Scofield whispered, kicking out of his stirrups. Kretch nodded, and both outriders dismounted and drew their pistols. Kretch slung his rifle over one shoulder as Scofield wriggled out of his long jacket, passing the six-shooter from one hand to the other as he slid his arms from the sleeves.

The two men approached the depression slowly, spreading out to close in at an acute angle relative to one another. The burrow was concealed by a large, circular tarp painted to match the desert floor and anchored by dozens of tiny copper stakes. The setup would complicate a swift removal. Using gestures, Scofield indicated for Kretch to take hold of one side and him the other, then for both to drag the cloth up and south. Wilton nodded, and they closed the last few feet to the tarp with painfully slow steps.

Scofield knelt and gingerly took a handful of canvas. When Wilton signaled that he was ready, Scofield fired into the air and both outriders heaved up on the tarp then lunged aside in unison, exposing the burrow.

Scofield dropped the canvas and spun to face the hole, his pistol trained with both hands. Peering out from heavy sleeping bags, two fearful sets of eyes stared back at him.

"Hands where I can see 'em! Real fast!"

The man was first to his feet, followed clumsily by the teenager. It was immediately clear that they were father and son: the same slender, hooked nose, same brown eyes, and the same dark hair, thinning and graying on the man; full and unkempt on the youngster.

"Get up here," Wilton sneered.

The teen crawled out of the burrow then turned to help his father, who rasped for breath after the short ordeal of climbing four feet up onto the desert floor. The pair stood before the outriders in matching gray uniforms. The boy's was ill-fitting, likely a hand-me-down. His boots, too, were oversized and clunky. His skin was pale and patchy but red with pubescence in places.

The father looked to be near fifty years old. The flesh of his face was tanned and tight, cut with the wrinkles of a man who had never known a desk job. But his shoulders drooped, rising and falling as he sucked in rapid, wheezing breaths.

"You gentlemen step towards me. Wilton, be so kind as to check out that hole, hm?" Kretch nodded and holstered his pistol, sitting on the ledge of the burrow before sliding down in.

"Anything on you I should know about? Things that shoot or stab or any of that?"

"Nothing, sir." The man said quietly. His voice was even; calm but humble. "We're just out here to—"

"Make a living or feed the family or whatnot. Yeah. Same shit thieves been saying for ten thousand years." Scofield waved the man's words away dismissively. "Now real slow, I want you boys to unbutton those jackets and toss 'em onto the sand."

The teen glanced over at his father, who nodded without returning the look. Both removed their coats and set them on the soil. The boy was wearing a long-sleeved white shirt. It was stained yellow around the neck and under his armpits. The man had on a sleeveless undershirt, and began to shiver almost immediately.

"Let's see them wrists."

Scofield looked at both sets of forearms and found them free of marks.

"Anything?" Kretch called from the hideout where he was busily searching through the pair's belongings.

"Clean."

"Wouldn't a'thought that," Kretch muttered, dusting himself as he crawled from the burrow. "C'mere, Scof."

Scofield backed away from the leeches, keeping his gun aimed at the man. Both the father and son had their arms raised, fingers intertwined behind their necks. Looking back and forth between the captives and the hole, the outrider followed his partner's finger as Wilton pointed out various items.

"That crate's got enough wire to stretch a half mile. Maybe more. They got the makings of three taps and pieces to repair a busted collector. See that sack there?" Wilton jumped back down into the burrow and hefted an olive green bag, shaking it up and down. Its contents clattered loudly. Kretch raised the sack out of the hole and upended it dramatically. Out spilled a random assortment of plugs and metal discs. Scofield immediately recognized the parts as fitting both the cable he'd found out east and the structure they'd discovered the night before.

Scofield knelt and sifted through the arcane hardware. Running his fingers across a smooth, steel disc, he looked over at Wilton.

"What's your gut?" he whispered.

"Not sure. But I think maybe these boys heard the horn and thought they could get in a day of heavy leechin'."

Scofield dropped the metal cap and scratched at the whiskers under his chin.

"Nah . . . they were sleeping when we tossed their hole open. Wouldn't have bedded down again if the warning was what brought 'em out here."

"True."

"And these things here match the taps on that big fucker we found."

"Yup . . . also true. Hm. What do you think?"

"Don't know yet. But we oughta bring 'em in. Fast. Maybe take some of this stuff with us."

Wilton crawled out of the burrow and stood. He tapped a few of the random plugs and discs with the tip of one boot. "Never seen this kinda shit before." He looked up at the shivering leeches. "What y'all got here, huh? What's this stuff?"

Neither spoke. The boy shifted his weight from one foot to the other nervously. His father stood still, his eyes on the ground.

"I'll bring the horses over," Scofield said, holstering his pistol and walking away. Kretch turned to face the leeches. A sneer lifted one corner of his lips. Unconsciously, he tugged at the buttons of his jacket then ran a palm across his chest. "Cold out, huh? Just about wintertime." He ambled slowly toward the men. "You boys smoke? Hm?" Getting no response, Kretch let out a short, sinister laugh. "Well, that makes one of us." He fished about in a pocket and found a cigarette he'd rolled the night before. Kretch placed the smoke between his lips and glanced up at the teenager. "You don't smoke? Huh, kid? No?"

"No," the young man murmured.

"Oh, so daddy taught you good, huh?" Kretch struck a match and held the flame to his cigarette, tossing the match at the boy's feet once the tobacco had caught. "Seems to me a man should share a smoke with his boy out in a place like this. Good thing to do. Good memory to share."

"He doesn't smoke. I don't either," the man rasped, his face averted. Slowly, the older leech lowered his hands from his head and began to rub his palms together. His son kept his arms tucked behind his neck. Scofield had looped Reese's and Shady's reins together and was leading the horses over.

Kretch glanced back at his partner, then fixed his gaze on the father. "You think I forgot you, ol' man?"

The leech raised his head and locked eyes with Kretch.

"Hitch up your shirt." Wilton snarled.

"Pa, we just—"

"Shut up kid!" Kretch barked. "Take off that shirt."

The humble pride in the man's eyes disappeared, replaced by fear. His hands trembled as he gripped the hem of his shirt, slowly raising it until much of his pale torso was exposed.

"All the way off," Kretch whispered, stepping closer. Scofield stopped a few paces back. He stood still, holding onto his horse's bridle with his right hand, his left awkwardly held before him where he had frozen upon seeing the old leech undressing. The boy's eyes whipped back and forth from his father to Kretch. Then he looked up at Scofield, his mouth opening slightly as if to speak.

The father held his shirt between both hands, clutching it to his chest like some talisman. His eyes were closed. Finally, after a long pause, he sighed slowly and let his arms drop, revealing a sinister scar just in from his right nipple.

"Just what I thought." Kretch hissed. "You remember what I told you, leech? You think I was playin' around?"

Kretch leveled his pistol and fired so fast none of the other three men had time to blink. The bullet tore into the old leech's chest opposite the shot that had taken out his lung two years ago. This one found his heart. He was dead by the time he hit the ground.

"No!" the boy shrieked, dropping to his knees. He took his father's head in his hands, whimpering. Blood stained the youth's white shirt. It spilled onto the sand. He looked up at Kretch, rage and hatred flashing in his eyes. Wilton lowered the gun down beside his hip but kept its muzzle loosely trained on the young man. A smile played across his face. He looked strangely satisfied, as though he had accomplished some goal. Kretch and the boy held each other's gaze for a long time. The outrider continued staring down at the dead man and his son after the boy finally lowered his tearful eyes, looking past the outrider.

Had Wilton glanced behind him, he would have seen what the youth did: Scofield quietly sliding his pistol back into its holster. He had drawn it instantly when Kretch shot the leech. His trigger finger had been taut, ready—a few more ounces of pressure and Wilton would have been dead. A silent, black rage grew in the pit of Scofield's stomach. He swallowed it down—for now—and approached his partner slowly. The boy looked up at him. Scofield curled his lips in over his teeth and gave the slightest nod. Then he turned away.

"Get your tarp," he whispered through clenched teeth.

Boss Hutton wandered about the room aimlessly. He walked up and down the rows of folding chairs, tested the microphone on the podium for the third time, and then just stood still in the middle of the plywood stage. Pale sunlight drifted through the dusty windows lining the sixty-by-forty foot room. His smoker's cough echoed off the cinderblock walls. It had been just over a half hour since he'd sounded the horns and the first of his outriders were sure to arrive any minute.

He dreaded the questions; could barely stand the thought of the usual bullshitting and banter. Not this time. This was no time for grab-assing. Hutton loved his boys but he knew them too well to let the fellahs in on what was happening just yet. *Bunch of hotheads*, he sighed, shaking his head. *They'll just wanna start hootin' and shootin' and take names later*. The Boss knew he'd have to explain why he'd called the men in early, but he needed more information before announcing a drain. Once the lid was off this thing, it would have to be seen all the way through. And as much as Hutton loathed the notion, he knew he'd have to consult Mayor Dreg and the Civil Defense Forces before an appropriate response could be mounted. There came a time when the field and the city had to come together.

The Boss had just taken a seat in one of the chairs somewhere near the middle of the room when the doors creaked open. Hutton was holding a slender cigar between two fingers, and he jammed the stogie between his teeth without turning around. An awkward, clunky shuffle announced the first arrival.

"Hey, Fischer," Hutton muttered.

"Howya doin', Boss man?"

Hutton rose and turned to face Noah Fischer. "How's the leg?"

"Oh, leg's doin' great. My hip bone's broken to shit in three places, but the leg's doing great." Fischer leaned down onto his crutches with a smile on his wide, flat face. He stood over six and half feet tall when on two good feet. His usual gait was heavy and loping, like each step was an effort. Now, with one hip cracked apart after a fall off a colt a few days back and leaning on crutches too short, he looked ridiculous as he hobbled into the room; looked like a kid who'd grown too fast to learn where his body stopped and the ground began.

"Starting a day early, hum?" Fischer asked, easing himself down onto a chair in the back row.

"Yep."

"Heard the sirens so I thought I should amble over. What's going on?"

"Usual shit, y'know" Hutton muttered. "Just rounding up my boys."

"Why early?"

"Hm?" Hutton grunted, looking away and hoping to deflect the logical inquiry.

"The horns."

"Didn't see any reason to put off the meeting. Got things to talk about now. We'll get to it all in time, Fish." This non-answer seemed to satisfy the broad-shouldered man entirely. Fischer leaned back in the flimsy plastic and aluminum chair and slid his right leg out in front of him. A white cast held his right leg immobile from waist to ankle and he groaned as pain shot through his side.

"Goddamnit . . . fuckin' horse . . . .."

"New mount that tossed you?" Hutton asked as he lit his cigar.

"No. That's the fuck of it all! It was Poppy. I got no clue what spooked him. We was just ridin' along when all the sudden he up and bucked like a son of a bitch. Like he stepped on something that messed with 'im, but I never seen a thing!"

"That'll happen." Hutton puffed at his stogie, then started walking toward the door. "Listen, Fischer, I gotta make some calls. Tell the boys to stay put in here and wait for me, OK? Tell 'em not to do anything stupid."

"Whaddya mean stupid?"

"Oh, come on Noah—yer one of 'em. I'm one of em." Hutton paused at the door, looking down at his boots. "You know us fellahs can't meet in a group bigger'n two and not do something stupid. Just say I said to not do shit and sit down and wait. I'll be back inside an hour and we'll get Round Up going."

"Sneaking into my own goddamn office," Dreg muttered as he gently keyed in the door code. The lock clicked and The Mayor slowly turned the heavy knob, easing the thick mahogany door open. He stepped into his outer chamber and looked around the room. The lamps were all lit, the overhead lighting turned off. Just as he liked it. From under the doorframe to Hale's office he heard the steady clatter of typing. His secretary had no idea he had returned—Franklin always entered his suite through Hale's office.

But something was up; The Mayor felt certain that his secretary knew something and was hiding it from him. *What the hell he could know is beyond me.* Dreg planned to take a thorough accounting of matters before confronting Hale and would then play dumb and see what his secretary disclosed. Those three receptionists in the lobby, though . . . Dreg didn't trust the way they'd looked at him. Did they know something, too? Had Hale coached them in some way? Their smiles looked the same; their eyes were nervous. In fact the whole city felt on edge.

Dreg made his way gingerly across the creaking hardwood and let himself into his private office. Maybe he had just been away too long. Four days was longer than he ever spent away from New Las Vegas. Perhaps he was in error leveling his anger at Hale and the city and the lot of it. After all, no one controlled snow storms. But the lack of communication—that was unprecedented. Why, anything could have been going on without him there at the helm!

The Mayor lowered himself into his soft leather chair and sighed, instantly more content than he had felt in days. The pitcher of ice water was perched atop his blotter, a crystal glass by its side. Three fountain pens lay next to a stack of documents awaiting his signature. Not a speck of dust on the desktop. He nodded slowly to himself. He was back. Dreg rifled through the papers, signing where Hale had indicated without so much as glancing at their headings. He poured himself a glass of water.

Turning to face the wall of monitors, Dreg unbuttoned his vest and loosened the plum-sized knot in his tie. He let his eyes drift very slowly across the sea of numbers, graphs, and tables. Everything looked stable. Perfectly so, even. Digits rose and fell smoothly and the tracking charts were near-textbook sine curves. *Ah, let it go old boy*, Dreg looked toward the door of his office. *He's good enough people. I must be remembering it wrong—all the booze that night.*

The Mayor rose and wriggled free of his pin-striped jacket, tossing it across a chair. He leaned against his desk and keyed the intercom.

"Tim! Get in here!" he rumbled.

Hale had been ready all morning. When The Mayor slipped into his office via the side door the secretary had feared the worst. But when Dreg used Timothy's first name in his usual booming voice, Hale figured he may yet be able to steer things his way. If Dreg was shouting things were usually fine: when he was angry he would positively roar; when he spoke quietly, he was beyond furious and only then to be truly feared.

Buttoning his suit coat, Hale hurried through the outer chamber. He paused before opening the door to Franklin's office just long enough to catch his reflection in a mirror across the room. Cleanly shaved, hair combed flat, shirt starched, story planned: nothing left but a touch of luck.

"Mr. Mayor! Good to see your face, sir."

"Yours too, Hale. And to hear your voice." Dreg rose from where he had perched on his desk and stood as Hale approached him. The two shook hands, making eye contact. Hale broke the gaze off after a few seconds and turned to the wall panel.

"Shall I get some light in here?"

"Oh yes, as much as you can, Tim. Depressing to leave the dreary Northeast and find home nearly as gray, though."

"Yeah, sorry about that storm, and as cloudy as it's been in months here!" Hale nodded, punching in a few buttons on the keypad. The steel shutters began to rise outside the windows and soft, diffuse light filled the room. The office grew brighter, but without the usual warming glow the bank of windows brought. Rather it was brighter but somehow colder. Hale turned and, spotting Dreg's jacked lying rumpled across a chair, he picked up the blazer and shook the wrinkles out before hanging it carefully on the coat tree in the corner. The Mayor watched this action with great pleasure.

"Now. Tim. Tell me everything I need to know."

Dreg sat in one of the two chairs before his desk, turning it inward to face the other. Hale eased down into the second chair, unconsciously sliding a few inches away from his boss. Franklin leaned forward, his face huge before Hale's eyes. The massive jowls, the mustache quivering above an awful grin, his nasal pores like impact craters. Timothy swallowed hard. He had not taken a good look at Dreg in some time, it seemed. Hale could feel his collar growing damp, his forehead pale. His handling of next few minutes would be pivotal.

"Well sir, where to start . . .. Basically it was business as usual . . ."

Boss Hutton ducked back behind the concrete wall, out of view from the street. Marc Alterman had just entered the meeting hall. That accounted for every one of his outriders save four: the bed-ridden Moses Smith, Tripp Hernandez, Wilton Kretch, and Scofield. Those last two had been scheduled to ride the field together for the past few days. Tripp, he was sure, would be late as usual but always showed up. It was unlike Scofield to be late to Round Up, though, especially in light of the warning horns.

*Somethin' ain't right here.* Hutton furrowed his brow and puffed several times at his cigar before realizing it had gone out. He threw the butt on the ground and pulled his hat low across his eyes. Walking quickly, he made his way across the road and took the long way around the building to avoid the open door. The boys were likely to hear his engine fire up, but they'd just have to wait and wonder.

Hutton turned the key then patted the dashboard in gratitude when the old jeep started right up. He tossed her into gear and set out heading toward the glowline. In the back of his mind, The Boss knew that driving out to the field in search of his men was near useless and perhaps even counter-productive: it was a big desert and he was unlikely to find them—especially if something were amiss—and if they were indeed simply late getting in, driving away from the meeting was the opposite move to make. But he couldn't bear the thought of sitting and waiting, fifty-odd pairs of eyes watching him skeptically.

Hutton jammed another cigar between his teeth and chewed at it, leaving the stogie unlit. The sun was well on the way to its zenith but a thick cloud bank hung in the sky and the land was gray and formless. He knew the pair of missing riders had been patrolling the west end of the field and kept the jeep pointed south by southwest, driving at around forty miles an hour. The Boss figured he would make two long, ovular circuits likely to intersect their route, then head in and figure his next move on the fly.

He tried not to, but often found himself looking down at his hands wrapped around the bouncing wheel. His knuckles were white with tension. So many veins and scars and brown spots and straggly hairs. A man knows certain things like the back of his hand, they say. *When did you boys get so damn gnarled? So damn . . . old?* he found himself wondering. *No one told me about it.* These two hands were foreign to him. Speckled and mildly arthritic and gripping the wheel so tightly, desperately. Hutton spent most of his waking hours alone and preferred it that way, but it was amazing how few of those solitary hours he spent reflectively. Or at least reflecting about himself.

But now, with the weight of the world on him—with his fields under assault and his best man missing—his mind opened up the floodgates and every doubt and fear flowed in. Each imperfection stood out stark-ly. How in the hell would his boys fare against a drain? What were they up against? When had these goddamn hands grown so twisted? *Christ, while we're at it, how long's it been since I had a piece of woman? That ever gonna happen again?*

Hutton was cruising roughly parallel to the glowline and a few miles north of the field. He figured he'd gone far enough west and began turn-ing to complete his first circle. Relief washed over him as he spotted two horsemen a mile off. He sped up to sixty. A smile raised the corners of his chapped lips. But as Hutton drew nearer to his boys, the grin flattened out again. One of the riders was dragging something and the other had a body across his horse.

"Hey Boss. Howya doin'?"

Hutton pulled up alongside the outriders and switched off the engine. He grabbed the roll bar and pulled himself up to stand on his seat.

"Well, I don't know, Kretch. How are we doing?"

Wilton watched as Boss Hutton surveyed the scene, noting the old man's distinct displeasure. Admittedly, it didn't look good. The boy was draped across the front of Scofield's saddle, unconscious. They'd wrapped the father in a drag tarp at Scofield's insistence—Kretch had wanted to bury him in his burrow.

"What's the story, boys?"

"Two timer here," Kretch spat, gesturing over his shoulder without a backward glance. "Ain't gonna have a shot at being a three timer, I'm afraid."

"This is his son," Scofield said quietly.

"How old's the boy?"

"Maybe fifteen."

Hutton climbed over the door of the jeep and lowered his boots down onto the cold sand. He walked over to Scofield slowly, his hips stiff from the drive.

"Hey, Reese. How you holdin' up, girl?" The horse tossed her mane and snorted, then lowered her nose into Hutton's outstretched palm, nuzzling against it. "You got a good goddamn mount, Scof. You know that, huh?"

"The best, Boss."

"Mhm." Hutton patted the mare's neck, savoring the musty-sweet odor of horseflesh. "Man I tell you if I still rode much, I'd be lookin' for any way to steal her from ya." The Boss nodded to himself, then pulled off his gray hat and ran a sleeve across his brow. Finally he looked up at the young man slung across the saddle. His face was buried in Reese' side.

"He out cold?"

"Think so. Hasn't made a peep in miles."

"You awake, boy? Young man?" Hutton whispered hoarsely. When no response came, he looked up at Scofield and asked: "What happened?"

"We seen some strange shit, Boss," Kretch called from where he perched a few yards off. Hutton glanced over at him, working his hat back on over his salt and pepper hair.

"Looks that way. What happened?" His eyes were on Scofield again.

"Long story, Hut. Not sure if the boy and his Pa figure in, but we found something last night. Collector I guess—like nothing I've ever seen. Nothing we'd ever seen. It was huge. Complex. What's the story with the horns?"

"That story's gonna have to wait a bit." Hutton looked away. Then, very quietly, he whispered so Wilton wouldn't hear, "The ol' man?" His eyes flitted to Kretch.

Scofield nodded so slightly Hutton had to read his eyes for the answer. It came unmistakably. The Boss sighed and dropped his head. He drew the chewed up cigar from a vest pocket and walked over to Kretch.

"You got a light there, Wilton?"

"Sure, Boss." Kretch pulled out his lighter and handed it down. After a few flicks Hutton got a flame and lit up his stogie. He handed the lighter back to Wilton and stared into the man's eyes.

"Seeing as I left Round Up in the hands of that damn fool Noah Fischer, and seein' as you already got a load hitched to uh . . . what's his name . . ."

"Shady."

"Yeah. Shady. Why don't we have you take the mounts in and I'll drive Scofield and the boy back with me."

Scofield shifted uncomfortably in his saddle. Reese seemed to bristle as well, though it was surely the outrider's imagination. Hutton looked over at the pair.

"Seems to me that's the best way. Ain't much of a load for two horses to trade off and I ain't much for corpses in my jeep. Kretch, you just get back fast as you can and put the body in the cooler. Tell the boys we'll be along by noon to start the Round Up."

"Boss, if we could—"

"Ride, Kretch. Just ride."

Scofield dismounted hesitantly, whispering a few words to Reese before he tied her lead rope to Shady's saddle horn. He and Hutton helped the boy, half-delirious and muttering, off the mare's back. They eased the youth into the back of the jeep. Then the two men watched as Kretch trotted north, looking back over his shoulder every few hundred feet.

The man nodded slowly to himself, rising from his knees to stand nearly six and a half feet tall. He raised the large binoculars to his eyes once more and tracked the jeep speeding north. Then he handed the field glasses back to his compatriot and began to strip off his beige cloak. The fabric, moist in the damp air, caught on his wide shoulders and then tore along a seam as he yanked it free of his body.

*Fuck it.* The man smiled. *Won't be needing you much more anyway.* He dropped the ruined cloak onto the sand and leaned his head back to survey the sky. The clouds were growing thicker, grayer. The wind was beginning to blow. It swirled around the men imploringly. Rain was coming. A storm.

The drone of the jeep's engine was all but inaudible now, its dust cloud ever more distant. Scratching at the thick bristles of his chin, the man turned to face the group and smiled broadly.

"Well, boys, this is it. The field is ours."

# 11

"It's quite alright," she said.

"No. It's not, though. I made a fool of myself and I'm sure I offended you. And embarrassed you."

"Um . . . you confused me . . . you definitely confused me."

Hale covered the mouthpiece and sighed, closing his eyes tightly. "You're being generous, Maria. I was a fucking idiot. I never drink. I mean I do—I mean . . . I'm never drunk is what I mean. I wasn't thinking."

"Of course not. You were drunk."

Hale thought he detected a smile speaking those words and found himself grinning. He leaned back in his chair and rested the heel of one shoe on his desk.

"Yeah. Good point. Listen, I . . . can I make it up to you? I just . . . I've always meant to talk to you. To really talk—not about work and the grid and all. I want to know you. It's stupid, I guess, but sometimes, you know you just meet someone and you feel like you should . . . Jesus, I don't know. Do you get what I'm saying some or am I rambling like an idiot?"

"You're making more sense than the other night, at least."

"That's saying a lot. Listen, can we meet up sometime?"

"I don't know. I guess. Maybe."

"That's all I could ask for, given my recent grace and poise. Alright, I guess I'll get to the point." Timothy sighed, switching back into his professional demeanor. "The actual reason I called—though you certainly deserved the apology—was to ask if you'd noticed any steady rises in the afternoon usage. Most grids seem to be using power steadily" he lied, "but Three has been hit extra hard." This last fact was true. It was as if half the electricity from Grid Three was disappearing daily.

"Hmm . . . no, it's been fine as far as my tracking, but this seems to be growing into a regular issue. Our lines and transmission beacons are due for inspection in a month, so why don't I just send the team to check them out early?"

"No!" Hale barked too loudly. Then, his voice measured, he added "No. Everything is fine. We've had some complications in the field but it's just a logistical thing. Just some maintenance so we already have men out there."

"You've already sent teams out to inspect?"

He paused, and then said "Yes" with resolution. "Any hardware problems and they'll find them. I'm on top of it. All you need to do is relax and track the numbers and give me a chance to make it up to you."

"I'll think about it, OK?"

"Think. That's all I ask." Timothy hung up without another word. He tucked his hands behind his head and leaned back again, conflicted. When The Mayor spoke Hale sucked in a bit of saliva and coughed. He had no idea how long Dreg had been standing in the doorway.

"Think about what?"

Hale sputtered, clearing his throat and hacking. "Sorry, Frank." He coughed again. "Down the wrong pipe. I'm sorry, what did you ask?"

"Who were you talking to and what did you want them to think about?" Dreg took a few steps into the secretary general's office. His pale blue shirt was open at the collar and hung down over his slacks, as if he had been caught in the midst of dressing. The Mayor often lounged behind his desk in this disheveled state, but rarely ventured farther than the door of his private office without his tie tied tight and his vest buttoned to the top.

"Maria Rodrigues," Hale replied evenly. "The lady from grid three."

"Right. Maria. What was the nature of the call?"

"Sir?"

"You said 'I'm on top of it' and 'think.' What was that regarding, Tim?" Dreg lowered himself slowly into one of the wooden chairs facing Hale's desk.

"Just that she should, um . . . not worry—"

"She should what? What were you talking about, Mr. Hale?"

"Mayor. Frank. If you doubt my integrity we can call back right now and prove that I was talking to her."

Dreg raised a hand, massive palm out, and bowed his head. "I don't doubt your integrity. I doubt your motives." The air hung thick between the two men. Dreg's beady, black eyes locked onto Hale's face. He felt his brow flush.

"Was this a business call?" Dreg practically whispered. Then, slowly, the corners of his mouth turned up. His eyes grew brighter and the fleshy, crowfeet wrinkles deeper. "Or did you finally make a pass at the pretty thing?"

"Well . . . I—I mean we talked . . ." the secretary exhaled, the tension in his neck releasing.

"Talked! Ha! I bet she positively swooned, old boy!" Dreg rose and clapped Tim on the shoulder, walking behind Hale's desk to look out the window. "What did you do? Offer a private tour of the executive office? A fine dinner? Was it wine or champagne?" The Mayor was chuckling, greatly amused with himself. He tucked his shirt in with forceful jabs, working the cotton between his trousers and paunch.

Still looking out over the city, Dreg went on. "When the cat's away, hm Hale? Come now, man. Tell me how it went?"

"It will be a . . . long pursuit, shall we say." He spun round in his chair to face The Mayor's back. "But I'm a patient man."

"Yes you are, Mr. Hale." Dreg seemed to stiffen. The warmth faded from his voice. "You are a very patient man indeed. I've always known that. The kind of man who waits for the right time. Well . . . I'm sure you'll get her."

Hale rose quietly and backed away from his boss. When The Mayor turned, Timothy feigned interest in a document lying on the sideboard, then stood facing Dreg. After an awkward silence, Franklin looked down and buttoned his collar.

"Such a gloomy day. Bitter out. Awful. But all my meters and tracking boards are running so perfectly smooth that I'm getting bored in that damn office." Dreg made for the door to his suite, pausing with a hand on the knob. "I thought I'd go around to a few municipal stations. Make sure everything is OK in my town—I can't rely on a bunch of monitors all the time, you know. Why don't you stay here and hold down the fort, alright Tim?"

"Sure. Of course, Frank."

"Atta boy." Dreg pulled open the door and stepped out of the room. Before shutting it behind him, he added casually: "Oh, and Hale—I think Colonel Strayer is going to be calling on you sometime this afternoon. Some new protocol he wanted to discuss. He seemed unhappy about the um . . . what did he call it—communication channels, I believe. Maybe something you said or didn't say or did or didn't do." With that, Mayor Dreg slammed the door. His feet fell heavily on the floor of his inner chamber.

"The thing I just can't figure," Scofield shouted above the whipping wind and engine noise, "is how someone got something that big there in the first place. And how in the hell they moved it out in one night. Not a track, Hut. Nothing. If I'd been alone I'd think I dreamt it. So much steel and copper and all the wiring—it must have weighed over a ton, easy."

Boss Hutton shook his head, chewing on his bottom lip in thought. "Don't make sense," he replied.

The boy was awake in the back seat. He had curled into fetal position and was staring at the sky, utterly despondent. Scofield had offered him water and food; the young man had not even glanced over. Hutton took a peek at the youth in the rearview mirror then looked over at Scofield.

Scofield met Hutton's gaze, his face grim. "Cold blood," he said just loud enough to be heard.

Hutton nodded. "We'll talk."

"Also, put the northwest holding cell on the route. I got a real son of a bitch leech locked up in there. I'll remind you later."

Hutton nodded. "Son of a bitch, huh?"

"Tried to jump me twice. Strange guy. Seemed like all he wanted was me to shoot him. Just wanted to be dead. Sebastian's the name if it matters."

"Not much. I'll put him on the pickup route."

They were nearing the Outpost. The Boss slowed the jeep as they crossed the glowline. A few pedestrians wandered between the charge station and shop, but the little township was quiet. It had begun to drizzle intermittently. Scofield desperately wanted to ask Hutton about the siren and tell him more about the contraption and the shooting and all of it, but they had to drop the boy off first.

It tore Scofield up inside to stick the freshly orphaned kid in a cell, but there was nothing else to do. They couldn't just cut him loose, at any rate. And maybe he had information. That, above all else, was what they needed.

Hutton parked next to the cinderblock jail—known as "The Office" among the men—and switched off the engine. Both outriders were taken by surprise when the young man immediately rose and climbed out of the jeep. He stood beside the vehicle, his face resigned. He had aged years during the short drive.

"I'll do this part. Watch my girl," Hutton muttered. He walked around the jeep and laid a hand on the boy's thin shoulder. "We're just gonna put you somewhere safe for a bit, young man. Somewhere warm and with food and a bed. It'll be alright."

The old man and young man walked toward the squat gray building. Some other day, in some other life, they could easily have been mistaken for grandfather and grandson walking side by side. Hutton held the door open for his charge and the two disappeared inside.

The rain was picking up and Scofield began to fidget with the jeep's old canvas roof. After a few minutes he had the cabin covered as best the worn vehicle would allow, and he climbed back into the shotgun seat and lit a smoke. Raindrops pattered off the fabric roof and drummed on the steel hood. The air grew musty and thick. Scofield watched the smoke curl slowly around his fingers as he held the cigarette near his mouth.

A door's slam snapped Scofield out of his reverie and he flicked a half-inch ash out the window as Boss Hutton hefted himself into the driver's seat with a groan.

"Never get old, Scof." Hutton pulled off his hat and shook the water from it. He looked down at his lap and sighed. "You got a cigarette for me?"

Scofield pulled out his pack and handed it over. Hutton muttered his thanks and struck a match, then sucked greedily at the cigarette. "Mostly I just stick to my stogies these days. One time a doctor told me I burned up five percent of my lungs smokin' these. I don't know if that's a lot or a little but it sounded bad." Hutton closed his eyes tightly. "That boy's broken now. He never said one damn word. Just stared at me when I locked the cell. You'd think it'd get easier, right? That you'd get harder . . . all these fuckin' years. But it just adds up."

"Just gets heavier."

"What happened?"

"It was fast. We pulled 'em out of their hole. Wilton checked their gear, I went for the horses. When I was leading the rides back, Kretch had the old man taking off his shirt. There was a scar on his chest. Bullet wound. Kretch said something about seeing him again and then bam, shot him as simple as you'd crack a smile."

"I loathe that son of a bitch," Hutton hissed, slamming a fist on the steering wheel. "We gotta do something about him. Soon. But not now. Scofield, you listen good, OK? This is just you and me talking, alright?"

Scofield looked over attentively.

"Say that for me. This is just you and me talking."

"This is just you and me, Hut."

Hutton took one more long drag off the cigarette and tossed it out onto the wet sand. "I sounded the horns because we got drainers."

"What?"

"We're being drained. Bad, I think." Hutton put his hat back on and cracked his knuckles. He turned the key and the engine rumbled but wouldn't take. "Not now goddammit girl!" he shouted. The Boss pumped the gas pedal and ratcheted the key again and, sputtering in protest, the jeep came to life. Hutton sighed, eyes closed.

"I haven't got a man to spare so the field is gonna be empty all day. This is gonna be a quick and dirty Round Up—we need to get our men back out there fast. Much as I hate to think it, we'll need help with this;

need Civil Defense. When the meeting's over, I'm sending you into Vegas to talk to the execs. I want you to sit in the back and not say much, OK? Just listen and learn. The boys don't know fuck about what's going on and I want it that way—bunch of hotheads. They'd just start shooting."

"Boss, I'll do what you need but shouldn't I be in the field? Not in the goddamn city? Why not send Tripp Hernandez or Haskell?"

"Hasky's too young. I thought about sending Tripp so I could have you right where you are now: next to me in shotgun. But he ain't checked in yet and there's no time to wait. Plus I trust you more. Look, I know you don't like Vegas. If I didn't hate it even more'n you I'd go. Besides I gotta be here with the gang. You're my best man, Scof—you're the best of 'em by long. At Round Up just sit and listen and don't talk, OK? You don't speak up often so whenever you do all them hotheads listen. And I need you to just hear right now, lie low. We're going to start putting together a puzzle with whatever pieces we gather, but without letting too many people see the big picture. OK?"

"OK. I get it."

Hutton nodded, then jammed the jeep in gear. They set off toward the meeting hall. "And we'll deal with Wilton fucking Kretch as soon as this shit is settled."

"Send a black pod to stop five-one-six." Dreg snapped his phone shut. He buttoned his overcoat as a shiver ran through his ample carriage. "Think I should have the street warmers switched on?"

The security officer beside him, a tall, wide-shouldered fellow whose name The Mayor could never recall—it was something Asian, though the man looked white save for his almond shaped eyes—shrugged and looked up as if doing so would help him better gauge the temperature. "It should get better out by mid-afternoon."

"Already one and still cold. I think I'll have them turned on."

The officer nodded, pursing his lips. Dreg may as well have been talking to a lamppost. The two men stood under the cover of a pod stop. The rain was falling steadily and the usually bustling streets of New Las Vegas were empty. People here had little experience being wet and even less patience for it. The first pod that had arrived was absolutely full, and while The Mayor preferred traveling among his people, he was in no mood to be crushed between damp, musty bodies.

When the executive pod arrived—jet black and about one third the size of the commuter vehicles—Dreg was only too happy to board and take a seat in one of the overstuffed leather chairs.

"Let's scoot over to grid three, alright? Power station."

"Of course, sir," The operator called over his shoulder, glancing back into the passenger compartment. The Mayor relished the notion of being chauffeured about; he alone had access to pods operated by humans rather than the computer network. He alone could disrupt traffic at will. The pod set off across town with a gentle hum. Dreg reached into his damp overcoat and pulled out his brushed steel cigar case. He selected a slender Dominican cigar wrapped in coffee -brown leaves.

"Can I offer you a light, Mr. Dreg?" The security officer asked, starting to rise from his seat with a lighter in his hand.

"No, thanks. Never use a lighter with a fine cigar, my man. The fluid taints the tobacco. I only use wooden matches." Dreg struck three matches, holding them together in a bundle, and puffed at his cigar. Blue-gray smoke drifted up into the stale air of the pod. "Do this for me, though. Call Strayer and tell him not to visit my offices until he's spoken to me."

"Would you like to talk to him? I'm sure he'll answer."

"No." Dreg blew out a great cloud of smoke. "Just tell him not to do anything for the moment. He'll get it."

The officer nodded and rose, walking to the back of the pod as he dialed his commander. The hushed conversation lasted longer than Dreg expected, and he peeked back at the man several times, his brow furrowed. The officer finally hung up and returned to The Mayor's side, tucking his black shirt more evenly into his matching trousers before he sat.

"What did he say?"

"Hm? I'm sorry, sir?"

"What were you and Mr. Strayer discussing?"

"Oh—nothing sir. I just relayed your message and he said he'd comply."

Dreg turned his head away, looking out the rain streaked windows at his city flying past at fifty miles an hour.

"And that exchange took several minutes?"

"Sir?"

"What else did he say?" Dreg looked over at the man again, placing his cigar in his mouth and lowering his hand. Two tendrils of smoke curled from his nostrils.

"Well it was unrelated, Mayor. I didn't want to trouble you." Wilting under Dreg's unyielding gaze, the man swallowed and went on. "It's just that we have a few Civil Defense men AWOL, apparently."

"How many are missing?"

"Six or seven. Colonel Strayer wasn't certain yet but a few of them are from my squad so he wanted to see if I had any information or . . . or thoughts on that."

"And do you?"

"No, sir." The officer looked down at his hands, locking them together in his lap self-consciously. The Mayor exhaled another puff. The cabin was growing hazy with cigar smoke. The officer stifled a small cough, which Dreg noted with derisive pleasure.

"Well, I'm sure it's nothing. Anyway, here we are."

Sure enough, not ten seconds later the pod eased to a halt.

"Station three, gentlemen," The driver called.

"You see? I know my city well." Dreg rose, smiling at the security officer. The two men stepped from the pod onto the slick sidewalk and The Mayor took a final puff of his cigar, then dropped it.

"Should I keep the pod here waiting for you?" The driver called through the open doors. But Dreg was already walking away. He hurried across the pavement, turning his collar up against the rain.

The doors to Power Station Three slid open and The Mayor entered, pulling off his overcoat. "Take this, would you," he said to the officer without the intonation of a question. "And wait here in the lobby. I won't be long." Dreg made his way toward the elevators, his shoes alternately clicking and squeaking on the marble floor.

When he arrived at the fourth floor—the operations department—Mayor Dreg ran a palm across his damp hair several times as the elevator doors opened. He straightened his lapels and put on a bright smile. Then he made his way down a short hall and turned a corner.

"Hello! Ms. Maria Rodrigues! How are you? I wanted to ask you a few questions, if you weren't too busy."

# 12

"Alright you sons of bitches, shut the hell up!" Boss Hutton bellowed into the microphone. A cacophony of shouts, curses, and laughter echoed back at him. Hutton closed his eyes and nodded knowingly, raising both hands, palms facing the assembly. The fifty-some outriders shouted, slapped one another on the back or face, swapped grandiose stories of bullshit, and generally had a grand old time.

Hutton had made his first attempt at order ten minutes ago and then immediately left the stage, knowing it would take a good half hour before the boys approached anything near calm. There was much ground to cover but, despite everything, The Boss loved this time. His crew got together in one big group only a handful of times a year, and seeing the genuine affection and kinship among the men was as heartwarming as it was reassuring: these boys would die for one another just as soon as they'd bullshit about their exploits or fight over women.

The Boss had made his way through the ranks, shaking hands and tossing a few punches (taking one or two himself) and reconnecting with the men he counted on every day. He'd listened to some gripes, taken a bit of praise, and generally tried to get a sense of things. There seemed to be remarkably little grumbling in the ranks. Which unnerved Hutton—this team was one of the best groups he'd ever worked with. Their lack of complaints and concerns didn't mean they were slacking at the job; it meant that the drain was being orchestrated flawlessly. Hutton's easiness dropped with inverse proportion to his comrades' excitement and happiness. *They don't know a goddamn thing*, he found himself repeating after each exchange.

Finally he took the stage again. "OK you goddamn bastards! Enough!" Hoots and hollers and curses and smiles. If anything, the hall got louder.

"Don't make me start shootin', lads! Y'all know I will!" Hutton counted out five Mississippi, then drew a small revolver from his back pocket. He fired three quick shots into the air. The reports reverberated deafeningly about the cavernous hall. For a moment, all was silent. Hutton lowered the pistol. Then came the first shout:

"Blanks!"

"Fuckin' blanks!"

"Blanks, Hut! Those're blanks!"

"He ain't shootin' shit, boys!"

Uproarious laughter filled the room. Smiles a foot wide spread across every face. Even Scofield, seated in the very back row and in a very black mood up to that instant, found himself smiling and shouting: "Blanks!"

Hutton flashed a shit-eating grin, then tossed the starter pistol aside. He paced back and forth a few times, his face growing serious. When he returned to the simple wooden podium, the men were finally starting to get the message. It was time to be serious.

"Boys . . . time for Round Up!" Hutton barked. "Anyone other than Moses absent? Look around some . . . take a minute . . . this is important this time—always important." Hutton shielded his eyes from the bright fluorescent lights and scanned the room.

"All here? Good. Now listen, the first thing all you assholes are gonna ask me, I'm sure, is why'd I sound those damn horns. We'll get to that. Don't you worry about it. Maybe I was just testing you. Maybe I figured it was gonna rain for the next week and we might as well get a move on things. After all, when it starts to rain, ain't so much work to do, and you boys tend to switch from business to bullshit pretty fast, fair? . . . Fair!?"

"Fair enough!"

"I sure as fuck do!"

"Fair!" came the cries.

Hutton nodded. He gripped the sides of the podium, praying no one could see how badly his hands were shaking. He had half hoped to be immediately overwhelmed with concerns and fears and reports of strange things out in the field. Going through the motions of Round Up—normally such a grounding, even joyous event—was draining the life from him. The boys didn't even know what they were up against. But he had to bide his time: until Hutton knew for certain what was going on, there was no way he could unleash his dogs. They'd end up dead or end up killing senselessly.

"So let's get into the shout-out reports. Who's got something worth all of us hearing?"

"I caught six leeches in one burrow two weeks back!" Shouted Noah Fischer.

"Yeah, then you fell off a colt and snapped your leg!"

"Well what's your count, Rush?" Noah raised his large carriage as much as he could given the cast on his leg, staring down his comrade.

"Got me five in as many weeks—ain't bad!"

"Were they a team or just bunked, Noah?" Hutton asked into the microphone.

"Team, I think," he settled back down in his chair. "They all had the same kinda yellowy-like robes on, anyway. But all first-timers. Notched 'em and sent 'em."

"OK, that's a start. Who else?"

Gregory White stood up and stretched his bull-neck from side to side. His voice was like steel on granite, and no one ever spoke over him. "Had to take out a couple fellahs last month. They had horses and one of 'em was branded ours. Must have come out of the stable. Any of you boys lose a horse?"

White looked around the room for a minute. Not a single pair of eyes met his. He was a known killer, and not for anything done in the line of duty. Greg White had spent almost ten years behind bars for the murder of two men in an alley—the circumstances were lost to all but him and the corpses.

"No one? Well it was one of our horses. They had it hauling cable."

"What do you mean?" Scofield called from the back of the room. Every eye turned to him, then back to White.

"What?"

"What do you mean hauling? What kind of cable?"

"Never seen it before. Thick. A few inches around. Almost as big as my cock and just as tan."

A few outriders burst out laughing. Scofield rose slowly, lifting one leg and resting a heel on his chair. He hooked one thumb in a pocket and took off his hat, tilting his head to one side.

"Well, cock aside, Greg, can you describe this . . . little wire? What did its, uh, head look like? The tap?"

White cracked his neck slowly from side to side and drew a breath in through his nose. He glanced toward the stage and Boss Hutton nodded emphatically, raising one hand to bid him continue. "There was a few taps. Four or five. Little taps like you use for a toaster or whatnot."

Scofield saluted in mock deference. "That's all I was askin' about. Maybe Boss Hutton would want to know if anyone else saw anything like that. That's the only reason I asked about your little wire, Greg."

"OK, what do we got?" Hutton called the attention forward again.

Kretch rose looking proud and smug. While smiling usually makes a person easier on the eyes, when Wilton flashed his tiny-toothed grin, his visage grew harder to look at: new wrinkles formed and his cold eyes grew smaller, darker. "Bagged me a two-timer just this morning. Fellah I'd tagged myself some time back."

"OK, Kretch. I meant the tap cable Scofield asked about. Anyone else see any wiring like that?"

Wilton's shoulders curled in. He lowered himself back onto the plastic and aluminum chair gingerly, silently cursing its loud creaking. His face flushed red. Perhaps Boss Hutton had meant nothing personal—perhaps it was just business—but Kretch was deeply insulted. Profoundly angry. He reached down to where he'd stowed his hat behind his boots and jammed the black ten-gallon onto his head. The brim cast a shadow over his eyes, which fixed Hutton in a searing glare.

C. J. Haskell stood up from the front row, clearing his throat. At just twenty-four years old, he already had six years' experience under his belt and was widely regarded as a good shot and an expert horseman. His beard still grew in patches so he kept himself clean-shaven, which only accentuated his youth. But Haskell was adept not only at gunplay and riding, but also at rolling with the punches and shrugging off all the bullshit. Even the senior men knew he was the real deal.

"I think I might have seen something like that, Boss. I found a few of these . . . kinda discs, I guess, that had receivers for four taps. There was a pile of them by a pillar out east. And there was a trail leading off a few hundred yards into the sand. Real thick—like ten feet wide and flat. Like something had been dragged."

"Then it just stopped? The drag mark?" Hutton asked, stepping away from the microphone and nearer to the young man.

"Yeah." Haskell looked down, fiddling with one of the buttons on his starched white shirt. "Just disappeared. I took one of the discs. It's over in my shack."

"Good man. Show me later." Hutton winked at Haskell and turned away, sighing with his back to the assembly. He returned to the podium. "What else, before we break down for route debriefs?"

"Hey, Hutton, y'know what?" It was Ryan Cannell, the second oldest outrider behind The Boss and a trusted friend. He coughed and wheezed as he half-rose out of his seat. His mind was quicker than his wrinkles and gray mustache suggested; Cannell's dark eyes were sharp as they darted about the room, taking in every little detail. "I don't think Tripp is here."

"What? Tripp, are you fuckin' here?" Hutton spat in frustration. Every head turned from side to side looking about the room.

"Don't he usually ride with Moses?" Noah Fischer called above the murmurs.

"Yeah, maybe he caught a touch of what Moses got!" Someone shouted from the back. Laughter filled the hall.

"Hold up! Shut up! Is he really missing?" Hutton shouted. The timbre of his voice cut the laughing short. The Boss looked out at the dozens of eyes watching him attentively. It had been unlike Tripp Hernandez to be late; unheard of that he not show at all. He was an awful drunk when off duty, but when sober, Hernandez was a consummate professional, often the first one to arrive for assignments, in fact—especially Round Up. *Fuck. Jesus H. fucking hell,* Hutton said to himself. He chewed on the inside of his cheeks.

"OK, I'll deal with that. Break into your teams and debrief. I want a ten minute summary from each group in one hour. And not one of you slips out to the goddamn bars, you hear me? Not this time! I'll personally drag any fuckin' one of you I find shirking business today. And with my jeep!"

Hutton hopped down from the stage, wincing as the sparse cartilage left in his hips ground between old bones. He made eye contact with C. J. Haskell and tilted his head toward the door. As The Boss walked hurriedly to the exit, avoiding any looks and waving off attempts at conversation, Hutton scanned the room for Scofield, but the outrider was already gone.

Hale snatched up the phone on the first ring.

"Hello? This is Timothy Hale."

"It's Hutton."

"Boss Hutton?"

"No, fuckin' insurance salesman Hutton. Yes, Hale."

"Where the hell have you been, man?"

"I said I'd call you back and here I am doing it." Hutton rasped then coughed loudly into the earpiece. Hale held the phone away from his head for a second, collecting his thoughts.

"You said you'd call me back three days ago."

"And lo and behold, I've gone and called."

A flash of anger surged through Hale. He gripped the edge of his desk and ground his teeth, desperately trying to remain decorous. He knew if he came at Hutton the wrong way, The Boss would just hang up and walk.

"Alright. Fine. Thank you for checking in. Have you had your meeting yet?"

"It's ongoing."

"Well do you know anything yet?"

"Let's cut to the chase, Hale. Yeah. I know things and so do you—we're being drained. Bad. I got horsemen with eyes in their heads and you got your computers and grids and whatnot; we both know what's going on."

"Can we contain it?"

"Contain it? What the hell does that even mean, kid? No. We can't contain it—it's not an 'it.' It's a 'who.' We have to fight *them* to end *it*. There's no containing."

"Alright, when can you be in town? We need to get a strategy together."

"I agree with the second part but there ain't a chance in hell I'm coming into that city. Listen, Hale—I'm gonna send you my best man, though. He'll be at your office within a few hours. You just be there and make sure The Mayor's there too. We gotta hit this hard and fast."

"I think I should take a report first and then—"

"No time for bureaucracy, Hale. No time."

"I . . . alright fine. I'll make sure The Mayor's here. What's the man's name?"

"Scofield."

"What was it?" Hale asked, but the line was already dead.

Boss Hutton shivered as he hurried across the cracked pavement outside the saloon. He tucked his chin against his chest and held his wide-brimmed hat down with one hand, trying in vain to keep the pouring rain at bay. But it found the space between his neck and collar, dripping down his back. It seeped in through the stitching around his boot heels. Everything was wet, clinging. Scofield pushed open the driver's side door as Hutton reached the jeep and The Boss jumped in as fast as his aged body would allow.

"Bad out today, boys."

"Haven't seen rain like this in years," C. J. Haskell said from the back seat. A small but steady leak in the canvas roof had banished him to the far right side of the worn bench. He leaned forward to hear over the throaty rumble of the engine as Hutton coaxed it back to life, his foot working the gas pedal ever so gently.

"Bad day for the field," Scofield muttered, as much to himself as to his comrades. "Arrays ain't gonna suck down much power in this shit."

"Real bad day for the field," Hutton echoed, his voice distant. He jammed the gear shift into first.

They drove in silence for several minutes, heading roughly west. The jeep bucked and swayed as it slogged through puddles and patches of mud and over little ridges cut into the sand by sudden runs of water. In a matter of hours the whole desert had transformed from a flat, barren expanse of loam to a dynamic, surging patchwork of countless streams and rivulets and pools of brown-gray water beside crumbling dunes. The rain drummed incessantly on the flimsy roof and metal body of the vehicle.

As they drew near his hut, Haskell leaned forward, ignoring the drops of water on his left shoulder to point through the windshield. "That's it, Boss. The third one on the right there."

"Home sweet home, huh?" Scofield flashed a smile back at the young outrider.

"Hey, it's walls, a roof, and a shitter, right?"

"This young buck ain't so dumb after all, huh?" Hutton cackled. "Took me damn near six decades to learn that's all you need."

When they pulled to a stop, Scofield leaned forward in his seat to let Haskell climb past and out of the vehicle. He ran to his door, keyed in the code, and let himself into the little concrete shack.

Once C. J. was inside, Scofield turned to The Boss. "There's one more thing I been meaning to tell you. Didn't even occur to me until we were in Round Up this morning."

Hutton pulled off his hat and ran the fingers of one hand through his thinning gray hair. He closed his eyes. "Go on."

"A few weeks back—better part of a month—Kretch and I were out on the eastern end. We dug up a leech. Old guy. Maybe seventy, even—"

"Hey now, I'll be there myself soon."

"No offense, Hut," Scofield said through a fleeting smile. "Anyway, I checked him and he didn't have any marks. So when I brought him in I just . . . you know . . ."

"You let him walk."

"Yeah."

"I trust your judgment. Sure it was the right call."

"Yeah . . . well, I thought so too. I sent Kretch to find his collector and took him back alone. I'd planned to let him walk from the moment I saw his arm was clean. Thing I just realized this morning: when I was leading him back in he was wheezing and stumbling and so I let him ride the last couple of miles. He thanked me." Scofield glanced over at Haskell's door. Then he pulled his pack of cigarettes from a pocket and put one in his mouth, offering the pack to Hutton. The Boss took a smoke and Scofield lit both of them and continued. "He thanked me by name. I never told him my name, though. And I'm pretty sure Wilton never said it aloud."

Hutton exhaled a plume of smoke through his nose. It swirled then seemed to freeze in the damp, thick air, curled about the old outrider's face.

"I can't believe I missed it until just today."

"There's no reason for a man to be surprised to hear himself called his own name. Makes sense you'd miss it. You're pretty sure he never heard the name though, huh?"

"I'd stake a good deal, Boss."

"Well . . ." Hutton cracked the door and tossed out his cigarette long before it was finished. "A month ago, ey? That ain't good." Unconsciously, Boss Hutton rested a hand on the grip of his six-shooter. The grips were cream colored ivory and the metalwork on the pistol was all polished brass. He'd had the mechanical components of the weapon replaced or refurbished dozens of times but the handle and inlay along the barrel were original, well over a century old. Most of the outriders used semi-automatics and, save for their tendency to jam with sand or dust, there was no good reason not to. But something about carrying the same kind of pistol men had been using for two hundred and fifty years brought comfort to The Boss. It was grounding. Just like the jeep.

"This thing is gonna get bloody. You know that, right?"

"I do."

"I need you to get into that goddamn city and then back out here as fast as you can. We're gonna treat this thing like—dammit . . . more to follow, bud." Scofield tracked Hutton's sightline and saw Haskell jogging back toward the jeep. He ratcheted his seat forward again and opened the door, allowing the young man to clamber past him onto the back bench.

"Here it is," Haskell said, panting as he held out a steel disc. Scofield took the piece from him and studied it. It had receivers for four taps and was cut with the same broad threading as the strange cord he'd found in the sand and seen on the wall of the massive apparatus he and Kretch had discovered.

"Yeah. It's one of them." Scofield handed it to Hutton, who gave the disc a cursory glance, then handed it back over his shoulder to C. J.

The Boss looked over at Scofield as he spoke, waiting for—and ready to accept—any signal to stop talking. "Listen, C. J. You're about to learn some very privileged information. Very secret info. Like don't fuckin' share this with anyone until I say so, you got it young man?"

Haskell nodded, leaning back against the bench seat and locking his eyes attentively on Hutton.

"OK. We're being drained. Real bad. Gotta be a lot of bad men out there, Hasky," he glanced over at Scofield and then back to the younger outrider. "And you two sons of bitches are going to be a big part of my response. So listen good as we head toward town. Scofield here is going to talk to Mayor Dreg. You and I are heading out to the field."

Kretch cursed the rain as he jogged through the muddy Outpost. He held a flimsy tarp over his head and shoulders but his jeans and boots were soaked through. He reached The Office—the nickname for this crude, all-purpose building—and ducked under a corrugated tin awning that stuck out over the iron door.

Wilton dropped the plastic tarp in a heap and wiped his damp hands on the inside of his jacket. He dug out his smokes, finding the pack soggy. A few of the cigarettes were dry enough, and he got one lit and stood there smoking and stamping his feet to keep warm. Through the gray haze of rain and fog Kretch could see only a few hundred yards in any direction. The world was monochrome, all outline and shadow free of detail.

*Fuckin' depressing out. Good thing Shady's at the barn. He'd be good and pissed at me riding through this shit.* Kretch began to rock back and forth on his heels, taking ever smaller drags off his cigarette as the ember crept closer to his fingers. When the tobacco was gone and he was sucking filter, Kretch tossed the butt away and considered lighting another. He thought maybe he should go and check on his horse after all. Make sure he had enough feed. Make sure he was dry.

After another minute of hesitation, Wilton shook his head and spat. Then he turned and keyed in the entry code and pushed the rusted door open. The Office was jail cells, storage, infirmary, and morgue all in one. This last detail was the thing that had unhappily summoned Kretch. He walked slowly down the dimly lit main corridor, his boots squeaking on the cement floor.

Stopping before the last door on the left, Wilton took in a deep breath and held it. Then he growled softly, getting up his courage, and entered the room. It was brightly lit and bitterly cold. A strange chorus filled the space: the whine of fluorescent lights mixed with the drone of an aging air conditioner that kept the ten-by-twenty foot room just above freezing.

There were three empty gurneys shoved into a corner and two draped with white sheets in the middle of the floor. Shivering uncontrollably, Wilton made his way to the closest gurney and checked the chart hanging off its side. The top line read: GREGORY WHITE. The report section of the form was already completed in angry, block letters. The outrider stretched his neck from side to side, making his way to the other bed. Sure enough his name was printed across the top of the page.

Wilton cracked his knuckles, then slowly drew back the white sheet.

The old man's face was a pale blue-gray. His eyes were open and his lips pursed. He looked strangely attentive, almost impatient. Bile rising in his throat, Kretch slid the sheet further down along the corpse. Back in the desert that morning, Kretch had worked the old man's shirt back onto his lifeless body, but it had now been cut away from the torso, leaving only tattered sleeves hanging irreverently off withered arms.

The gunshot wound was savage. Wilton's pistol had been close enough to cause powder burns around the gaping hole. Blood was caked all over the old man's chest; brown where it had flowed down his flesh, crimson and congealed in the ragged wound itself.

*OK, just do this goddammit.* Kretch began to search his pockets for a pen. "One of yours, huh?"

Wilton literally jumped, gasping in terror. He wheeled, beginning to draw his pistol, to find Moses Smith framed by the soft light from doorway. The heavyset man ambled into the room, wheezing and with a slight limp in his left leg.

"Yeah," Kretch forced out, his heart racing. "Had to take this one out."

"Old timer. Hoo boy . . . that's a game-over shot right there." Moses studied the body clinically, his large brown eyes looking the dead man up and down. "Cannell come by earlier. He took a look in here but I was achin' goddamn bad then. Meant to get my ass out of bed and ask him about it—makes sense that ol' boy weren't the one that bagged him. Can you imagine riding the field pushin' sixty five? Hell if I can." Moses turned away from the gurney, wincing as pain flashed through his crotch.

"How you doing, Moses? What is it—pneumonia?"

"Something like that," Smith snorted. "Doc's got me on these fuckin' horse pills and bed rest."

"That's what a body needs, I guess. That and a stiff drink now and then."

"Less drinkin' and I'd find myself a bit healthier right now, you get my drift." Moses smiled sourly and turned back to the dead leech. "Looks like this fellah took a bullet in his chest once before."

"Yeah, that—that's what it looks like."

"They never learn, huh?"

"Never."

"So you make it to Round Up?"

"Yeah." Kretch nodded, awkwardly stepping in front of Moses and covering the corpse again. "The morning session, anyway. We're gonna pick it back up in an hour or two."

"Hutton say what them horns were about?"

"This morning? No. Not really. He just said what with the rain and all he didn't see a reason to put it off."

Moses casually leaned against the gurney, sighing as he took the weight off his legs. He looked down at the floor and Kretch could finally study his face for a few seconds. The man's fleshy cheeks were sallow and covered with an oily sheen. Massive bags hung beneath his eyes and his hair was damp with perspiration. Moses was wearing a loose gray shirt and ill-fitting canvas trousers. His feet were bare.

"Well, I wish I could be there."

"Yeah, well, I'd trade you if I could." Kretch reached past Smith and grabbed the chart from beside the old leech. "Listen I gotta fill this out and get back."

"OK, Kretch. You do that. I'm not supposed to be on my feet anyway." He limped slowly back toward the hallway. "I'll leave you to pay your respects and whatnot. It's the worst part of the job, ain't it?"

"Yeah. Guess so."

# 13

Scofield ran his palms together nervously. His back was ramrod straight, glued to the plastic seat. Each time the pod stopped more people got on. When Boss Hutton dropped him at the third station east of the Outpost, he had been one of only three passengers and sat a good twenty feet from the nearest rider.

Now the pod was nearly full and there was a person sitting on either side of him. Among the growing throng of commuters, with their business suits or workman's jumpers or damp, musty coats, Scofield stuck out like a sore thumb. He felt ridiculous in his leather boots, black trousers, and canvas jacket. His wide-brimmed hat rested conspicuously on his lap. He'd removed his holster, pistol, and ammo pouch and crammed them into a leather satchel. Also in the satchel were a canteen and a day's rations. This made him feel all the more foolish. *Christ sake I ain't going to camp out somewhere—it's a goddamn city. There's stores and . . . and restaurants and all.*

He shook his head at himself, sighing. His thoughts drifted to Reese alone in an eight by six pen. That just about ate him up inside. The screens flickered with the name of the next stop, announced by a female voice: "New Las Vegas City Limit Station." Not much longer until he was deep in it. The sprawl had begun miles back but now the buildings began to grow taller and larger and ever more closely spaced. The desert sands were replaced by endless concrete and pavement. Now even the gray sky was obscured by towering construction. Scofield looked around the pod, scarcely believing how casually the other passengers accepted this transformation; this self-imposed plunge into the labyrinth. For them it was just another afternoon. Alone in the crowd, Scofield traveled into the heart of his hell to face Dreg; to face the future on behalf of his boys.

*Some fuckin' ambassador I am.* Again he looked down at his boots. They were mostly dry now, and the salt-stained, scuffed leather stood out against the white tiles of the floor. Thankfully an even number of commuters exited the pod as boarded at the next few stops. Then the screens flashed and the digital woman spoke the words he'd hoped in vain would never come: "Executive Center Station."

Scofield rose stiffly as the pod came to a gentle stop. He allowed several passengers to exit before him, ignoring their eyes as they looked askance at the strange man in the long jacket and cowboy hat, then stepped out into the streets of New Las Vegas.

"Thank god for the rain," Scofield muttered as he looked around to get his bearings: the streets were all but empty. Drizzle pattered steadily on his hat and shoulders but the outrider was in no rush to enter the Executive Building. He ambled across the wide sidewalk and leaned under a glass overhang.

Lighting a smoke, Scofield ran through all the things he and Hutton had discussed that afternoon. He had much to tell The Mayor, but an equal amount to learn. And while the outriders and the City were all on the same team, there was little love lost between them and even less trust. Scofield needed to play his hand tightly; he needed to keep the sunfield the domain of the riders as much as he could, or else risk a botched response. These people—these boardroom and condominium air-conditioning people—had no grasp of the realities of the field. Fuck up the response and good men would die. A leech, or, for that matter, a drainer, had no one to report to and no one to worry about: they'd just start shooting. There was nothing for them to lose, everything to gain. A man can never face a more dangerous adversary. This the outrider knew well. This he knew personally.

Of course, on the other hand, Scofield was the one on foreign ground at the moment. The polished granite of the sidewalk was hard beneath his feet. Even muted by steady rain the city was a cacophony of humming rails, clattering machines, and human voices. Scofield exhaled a thick plume of smoke into the air and, figuring it was the right thing to do, he looked around for a receptacle to toss his cigarette in. Finally he dropped the butt on the ground. It didn't feel at all like he was polluting.

"He's here, sir," Hale's voice came quietly from the intercom.

"Are you on speaker?" Dreg asked, leaning forward in his chair.

"No."

"Alright. Show him into my chambers and leave him there alone. Let me know when he's in." The Mayor rose and stretched his back, twisting from side to side with a groan. Outside the bank of windows, the gray afternoon was slowly yielding to night. Dreg stepped before a mirror hanging near the coat tree and re-tucked in his white shirt. He straightened the knot of his tie and then took his blazer from its hanger.

"Alright, Frank. He's inside."

"What was his name again?"

"He didn't give it."

Dreg took in a breath to berate the secretary general for not asking, but changed his mind. There was something more important to be said. The Mayor took a step closer to the intercom panel on his desk and spoke in a hushed voice.

"Mr. Hale, what I'm going to talk to this fellow about is our drain. I remember now that you told me about it on the phone in Boston. Days ago. I have no idea why you haven't brought it up since, and I don't know how the hell you could think I haven't known about this for a while now, but I decided to leave those facts alone until I find out for myself what happened on the ground while I was away. We'll deal with you later."

"Sir—Frank, wait! I'm going to come through the side door. Just—"

"Just nothing, Tim. Go home. You've always been a trusted ally and don't think I've forgotten all you've done for me overnight, but that trust is shaken for the moment. I'm confused. I'm displeased. I don't want to see your face again today. Go home. Now."

As he said this, The Mayor's voice had been perfectly calm, measured. Hale knew all too well what that meant. He was out the door before Dreg had even one arm in his jacket sleeve. The Mayor jostled his heavy frame into the blazer and turned back to the mirror.

*It's always the patient ones you have to worry about, isn't it old boy?* He licked the tips of both index fingers and smoothed down his eyebrows and mustache. *Impatient men gain quickly but often gain little . . . patient men can gain much.* He had asked Colonel Strayer to pay Hale a visit at his home that evening. Not for an interrogation, per se, but for a very thorough . . . debriefing. The number one question he'd instructed the security officer to ask was why Hale thought he'd get away with resetting the executive password for the central tracking systems. *Thought I had no idea what goes on around here, ey Tim? Thought I trusted you fully, you pissant? I trust only one man fully. Only one.* He would deal with Secretary Hale tomorrow. Tonight, The Mayor would personally address the crisis facing his beloved city's power fields. He had waited, watching, long enough. Now he would start the ball rolling; he would take action.

"Now," Dreg said aloud to himself, taking one last look in the mirror. "Let's see about this fellow."

Mayor Dreg pulled wide the double doors of his office, stepping into his opulent receiving chamber with pomp. He smiled brightly and took in a deep breath, practically bellowing: "Good evening, sir!"

Dreg stopped short. His head whipped from side to side. The room was empty. His shoulders slumped, his chest dropped its regal thrust. "The fuck?" he muttered. Growling, The Mayor began walking across the room to Hale's office, assuming the foolish executive had left the visitor there after all.

"Evening, Mayor."

Dreg gasped, wheeling about. There, leaning against the doorframe, was a tall, striking man. He wore a dark canvas jacket and knee-high boots. A leather satchel was slung across his chest and he was wearing a gray, wide-brimmed hat. His face was made up of strong lines and sharp angles, handsome in an imposing way, and covered in a five-day beard.

As Dreg regained his composure, embarrassed and shaken, the man stood up to his full height and pulled off the hat. "Name's Scofield. Sorry to give you a start, Mr. Dreg."

"No, not at all, Mr. Scofield. Call me Frank, please." Dreg grinned and extended his fleshy hand. Scofield's grasp was firm, the handshake brief.

"Well do feel free to drop your bag, hang up your coat. Make yourself most comfortable, Mr. Scofield." Dreg began to amble about the large room, switching into the warm tone he used when addressing constituents and investors. "Do you get into the city much?"

"No."

"Must seem rather boring here compared with the open range, I suppose. Stuffy. And on a day like this! What miserable weather, right?"

"Lots of rain," Scofield replied, sliding between two of the couches. Selecting a loveseat perpendicular to both doors, he rested his hat and bag on one cushion then lowered himself down onto the other.

"Lots of rain indeed. I haven't seen it like this in years. I was in Boston earlier this week on city business and it was a genuine blizzard, I tell you. Snow for days and flakes as thick as my fist. Have you ever been?"

"To Boston?"

"Yes."

"I have, yes. Many years ago."

"Beautiful city! And so much history. A bit dreary of a place, but a fine town to visit. Seeing as it's after five, may I offer you a drink?"

"I wouldn't say no to bourbon, thanks."

"Bourbon!" Dreg slapped his thigh. "I think I'll join you in that. Sounds divine. So tell me about yourself, Mr. Scofield."

Scofield leaned back against the soft leather of the sofa but kept both feet planted on the floor. Without staring, exactly, he kept his eyes on The Mayor as Dreg made his way to a corner bar.

"Not much to tell, Mayor. Frank. I spend all my days out in the field. Riding 'til it's time to sleep, you know."

Dreg selected two wide tumbler glasses and put a few ice cubes in each. "Oh, there must be more to you than that. I can see it in your eyes, Mr. Scofield." He poured himself a modest amount of whiskey, then filled his guest's glass with several fingers of liquor. "You have a first name, Mr. Scofield?"

"Yes."

"Well," Dreg smiled gamely, cocking his head to one side. "Scofield it is, then."

He made his way around a couch, cupping his glass to keep it obscured from his visitor, and handed Scofield the other.

"Thanks."

"Most welcome, sir! Let's make it the first round of many! You've traveled far enough to deserve it, I'd say. Now, really, there must be some story you can tell me before we get down to business. You outriders have all the adventure in these parts. It's my job to ensure things stay good and boring around here."

"That's my job description too, Mayor. Just a different part of the equation. The parts you might think of as adventure are the parts I hate."

"Mm," Dreg nodded solemnly, "I think I know what you mean. Well, to the hard parts, sir." Franklin raised his glass, then took a small sip. The outrider nodded, looking down. He took a long draught of his bourbon, his eyes focused on the table. For a moment he seemed lost in thought; in remembrance.

"May I tell you a bit about myself, then? About the city?"

"By all means." Scofield set down his glass and looked up at The Mayor.

"I've served New Las Vegas for most of my adult life. For well more than a decade now as its chief executive. It has been a wonderful and humbling experience. Those two words are the only two for it. I didn't grow up with much, Scofield," Franklin looked down at his hands, as he had a thousand times when delivering this monologue, "and it grounds a man to remember where he's been when he sees where he is. It makes a man wiser, more patient and more . . . convicted, if I may. And dedicated—this city is my love; my passion. What's something you're passionate about?"

"My horse."

"Ha! Goddamn, what a good answer! I'll drink to that! I've asked so many men that question and it's all bullshit, Mr. Scofield! All bullshit. Not with you though. I can see that clear as day." Dreg set down his drink and leaned back, loosening his tie. He reached into a pocket of his blazer and drew out the cigar case. "Cigar?"

"No, thanks. But if it's alright with you I'll smoke a cigarette."

"Please, please," The Mayor grunted, twisting to reach for a brass ashtray perched on the table behind his couch. He placed it between the two men. "That was a gift from the Prime Minister of India. See the inlay? All twenty-four karat gold." Dreg smiled proudly at the large, gaudy object. "Sometimes I feel badly tapping ashes into it. That's why I only smoke fine cigars. A man must be humble, but that doesn't mean he can't enjoy the finer things, yes?"

"Sure."

Dreg looked askance at the outrider, remaining coy but inwardly angry at how under-whelmed his guest seemed to be. It was surely pride keeping this provincial fellow from marveling at the opulence around him—the artwork, the fine craftsmanship of the furniture, the collection of curios from around the world.

Scofield lit a cigarette, exhaling through his nose. Dreg held three wooden matches to the tip of a thick cigar and puffed away until it glowed orange. He blew a perfect smoke ring into the air, watching as it grew larger and then dispersed in the gentle breeze of the air conditioning.

"Look around this room for a minute, if you would, Scofield," Dreg said, trying a more direct approach. "You see all these . . . these things? The paintings? That statue? The art and artifacts, if I may? These were most all gifts. Tokens of appreciation or thanks for this meeting or that deal or this trade and such. I love this room. I love it not as a testament to myself. That would be the height of hubris, and I know how it may come across, but I also know why this room is here and why it's appointed the way it is. It's here because of the tireless labor of thousands of men and women—yourself well counted in that number. We have built as perfect a place as human history has ever seen. I know that sounds dramatic and, well, it is dramatic. But it's true."

Dreg leaned forward to set down his empty tumbler then rose, helping himself to his feet with a hand on the armrest. "Do you know what has been the one most persistent, most dominant, and most difficult challenge mankind has struggled with, Mr. Scofield?"

"Death, I'd say." He smiled ruefully, his eyes on The Mayor's. Scofield crushed the ember of his cigarette on the rim of the ornate ashtray and leaned back against the plush cushions. "But that's not what you have in mind, Frank."

"Power. That's what it's all about. Be it the oil to light a lamp, the river's flow to move a barge or turn the millwheel, the fire to heat a home, or the electricity to run a metropolis. Such as mine. Ours. Power. And with power—the control of power, I mean to say . . . the control of the dam or the crude oil or the firewood—has come might; influence. Since time immemorial. As Mayor, the responsibility for this city rests ultimately in these two hands. It makes me proud, but it's also robbed me of many a night's sleep and cost me many a gray hair. The crown sits heavily, as they say."

Dreg paced about the chamber, silent for a while. He paused before a painting of a ship that had just emerged from a mighty storm. The Mayor studied the piece, sure that Scofield would be watching him. He leaned in toward the canvas, squinting, then backed up a few feet to admire the work as a whole. Behind him, Scofield's lighter crackled and cigarette smoke scented the air. Franklin's jaw clenched involuntarily. He stepped a few paces to his right and pretended to study a small vase, glancing into a silver-framed mirror hung above it. Scofield was picking at the nail of one thumb with the opposing index finger.

Dreg wheeled around. The inch-long ash from his cigar fell to the floor. He pretended not to notice. "So power, then, Scofield. That's the matter at hand. You know that well. You live it every day all the way out there." Dreg rested a palm on the back of the couch before him and leaned forward. "It's both of our lives, yes?"

"It's my livelihood, yes. But life? I don't know about that. When a man starts defining himself by his day-to-day business, he starts to lose sight of himself, you ask me."

"That's very wise, my friend. Sage," Dreg nodded.

"However," Scofield ran his tongue over the point of his left canine tooth, "seeing as it is the business of the day—and forgive me for being blunt—can we get into it, Mayor? The sunfield is drained. Bad, I think. And I'll wager you know the extent. My boys will be keyed up to fight back by this time tomorrow, but I gotta learn what you and your people know tonight, and what you're ready to do in response."

"I admire your forthrightness. It's refreshing. I'm so often surrounded by these goddamn politicians and bureaucrats. Bunch of bastards never saying what they mean, the lot of 'em. Yes, then. The drain. That's the business at hand. May I offer you a refill?"

"No. Thanks just the same."

* * *

"So now you know. And you know just about as much as I do, so if you got questions, don't make 'em damn fool questions." Hutton looked at each man gathered around him, studying their faces.

He'd told C. J. Haskell about the drain earlier, and the young man's features formed a mask of resignation. Gregory White looked about ready to rip the head off a preacher; his thick jaw was grinding from side to side and his cheeks were beet red. Joseph and Eric Bay, the half-brothers separated by a good ten years, were both nodding grimly. Matching silver crosses hung from the brothers' necks. The older, Joe, whispered something to his brother that caused Eric to cluck his tongue, eyes closing for a long moment, gently taking hold of his cross. Wilton Kretch had gone pale and was doing his best to keep his bottom lip from quivering.

The rainfall had slackened but the individual drops were bigger. They hammered against the tin roof of the stable. The long, single-story building echoed with dull thunder. It would have been sunset out if not for the storm. Instead the evening bled from pale gray to charcoal black. The odors of damp straw, manure, and sweat mingled in the stagnant air, filling the massive stable with a musty but comforting smell. It was familiar. Now and then a horse whinnied or snorted or stamped a hoof. Somewhere a few stalls down a stable-hand cursed. None of the outriders spoke for a long while. Boss Hutton rocked back on his heels, chewing on an unlit cigar and letting reality sink in to his boys' heads.

"I got Ryan Cannell briefing the rest of the fellahs. And I mean brief, they won't know as much as you, just that we got some bigger problems'n usual. So if you cross paths with any other riders in the next twenty-four hours, ask questions but don't say much. Don't say shit, I mean. I'll send runners to brief you boys deeper into this mess when Scofield gets back from town.

"For now," Hutton paused and leaned forward, his voice deadly serious, "you five are going to be the only men in the field. Stick to the routes I assigned and do not move into the interior. At all. Just ride your perimeters and don't stop for anything but a piss break or to water your horses. This is smoke and mirrors: we gotta make our presence known, but it ain't time to show our hand. You see a tap line, you ignore it; you see a collector or hook-up, put a bullet in 'em and move on. And if you see a burrow, note the location and you fucking gallop."

Hutton fished a lighter from his vest pocket, finally lighting the cigar. He sucked at the soggy tip, chewed halfway through. "You'll be heading out in fifteen minute intervals. Greg—you're first."

"Hut?" C. J. spoke up.

"Go ahead, Haskell."

"What if something happens? What if we run into someone? Do we engage?"

"Shoot and ride. Ask questions later."

Scofield scratched his chin, making no attempt to hide his lack of understanding.

"This graph tracks daily averages. You see the pale blue line? That's the good line. All these thinner strands are outlying trends. Red is bad. Red means over-consumption and strain." Dreg ran his thick index finger along a glowing amber trail of information. It rose and fell erratically. "Green means under-consumption, which is good in theory but means fewer billable kilowatt hours, so too much green, well, that's bad too! It's always a balancing act. Of course, that's all rhetoric these days—there's not a hint of green to be found, between the weather," he waved his hand in a loose circle "and the rest of it."

The Mayor took a few steps to his right and pointed to the next screen. "I'd hate to raise the rates on my fine citizens, or on any of our many dependable client cities around the western states, of course, but you know how 'they' say money is power? Well, power is money these days." Dreg chuckled at his own wit, glancing over at Scofield. The outrider's face was implacable. "Anyway, this monitor tracks consumption in real time."

"OK."

"What time is it right now, Scofield?"

"About seven, I guess. Not sure. I got a watch in my jacket."

"Don't worry about it—just making conversation. Every one of these screens has a clock. I prefer that old girl in the corner anyway," The Mayor hooked a thumb toward his grandfather clock without looking. "Seven fourteen, though. That's what this monitor says. Seven fourteen and twenty-three seconds and right down to the damned hundredths. At any rate—normally at this hour this screen here would be all soft blues and greens. But it's not. It's mostly orange with some fucking red! Do you know what that means?"

"I . . . well, yeah—means we're not collecting near enough power, right?"

"More or less. Enough," Dreg said icily. "Yes, losing power every day, but it's worse than that. We're losing what we already have, too. You see, it means the bastards are into our molten salt stores. We can always stand a week or two of bad collection. We can't stand more than a few days of the salt stores being reduced like this. They're into the lifeblood." Dreg took in a long, deep breath. He closed his eyes and pressed his thumbs against the bridge of his nose. His shoulders were tense, quivering. Scofield could sense The Mayor's simmering rage. This was, for the moment, not a politician—it was a man who had been robbed. "This needs to be stopped. Fast."

"Agreed." Scofield nodded, taking a sip of bourbon. Dreg had insisted on refilling their glasses. The outrider noted that on the second round Franklin had actually served himself a full pour and thus he'd allowed himself a bit more liquor as well. Scofield could hold his liquor against any man, but it was never wise to take a drink when the other man wasn't. He knew that Dreg was trying to loosen his tongue. But that could work both ways—whiskey, after all, is ambivalent.

Scofield had already learned enough in the half hour spent studying this bank of monitors that he had decided this would be his last drink anyway. He didn't understand every sine curve or median usage chart, but he got the picture: the drainers were now tapped in at all times and in myriad, evenly spaced locations, and they had even begun to siphon power at night. That was the biggest issue: it meant that not only were they sucking down massive amounts of wattage, but also that they were extremely well organized and advanced in their approach.

Any fool could hook a tap line to a QV pillar; any group of fools could hook up lots of tap lines to lots of QV pillars. It took not only manpower, but strategic thinking to siphon off as much power as the daily charts showed missing and as the salt caverns were losing at night. It meant lots of people working in concert. And what's more, it was likely the drainers were in it for more than material gain—there was no reason to go after the salt caverns or to work in the rain unless at least part of the motivation was disruption. Or destruction.

It was a safe bet that this drain was either about terrorism, or else about insurrection.

Scofield wasn't sure if Mayor Dreg knew just how serious the data were. He resolved to himself to get out of town as quickly as he could without seeming an alarmist in order to report to Boss Hutton. Had Scofield been in charge, he would have told Dreg to call out the Civil Defense Forces right then and there. He would have mobilized every martial resource New Las Vegas had at its disposal. But it was his duty to report, not to incite. So he finished his bourbon and turned to Dreg.

"Where should I set this glass?"

"Hmm?" Dreg leaned away from the monitor he was studying. "Empty? Need another splash?"

"No, thanks, Mayor. Just don't want to damage the finish on your nice desk here."

"Ah, yes. I got that piece custom made. It's a mixture of cedar, mahogany, and teak. Each wood plays a specific role, you see," Dreg took a step toward the large desk and took in a breath to continue. Scofield wasn't looking and didn't realize he was interrupting a monologue.

"Yeah, I'd hate to stain it. I'll just set the glass down on the way out. Listen, I think I have a good enough sense to get the ball rolling now. Anything else you want to make sure I tell the boys?"

"Wait, you're going?" Dreg fixed Scofield with an incredulous glare.

"Yeah. Gotta get back to the fields. Where I belong. We'll make sure to report in every time there's something worth reporting."

"Mr. Scofield, I don't think you entirely grasp the nature of your visit here . . . the nature of our relationship." The warmth was gone from Dreg's voice. The politician's smile had flattened out below that thick mustache. "You and your men do what I say. I have no intention of sitting back and waiting for reports, sir. I have, on the contrary, every intention of singlehandedly directing the response to this fucking catastrophe."

"Mr. Mayor, all due respect, that ain't the way to handle this. Not yet, at least." Scofield was entirely unfazed by Dreg's icy glare and widened stance. Only half aware of himself, the outrider did, however, casually button up his vest.

"Oh? And why ain't it?" Dreg asked, subtly mocking the outrider's speaking.

"You keep your Civil Defense boys pretty well trained? Lots of drills for the troops and such?"

"Near constant. They're a precision machine. Thousands of men ready at all times." Dreg did not, in fact, know just how many thousands or know anything at all about their training.

"Mm. That's good. Your men got good gear? Good munitions and transports and communication gear and all?"

"The very best this city's rather plentiful money can buy."

"Course. And how much do they train without all that fancy shit?"

"What?"

Scofield took three confident steps toward The Mayor. His gaze was firm; his voice even; the outrider neither sought to intimidate nor to demur. Franklin took an unconscious step back nonetheless, brushing against the coat tree and steadying himself with a hand wrapped around its thick bronze pole.

"Out there in the fields, Frank, there's no radios. There's no satellite links. There aren't any transports or armored vehicles or anything. It's just men and horses and guns, you get me? You can have the best army in the world, y'see, but if they don't know how to fight the war at hand, it ain't worth shit. At day's end, yeah, we work for you. But how we do that has got to be left up to us, just like it is day in and day out. At least for now. Give us some time. Let us find out exactly what we're facing. That make sense?"

Dreg nodded slowly, with grudging sincerity. "It does indeed. Perhaps I was too hasty just there, Scofield. Patience is a virtue I've struggled with my whole life. I'm not sure if its absence has driven me farther or held me back."

When Scofield said nothing, Dreg sighed and turned toward the door. "Well, lend me your ear for five more minutes."

"Sure, Frank." Scofield followed Dreg back into his outer chamber. The Mayor walked slowly toward the large bank of windows and flipped a switch set in the wall beside him. With a metallic whine, the steel shutters outside the glass rose, revealing the night. It was still raining and foggy. The pulsing glow of New Las Vegas painted the air a gauzy amber-gray. Rivulets of water ran down the windows, their trails orange.

"A thousand years ago it was fire. Three hundred years back, steam. Then oil and coal. We live in the future, Scofield. The system is almost perfect; perfect because it's endless. But it's vulnerable. You know, even thirty years ago there were still nuclear plants, many of them not far from here."

"I remember 'em."

"There's a reason most every major city within five hundred miles gets its power from NLV, sir. Because we figured it out, we got the power, dammit! Photovoltaic panels have been around for years—a century!—but it was here that we first got things really right. Here. Quantum bundling. QV! Such a simple thing: just let the particles move as they want to right there in those millions of little bundles . . . and it's solved, the riddle is cracked! Those arrays you ride beneath every day? Do you know what they look like under a microscope?" Scofield shook his head. "They look like the inside of a lung. The alveoli. Little bundles of electrophilic nodes. Every one of them . . . the billions of them . . . here we stand in the soft light of their work. They are the lungs and heart and soul. And now this . . . cancer."

Dreg had left his glass sitting on the desk in his office. He walked to the bar and grabbed a fresh tumbler, then selected a bottle of thirty five year old cognac.

"I'll drink this alone, then." He poured an ample dose of liquor. "But remember what we're fighting. Not men, not mere thieves—cancer. It must be stopped. It must be extinguished. However necessary."

"I get it."

"I believe that you do." Dreg took a large sip of brandy, coughing as the liquor caught in his throat. Scofield went to the sofa and gathered up his hat and satchel. He buttoned his coat and turned to face Dreg. The Mayor was leaning down toward a shelf, inspecting several of his curios.

"Do you know what this is?" The Mayor asked, a bemused smile tugging at the corners of his wormy lips. He held up the odd, carved staff for the thousandth time, hefting the short length of hardwood. Scofield approached and studied the object.

"Spear thrower."

"What?" Dreg asked too loudly.

"It's a spear throwing stick. You rest the back of the spear in this notch," Scofield reached out and took the piece from Dreg, pointing to the divot cut near its thicker end, "and hold it like this." Scofield mimed resting a spear against his forearm, then whipped the thrower forward.

"It adds range and accuracy to your throw."

"Amazing," Dreg chuckled, taking the spear thrower back from Scofield and shaking his head. "I've had this damn thing for a decade—never knew. My God, can you imagine a time so primitive! So savage!"

"It's simple, sure. I'll give you that. But if I had one and you didn't, I'd be the man that made it home that night."

# 14

Timothy Hale trembled in the cold night air. He was standing in the middle of the sidewalk outside his apartment building, dripping wet. The rain had grown heavier again in the last half hour, the entirety of which Hale had spent wandering around a few city blocks near his home. His tie was ruined; his loafers were overflowing. The golden lapel pin that marked him as a man of clout dug into the flesh of his left hand. He gripped the little chevron so tightly his palm was riddled with puncture wounds.

Hale was angry, terrified, and very much alone. A crippling undercurrent of sadness swirled beneath more tangible emotions: rage at Dreg for so quickly casting him aside after his years of service; abject terror as Hale realized he had nothing to fall back on—no backup plan for his life. The sorrow came from finally confronting the long suppressed reality that Hale had no one to turn to. There was no shoulder on which to lean; no smile from which to draw comfort. He had no real friends, no family with whom he'd spoken in years. He had no one, and now, quite possibly, he had nothing. *What the fuck was I thinking? Who the fuck do I think I am!*

It had yet to dawn on him that, earlier, as he rode the elevator down after leaving The Mayor's office, it had stopped once, allowing several bureaucrats to board. The golden chevron—the executive pin he'd worn so proudly for so long—had been deactivated. When not lost in abject self-pity, he kept returning to the horrifying knowledge that The Mayor said he had known of the drain for some time. What else did he know? *That I went snooping around his office and computer? That I'm a fucking rat playing hero? A fucking manchild fool?*

The wind picked up and the rain began to assail Timothy. It was not enough to drench him; now the raindrops attacked, coming sideways down the street, seeking his face, his eyes. Cold and miserable though he was, somehow the thought of entering his home only brought more weight down upon Hale. The matching couches, the brushed steel appliances, and the faux-Tiffany lampshades ... *a store-bought life—nothing more. That's what I have. That's what I am goddammit. Fucking store-bought forty years.*

Strayer had called him seven times in the past two hours. Hale had turned his phone off after the last call. *Why won't he just leave a fucking message?* Timothy turned toward the brightly lit alcove of his building, determined to finally get on with things and go home. A few glasses of wine, a hot shower and then, with any luck, dreamless sleep. He could explain himself in the morning. With the right mix of contrition and deceit, no doubt he could talk his way back into Dreg's good graces. The Mayor needed him, after all. Perhaps the few hours he'd spend without his right hand man would prove how much, in fact. Perhaps tomorrow would be handshakes and "Hale, fellow, well met." The secretary general smiled at his pun. Logically, the worst that could happen would be a stiff rebuke and a period of reconciliation. In the face of the impending crisis, surely he could make his value clear.

The bright glow of the lobby, so menacing from the rain-slicked streets, was warm and comforting as Timothy finally entered the building. He shivered violently as his wet suit clung to him in the temperate, dry air. Hale stripped off his suit jacket and tie as he rode the elevator up to his floor.

By the time he opened his door, Timothy was almost entirely relaxed. He had been deluding himself—panicking for no reason. He stopped just across the threshold of his home and stripped to his sopping briefs. Hale threw his wrinkled tie into a trash can in the kitchen, then draped his wet suit over the laundry basket in the closet. He grabbed a thick, white robe and relished the feel of the heavy cotton cloth as he wrapped it around his body.

Hale turned his phone back on as he walked into the kitchen. After briefly debating between opening a bottle of '84 Cabernet and finishing the Chardonnay in the fridge, Timothy smiled to himself: it was time. He threw open the cupboard above the sink and pulled out a thirty-five year old bottle of cognac. He'd received it as a gift the day he was appointed Executive Secretary General to the Office of The Mayor of New Las Vegas. Optimism tinged with resignation for what the morning would bring convinced Hale that this was the exact moment to crack open the prized bottle.

It was not until Hale was savoring the first sweet sip of the liquor that he realized he had left all of the lights on in his apartment that day.

Swirling the snifter below his nose, Timothy admonished himself silently. Though his electricity was free, he felt it a civic duty to conserve when convenient. *Certainly no time to be wasting power, man.*

He keyed off the lights in the kitchen and walked through the dining room toward the panel that controlled the lamps in that room and in his den.

"Leave them on, if you would."

Hale stopped dead in his tracks. His knees buckled and a few drops of urine leaked out into his underwear. He turned slowly from the wall panel to look into the living room.

There on his couch sat an elderly woman dressed in a fine tan skirt suit. Her long white hair was coiffured around ruddy cheeks and a bright smile that deepened the wrinkles lining her face. She wore tortoiseshell glasses. A blue silk handkerchief peeked out of her breast pocket.

"I apologize for startling you, Mr. Hale. I thought it fitting to let you get comfortable in your own home before engaging you."

Timothy shrank back a step, gripping the molding around the doorway for support. He was utterly shocked, his mind blank. He raised the glass of cognac as if to take a sip, freezing with the snifter inches from his face. A long moment passed. The old woman looked away, inclining her head to one side and gently raising a hand as if to say: "take your time."

Slowly Hale's mind began to work again. His eyes darted about the room. There was no one else there. And nothing seemed amiss. Then he spotted it. Behind the couch stood an IV tower. Timothy's eyes traced along a slender tube suspended below a fluid-filled sack. It ran down the back of the woman's blazer. Hale looked again at her smiling face, gawking as if just now seeing the woman for the first time. Then it clicked . . . the lobby all those times . . . the incident outside the elevator . . . the . . . janitor?

"My God . . . Wilbee?"

"You know, Timothy, I've always hated my surname. More than seven decades on and I still hate that name. I've been thinking maybe I should change it. If I do, you know what I'll change it to? I think I'll change it to: 'Is.' Doesn't that have a ring to it? 'Candice Is.' I love it."

"What are you doing in my home, Wilbee?"

"See, it just sounds all wrong . . . just sounds so desperate. I really think 'Is' suits me better. Suits things better. Now, listen well Mr. Hale—I'm going to afford you a bit of respect even though you never saw fit to do the same. Go and change. Put on some warm, comfortable clothing, and if I were you I'd set aside that liquor and take a good long drink of water. Please be efficient. We're on a schedule."

Hale hurled the snifter against the wall. The glass shattered, splashing liquor across the Maplewood floor. "We're on your schedule, are we old lady? We'll see about that!"

Hale had not taken two steps toward Candice Wilbee before another voice came from behind him, this one unmistakably male.

"Yes, we will." Vice-like hands gripped Hale's shoulders. He was spun about and came face to face with a giant of a man. Hale scarcely had time to see dark whiskers on a wide chin as a fist closed in and then his world was all flashes of reds and yellows and dull pain and the floor rushing up toward him and then black.

C. J. Haskell had been riding hard for over an hour when he spotted Tripp Hernandez, the one outrider who'd missed Round Up. Tripp had a reputation for both kindness and drunkenness. With some two decades of experience under his belt, he often helped mentor the newer riders, showing them the tricks and traps of life in the sunfield. When drunk, he was always smiling that lop-sided, yellow-toothed grin. While certainly no philosopher, Tripp had a way of reading things—both people and situations. His gut instincts had saved him many times. But not this time.

It would later bother C. J. Haskell that his first thought upon seeing Tripp was not filled with sadness or even anger, but instead consisted of rational confusion: *How the hell did they get him up there?* Haskell reined his horse to a stop and peered up through the fog and drizzle.

Hernandez hung dozens of feet above his head, dangling from a noose strung below a QV array. His soaking body swayed gently in the breeze. Haskell shielded his eyes from the raindrops dancing in the wind and set his jaw, staring at his dead comrade for a long time. It seemed like a goddamn shame and insult to leave a good man just hanging up there, but C. J. knew there was no time to pause now. Trying to shoot down the rope would telegraph his position to anyone in the area. And furthermore, he knew that Tripp could have been trussed up as part of a trap; a lure. It was entirely possible that the three minutes Haskell had spent sitting still were three minutes too long.

His blood growing hot with anger, C. J. spurred his colt back up to a canter and continued west. It was true night now, though through the storm the only perceptible change was a darker gray than the slate color the sky had borne all day. Far ahead, toward what would have been the horizon, a few darker patches of sky hinted at a break in the weather. The rain, steadily drumming all day, was at least falling in smaller droplets.

If the storm were lifting, though, it was unlikely to break up anytime soon. It was going to be a long, cold night.

Haskell wrapped the reins around his left hand and gripped the collar of his long duster shut with his right. His boots were soaked through and his toes numb. Before long, his mind joined them. No thoughts of Tripp Hernandez. No thoughts of what the night may bring. Shoot and ride. If given the opportunity, shoot and then ride.

Scofield had been the only passenger in his pod for the last three stops. Only two other passengers were on the four-car train when it eased to a silent halt at the end of the line. Scofield stepped out onto the cement platform of the Outpost station. It was shortly before midnight. The rain had stopped but the air was still thick. Within seconds his exposed flesh was cold and damp. He pushed his hat down low on his brow and readjusted the satchel slung across his chest. Taking a few steps out of the pool of halogen light cast by the station lamps, Scofield pulled his holster and pistol from the bag and returned them to their proper positions.

He took in a long, slow breath and let it out as a sigh. Despite any potential peril ahead, it was a great relief to be out of New Las Vegas. The city always had an oppressive effect on Scofield; this time the usual discomfort had grown to a profoundly crushing level. His breaths were coming short and his heart had been pounding by the time he left Mayor Dreg's office and boarded the commuter line.

Scofield slid his hands into his jacket's deep pockets and began to walk south, his pace as fast as he could muster without breaking into a jog. The Outpost was oddly quiet, muted both by the heavy air and as if by some sense of looming dread. Surely it was all in his mind, but as Scofield crossed the dark threshold between the lights of the pod station and the few lamps still glowing on the Outpost's buildings, he began to feel as if his world was coming unhinged. His mind raced. Familiar though this place was, every shadow, every alley or doorway, concealed a threat. The few muffled sounds that made their way through the dampened night brought fear rather than their usual comfort. The thought of a night in his lonely shack—normally a haven—made the outrider shudder.

Of the several taverns that catered to the outriders, Scofield knew the first one to check. Matteson's Place. Matteson, the middle aged, craggy-faced proprietor didn't even own the unnamed bar, but he'd worked the counter for some thirty-five years and never seemed to sleep. Ten a.m. or hours past midnight he was there, wheezing under his breath and serving the boys whiskey. It was Matteson's Place just as sure as if he'd built it brick by brick.

Sure enough, Boss Hutton was at the bar. Ryan Cannell was beside him, both men hunched over glasses of whiskey. The two old men were talking quietly, then Hutton's shoulders blades poked up through his flannel shirt, rising and falling rapidly as though he were either laughing or sobbing. A few other riders sat at tables, chins resting on fists. They looked up then back down as Scofield walked slowly across the low lit room and eased himself onto a stool next to The Boss. Just as Scofield sat down, Cannell rose. He pushed his half-full highball of bourbon across the bar and muttered: "Good evening and goodnight," then walked away without so much as looking up. Scofield watched him walk away, then turned to look at Hutton.

"How we doin'?"

"Hey, Scof." The Boss glanced over then turned his eyes back to his glass of liquor. The old man shook his head slowly from side to side and waved his hand in the air without looking up. "Round for us both."

Though Hutton had barely spoken above a muttered whisper, Matteson was there within seconds, placing a fresh glass before Scofield and pouring a generous dose of whiskey for both outriders. Scofield took a hearty swallow of bourbon and unbuttoned his jacket and vest. He placed his hat on the bar and fished a pouch of tobacco from his satchel. A thousand questions raced through his mind, but Scofield read Hutton's mood and leaned back, slowly rolling a cigarette and letting the moment linger.

Both men sipped their whiskey. Occasional bouts of laughter and cursing pierced the smoky air. Boss Hutton pulled off his hat and lowered his head, eyes shut tight, and ran a hand through his gray hair.

"They don't know yet?" Scofield asked finally.

"They know some. Not much." He put his hat back on, eyes still closed.

Scofield took in a breath to say more but looking askance at Hutton decided to wait a little while longer before getting down to business. Just one more minute waiting wouldn't hurt. Scofield sat up on the stool, feeling the hard oakwood beneath his legs. He hooked his bootheels over the brass rod fastened to the bar. Matteson was pouring himself a glass of gin, trying to be subtle by leaning near the cash register. In the hazy, smoke-stained mirror Scofield watched his compatriots drink and joke and smoke.

Finally Hutton raised his head again. "I sent Greg White out first. He went east. Sent him with extra chow for a long ride. I asked him to check on your leech. He called in from the line box out near the depot. Gone. Lock was shot through from the outside."

"Fuck," Scofield muttered. "Guess he wasn't just some lone leech, then." Scofield cursed again under his breath and took a long pull of bourbon. "Fuckin' hell—I should have brought him in then and there."

"Weren't no way for you t'known. No worries 'bout it. Worry about—shit, Scof, how could you have known about that shit?" Hutton downed his glass and slammed it angrily on the bar three times. Matteson set down the ashtray he'd been wiping clean and hurried over, filling Hutton's glass and leaving the bottle. The Boss took a few small, quick sips of whisky, slurping the amber liquid sloppily, before a coughing fit took him. He hacked and sputtered, then drew in a long, ragged breath. Wiping a sleeve across his mouth, he asked "You got a cigarette, Scofield?"

"Sure." Scofield dug out his pack of store-bought smokes and offered it to Hutton. The Boss fumbled around with the pack for a few seconds before managing to get a cigarette out and between his lips. He leaned toward Scofield and the outrider lit the smoke for him.

"C. J. Haskell checked in, too. He was out west. He uh . . ." Hutton's mouth twisted into a sneer. He took another sip of liquor, slowly, deliberately tilting the glass against his lips. "C. J. checked in too."

"Hut, listen, I get the gravity and the pressure and the what-the-fuck of it all, but I'd be lax or remiss or whatever if I didn't say it . . . maybe this ain't the best time for you to be drunk?"

Again Boss Hutton pulled off his gray, wide-brimmed Stetson, dropping it on the stool beside him. He sat up, steadying himself with one hand against the bar. His other hand was wrapped so tightly around his glass the knuckles were white.

"Tripp's dead."

"What?" Scofield gasped.

"Dead. Hung. They fuckin' hung him."

Scofield took in a breath to speak but it came out as a dry rasp.

Tripp Hernandez was dead. Crooked-toothed, lovable, stumbling, smiling Tripp. Scofield caught his own eyes in the mirror. He could picture Tripp there grinning beside him as he had so many times for so many years. As he had mere nights ago. Turning to his right, Scofield nodded to the empty stool beside him—just the slightest nod; one that no one in the room could have perceived—and raised his glass off the bar. After a long pause he drained the bourbon in one gulp. When Matteson walked over and reached for the bottle, Scofield shook his head, whispering "Just water."

Scofield muttered his thanks as Matteson set a glass of tap water down before him. He glanced over at Hutton. The Boss was smiling and looking down at his hands. They were resting on the bar, palms up with the fingers curled halfway into fists. Hutton's mouth was moving slowly. His eyes were distant. Almost falling into a trance, Scofield turned farther toward Hutton. He sat staring right at the old man's face.

Finally Hutton snapped out of his reverie and folded his hands together in his lap. Eyes still staring a thousand yards, he asked quietly, "So what did the good Mayor Dreg have to say?"

"He knows about the drain. Knows it's bad. He did the whole dog-and-pony bullshit. Showed off his art and cigars and all. He wants to send in the troops."

"Go on."

"I got a feeling like he didn't tell me a damn thing that was actually on his mind. That he was planning the whole time. But I bought us a day. I know that. I got us at least one day. I think I convinced him that he needs to wait for our move before he sends in Civil Defense en masse; needs to wait for your cue."

"One day . . . maybe that's all we need." Hutton smiled again, then began whispering something under his breath. After a minute spent muttering he went on, just loud enough that Scofield could hear. "The field's been uh . . . been home for most all my life. Yours too, I know. Lots of ours. Ours. These boys," The Boss waved a hand in a circle over his shoulder, "they're my boys. My family. My brothers."

Scofield impulsively grabbed the bottle of bourbon from where it sat on the bar and took a long pull. "Mine too," he whispered through clenched teeth.

"I don't much give a goddamn about what happens in the city or in the towns," Hutton said. "I just know that me and you and our brothers are out here, and that for being out here we're free. We're . . . we're alive out here. Tripp was a good man. Good friend."

Hutton slowly worked his way to his feet. He kept one hand on the bar to steady himself and turned to face Scofield, head tilted down. He was swaying slightly but managed to look dignified; resolved.

When he raised his eyes they were made of ice. "I want blood."

# 15

Timothy Hale woke up into a nightmare. Searing waves of heat washed over his body. All was black. The world quaked and writhed around him. A strange, deafening roar thundered in his ears and he was tossed about, bouncing painfully off the hard floor and against unseen objects. Abject terror kept any attempt at rational thinking from his mind and, unaware of himself, Hale was screaming and thrashing.

Only after several minutes of this half-conscious hell did Hale form a single cogent thought: *You're alive . . . you're alive it'll be OK. Oh God what's happening to me! You're alive, Tim! You're alive, goddammit!*

Slowly, in broken fits and starts, reason began to make its way through the awful, shaking din. Hale was bound and blindfolded, hands and feet tied tightly into a ball in front of him. The rough cord cut into his flesh. As he got his ragged breathing under control, Timothy began to perceive a rhythm in the violent, shaking clamor. Two loud, bass booms were followed by a quick succession of higher-pitched clattering. The room seemed to heave and roll in a steady—though turbulent—pattern.

*I must be by one of the generators*, Hale thought suddenly as he tried to roll onto his knees. Only in the salt store power stations had he ever heard such a racket. But as soon as the notion had come to him, he dismissed it, somehow innately knowing there was no way he was in a power station, despite all the noise. The stations used direct electron transmission and heat transfer; all the noise came from cooling systems and the buildings themselves were temperate and remarkably still.

Hale rocked back and forth in his blind, sweltering, deafening bad dream for what seemed an eternity. Time and again he tried to reconstruct the last few hours and days but nothing made sense. How had Wilbee gotten into his home? And why—never mind the how at all, why! And the giant of a man who'd knocked him out—why? Why! Despite his best efforts at constructive analysis, a consuming fear filled Hale and he couldn't get past the vision of Candice Wilbee perched comfortably on his sofa and then the huge fist closing in on him. His head ached. He was bathed in stinging sweat and he itched all over. Gradually, despite the terrible shaking and roar, Hale's mind grew numb. The dark world grew ever more distant as sleep mercifully took him.

The horror of the waking world slipped into a restless dream. Hale stood in the hall outside his office, staring at the janitor cowered behind the terracotta planter. Timothy was pointing at the frail woman and trying to shout but his voice failed him. Wilbee was wearing an elegant dress and looked younger and ever more poised, almost elegant as the seconds passed. She rose slowly to stand at her full height. Soon she towered over the secretary, looking down with fiery eyes. *Candice Is*, she whispered, though her lips did not move. *Candice Is. Candice IS . . . I . . . AM.*

Shady tossed his mane and snorted, digging at the damp soil with a hoof. Kretch clicked his tongue loudly and raised a hand over one shoulder, not looking back. The horse fell silent. Again Wilton lowered his cheek down against the rifle stock and closed his left eye. He lay prone behind an outcropping of rock and brush atop a small dune. The sun had begun to crest the horizon not five minutes ago.

About a hundred yards to the west, three hooded men were hauling a heavy object wrapped in drab cloth across the sand. Each man had a thick rope over one shoulder and they trudged slowly, bent nearly double with the weight of their load. The swaddled object was no larger than three or four feet cubed, and Wilton scratched his chin, wondering what it could be. No matter: there was not another soul in sight and even if the men were armed with rifles, which they did not appear to be, Kretch had the drop on them. And an elevated shooting position, no less—these would be clean kills.

Wilton slid open his rifle's breech and pressed the thumb of his right hand against the back of a brass casing, applying enough pressure to be sure his piece was at its full capacity of eight rounds. He clicked shut the load lever and worked his way up onto his elbows. *Shouldn't've fucked with my field, boys.* The stock was damp against his cheek, the gun metal cool on the flesh of his hands. *You shouldn't have fucked with ol' Kretch.*

His shooting finger tightened. One more second . . .

"Relax Wilton, it's Haskell!" C. J. shouted as he dove on top of his comrade, one hand batting away Kretch's shooting arm, the other clamping down on the gun barrel for good measure. The young outrider rolled off Wilton and rose to his knees, making sure to get his face down where Wilton could see it.

Kretch let out a piercing shriek and clawed at the rifle, trying to get his hand back on the trigger. His eyes were wide and wild. Only after C. J. let the rifle go and gripped Kretch's shoulders firmly did Wilton take a clear look at his assailant.

Rage instantly replaced terror, rage both at his kill interrupted and that the young man had seen the abject fear in his face. "What the fuck are you doin', kid!" Kretch spat.

"Might ask you the same thing, Wil." Haskell replied calmly. He released Kretch and dropped down to his stomach, peering past the older rider out across the sand. "Get down, man! Get flat."

Kretch swore under his breath and lowered himself, lying down beside the young man. Both sucked in heavy breaths, Haskell's eyes were glued to the men below, while Kretch looked askance at C. J., his eyes cold. When it was clear that the trio had not noticed the scuffle, Haskell rolled onto his back.

"What the hell were you thinking, Wilton?"

"What's that, boy?"

"Ain't but five of us out here. In the whole field. How long you been staked out up here? How many miles we got uncovered out there?"

"You don't see them three out there, Haskell?"

"Yeah, I see—"

"Oh, so you do see 'em? You see those three fuckers dragging whatever they got towards our field? You think maybe we oughtta just let 'em—"

"I could also see your damn horse standing behind you from near a mile off. Fucking miracle you ain't drawn fire!"

Wilton was silent for a moment, realizing the young man was right. He hadn't checked his flank once in the whole time he had been atop the dune. Wilton sneered, glancing out across the sands, and then turning back to C. J. "The second I drew them in they'd a'been dog meat. If you hadn't fuckin' jumped on top of me."

Haskell rose to his knees and crawled backward a few feet until he could rise into a low crouch. He waved at his horse, Duncan, a jet black colt, to come up the dune; he'd dismounted a hundred yards back and jogged up to Kretch. Turning back to Wilton, Haskell was about to issue some further reprimand when he noticed the outrider's right hand resting loosely on his pistol's grip.

"Look, man, The Boss told us to shoot and ride. Not dig in and shoot. You and me gotta head away from these three and then split up again.

Keep the field covered. No sense in starting a hot war before we know what we're up against, right?"

Kretch said nothing, staring daggers at C. J. His pants and duster were soaked through on the front, leading Haskell to assume he'd been lying still on the damp sands for a good long time. At the rate the three men were making, what with towing their heavy load, it may well have been since before dawn when Wilton dug in. It occurred to Haskell that perhaps Wilton had even spent the night bunked down up here and had spotted the group by luck—it was still barely light enough to see, after all.

No good pressing the issue, though. Kretch was grinding his teeth, livid with the situation. The fingers of his right hand were still teasing his pistols. C. J. couldn't tell if Wilton was conscious of the action. So much the worse if not. Haskell was well aware that Kretch had it out for him—Wilton was an inferior rider, a worse shot, and disliked. Time and again Kretch had let his jealousy and enmity out in the form of barroom threats or jibes at Round Up. Alone in the middle of the desert was no place for Haskell to toy with a live wire.

C. J. considered asking the outrider what he'd seen so far; to try to turn things back to business. But he feared his professional intentions would be construed as inquisition and made up his mind to just get the hell away from Wilton Kretch. He wanted to at least break the news of Tripp's death, but decided to withhold the information. No telling if word of a fallen comrade would sober the impulsive bastard or fill him with bloodlust. Nothing to do but get away and keep on riding.

"I'm gonna mount up and head well north of these boys then keep on the westerly route. You're due to head east near the field, right?"

"Guess so," Kretch mumbled in reply.

"Well let's light a smoke for luck and get on with it," Haskell said, forcing a smile he hoped would look genuine. He dug in a pocket of his scuffed suede jacket and drew forth a pack of cigarettes. The tension seemed to leave Wilton as he reached out to accept a smoke. Behind them, Shady let out a whinny.

"Pipe down, boy!" Kretch rasped.

Haskell had just flicked his lighter when the first shot came.

"Goddammit, I'm still drunk," Boss Hutton croaked out amid a coughing spell. "Shoulda listened to you, Scof. I shoulda backed off from the bottle last night."

The jeep skidded to and fro on the wet sand, Hutton overcorrecting each time the tires slipped. They were heading back toward the Outpost at over sixty miles an hour, and while Scofield wasn't quite prepared to tell Hutton to ease off, he was certainly ready for a rollover. He gripped the handle by his door with white knuckles and found his eyes upon the frayed canvas seatbelt every few minutes. Time was certainly of the essence, though: the sooner they got back to the Outpost, the sooner Scofield could grab Reese and get back out into the field.

It was just between daybreak and morning. The sky was still a patchwork of gray above but the day promised to be clear. As soon as The Boss had been capable of action, he and Scofield had set out to give a cursory inspection of the stretch of Sunfield closest to the Outpost; closest to New Las Vegas. Their findings had been grim. For a solid five miles east, all had seemed normal. Then, about a mile past the first satellite outpost—simple concrete buildings used as store houses, jail cells, and temporary bunks—Scofield had spotted one of the contraptions. The outriders were cruising along two miles south of the glowline, well past where a sober and clear-headed Hutton would have ventured in his vehicle, and Scofield had kept a pair of binoculars trained on the field the whole time. When through the wildly bouncing field glasses he'd spotted something by a pillar, he bid Hutton stop, and then, to his dismay, confirmed seeing the same type of construction Kretch and he had first discovered a few nights back.

A mad dash back nearly twenty miles the other way confirmed what both men feared. Scarcely ten miles west of the Outpost, they spotted another of the contraptions built around a QV pillar, this time set a few rows into the sunfield. It was a safe bet the damn things were everywhere.

"They're comin' at us hard, man. They're comin' at us full tilt." Hutton practically moaned out the words. "Jeezus H, Scof, I think we gotta call out Mayor Dreg and his boys right quick after all."

"Gonna turn into a war then, Hut. You know that."

"Sure I fuckin' know it! The fuck else we gonna do here?"

"I don't know."

Hutton swore as the jeep bucked over yet another rut carved by the downpour, wrenching the wheel to keep the vehicle driving straight. "I don't mean to shit on ya, Scof. But we never seen anything like this. All my years riding the fields don't add up to shit when I ain't seen anything like this."

"Fuckin' Hell, Boss—don't apologize for calling it like it is. You think I don't know how bad this mess is? I just know what I saw in Dreg's eyes. Almost seemed like he was thinking like this could be—I dunno exactly—like his . . . his shot or something."

"What do you mean?" Hutton's foot eased up on the gas pedal and he looked ninety degrees over at Scofield, not bothering to watch the land ahead.

"I think he may see this as an opportunity. I don't know, man. Just something that occurred to me. I'm just talkin' here. Seemed like he was calculating beyond dealing with the field."

Hutton snorted and shook his head. A cryptic smile played across his face. "Maybe that's so. Maybe not. Dreg's got a big hand he's been playing, if what folks whisper is true. Maybe he wants to double down. We'll see later."

The main Outpost was visible ahead now, a smattering of concrete and brick buildings still gray in the quickening dawn. Boss Hutton shifted up into fifth gear and pressed home on the accelerator, steering north toward the stables.

"I guarantee you he's awake right now."

"You're probably right." There was a pause, and then the second voice went on, a lady's voice, speaking more quietly than before. "In fact, I'm certain you are."

Slow, shuffling footsteps made their way toward Hale across the thin carpet, accompanied by a soft clatter and metallic squeaking. When the second voice rose again after a long, wheezing breath, Hale recognized it as belonging to Candice Wilbee.

"He doesn't look too much worse for the wear. That chin is pretty bruised where you laid him out."

"I'll be sure to apologize for that." The first man said with a laugh. It was the gigantic sonofabitch who had accosted Timothy in his home, no doubt.

"Well," Wilbee replied, "as you see fit. I'm going to head back to . . ." she paused and then moved away again, her retreat marked by the same clattering. Hale could not make out the next few words she whispered.

"But give Mr. Hale my best, as it were," Wilbee said aloud.

"Of course." A door opened then shut. All was silent for what felt like minutes. Then five heavy footsteps.

"You're awake, aren't you Timothy?"

With no calculable reason to lie, Hale answered, his words rasping dryly through his parched throat. "Yes, I'm awake."

"I thought so." The man's voice was calm, even friendly. "Listen: I'm going to cut you free, then remove your blindfold, then get you a glass of water. I'd like you to stay still on the floor until all that's done."

Without waiting for a response, the man went to work. Large, strong hands gripped Hale's wrists and he felt the sensation of a blade working at the ropes. Suddenly his hands were free, his arms involuntarily flying apart as the strain released. Then the cords binding his ankles were sliced. Once all his limbs were freed, fingers worked their way under the black cloth bound tightly around his eyes and suddenly he was blinking, half-blind, at the giant silhouette before him.

"Fingers OK? You have feeling in them?"

It took a second for Timothy to process the question and then to make and release fists to check.

"Yes."

"You have feeling in your feet?"

"Um . . . pins and needles."

"That's feeling. That'll be just fine. Work the ropes off yourself, alright? I cut all the knots." The big man walked past Hale, who had yet to roll off his side, and searched through a cupboard. Hale's vision was poor in the light after so many hours spent in darkness, though the room was lit by only a few lamps and a weak, naked bulb overhead. He sat up, blinking, as the large fellow knelt beside him and offered a glass of water. Several iced cubes floated in the glass. Hale drained it in one long pull.

"It gets pretty hot in there, huh?"

"In where?" Hale asked, his throat still dry despite the liquid. The man made no answer, reaching out to take the glass back from Timothy and rising again. His eyes finally adjusting to the space, Hale looked around. He was in a motel room: floral print bedspread, a loveseat and wooden chair by the single window, and a sink outside the bathroom over which his captor now stood, refilling the glass from a large plastic jug. Looking down at himself he realized he was wearing blue jeans, a gray sweater, and brown loafers. They were his clothes.

"Where the hell am I?"

"Sandy Dunes Inn."

"What?"

"Nothing. Don't worry about it." The man turned and stood still, holding the glass of water in his hand. "Why don't you have a seat. Or lie down if you'd like."

Hale rose shakily to his feet, his joints creaking and popping. He held himself as tall as he could against the myriad aches and pains suddenly assailing him.

"Or stand," the man smiled. He stepped closer to Timothy and handed him the water. "Sorry about the crack on the cheek, Tim. Far from personal. I'm Russell Ascher. Russ is fine if you'd prefer."

"What's going on, Russ? Where the fuck am I?"

"Like I said, you're in the Sandy Dunes Inn."

Haskell and Kretch were both so surprised by the flying dirt and echoing report that for a moment they merely blinked at one another. A second shot crackled through the air between them and C. J. dove to the ground. Kretch, petrified, remained standing and even took a drag off his cigarette.

"Hit the fuckin' dirt, Wilton!" C. J. bellowed, grabbing at Kretch's jacket and hauling him to the ground. Wilton collapsed into a pile and Haskell rolled away, pulling off his hat and rising onto one elbow. With his other arm he held the white, wide-brimmed Stetson away from his head and a couple feet off the ground, surveying the desert below. The bullets had come from the north. There wasn't another dune half the height of this one anywhere near firing range in that direction and Haskell strained to spot the source of the shots.

The three men out on the sands below had abandoned their load and were sprinting away to the west. Three more shots rang out, though C. J. heard neither rippling in the air nor impacts as lead met earth. He pressed one cheek to the damp soil as he looked behind him to find Wilton still curled in a ball, fumbling to draw his pistol.

"Here," Haskell whispered loudly, kicking the rifle Kretch had dropped closer to him. Then he tossed aside his hat and turned to look over the other shoulder. "Duncan! Down, boy! Down! Down! Get down, Duncan!" He held his palm parallel to the ground and made a rapid pushing motion. The horse immediately obliged, lowering itself onto its knees and then rolling onto one side, black withers twitching with excitement.

Haskell spun around and then clawed and kicked at the dirt, crawling to his horse as fast as he could while keeping himself flat. A sustained hail of gunfire rang out, this time aimed close enough that dirt clods and pebbles flew into the air then rained down on the outriders. C. J. scrambled faster down the dune toward Duncan.

"Hasky! Where are you goin;?" Kretch veritably shrieked. The younger man paid him no attention, his mind racing. *Where the fuck are they shooting from? Ain't a goddamn place to hide out there!*

Again Kretch called out. "Haskell, come back here!"

C. J. reached his horse and threw one arm around the colt's neck. "Just stay down, honey! Stay down, Dunc!" He sat up enough to reach over the horse's flanks, pulling his rifle from a saddlebag. Then he grabbed the satchel slung from the saddle horn and began to work his way back up the dune, wriggling his shoulders and using his heels to propel him, staying belly-up and digging through the satchel.

Wilton craned his neck to see out into the field. He tossed another look back at his comrade, and upon seeing Haskell returning, Kretch managed to get back a bit of nerve. Wilton grabbed his rifle and swung round again to face out over the desert. He checked the muzzle for sand or other debris and then jammed down the brass load lever, chambering a round. No shots had been fired for what felt like a minute or two; it may have been seconds. Kretch tucked the walnut stock against his shoulder and slowly raised his torso off the ground into a shooting position.

"You got any bead on 'em?" he called back to Haskell, his voice taught.

"Nothing." C. J. crawled up beside Wilton, then rolled twice to put about six feet between them. Ratcheting back on his rifle's bolt, Haskell said: "You got them sharp eyes, right? You keep sweeping and I'll use my glasses."

"OK," Kretch nodded. Keeping his cheek down by the gun barrel, he panned back and forth across the land below. C. J. raised a pair of binoculars to his eyes and began a careful albeit swift inspection of each little dune, outcropping, or stand of brush within what he gauged was the range the shots had come from.

Four or five bullets slammed into the dune not ten feet from the outriders and Haskell dropped the field glasses, impulsively grabbing his rifle. Wilton squeezed off three shots, deafening so close to Haskell's ears. The young man could barely hear Kretch's voice over the ringing in his skull.

"Got movement on that low dune! Due northwest two-hundred yards!" Kretch pointed and fired another volley, then rolled onto his back to reload.

C. J. set his jaw and wrapped his left hand around the smooth wood of the rifle's stock, his right index finger finding the trigger. He lowered his chin against the weapon and closed one eye, sighting between its three iron pegs and cursing himself for not using a scope. *The fuck did he see?* Haskell's breaths were short, his heart pounding. There was scarcely a shrub on the dune Wilton had indicated. He stayed perfectly still, watching the hill. All was silent save for the methodical click of Kretch jamming rounds into his repeater. The sun was breaking through the clouds of the eastern sky, painting little pockets of the desert gold while leaving the rest a soft purple-gray. A bead of sweat trickled down Haskell's brow and crept into the corner of his left eye. As he wiped it away with the thumb of his shooting hand suddenly Wilton began firing again.

C. J. immediately opened up as well, firing six or seven fast shots from his semi-auto. Multiple puffs of dust rose from the little dune.

Ten or fifteen reports rang out from several distinctly different weapons. Only one shot landed close to home, caroming off a rock between the two outriders with a wicked clang.

"Fuck! I didn't see shit! You got anything?"

"Nothing." Wilton's voice was reassuringly calm for once; he had stayed up and ready, watching for muzzle flashes or smoke. "Gonna let these sons of bitches know we ain't playing with quits."

As Haskell looked over at Kretch, not understanding what he meant, Wilton closed one eye, steadied his hand, and squeezed off a single shot. Far away across the desert below, one member of the retreating trio stumbled, then fell to the ground. C. J. could scarcely believe Kretch had made the shot; they had to be three hundred yards off by now. Sneering, Wilton ratcheted down the lever of his rifle.

"It ain't them, Wil!" Haskell barked. "Just keep your—" His words were drowned out by the savage howl of machine gun fire. It was close. Maybe a hundred yards. Just below them. The earth came to life, sand and soil and rock dancing in the air as lead ripped through the sky; tore the dune apart. Haskell flattened himself against the ground, screaming. Unthinking, Kretch rose to his feet and then dove backward away from the murderous assault.

For a torturous minute the firing kept up, unceasing at first and then in sustained bursts. The silence that followed the hail of gunfire was absolute. Slowly, half-numb, Haskell thought through the various parts of his body, amazed to find himself unscathed save for a few scratches.

"Kretch . . . you OK?"

There was a long pause, during which C. J. didn't dare move a muscle. Then Wilton whispered back: "Yeah. I'm good."

"I saw them. Did you see them?"

"No."

"They're dug in everywhere. I saw at least five different muzzle flashes. They're spaced out in the sand just below us. Some farther out too. They're dug way in. Bunkers, I think."

"Jesus," Kretch stammered. "What do we do?"

"They were all west of us. We crawl off this dune and then get the fuck out of here heading east full gallop."

# 16

"What do you mean gone! He has to be there, the man's got no fucking life outside my office!"

"Mr. Mayor, he's not home. His phone is. The door was locked. I don't know what you—"

Dreg interrupted, shouting at the speaker phone on his desk. "Don't take that fucking calm-him-down tone with me, Strayer! Don't you condescend to me you mental midget of a man! Why don't you have men checking the cameras? You can't walk two steps in this city without being watched!"

"I already have men doing that, sir."

"Well then reactivate his chevron pin and track it!"

"The pin is here, Mayor. I already thought of that."

"Well think of something else goddammit!" Franklin pounded a fist on the desk so hard the shade slipped halfway off his gold-plated desk lamp. Dreg leaped forward out of his chair to catch it. He loved this lamp: its pale alabaster, ochre, and beige lampshade had been a gift from the Saudi ambassador. Its various inlays and facets came from no fewer than ten nations; the shade alone worth a small fortune.

Dreg sighed as he righted the lampshade, not speaking for a moment to let his blood cool. When he continued, his voice was quiet and measured. "Listen, stay right where you are. Call a few men you trust to Hale's apartment. I'm coming over there myself right now."

Colonel Strayer clicked shut his mobile. He took two slow, deliberate steps and set the phone down on Timothy Hale's large dining room table. Then the security officer closed his eyes and, channeling his special forces training, counted out a few long breaths and forced the rage from his head. His thoughts were calm and lucid within seconds. Opening his eyes, Strayer ran his fingers through his short blond hair, then began to walk through the apartment for the third time. There were shards of glass on one section of the floor. An amber stain on the wall above was tacky to the touch and smelled sweet and vaguely pungent. Surely alcohol and a few hours old.

Entering the kitchen, the officer slipped on a pair of thin black leather gloves and began to open cabinets. He found a bottle of cognac front and center in the third cabinet he checked. It was missing only a finger or two of liquor. That had to be the one. Strayer shut the cabinet and moved into the bedroom.

The bed was made, folded down tightly enough to bounce a coin off it. *Retentive prick*, Strayer thought with a rueful smile. Every drawer contained neatly folded clothing. The drapes were drawn and there was not a single random object upon any of the furniture in the austere room. Above the headboard of the king-size bed hung a large canvas entirely covered by circles of white paint. They were layered over one another thickly, with hints of color tinting an arc here and there. Strayer found himself studying the painting for a long time before he snapped back into the moment.

He returned to the dining room and retrieved his phone to summon a small security detail to the apartment. As he dialed he shook his head, looking down at the large table. There were chairs for eight. Strayer would have bet his last dime the table had never once been set for that many guests.

Scofield lit a match and held it to the tip of his cigarette, taking a long drag. He shook the flame out once the tobacco had caught. He held the extinguished match for a minute, watching a thin trail of smoke dissipate from its smoldering head. Then he snorted out a little laugh, dropping the matchstick on the sand.

"We had a lotta good times, didn't we?"

Reese neighed softly at hearing her master's voice. "You remember back in, uh . . . shit what was it . . . late seventies I guess . . . maybe eighty . . . remember that bar fight with those Comanche sons of bitches where I grabbed your shoulders and you wheeled round and clocked me upside the face? Man . . . I got a lot of drinks off you after that."

Scofield laughed out loud for a moment, then took a drag of his smoke as a tear formed in the corner of his left eye. "I'm gonna pay you back for that the way you deserve, bud. That hit wasn't meant for me . . . or this for you. I always owed you one, even though you clocked the wrong sonofabitch. You were lookin' out, anyway. Just not looking straight."

Scofield found himself laughing again at happy memories as he ratcheted back the bolt of his rifle. He took careful aim at the rope right above Tripp's neck. "Shot coming, Reese!" He bellowed. Then he fired a single round. It cut through the nylon cord a few feet above the dead outrider. For a second the body swayed, and then the remaining fibers conceded to the large man's weight and he fell down . . . down for what felt like ages but was barely seconds . . .

The corpse of Tripp Hernandez landed with a dull thud.

Reese lowered her head as if in deference to the fallen man as Scofield tapped her flanks. He rode over to his dead brother-in-arms at a slow trot, reining the mare to a halt a few paces away. Scofield slid from the saddle and pulled off his hat. He walked over to Tripp, who had landed in an inglorious pile, his torso twisted half over legs splayed out in op-posite directions, and took a final drag off his smoke.

Grinding his teeth, the outrider began to inspect his friend's body. The flesh was sallow and bloated, already beginning to rot near his eyes, mouth, and ears. Hours spent hanging in the rain must have sped the decomposition. It still looked like Tripp, but Scofield found himself keeping his eyes off the dead man's face. The faint odor of decay drifted off the corpse when the breeze stirred.

Scofield forced himself to think not of this as a man he had once cared for but rather as an object to be inspected. There were no bloodstains anywhere on Tripp's clothing save for a few splotches near his collar where the rope had flayed the flesh of his neck. Scofield peeled back his jacket and shirt. No trauma on the chest. No bones seemed to be broken. *Fuckin' Christ . . . he died by the hanging, then,* Scofield bit his lip, both angry and overcome with grief. What an awful, terrifying way for a man to go. What a lonely way to go, out here surrounded by hateful men in the middle of a thunder storm.

There was nothing more to do for now. Scofield hooked his hands under Tripp's shoulders, reprimanding himself silently for the queasiness in his stomach, and dragged the body toward the nearest QV pillar. He drew a little notebook from his pocket and scratched down the serial number stamped on the column's base with a pencil. Then he straight-ened out Hernandez's limbs so the outrider would at least lie in repose beneath the morning sky.

Scofield knelt, slowly putting his hat back on. He stayed crouched for a long while, his eyes drifting across the field. It was a remarkably clear day, the sky a brilliant blue above, still punctuated here and there by milk-white clouds. Visibility seemed endless. Scofield could count no fewer than fifteen of the massive, sinister arrays he had first encountered just a few nights before with Kretch. The strange constructions were wrapped around the base of every interior QV pillar in view. It was hardly believable—picturing the manpower needed to haul that much poundage was blood chilling.

As Scofield walked slowly into the sunfield, he tried in vain to sort through the myriad facts and assumptions cluttering his head. A few words muttered by Boss Hutton got mixed up with something Sebastian had hissed. Fresh images of Tripp Hernandez's bloated corpse were superseded by a memory of the old leech bleeding out as the boy knelt beside his stricken father. Mayor Dreg's wormy lips drooled out aphorisms and condescension. The outrider's mind slowly grew numb, aware only of his immediate surroundings. There was a mustiness to the air as the brilliant sunshine spilled down upon the still damp sands. The sun was warm on Scofield's back, but not in the way a of a cruel desert sun—it was comfortable; comforting, even. The heat soothed the tense muscles of the outrider's shoulders. It caressed his neck, sneaking under his wide-brimmed hat as it made its way higher in the sky and he made his way a few more strides southwest to the nearest pillar and its Byzantine parasite.

The array looked by daylight much as it had at night, save for gradations of color where brass tubing intersected copper wires and steel support bars. The back plate and its thick couplings were cast in rough iron. Hairline cracks and imperfections marred the slate-gray surface. As Scofield drew to within three paces of the structure, the hairs on his arms and neck began to rise. He froze, then took a step back: the outrider knew all too well what this tingling could mean. He took stock of the items he was carrying; there was nothing likely to hold a static charge but his six-shooter. Scofield rested his palm over the hammer of the pistol, then walked over to the array and touched a steel strut with the index finger of his left hand.

Nothing happened. So the circuitry of the device was closed. Scofield shook his head in grudging admiration: a mechanism that could stably generate that powerful of an electric field was damn well made, hate the maker or not. He made his way around the pillar, studying the apparatus with something near reverence. Scofield stopped walking after a complete pass of the device and leaned in to more closely inspect the band of strange bulbs set waist-high atop aluminum posts. He squinted, shading his eyes with cupped palms. Maybe it was a trick of the light, but it seemed they were glowing.

Scofield pulled off his hat and lowered it over one of the glass spheres. Sure enough, the bulb shone with a pale greenish light. A filament inside the smoky, yellowed sphere, visible with the sun's glare softened, glowed as if with a charge. *How the fuck is that even possible?* There was clearly a current flowing through the bulbs, here in the very middle of the sun-field. The filament seemed to pulse and undulate, shifting from blood red to ember orange. *The lifeblood . . . right there . . . the fuckin' blood . . .* Scofield began to whisper out loud "sucked out . . . before my goddamn eyes just draining away . . ."

For this Tripp Hernandez had died . . . . For this his boys had been called to war . . . . For this the world turned, love it or hate it. Or, for Scofield, tolerate it with ambivalence. At least things had always been stable before. His blood ran hot. The outrider straightened up again and jammed his hat down on his head. He dug in a pocket of his jacket and drew out the sack of tobacco and papers; he needed a stout smoke. As he rolled a clutch of tobacco into a cigarette, Scofield whistled twice, summoning Reese to him. He placed the smoke in his lips and then patted the mare's flanks as she came to a stop beside him.

"Good girl," he whispered through clenched teeth. Scofield struck a match and lit his cigarette—practically a cigar he had rolled it so thick—then walked around the horse. The outrider tried not to look at Tripp's corpse but there it lay in his peripheral vision. Scofield drew his carbine from its saddle holster and walked back over to the apparatus: the embodiment of his blackening rage.

Two thick tendrils of smoke drifted from Scofield's nostrils as he gripped the rifle barrel and raised the stock above one shoulder. He checked himself just before smashing one of the glowing bulbs. His anger was getting the best of him. *Fuck you thinkin', Scof? This damn thing may blow sky high for all you know. Leave this to cooler heads.* He lowered the rifle and stood still, taking in heavy breaths. He began to dig at the thick tapline connected to the array with the toe of one boot.

The outrider spotted the figure slip from behind a QV pillar to the east but made no move yet. He kept on kicking at the soil, subtly easing the rifle's strap to the very edge of his shoulder. It looked to be a man of above average height. He wore a long beige robe with a hood obscuring his face. His steps were slow, measured. Scofield trusted his own quickness enough to wait a second longer before engaging. If he could get the rifle aimed square at the man fast enough, perhaps they could trade in words rather than lead.

But the drainer had other ideas. Scofield whirled about as the man dropped to one knee, raising a pistol. The outrider spun his rifle off his shoulder and up into a shooter's stance, firing three quick shots as the drainer squeezed off two. No bullets found their mark and both men scrambled for cover, the outrider behind the iron plate of the apparatus, the drainer back behind the pillar.

"Fuck!" Scofield swore under his breath. Why the hell had he moved? He had a rifle squared off against a pistol! He knocked his hat off and dropped down onto his belly. Working his way quickly to the edge of the metal plate, the outrider found himself strangely energized; nearly elated. Adrenaline was pouring into his bloodstream. His heartbeat quickened but did not race. Here, finally, after days of confusion, fear, and fury, was definitive action. *You better be ready, you sonofabitch . . . I'm ready for you.*

Just as Scofield sucked in a breath to pop clear of his cover, a burst of three shots rang out. The bullets impacted inches from the outrider's right thigh. Time slowed to a crawl. Or rather Scofield's thoughts sped up tenfold: the drainer was east, the iron plate directly between them—these shots had come from south. From deeper within the field. Second shooter.

Scofield leapt to his feet and stumbled backward halfway around the pillar, trying to get cover between both the established contact and the likely vector of the new assailant. He drew his pistol and fired two shots into the sand for good measure—keep their heads down for a second. Jamming the six-shooter back into its holster, Scofield pressed the rifle stock against his shoulder and pressed his cheek down along the weapon, getting his eye lined up with the sights. Then he spun around the north side of the pillar. The first drainer was leaning out from his column. He ducked behind it just as Scofield pulled the trigger.

Immediately, the outrider wheeled to the south. There he was: a shorter man wearing the same beige robe but with his head exposed. He was running toward Scofield full tilt, an assault rifle in his hands. The man raised the weapon, erratically spraying bullets, but it was too late—Scofield had already zeroed in on him. He fired a single round. The man spun a full three-hundred and sixty degrees, ending up face down on the sand. This was no time to take chances: Scofield took a step backward to where the first drainer would be unable to draw a bead on him and fired three well-aimed shots into the fallen man. His body shuddered slightly as each piece of lead found its mark.

Scofield dropped the clip from his carbine—he still had two, maybe three rounds in it but no reason to be conservative at the moment—and jammed a fresh one home. He ventured a quick glance around the apparatus to be sure the drainer hadn't broken cover, and began to hash out a quick plan. If the man had a rifle he'd have readied it by now. Hitting a person on the run with a pistol was tricky business even for a seasoned, steady hand, so the outrider could be safe enough in the open for just—

Suddenly two pistol shots rang out. Scofield was confounded—he was totally hidden behind the apparatus. What could the drainer possibly be shooting at? A third shot followed by a whinny from Reese gave answer. Scofield broke cover and was charging in a split second.

"Don't shoot at my girl you motherfucker!" Scofield screamed, his voice cracking. His feet flew across the sand, carrying him faster than he'd ever run in his life. The drainer stepped out from the pillar, then balked at the sight of this raging man bearing down on him. He raised his pistol and fired a few rounds before being cut down by a hail of lead Scofield squeezed off from the hip. The outrider reached his crumpled foe and landed a savage kick into the man's ribcage. Bones snapped and the drainer bellowed, suffering as much pain from the blow as from the searing lead in his belly.

Scofield swung his rifle around like a baseball bat. The stock connected with the man's head just below his left ear. No way he'd be putting up a fight any time soon, if ever again. The outrider wheeled and set off sprinting toward his horse, which was standing only a few feet from where he'd left her.

Reese tossed her mane and snorted as Scofield reached her, dropping his rifle and throwing his arms around the horse's neck. "Are you OK baby? You OK girl?" He made his way around the mare, running his hands over her velvety flesh. She had a scratch across her withers. A thin trail of blood trickled from the glancing wound, barely visible against her chocolate-colored side.

"Is that it girl? That all that got you?" Scofield began to smile, resting one hand on her sinewy neck. Then something caught his eye: there was a small hole in the leather of the saddle. Scofield's hands broke out in a cold sweat as he ripped at and fumbled with the bridle and stirrup straps. Once the saddle was unhooked he practically ripped it off the horse's back. Nothing. The pooled blood the outrider had already begun to picture in his mind was not there. Incredulous, Scofield turned and picked up the saddle.

*I don't fuckin' believe it . . .* There it was. "You got some angels watching over you, Reese." The bullet had almost penetrated the thick saddle, stopping with just a hint of its brass casing sticking out from the burnished leather. It was unlikely the horse had even felt a thing. Scofield dug the deformed slug from the saddle with the tip of his knife, wrapping his fist tightly around the bullet. He stepped back from his horse, smiling at her.

Then he turned around slowly. His smile flattened out.

* * *

"What's this stain on the wall here?" Mayor Dreg asked, pointing at the honey-colored splotches covering a portion of Hale's dining room wainscoting.

"Liquor, I think. Or rather it is liquor. I'm sure of it." Colonel Strayer glanced up from his mobile and nodded, affirming his words.

"How are you sure?"

*Must you question every goddamn detail to feel like you're relevant, you fat fuck?* Strayer took in a breath and let it out slowly enough to make a point. "Because . . . sir . . . it smells like it. And there are shards of a crystal glass on the floor and because there is a bottle missing one glass worth of alcohol in a kitchen cupboard that's not tucked neatly back in among the others. I feel we can safely assume that a retentive—or rather . . . meticulous man like Timothy Hale would have realigned all of his bottles were he done drinking for the night." Strayer walked into the kitchen, beckoning for Dreg to follow him.

"Do you agree? Sir?"

"Frankly, yes," The Mayor nodded and crossed his arms over his large belly as the security officer pulled open the liquor cabinet and pointed to the shelf of bottles. In the living room, the other three security personnel Strayer had summoned were having a quiet debate. The officer strained to listen in while feigning attention to Mayor Dreg. *Had he heard what he thought he did? Was word spreading among the men?* He managed to tune out Franklin's muttering and distinctly heard one of his men utter both the words "sunfield" and "drain" twice before Dreg let out a gasp.

"Fuck's sake . . . this is the bottle of cognac I gave him the day of his appointment! I remember it well! This liquor is nearly as old as he! Fine stuff . . . fine, fine stuff . . ." Dreg pulled the bottle down from the shelf, and admired it for a good long time, seeming to lose track of the present. A private smile tugged at the corners of his lips. Then, abruptly, he tapped on the cork to make sure it was secure in the bottle and then returned the cognac to its shelf, carefully sliding it in among the other liquors and closing the cupboard.

"What do you think, Strayer? Think he flew the coop?"

"Sir?"

"He could have realized his executive chevron had been deactivated and hit the road. Hale's a smart man, though—I can't see him fleeing without a damn good reason; more than that rot about the computer passwords. Christ I hope I didn't scare him off—just needed to dress the bastard down bit. . . ."

"I highly doubt he left of his own volition, Mayor."

Dreg sighed, leaning heavily against a marble countertop. Had he imperiled his strongest ally and shrewdest advisor in a moment of foolishness? Had his anger and tendency toward mistrust caused a lapse in judgment that had in turn landed Timothy in some trouble?

"So you think he was . . . forced from here? Snatched away?"

"That or he was compelled to leave in a very big hurry. All I think we can be sure of is that this was not a choreographed exit. He—"

"Colonel Strayer!" One of the security officers in the next room shouted for his commander.

Strayer turned and walked from Hale's kitchen into the living room where he was met with three stony-eyed stares.

"Well, what is it boys?"

"Nothing good." The officer who had called him, Major Engel, a man of medium height with wide shoulders and coffee brown skin framing an angular face, lowered his voice as Dreg came out of the kitchen.

"We've got shots fired out in the sunfield."

"Multiple incidents, sir," the tallest of the three security men added through clenched teeth.

"What does that mean?" The Mayor asked quietly, standing behind Strayer.

"It means a war is starting," The colonel answered, barely above a whisper. He slowly turned to face Dreg. His voice was even softer when next he spoke. His lips barely moved and his eyes were aflame. "I guess that's what you wanted." *Easy enough to change anything you want now, you megalomaniacal bastard.*

Scofield polished the lenses of his dark sunglasses then slid them onto his face, hooking the metal loops behind his ears. He hardly ever wore the glasses except when there was a sandstorm. Better to let your eyes adjust than to shade them when on patrol, he found; the minutest gradations of color in the sand often led to a burrowed leech or tapline. Right now, though, he wanted his eyes covered.

The drainer was propped up against the QV pillar from which he'd been shooting, legs splayed out before him and hands bound behind. He was unconscious. A savage purple and black bruise spread from his right shoulder up to behind the ear where the outrider had struck him with his rifle. The bloodstain on his beige robe was still spreading slowly, and Scofield could only imagine how much had spilled out beneath the thick garment.

The outrider slung his rifle and began to draw his six-shooter, then, thinking better of it, he slid the long knife from his belt, admiring the polished steel blade before slowly crouching until his face was inches from the drainer's.

"Wake up, you piece of shit." He waited a few seconds, then slapped the man roughly across the cheek. "Wake up, motherfucker!"

With a pitiful groan, the man came to, his thin face twisting into a grimace. He blinked in the bright sunlight, disoriented and in agony. He was maybe thirty-five years old, with close-cropped golden-blonde hair and pale gray eyes. His face was ruddy with sunburn, and the lines of his crow's-feet wrinkles stood out bright white against the red flesh of his cheeks and forehead.

"You with me? Hmm?"

The man nodded slowly, gritting his teeth.

"It takes a real lowdown fuckin' coward to shoot at a horse. Horse that ain't even being rode, no less. You rank somewhere between shit and a mosquito to me right now, so keep that in mind as we chat."

"All's fair, don't they say?"

Scofield cocked his head to one side, making no attempt to hide his surprise at the man's thick Australian accent. He casually tested the edge of his knife against the tip of one index finger.

"You're a long way from home, huh?"

"I'm right where I want to be."

Scofield rose to his feet, eyes locked on the drainer, who stared right back at his black sunglasses. The man's chest rose and fell quickly. No doubt he was in excruciating pain, but he managed to keep his face impassive save for a clenched jaw.

"Right where you want to be is gutshot, bleeding out on the sands of Vegas County, huh? I guess we kind of have something in common, leave out the lead in the stomach. See, I like it around here. But I don't like you being here. And you're remaining here, or anywhere, is up to me right now. Puts me in the catbird seat, Aussie."

The drainer struggled to sit up farther, gasping in pain and ultimately achieving nothing; he slumped back down against the pillar, leaning against a steel strut to his right to favor the bruised ribs on his left side. "I'm not . . . familiar with that little . . . turn of phrase."

"What it means is if you so much as look at me in a way I don't like, you're dead and I'm smiling about it. Does that translate?" Scofield pulled out his pack of smokes and put a cigarette between his lips. "You smoke?"

"Who doesn't?"

"You, for right now." The outrider lit the cigarette and savored a long drag, pulling off his sunglasses and making eye contact with the drainer as he spoke. "Here's the short version of a long story," Scofield said quietly, smoke drifting from his mouth with each word. "I'm going to bring you back to my headquarters and if you expect any kind of medical attention or even a goddamn glass of water, you're going to be a good little drainer and tell me everything I want to know."

"What are you going to do with that knife? Try to loosen up my tongue?"

"We'll see." Scofield crouched and took hold of the drainer's thick beige cloak. He pulled a section of the cotton garment taught, then cut a long slice into it. Sliding the knife back into its sheath, he took two fistfuls of fabric and ripped the cloak wide open. The drainer groaned as his body was jostled. Beneath the robe he wore blue jeans and a worn gray sweater. There was blood everywhere. It looked like one of Scofield's shots had caught him dead in the navel.

"This ain't too good, mister. You're on the clock, as they say."

"We're . . . all on the clock . . ." he gritted his teeth as Scofield roughly pulled up his sweater to examine the gunshot and cracked ribs. "Just at different . . . times."

"That's a nice philosophy. I hope you take some comfort in it." The outrider stood up and stretched his legs, letting out a sigh of satisfaction. "I reckon we got a little time, just us two. Then, you behave, and I'll take you to see some real nice fellahs. They'll patch you up all ship shape." His face grew hard. He took one last drag off his cigarette and dropped it between the drainer's feet.

"How many of there are you?"

"Five."

"Real cute. Listen, bud, I'm not gonna fuck around here. You're dead or alive based on the next few answers. How many men are out here draining my goddamn sunfield?"

"Maybe I meant five hundred. Maybe five thousand." The man forced a saccharine smile. "There are lots and lots of us, that's the truth."

"Who's behind it? Who's in charge? I'm going to guess this ain't some Australian conspiracy—why are you here?"

"I'm here because this is where it's happening this time."

"What's happening?"

"The change. The shift."

"Go on, and make some goddamn sense." Scofield pulled off his hat and ran a hand through his salt and pepper hair. A single bead of sweat trickled down his brow despite the cool air.

"You don't know a goddamn thing, mate. You couldn't even start to understand."

"Try me."

The Aussie shook his head, a look of profound resignation on his face. "If you only knew . . . perhaps you wouldn't be fighting back. Listen—I don't wish you any harm. If I'm going to die out here that's fine but it's important to me that you understand that. It's not about you or your comrades. It's about the change that's coming. I . . . I'm sorry I shot at your horse . . ." he trailed off for a minute, his eyes seeming to lose focus.

"I'm sorry you did that too. You're goddamn lucky you only nicked her. If you'd hit my girl square on, I—" The drainer cut Scofield off with a violent coughing fit. Flecks of blood dotted his lips and chin by the time he got himself back under control.

"Listen: I'm dying. A man knows when it's coming. Never knew that until this very moment, but now . . . I can speak to it with conviction. I won't tell you anything you want to know so do whatever you want. I'll tell you this, though—we won't stop. For anything. You can't win unless we're all dead and you'll never kill us all."

"Who is 'we'?" Scofield asked, his voice involuntarily raising an octave.

"Just . . . people who think differently. That's all. People who see that the world is never going to change itself and so . . . " the drainer was fading, "so we're . . . forcing it to."

"Just hold on, you goddamn bastard. I'll get you some water and take you in."

"Don't bother." The drainer closed his eyes. His eyelids were milk white against ruddy skin slowly growing pale.

"Look, if you're going to fucking die then what's the point, man? Just answer what I ask—how many of there are you? Who's leading you?"

"If I didn't think that we were right, mate, I'd tell you all about it. If I didn't know. But if you think I'll use my last breaths to piss on all I believe . . . then just get that knife of yours back out and get to work."

"I don't *want* . . ." Scofield trailed off, the words 'you to die here' staying in his mouth. Again the man was wracked by coughs; this time a thin trail of blood dripped from the corner of his mouth. His breaths were growing short. The outrider thought to offer him a cigarette, but looking down at the broken wretch figured there wasn't enough time left for him to smoke it. He figured maybe he should untie the man's hands and let him expire with dignity, but already the Aussie's eyes were glazing over. Once more he looked up at Scofield, then, slowly, his chin lowered down onto his chest. His shoulders rose and fell as he rasped out his last few breaths and then he was still. Gone.

Scofield waited a minute, then checked the drainer's pulse to be sure. There was none. He sighed, shaking his head slowly.

Scofield turned away from the dead man and looked at his horse, casually swishing her tail at flies while she waited for him. He looked out toward the western horizon, so distant and crisp, all soft dunes and faraway brown mountains beneath a deep blue sky. The arrays hummed above him, a sound so familiar he never heard it except when he focused on the noise.

This was the second man Scofield had ever killed. And the first lay not fifty yards away. As the realization that now he was a killer settled in on him, a profound weight lowered itself onto his soul. Strangely, the burden was made harder to bear by Scofield's summary acceptance of it. He was acutely aware that having crossed the line he could never go back. And, undoubtedly, he would soon wade deeper into the blood that lay on that boundary's far side.

How was this so effortless for some men? So simple to rectify and repeat? Scofield could scarcely have been less of a coward; could hardly have had more courage and confidence. Yet these attributes did not make a man ready to kill. They had nothing in common with comfort in the letting of blood—quite the opposite, even, as he figured it. There had been no other recourse today, and the outrider knew his soul would rest easily in the days and years to come, but for now he was shaken, saddened, and confused. This was not the first time he had shot to kill, but it was the first time he had completed the task. He felt sick with himself for his cruel, threatening bravado knowing now that the death rattle had echoed in the man's ears. But he hadn't known—it was just another incident until it wasn't. He didn't know the man's liver had been ripped to shreds; that his stomach had filled with blood.

Scofield shivered involuntarily as he looked down at the fresh corpse. He knelt and pulled the man's hood over his face. Resigned to searching the body—and then inspecting the other man he'd killed—Scofield found himself for the first time questioning his line of work; his life. What was really out here that was so precious men had to die for it? Power?

# 17

Kretch had never ridden so hard in his life. He was exhausted, near delirious. Shady's breath came out in ragged wheezing; foam frothed at the sides of his mouth. Wilton's spurs had torn the colt's flanks to shreds. Crimson blood glistened against the horse's gray hair beneath the noontime sun. *Just keep goin' goddammit, boy! Just keep going.*

He was riding due east, several miles north of the field. He'd told Haskell when they split up a few miles back that he would head straight to the Outpost to debrief. Kretch let himself think this was honorable adherence to duty, but somewhere deep inside he knew he was terrified and just wanted to be in a place he'd feel safe. *This shit ain't fun when they're shooting back,* he thought to himself with a grim smile.

The horse was fading. Grudgingly, Kretch reined the colt down to a trot. His eyes were constantly roving, his head twisting from side to side. He pulled his rifle out of its saddle holster and began to reload. The desert was quiet save for a gentle, welcome breeze. Miles ahead, Kretch could see the vague gray outline of New Las Vegas. The sun was bright but the day cool. Wilton's neck and armpits began to itch as his sweat dried. As soon he scratched those places, new itches appeared: on his thighs, his chest, his crotch—in his goddamn boots. *Gotta shit, shower, and shave before I head in. Get some new threads on. I gotta get my boy watered up and fed—wouldn't be right by him not to,* he nodded to himself, sliding the eighth round into his rifle and ratcheting down the load lever. He placed one last bullet in the weapon then rested it across his lap.

"Not a bad day out, huh boy?" Kretch said aloud, his voice strong as his nerves calmed. "We hit a pretty rough patch there, ey Shady? Got out of that one real good, though."

The gravity of the day was lost on Kretch as soon as he had regained his cool—it had been a tense moment; that was all. Already he had suppressed the sensation of abject terror that had gripped him not an hour before and was planning how he would describe the gun battle to his comrades: he'd acted bravely that morning, holding his ground amidst an onslaught of goddamn machine gun fire—why, he'd even dropped one of the bastards at three hundred yards all while lead was ripping through the air inches from his head! *What have you boys done today? Hmm? Had some coffee and a piss? Well I was out dodgin' machine gun bullets, you sonofabitch! How about that for a morning wake-me-up?*

He smiled to himself. Sure, he'd been lucky. But luck only ever counted when you were neck deep in the shit out there where the shit mattered. Kretch dug in his saddle bag and pulled his little cigar case from beneath a few crumpled shirts and random sacks of chow and ammunition. It was time for a good honest victory smoke.

"This'll be for both of us, Shady," Kretch said with a cackling laugh as he struck two matches and held them to the tip of a cigar. The horse plodded along unevenly, favoring its right hind leg. Wilton hardly noticed as he puffed out thick plumes of smoke. He took a long pull from his canteen, then splashed a handful of water over his face and neck. Slinging his rifle over one shoulder, he kicked free of the stirrups and leaned back in the saddle, riding easy.

Kretch thought he imagined the sound at first. It was distant and indeterminate—a sound that didn't fit the tableau of calm desert but was so faint he could easily write it off. Once, at least. The second time the low, baleful moan drifted across the sands, all the calm and happiness Wilton had felt just a minute before turned to a creeping fear. He'd heard this sound before; just a few nights ago when he was patrolling solo he'd heard it.

He clenched the cigar between his teeth and pulled the rifle back off his shoulder, gripping the gun tightly as if it could ward off the unknown menace. Where the hell had the ominous noise come from? And more to the point, what had it come from? It was like nothing he'd ever heard before. Something caught the corner of Wilton's eye to the distant south, but when he whipped his head around to peer into the sunfield, nothing remarkable stood out.

There it was again, almost like some great pipe organ sounding a single note; a distant dirge. Slowly, the sound faded. Or rather it wasn't fading, it was being replaced. Far away—Kretch couldn't tell from which direction—a deep, powerful rumble had begun. It sounded like thunder but it was constant, rhythmic. And growing. Louder and nearer. The very air seemed to grow heavier.

Suddenly, with an awful crackling roar, a group of fighter planes ripped through the sky above the outrider. They had passed him not a second after he even realized they were there, zipping over so quickly he could barely see the sleek, delta winged aircraft as he tossed his head back. There were five planes in the formation, flying at about twenty thousand feet—near to their operational floor this close to the sunfield.

As the jets passed overhead, a mighty sonic boom shook the desert floor, the shriek of their engines trailing behind them. Shady bucked twice then leapt into the air and Kretch threw his arms around the colt's neck to keep from being thrown. His hat fell from his head and he closed his eyes and gritted his teeth against the deafening cacophony.

"Easy boy! Easy now!" he shouted as much to himself as to the horse.

As quickly as the terrible thundering had come it was over, a distant rumble on the horizon. Shady calmed, still side-stepping and tossing his mane, but no longer jumping. Kretch slid off the colt, taking the reins in his hand and leading Shady back to where his hat had fallen. He grabbed the Stetson and was placing it on his head when a new sound began.

This time the outrider could clearly see the source of the din: no fewer than twenty helicopters were approaching from the east. There was a mix of sleek attack craft and heavy transport birds. As the choppers drew nearer to Kretch, several branched out to cruise due west, a few seemed to be banking east, and several maintained their course toward the field, rising higher into the sky as they passed overhead.

Wilton wrapped Shady's reins around his right fist and took his hat back off. He stood next to the horse, the cigar hanging from his mouth, staring up at the helicopters. His throat went dry. The tobacco smoke drifted into his eyes and nostrils, stinging and acrid, but he felt nothing. He was profoundly numb, body and mind.

Timothy Hale wrapped his fingers around the doorknob. He twisted it slowly and, to his surprise, the door clicked open. He took in a deep breath, glancing once more around the simple but clean motel room where he had spent the morning, then exhaled and pulled open the door. Bright sunlight spilled into the dimly lit room and Hale shielded his eyes, squinting, unable to see anything of the outside world.

A minute passed before Hale could discern shapes and colors in the brilliant early afternoon. Still half-blind, he stepped out onto a porch of faded but evenly cut and measured pine planks. An awning of matching wood hung a few feet above his head, the floorboards and deck running the length of what Timothy could now see was indeed a long, single-story motel. He had half-expected he was being held in a room appointed as a residence but built into some strange citadel or bunker or . . . or something other than the quaint town he now found himself looking around.

As his eyes adjusted, Hale scanned his surroundings. He was standing beside what could well have been the main street of most any little town in America, save for pale yellow sand replacing the usual swaths of green grass and pavement. Not a soul was in sight. There were a few shops across the street, all with clean windows reflecting the sunlight and carefully lettered signs above their doors. A row of houses sat a bit up the street to his right, each with white siding and red doors. Three horses were tied to a hitching post at the left end of the motel's porch, and beyond them a larger brick building looked to be a town hall.

"Nice place, isn't it?"

Hale wheeled to face the voice. It came from a smiling man with ruddy cheeks and warm brown eyes twinkling beneath a formless tweed hat. He was maybe fifty years old. His fingers were intertwined, palms resting on his round belly as he leaned back in a wooden chair, his head against the motel's stucco wall. The man wore drab green canvas pants and brown boots. His tweed jacket matched his hat both in its gray-brown color and its well-worn condition.

"I'm Dave. David Flint. Dave's fine . . . Flint's fine—whatever suits your mood, Tim. Is Tim OK?"

"Where am I?" Hale whispered between clenched teeth, ignoring the question. David smiled even wider, looking away, and disregarded Hale's inquiry right back.

"We thought you were gonna sleep all day. Ms. Wilbee was by a few times to see if you'd come out yet. Actually, were you asleep, or did you just assume the door was locked? People always think the door's locked."

Timothy took a few steps away from the door, the floorboards creaking under foot. He heard the front legs of David Flint's chair touch down as he stepped out onto the sand. The sun was warm on his shoulders.

"Yeah, sure, look around all you want." David said from behind him, rising with a slight groan. "In fact, you're free to go anywhere you want in this town."

"Where is this town, Flint?" Hale looked over his shoulder.

David dug his hands into the pockets of his blazer, cocking his head to one side. "Well, that's a tricky question to answer. See, as far as the world knows, this town ain't anywhere. Doesn't exist. It's our little secret, so I'm not sure the best way to answer. Best to say nothing—just right now, at least. For me, at least."

Hale's shoulders drooped. He closed his eyes tightly. He had spent the morning running through all that had happened and trying to calculate what was likely to come next. This strange, provincial man in his slouch hat, leaning casually against the wall with a friendly smile, didn't square up with anything he'd imagined.

If the door was unlocked, why had the windows been painted over? If the lights and ceiling fan worked, why was the tap dry? Why had he been assaulted and dragged from his home, writhed for hours in some awful, deafening, smoldering hell only to be deposited in a clean motel room and now free to wander about this tidy, deserted town?

"I can tell you have a lot of questions. That's only fair. Ms. Wilbee and Russ Ascher are waiting for you. You know Ms. Wilbee and Russell is the big guy. Oh, wait—you know him too." David laughed, tapping his jaw. Hale involuntarily raised a hand to his own bruised cheek. He couldn't be sure, but it seemed as though Flint's pause and even his laughter had been calculated, rehearsed. "Sorry. I don't mean to make light. Anyway, they're over at Town Hall. It's the big brick building. Pretty obvious, I guess. So poke around if you want, but make your way over there soon, hmm?"

Timothy turned and took a long look at David Flint. The squat man held eye contact, regarding Hale with the same calm a man might reserve for a signpost: something to study, nothing to fear.

Hale spun on his heel and began to make his way down the dusty street, away from Town Hall.

"Plenty to see that way, Tim. Plenty of miles and miles of open desert to see. Just one thing!" Flint called from behind him. "Don't think you're getting out of this!"

Hutton's right hand draped limply over the gear shift. His left fist was wrapped tightly around the steering wheel. The jeep's ancient engine alternately purred and coughed beneath the hood. The Boss had stopped the vehicle right between the meeting hall and Matteson's Place; logic and desire were battling one another in his head. The early afternoon sun was bright, but already the shadows were beginning to stretch longer across the sand. The days grew shorter so quickly it took the old outrider by surprise every year.

This was usually the start of the quiet season. Fewer hours of sunlight meant fewer leeches. More time with feet kicked back and a glass of bourbon. More sleep. More calm. Miles away Hutton heard the deep reverberations of a second squadron of helicopters making its way from their base north of Vegas. All goddamn day the desert had been a din of machines overhead. These last few minutes had been the first quiet he'd heard, save for the comforting rumble of his old jeep.

The Boss figured one drink was a solid compromise between reason and longing. He threw the stick back in gear.

It was dark inside. Just a few lamps shone in the corners and one rested on the bar itself. Hutton blinked repeatedly, navigating the familiar space as much by memory as by sight. He sidled up to his regular stool but remained standing. There wasn't a soul in the place. Hutton cleared his throat loudly and heard a cough and some shuffling from the back room. He turned and looked around the bar—it was the first time he had ever seen it empty. Every one of his boys was now out on assignment, save the few awaiting him in the Meeting Hall.

"Hey, Hut," Matteson said as he came through the door from his living quarters. His voice was dry and rasping like he'd been asleep. "How bad is it?"

"Ain't good, buddy. Sorry to wake you."

"No, no—I'm up. Glad for the business." Matteson grinned, though his bleary eyes and sallow cheeks made it clear the smile was forced. He looked utterly exhausted.

"Double me up then cut me off, if you would."

The bartender nodded, reaching for his black apron out of habit, then shaking his head and turning the other way, leaving his shirt tails untucked. He scanned the back row of whiskey bottles and then selected a fifteen year old rye, placing two small glasses on the bar.

"Figure this might be a good time for you'n me to share something," the bartender said, pointing to the glass closest to him. "I heard a lot of planes goin' over?"

"Yeah. Choppers, too. And there's gonna be trucks and half-treads soon enough."

"That so?" Matteson poured a few fingers into each glass, setting the bottle down uncorked.

"That's so. Do me a favor, Matt—put the bottle away now. I don't think I'm fit to fight temptation. Be way too easy for me to drink myself outta this shit for the day and I can't afford that."

"Course. Wise of ya." The bartender returned the bottle to its place, then walked around the end of the bar. He was barefoot. Matteson eased himself down onto a chair at the table nearest Hutton as The Boss took a seat on his stool, resting his back against the bar. He pulled his cigar case from his vest and looked up as he lit a stogie.

"How long you been here?"

"Forever I think. It's twenty years if it's two."

"Feels more like the former. The forever I mean. Christ man, we seen it all, ain't we?"

"All that's to see around here, sure."

"What did you always want to do, Matt? When you were a kid, I mean."

"When I was a kid?" Matteson laughed, running a hand through his thinning black hair. "I wanted to be a knight. And if that didn't work, I was gonna be a pirate."

Hutton laughed quietly, cigar smoke drifting from his nostrils. "I think all the knights are dead. Plenty of pirates around though."

"Not quite so romantic now, hmm?"

"Not quite so much."

"So what do you think's gonna happen, Hut? Shoot me straight. You think there's gonna be a war here? Think they got the numbers, whoever it is? Or is this shit blown out of proportion?"

Boss Hutton sighed, pulling off his hat. He rested an elbow on his thigh and cupped his chin in one palm. His five-day whiskers were coarse and his face itched where his hand bent them back. The whiskey warmed his throat and belly and it occurred to him that he couldn't remember the last time he'd eaten an honest meal. Yesterday's breakfast? Had he had anything but a hunk of wheat bread since then? A few bites of corn cake an hour or two back. Or three hours or five.

He was feeling the few sips of liquor; feeling them work their way into the darker reaches of his mind. When the South Australian Field faced a drain some seven or eight years back, the assailants had drawn down enough power to fuel their insurgency for weeks and then run a thriving black market for months. What was worse, they had destroyed half the S.A. Field's infrastructure, leaving their illegal power taps an economically viable source for several years.

That was the greatest danger here: a group of boys as fine as his riders could keep the field safe against any normal threat; the martial force of greater New Las Vegas County could keep the field safe against most any army in the world. But if the field was damaged—if much of it was destroyed—there was nothing to do but weep and moan. The drainers could suck as much power as possible, then sabotage the rest and leave, selling what they could to who they could and ultimately doing what they pleased. How to beat an enemy you can hardly define? They weren't up against a real army; certainly there was no government to topple and sign a surrender. It was an outrider's lot to fight a battle of attrition, and this time that conflict was sure to cost dearly.

And why, given all that, given that there was no "army" to fight, why in the hell had Mayor Dreg been so cavalier to send out his troops? Was he hoping to win a battle, or to merely show off on a grand stage? And to who? *Most likely just beats jackin' himself off,* Hutton thought as he looked up, breaking free from his long brooding.

"I'm sorry, Matteson—what did you ask me? Sorry, I get wrapped up in my own cobwebbed old head. Just . . . I get mixed up thinking about this. Sorry, bud."

"You apologize to me again and I'll make you start paying around here. I just asked how bad you think it's gonna get."

"Christ I wish I knew. I got all sorts of theories and all, but between you and me, for all my years spent neck deep in this mess, I've never seen anything like this. I hear Kretch and C. J. got sprayed by machine guns. You've heard the jets and choppers. And smilin' Tripp Hernandez. It's just . . . it's so much different than any other given day—so much worse than a given worst day, and the thing that kills me is that I don't get the motivation. It may come as a surprise that ol' Hutton's a student of history, but I'm too old to fuck and fight much, so when I ain't on the move or piss drunk right here, I study. And I can't square this up. Country's stable. Which is to say the economy's stable . . . there's no foreign aggressor could muster even a bow and arrow against the interior of this nation . . . so what the fuck, Matt? That's why I'm here having a drink instead of dealing with the goddamn mess at hand—I don't know how to fight back against something when I don't know what's driving it!"

Hutton slammed his empty glass on the bar and rose suddenly, grabbing his hat so hard the firm felt brim folded in half in his fist. He immediately loosened his grip on the Stetson, massaging flat the crease he'd formed.

"I got to face the music. Face the bullshit. See you around, Matty."

"Yup. Soon and better I hope." Matteson rose as Hutton strode toward the door.

"Just one thing I thought I'd add, Boss." Hutton turned around, looking attentively at the disheveled bartender. "I don't know a hell of a lot about history but it may surprise you to know that I'm a . . . well, a lover of poetry."

"Does indeed," Hutton said, a broad and genuine smile turning up his lips.

"Yeah, well, keep it quiet. But a quote I thought may bring some . . . some thoughts to you. Fellah named W. H. Auden wrote these words—part of a longer piece—but he wrote 'em just when World War II was sweeping over everyone a century and a half or so back. He said uh . . . he wrote— wait let me get it just right . . ." Matteson closed his eyes, then whispered:

"What huge imago made a psychopathic god: I and the public know what all schoolchildren learn, those to whom evil is done, do evil in return."

He opened his eyes again. Hutton waited a moment before responding.

"You saying you think this is . . . like some retaliation? What would anyone be fightin' back against? Is that what you're saying?"

"No. Not at all, in fact. And what do I know, anyway? I just know that even the drunkest bastard I ever seen in here usually don't throw a punch when there weren't some reason, whether it was bad blood stirred up that very night or bad blood flowing underneath a long time, you know?"

Boss Hutton cracked open the door, sliding into the meeting hall as quietly as possible. He leaned back against the cool cinderblock wall and looked around the familiar space as if seeing it for the first time. Most all of the chairs had been folded and stacked against one wall. There were hundreds of cords crisscrossing the floor leading to banks of screens, tables piled high with computers, and monitors and stacks of communication gear. Antennas stretched up to the rafters thirty feet above.

The cavernous room was bustling with strangers wearing the black fatigues of Civil Defense forces; an unfamiliar cacophony of static, beeping, clicks and the constant drone of machinery echoed off the walls. *Jesus H. Fuckin' Hell—this is goddamn terrible.* Hutton pulled off his hat, sighing and massaging the bridge of his nose between two fingers. *I always liked to think I was in control of everything, didn't I? Didn't you? OK, old man . . . face it. Face it straight on.*

"Who thinks they're in charge here, huh?" The Boss barked loudly, standing tall with his feet spread wide.

For a moment the room grew quieter; the murmuring of voices dropped off. Mere seconds later, most every face that had turned to look at him was back on its console or phone or charts. Only a few people paid attention to Boss Hutton—his boys to a man. Noah Fischer was the first to reach Hutton. He was limping badly, dragging his right leg, but the heavy white cast was gone, replaced by a flexible brace.

"You sure you should be walkin' around on that thing, Fischer?"

"Good as new, Boss," Noah smiled. "Assuming I bought a brand new piece of shit busted ass leg, but I'm just fine, sure."

"OK, good man. How you doin', Greg?"

Gregory White nodded slowly, rolling out his thick shoulders. "I'm alright, Hut. Except for all these goddamn assholes crowded up in here. Fuckheads don't know shit about shit!" he said loudly, his eyes seeming to find one soldier in particular. Then, dropping his voice again, he added: "Good to have you back here."

"Yeah. Good to be back. How was your patrol?"

"Field was quiet for me. Seems that's the exception, though. You see anything out on the line?"

"No. Not really," Hutton shook his head, looking away from Gregory and reluctantly making eye contact with Wilton Kretch. "So what happened, Kretch? Heard you and Haskell got lit up pretty good."

"Bullets like raindrops, Boss. I ain't ever seen so much lead in so little time. The kid's lucky he weren't alone. I managed to drop one of the fuckers before the shit got too thick and I figured we had to ride out. Gotta fight another day, y'know?"

"Sure." Hutton looked away, again scanning the room. "So what's the story here—they got our hall set up as their command center, that right? Fischer?" Hutton added this last question as Kretch opened his mouth to answer the first.

"Yeah. Pretty much. Bastards started pouring in around ten, maybe ten thirty. Didn't ask anything; didn't say much. Just took over the place."

Hutton put his hat back on, shoulders sagging in resignation. There was nothing he could do to stop it, after all. "OK . . . any one of 'em seem to be in charge?"

"Yeah. I'll send him over," Gregory White answered quietly, turning around and making his way through the jumble of cords and desks and men scurrying about in black uniforms.

"Any word from the field? From anyone?"

Fischer lowered his head, his fleshy chin compressing against his chest, and shook his head slowly. Kretch glanced over his shoulder, then whispered: "Ol' Ryan Cannell came back in from a short ride and a few of these security bastards led him off somewhere. Said they had questions."

"Where was he ridin' from?"

"Checking out the cage closest west of here. We heard there was a fellah got locked up in there and the ol' man said he'd go look himself."

"Watch it with that old man business, Wil—he's younger'n me, dammit."

Wilton cracked a smile which Hutton tried to return, but it came out as more of a sneer. Kretch took in a breath to say more, but The Boss quieted him with a subtly raised hand. Greg White was walking back toward the group, trailed by a tall man with square shoulders, a square jaw and pale blue eyes set beneath close-cropped blonde hair.

"I'm Colonel Ridley Strayer. As ranking Civil Defense officer and the head of executive security, I'm the one overseeing this operation. I take it you're Mr. Hutton?"

"Boss Hutton," Gregory growled over the colonel's shoulder. Strayer ignored him.

"I need you to send each of your men to me as soon as they report in from the field. I'll want to interview each separately before they so much as take a piss. And no one heads out into the sunfield again without my clearance, is that understood?"

"Don't you fuckin' talk to The Boss that way, you cityboy pissant of a—"

Strayer spun on his heel, locking eyes with the large man glaring down at him. "Gregory White. Four sets of charges dismissed, three felony convictions, two of which resulted in jail time—the first for manslaughter the second for rape, if I'm not mistaken. Father deceased, mother and two sisters living in Mobile, Alabama. And kindly slide your hand back off that pistol, if you would. If you really think drawing it would be a good idea I won't object, but I guarantee it will be the next to last action of your life, followed quickly by the ground rushing up to meet your very dead body."

Greg blanched and took an involuntary step back, dumfounded upon hearing his darkest secret casually revealed. He had bragged about the man he'd killed more times than he could count, but about the girl— about the girl he'd poured vodka into and then punched square in the jaw when she tried to keep her skirt down, the girl he'd mounted while she lay there unconscious and bleeding from the nose, the girl whose face he saw every night before sleep took him . . . .

"That's better." The other outriders looked askance at Greg White as Colonel Strayer turned back to Hutton. "Now, I'm sure you have many questions and we'll try to answer them and to accommodate your men. We're in this together, after all; we're partners. But you are not in control. We are in charge. You don't have to like it—if I were you I certainly wouldn't, OK? Know that. But also know that this goes a bit beyond petty thieves and little generators. This goes a little bit beyond fifty-odd men and a stable of horses."

# 18

Scofield was riding at full tilt. Reese's hooves thundered against the desert floor, sending up a trail of dust. The corners of her mouth were dripping with foam.

"Come on girl! Just a little while more baby, keep it up!" he shouted as he craned his neck to look back again. His hat bounced wildly in the wind, flapping behind him on its lanyard and blocking his view. He dug his fingers between the flayed flesh of his neck and the rawhide cord and pulled the hat flat against his back. Finally able to see clearly, he swore under his breath. It was no use—it was still gaining.

Scofield faced forward, scanning the terrain. He'd just broken free of the sunfield and had been making for the nearest dune, but the massive, awful machine bearing down on him was just too fast. The outrider had never thought he'd flat out escape the damn thing, but he'd hoped to gain elevation.

Not five minutes earlier, Scofield had been making his way back toward the Outpost at an easy canter. He had to report the two men he'd fought and killed. He had to get water for himself and his horse. He had to get more information. All had been perfectly tranquil in the hour following the gunfight. Then, suddenly, a deafening wail sounded behind him. His horse had picked up to a full gallop without Scofield's consent but the outrider could hardly fault her. All he could see behind them was a massive cloud of dust and sand surrounding some strange, speeding behemoth.

A moment of abject terror had quickly given way to the lightning fast calculations some men make in moments of great trial. He knew he'd never outrun it, but if he could get to that dune, maybe the machine couldn't climb. There was a chance it would be slow in turning, but out in this wide open swath of land, he could spend the afternoon feinting left and wheeling right and still not get away. *How the fuck is this even possible?* It occurred to Scofield that there was a good chance the sunfield was shut down, taken out. A vehicle this big could scarcely come within six miles of the field under normal circumstances; this thing had driven right under the stacks. *I could be royally fucked here. This could be real, real bad. This could be it.*

Scofield reined his horse to a stop. In one fluid motion, he grabbed his rifle and the submachine gun he'd taken from the drainers and leapt off the mare.

"I love you, Reese. You're the best there is." He cupped her soft muzzle in one palm, looking into the horse's large brown eyes. Then he barked at her to stay still, and jogged away from the horse.

The dust cloud surrounding the approaching vehicle grew smaller and Scofield could hear the rumble of its engine lower in intensity. As it drew ever closer, he could finally see his pursuer. It wasn't only dust and sand forming the haze around the machine. It was also steam.

The locomotive came to a stop fifty yards from the outrider. Great clouds of white steam and gray smoke belched from the iron stack atop the gigantic tank engine. It sat upon three pairs of massive treads. The whole vehicle was painted matte black, from the savage-looking scoop jutting off its front to the myriad gears idling along the sides. A large wheelhouse with small windows sat just below the smoke stack. Deep, staccato huffing rumbled across the sand, like the breath of some predator crouched and waiting to attack.

Mayor Dreg wiped droplets of coffee off the desk with his sleeve. He had slammed a fist down so hard his mug had bounced off its leather coaster, jumping an honest inch into the air. "I can't tell what the fuck I'm looking at, man! What are these goddamn dots and circles?"

"Those are probably helicopters . . . half-tracks or . . ." Strayer's voice crackled through the speaker, a syllable dropping here, a word garbled there.

"I can barely understand you, Strayer! Speak up!"

"I'm shouting, Dreg!" The absence of the words "Mister" or "Mayor" was not lost on either man. "I'm two miles south of . . . glowline on a satellite phone. I shouldn't . . . using . . . thing as it is!"

Franklin leaned closer to the screen set in his desk, straining to make sense of the pixilated image before him. He could see about a mile-long stretch of the sunfield and in various places there were strange objects that looked like smudges to him. Supposedly these were the various vehicles of his defense force taking position, but the pattern of deployment and the snail's pace at which it was happening consternated The Mayor. He could not unveil the full sweep of his plans and ambitions until the Civil Defense Forces were in place. Sweat dripped down the rolls of his neck and pooled in his bushy eyebrows. He loosened the thick knot of his crimson tie.

"Why can't you get me better images of my field?"

"The aircraft . . . stay above twenty-thousand feet, Mayor. We have one glider and an analog film camera. That's . . . blurry you . . . . It . . . at least another two hours to divert lower orbit satellites . . . problem . . . higher resolution aerial reconnaissance . . . and are . . . but from Oregon. Maybe by sundown. Not . . . but we'll see. We're doing all we can."

"Have you engaged yet?" Dreg growled between clenched teeth.

"Say again."

"Have you engaged!"

"With who? Ghosts? We haven't seen a single soul out here."

"What's the name of the deputy head of security forces? Black guy, wide shoulders? Not you. What's his name?"

"Major Engel?"

"If that's his name, then yes, Engel. He's the one right below you, correct? Federal Military background? Former Air Force man, I think. He was there at Hale's apartment. That's Engel?"

"Yes."

"When next you have something to report, have Major Engel call me, Strayer. I get tired of your insubordinate bullshit."

Franklin wished he were holding a handset so he would have something to smash down. Instead he jammed a stubby index finger against the red button at the top of his phone console, hanging up on the security chief. He was livid, his mustache quivering, toes curled into balls and stretching the thin leather of his wingtips to the very edge of ripping apart.

His anger was fueled by both edges of the same sword: First, Strayer was acting like a mutinous prick and had taken the execution of the response into his own hands, treating Dreg as a man to be read reports to rather than the man he reported to. Second, The Mayor had absolutely no grasp of martial issues and, while he never quite admitted it to himself, he was innately aware of his own impotence in that arena. He had neither the experience nor the mind for matters of tactics and strategy.

Mayor Dreg didn't even know how many men he had in his defense forces, never mind who took care of logistical re-supply for vehicle batteries or ammunition or who was cooking the soldiers' meals or what kind of aircraft were circling the sunfield. A glider? Had Strayer really said there was a glider? Why was there a goddamn glider!

All that compounded with the fact that he had arranged for a division of Federal Forces to be waiting the day after he returned from Boston, and now had no clue what to do with them. Where to put them and when? He feared he would have to reveal his trump card to Strayer, essentially ceding full control of the operation to the colonel and thereby losing his triumphant moment—his hero's victory; his display to centers of power ranging from Los Angeles to Austin to Washington itself that there was much power indeed in the hands of Franklin Dreg.

Dreg had been long accustomed to issuing orders and having them carried out. Only now, when his city faced a crisis that demanded reaction rather than action was he finally, acutely aware of his plight: quite simply, he did not know what to do. Instead of rationally delegating duties to those fit to carry them out, he became increasingly furious and increasingly bent on managing matters directly, despite his total lack of ability to do so, and despite the fact that his intentional delay of a response had let the crisis grow so large.

Curling his bottom lip over tawny-speckled teeth, Franklin pulled open the top right desk drawer and opened the cigar box within. He chose a thick, rum-scented corona and laid the cigar on his desk, turning back to his computer screen. Toggling through pages of data on troop movements and flight patterns, The Mayor soon accepted that the information before him might as well have been Greek. He shook his head, wishing he could tap the com button and call Hale into his office. *Tim would have made sense of this mess for me. I'm a goddamn bastard for running him off.*

Dreg let his chin sag down onto his chest, thinking wistfully of a time not two weeks ago when he casually oversaw millions of stable lives. He and his trusted executive secretary. But just as soon as this nostalgia had come, The Mayor thought of Hale's lies and his conniving; his changing passwords and withholding information. Everything was in flux, everything was different.

Dreg tapped his screen twice to darken it; the data were all a meaningless jumble to him anyway. He grabbed the cigar, slipped off his shoes and stood, slowly making his way over to stand before the bank of screens on his office wall. Here was logic. Here were numbers he could understand. And all the worse for it: everything was in the red. Power was literally draining from his city. *And they haven't seen a fucking one of them? Idiots! Fools!*

Dreg ground his teeth as he fished a pewter cigar cutter from his vest pocket. His eyes were on the screens as he slid the tip of the corona into the cutter. The salt stores and PV arrays were being drawn from simultaneously, and this on a sunny day. It was truly staggering to grasp the scope of electricity lost. Almost as much power as was flowing into the city to keep life moving along was being drawn out to God knew where. How long before the fulcrum tipped? The Mayor made up his mind to travel personally to the command center. It would be good for the soldiers to see their chief, he reasoned. If only he had some kind of uniform . . .

No time for that now, of course. Dreg slid his fingers into the cutter, sighing as he paced before the monitors. He bungled the slice, leaving dangling flaps of tobacco hanging limply from the cigar.

Hale made his way down the deserted street slowly. The shadows were growing longer and a breeze had started, lifting sand and dust up into the air and howling softly among the buildings; whispering gently across the distant hills. He had hiked more than a mile south of the strange town and clambered to the top of a high dune. As far as he could see there was nothing but rolling desert rimmed by distant mountains. Without food and water, Timothy knew trying to escape across the barren landscape would be suicide.

And his captors knew it too, of course. They would never have let him roam free if not to demonstrate just how very trapped he was. So what was left to do? Hale was making his way toward the large redbrick Town Hall. He passed the Sandy Dunes Inn where he'd awoken that morning. The chair where the portly, enigmatic David Flint had perched sat ominously empty.

It was as if the whole town was one huge conveyor belt, pulling him along. There were shops and houses and the motel, all of them clean and in fine repair but utterly lifeless; nowhere to go but to the center—to the place they knew he had to go. Hale had the uneasy feeling that he was on the set of some play with the action preordained, the script written. He need only follow his stage directions to reach the inevitable denouement.

He paused at the gleaming white steps of Town Hall, looking up at a brass plate mounted beside the building's broad double doors. The top line of the plaque—surely the town's name—had been buffed out. Below the scratch marks read the words:

PROUDLY INCORPORATED IN
1982 BY THE PEOPLE OF
. . . . . . . . . . . . COUNTY

Again there was a word erased. Hale took in a deep breath as he slowly raised his left foot, lowering it onto the first of seven steps but not yet ascending the stairs. He looked off toward the horizon, squinting in the bright afternoon sun. Then he ran a palm across his hair and cleared his throat a few times.

Timothy strode up the steps with confidence, and took hold of both heavy bronze doorknobs.

It was dark inside Town Hall. The doors opened into a narrow, high-ceilinged vestibule. Hale blinked repeatedly as he stepped across the threshold from sunlight to interior gloom. A faint scent of ammonia mixed with tobacco smoke drifted through the air. Timothy eased the doors shut behind him, much of the determination he'd mustered mere seconds before now fading.

He was standing in a corridor some thirty feet long by eight feet wide. The floor was polished black granite and the walls half wood paneling, half painted dark burgundy. Several doors were spaced evenly along either side of the hall and one large window above the entryway, paned with smoky glass, provided the only light in the space. The end of the hallway was lost in shadow; Hale couldn't tell if it stopped in a wall or led deeper into an open space. Faint murmurs drifted from somewhere.

Maintaining what resolve he could, Hale walked down the dark hall, wincing as his loafers squeaked on the smooth stone floor. His eyes were slowly adjusting to the darkness and ahead at the end of the corridor he could now see two large wooden doors propped slightly ajar. The sound of voices grew louder the nearer he drew to the doorway. Several people were speaking all at the same time, each in hushed tones. Timothy sidled up against one of the doors and strained to make out what was being said but any specific words were lost in a gentle echo off the stone floors and wooden walls.

Finally Hale sighed, then slid between the open doors. He entered a cavernous room. At the center of the Town Hall proper was a massive table laden with documents, maps, phones and various communication gear. The space was lit only by six or seven tall lamps, the same as one would find in any parlor, and a few naked bulbs suspended above the large table. Twelve or fifteen people leaned over the table, variously muttering to one another or studying paperwork. There was a large bank of windows around the top of the room but every pane was papered over.

Hale stood just inside the room for the better part of a minute before he was noticed.

"He's here," a voice said above the quiet din. Instantly the room became a hive of activity, bodies scrambling to roll up documents, cover images and terminate conversations on the various equipment.

"Clear it out! Clear it all out!" Hale recognized Russell Ascher's baritone voice and then spotted the massive man making his way toward him.

"Mr. Hale, please just stay where you are for a moment." Ascher approached with his hands raised, palms out but with a look of deference on his square face, stopping a few paces from the Secretary General.

"Do you need water or something to eat? Anything?"

"I need answers."

"Sure. That's coming very soon, I assure you. But if you're thirsty or hungry or . . . or need to piss or anything, believe me, now is the time to take advantage."

Hale stammered. What did that mean? He sucked in a breath to respond with defiance but was shocked to instead find himself quietly saying: "A cup of coffee wouldn't be so bad."

Ascher nodded, a faint smile turning up the corners of his lips. "I think we can arrange that." He glanced over his shoulder, watching as the room's inhabitants shuffled out a side door. Then he turned back to Hale. "Why don't you grab a seat? I'll see about some coffee. Just cream OK? We're out of sugar."

"Yes. Fine," Hale said, looking down. He always drank his coffee black.

The large man walked away and Timothy slowly approached the massive table, now covered by only a few random documents and a plethora of half-empty mugs and leftover food. Two men sat at the far end of room, casually watching Hale. Only one person remained at the table, stooped over a map.

"How are you holding up, Mr. Hale?"

"I'm honestly not sure how to answer, Ms. Wilbee. Or are you going by "Is" yet?"

The elderly woman raised her head and smiled warmly, cocking her head to one side and scratching her chin. "Hmm . . . no, I think I'll wait a bit longer. A lady my age has learned patience, you know." She beckoned Hale with a gnarled finger. "Come over here, Timothy. Come have a look at this."

Hale made his way around the table slowly, trying to study some of the graphs and writing that had been left behind. None of it made sense to him at a glance. Wilbee was looking down at a large topographical map.

"See, here about in the center is New Las Vegas. Can you believe I remember a time before they added that damn word? New—ha! Lipstick on a pig is all. Anyway, that was then. See, here is the sunfield. These here," the old woman pointed to a number of dark blue triangles, "are some things we'll get to a bit later and last . . . over in this corner . . ."

she pointed to a green square, "is where we are. Home sweet home. We keep it nice and clean, as I'm sure you've noticed. There is civilized life left yet, Tim."

Hale was studying the map incredulously. "That's not possible. There's nothing for . . . for thirty miles in any direction from there." Timothy stabbed a finger against the section of map Candice had indicated.

"Yet here we are." Wilbee straightened up, her spine popping. She was wearing a gray sweater and a long crimson skirt, looking every bit the grandmother rather than the master tactician. Her white hair was combed straight, though wiry strays escaped the coiffure here and there.

"There's nothing there on any of the maps you've seen, Mr. Hale. Nor is there anything where the blue dots or red squares are. And as far as you and most City people are concerned, there never has been."

She turned and looked up at Hale's face, still smiling but with a strange intensity in her watery eyes. Just then, Russell Ascher reentered the room holding two coffee mugs. Wilbee lowered her voice, maintaining eye contact with Timothy. "But there was."

Candice Wilbee winked and turned to leave. Ascher leaned toward her as he drew alongside the table, whispering something to the elderly lady.

"Yes, send her in, I suppose," Wilbee replied with a slow nod. She made her way toward the back door limping slightly, her feet dragging across the granite with a rhythmic whisper.

"Grab a seat, Tim," Russell set down both coffee mugs and turned to leave. "You guys come on with me." The two men seated against the wall rose and followed Ascher out.

Hale stood perfectly still for a long while, rooted to the spot by confusion. The large room was utterly silent save for the sound of his own breathing. He thought of grabbing up all the documents he could and stuffing them in his pockets. Or of trying to use some of the arcane, antique communication gear to raise someone back in the city. He thought of fleeing the building and taking his chances on foot across the sands. Then, reluctantly, he eased down onto one of the wooden chairs set about the table.

Two thin columns of steam rose from the mugs. Tim could smell the mildly acrid coffee. A cigarette butt smoldered in an ashtray on the far side of the table. Then from behind the closed doors Hale heard heels clicking as someone approached. The knob turned and the hinges creaked.

He sucked in a breath as she entered.

"Hi, Timothy."

"Maria?"

Maria Rodrigues walked over to Hale and stood before him, looking down. She was wearing a gray sweater above blue jeans and heavy black boots. A beige cloak hung from her shoulders, gathered at the small of her back by a thin cord.

"Fancy meeting you here," she whispered, a sad smile on her face. She tucked a few errant dark hairs behind her ears as she sat down beside him and wrapped her hands around one of the coffee mugs.

"What the f—what the hell are you doing here, Maria?"

"You'll never understand, I think. You'll never . . . you won't see. I'm sure of it, actually. But I asked Candice to let me talk to you for a minute before they show you."

"Show me what?"

She took a sip of coffee, her eyes on her knees. "Show you why we're here, why we're anywhere, why we're together, and have been for a long time."

Hale looked away, shaking his head as he exhaled heavily. His throat had gone dry. He grabbed his cup of coffee and took a large, noisy slurp. Then a circuit in his brain closed—he had been so dumfounded by her appearance that only now did he realize that she spoke with an accent. He leaned forward suddenly, staring at her face.

"Where are you from, Maria?"

"Lisbon. Portugal."

"Then what are you doing here? What the hell were you doing in the city? What . . ." he trailed off. She held his gaze, her eyes soft.

"It's not just here, Tim. Believe me. And please, just try to keep an open mind."

Candice Wilbee had been standing just outside the door as Maria and Timothy talked. She was not eavesdropping, exactly, having been unable to hear their words, but she had caught the tenor of rising fear in the man's voice and the calming, almost warm tones with which Maria seemed to be soothing him. Wilbee smiled to herself, momentarily thinking of Maria not as an able comrade but rather as *such a nice young lady, really.*

Wilbee was still smiling as Maria stepped out into the hallway beside her and gently shut the door.

"How is he?" Candice asked, looking up into Maria's dark, brooding eyes.

"Fine, I guess. Considering. Actually . . . not fine. He's so far out of his element I'm not sure he'll ever make sense of a single thing again."

"It's a lot to understand so fast, Maria. I remember when I first met you—you were a bit dazed by all of it, and you were already, dare I say, simpatico?"

Maria smiled at the shared private joke playing off her native Portuguese. "That's still Spanish, Candice."

"Well, at least I try. Now tell me . . . how are you?"

Maria looked away, her eyes staring off down the darkened hallway and slowly losing focus. "I'm scared. I'm excited. Or anxious, is more like it. I just . . . I know what we do—what we're doing—I know it's right . . ."

"But . . ." Candice led her, gently laying one of her wizened hands on Maria's left forearm.

Maria took in a deep breath and turned her head back to meet the elderly woman's gaze. "But I know lots of people are going to die soon."

Wilbee lowered her head, her eyes closing. She was silent for a long while. Finally, taking her hand from Maria's arm and turning to walk down the hall, she whispered, as much to herself as to her companion: "What we're doing is right."

# 19

The sun was just beginning to dip below the western horizon. Impossibly orange, it slid behind the distant hills, painting the sands with a rich palette of reds, purple, and gray. A solitary evening star pierced the darkening eastern sky. More likely it was a planet, actually—probably Venus. *Yeah, gotta be, in fact,* C. J. Haskel nodded to himself in silent confirmation. Still too early to see true stars. *Guess I've got nothing to wish on, then.*

He tried to force a smile as he dug in his vest pocket for cigarettes. Boss Hutton had counseled his boys a thousand times not to smoke when there was a potential engagement; the scent of the smoke could carry for great distances. It didn't much matter, Haskell figured, when you were already pinned down. He slid a few inches up the QV pillar he was propped against to dig in his blue jeans for a pack of matches, keeping his shoulders pressed against the cold steel and his legs close together and stuck straight out, just inside of what he reckoned was their firing line.

His lungs filled with smoke and he let his hatless head lean back against the column. The outrider had three rounds left in his rifle. His .45 had a full magazine loaded and one in reserve. Seventeen bullets total. He had counted at least five shooters, not including the one he knew he'd dropped. There were probably more. At this rate, they could practically charge with knives and still best him. His horse had run off a half hour ago. He was glad for it—better to have Duncan alive and gone—as he'd surely have been shot had he made a break for it on horseback, anyway. No reason to have his boy in the line of fire, too.

As he smoked, C. J. began to mull over the questions that only matter when their answer is no longer academic. He was happy with the life he had lived; the life he had chosen. But the young man felt distinctly cheated by fate at only twenty-four years. There had been women, there had been challenges met, there had been camaraderie, there had been tears. But Haskell was sure he would die missing out on that indefinable but perceptible "It" that let a man nod as the light grew dim and accept the end with equanimity. *Fuck, maybe it's all just bullshit, anyway. Maybe it's not worth fighting for; maybe it's not worth fighting against.*

Haskell didn't consciously know what the "it" he now singled out was, but he figured somewhere in his mind—somewhere in the mix of surging emotion and lucid perception that fought for control—that "it" was a convention men with years left to live and no fears to face brought out in pleasant conversation. The meaning of . . . of life? Was it not merely to be alive without suffering?

A rapid burst rang out from an automatic, quickly followed by three deeper reports from a large caliber weapon. A few of the bullets from the first barrage caromed off the QV pillar and C. J. heard the lead of the second rifle crackle past him at the same time as the awful echo of the shooting rippled by. There was a chance they figured him dead by now, but it was unlikely—no reason to fire for effect if you think your target is gone. If they took him for dead, the logical thing to do would be to lie low for much longer than they had, then spread out wide while leaving a couple of men spotting for movement. So likely they were patiently waiting for his move and occasionally firing to hope for a lucky hit. *Goddamn, if only I could've taken two of these fuckers out—wish I was gonna give 'em less than a fair trade.*

He had all but forgotten his cigarette as he hunched over when the shots were fired. Now suddenly came a burning between his left index and middle fingers and at first Haskell was confused, thinking somehow he had been injured, before he looked down at his hand and then shook the smoldering cigarette butt free with a quiet yelp.

Haskell scratched off a small blister that had already formed on one finger, exposing the tender red flesh beneath. As he studied the little wound, staring intently at the small droplets of blood forming, something suddenly occurred to the young man. The thought shot through him like a bolt of electricity, literally jolting him back upright: if they wanted him dead, he'd be dead. One man on six, seven? Maybe more? They were trying to take him alive. Had to be.

This new assumption became an immediate certainty. Haskell was unsure whether he was more at ease with a definite end or the unknowable abyss of captivity. Would he be tortured? Starved? Locked away in a little cell? What would they try to get from him and what the hell did he really have to offer, anyway? For the first time that day, he found his mouth going dry. His fingers no longer stung from the burn, but rather his hands were cold, damp. The half-thought faded before galvanizing but he had begun to think of charging to assure a set conclusion.

His thoughts were racing so fast that it took Haskell a few seconds to notice the strange whistling noise. As soon as his mind cleared enough to isolate the new sound from the racket in his head, the whistle had become a whine, louder and louder and then suddenly he was lifting and then falling, a deafening roar and a mighty pressure wave all around him. C. J. landed flat on his chest as a second concussion rattled the earth, followed quickly by a third and fourth. He felt the heat and crushing power of the last two blasts but could scarcely hear anything but a persistent ringing in his ears. A long, bass groan made its way through the tinny echo, followed by a crash that shook the ground.

As suddenly as the awful, earth-shaking attack had come all was silent. Haskell rolled onto his back, staring up into the twilight sky. The arrays above hung black beneath the crimson evening. A cloud of dust, sand, and smoke hung heavy over the area and the outrider could smell an acrid mix of cordite and petroleum. The ringing went on in his skull but as he ran his hands over his face and neck he could hear the quiet shuffling of his fingers and knew his eardrums had not ruptured. He was not injured; the wind had been knocked from his chest but that was all.

Slowly, dazed, Haskell rose to his feet. He forgot his adversaries entirely and took a few stumbling steps away from the steel column where he had sheltered to look around. Through the dusty haze, now barely backlit by the sun's last rays, Haskell could see that one of the massive QV pillars had fallen. There were three distinct craters in the acre or so around it, thick trails of smoke rising above them. The photovoltaic array had been thrown clear as the column fell and lay a good hundred yards away, cracked in half on the desert floor.

Haskell stood perfectly still for a long time. He could not fathom what had just taken place. Slowly, his ears stopped ringing and he was left with the silence of the night. It was a full two minutes before he realized he was standing in the open and that there could still be a drainer alive and ready even after whatever the hell had just happened. He turned and walked the few feet back behind the pillar, and leaned against it as he dug out his cigarettes. The pack was crushed. Haskell could find only three cigarettes worth smoking. He ripped the filter of one of them and stuck the smoke between his lips, his hands suddenly beginning to tremble.

As C. J. lit the smoke, he caught a familiar sound: galloping hooves. The rhythmic pounding was growing closer. Haskell stayed leaning against the QV pillar and slid his pistol from its holster. His rifle lay only a few feet away where it had fallen when the explosions began but he thought better of going for it. The tobacco smoke was rich and fine. He was perfectly calm. He was ready to die fighting.

Haskell raised the .45 as the first rider came into view, but left his finger resting on the trigger guard, hoping against hope . . .

The horseman drew closer. The sun had set but there was still light in the sky. Haskell dropped the cigarette and, out of habit, stomped it out. Their eyes met.

"I never thought I'd be so happy to see your face."

"What's that mean, asshole?" Gregory White smiled from atop his black steed.

"Aw, don't mean shit, Greg."

White slid from atop his massive thoroughbred and walked over to C. J., clapping his comrade on the shoulder. "We heard you needed a little help out here."

"You heard? How the fuck did you 'hear'?"

"Got some help as of today, young buck. We got eyes in the skies and boots on the ground."

"Civil Defense is in the game, huh?"

"Civil's playing a whole new sport." The smile left Greg's large, square face, replaced by his customary scowl. "They've taken over. And you know what? I can't say I mind, this time. Do you know how many men that strike just took out?"

"Counted seven, maybe a couple more. I got—"

Greg interrupted, whispering "Thirty. Maybe thirty-five." He paused to let that figure sink in.

"Jesus Christ . . . you know . . . I wondered. I wondered if they were trying to take me in alive."

"Had to be. You're goddamn fortunate one of the planes picked them up. They got birds up there with cameras and heat sensors and all. And as you may have guessed, some pretty fuckin' angry rockets. It's a brand new sport. Anyway, we come to get you out. Looks like your horse ran off."

C. J. nodded slowly, half-listening to the last few words the big man had said. "Yeah . . . little while back. Hope he didn't . . . didn't get hit or . . . ." Haskell shook his head to clear it, looking over at Greg again. "Wait, whose we?"

White laughed, looking back over his shoulder. "Motley crew, your rescue team. Just me and Moses Smith and some old pony."

"Moses? He dragged his ass out of bed?"

"Yup. You shoulda seen his face when his crotch hit the saddle. Looked like he was sitting on hot coals!"

Both outriders laughed good and long. C. J. felt the tension of the evening finally leaving him. White went on: "He had to slow down because the bouncing hurt too much. I told him to ride back but he wanted to come on along; feel like part of the gang again. Me? I'm happy to sit this fight out. There's hundreds of 'em, Hasky. Hundreds. I kept trying to listen in to what the Civil D officers were saying back at the Outpost—none of it seemed good."

The two outriders went on jawboning for a time. Greg bummed a cigarette off Haskell who decided not to mention it was his next to last. After all, the man had ridden out to help him. It was a few minutes before they finally heard two sets of hooves drawing nearer. A faint glow still lit the sky but it was mere minutes from true night, so Moses Smith was less than thirty yards away before Haskell spotted him lurching about atop his horse, a little ten-hand colt in tow.

"How you feelin', Moses?" Haskell called out as his comrade came into hailing distance.

"I feel like shiiiiiiiit!" Smith bellowed back, drawing out the expletive. He was smiling nonetheless as he reined the mounts to a halt beside his buddies. "Jesus H, C. J., we could hear those goddamn explosions for miles. I can't hardly believe yer in one piece."

"Woke me up good—I'll tell you that."

Moses kicked free of his stirrups and gingerly swung one leg over the saddle then slid to the ground. He accepted Haskell's outstretched hand with a vigorous shake.

"Thanks for coming out. Both of you." C. J. looked into each man's eyes.

Greg White took a long drag off his smoke, the ember illuminating his face as he met the young man's gaze. His jaw was set tight, his nostrils flaring suddenly. He lowered the cigarette, whispering: "You boys hear anything just now?"

It started as a few loud clicks and some distant mechanical grinding. The clicking grew faster and louder and then, initially with a faraway ripple but soon a surrounding drone, the sunfield was alive. Above the three bewildered men, the arrays slowly shifted to face their photovoltaic panels west. Every night, once finished tracking usable light, the arrays flipped back to face the sunrise—now they came to a gentle stop one hundred eighty degrees opposite their standard alignment.

"OK . . . what the fuck?" Moses muttered.

"Don't know, hell with it, let's ride," Haskell hissed through his teeth. As he took a step toward the colt lashed to Smith's horse, he felt a sensation like someone was fanning his neck. Then the air inches from his nose was crackling. By the time he heard the distant reports he was already reacting to the bullets, dropping to the ground.

"Cover!" Greg shouted as he threw himself flat beside C. J. The air was alive with the racing, raging hiss of lead and the echo of shooting rumbled across the sand. *How the fuck did anything live through the bombs?* White thought.

The firing kept up for no more than fifteen seconds, but it was enough to rip Greg White's horse apart. The black steed crumpled without so much as a whinny, six fifty caliber rounds having passed clear through it.

White watched his horse fall with a breathless gasp. He scrambled toward the animal on his hands and knees but by the time he got to it, the horse was dead. The outrider didn't have long to dwell on it.

"Oh fuck! Greg, they got Moses!" Haskell called out as he lunged toward his fallen brother-in-arms. Greg rose to his feet and sprinted over and together he and Haskell dragged Smith back behind the nearest pillar.

Moses was coughing and wheezing, half his breaths coming out as a sickening gurgle. One lung had been shredded, among other body parts. In the gloom, he could barely see his comrades' eyes as he rapidly looked back and forth from C. J. to Greg's faces. He couldn't feel anything other than an immense pressure on his chest. A great weight was crushing him. One of their knees maybe or a stack of bricks. But why would there be bricks out here? It was someone on top of him or it was a great vise or something that was on his ribs and was making him so thirsty. So god-damn thirsty and his feet were so cold and his hands were cold and he was all alone and then C. J. was there again and his hands weren't cold but they wouldn't reach up to scratch the itches or to wipe the sweat off his brow and in his eyes and there were no more bricks on him but now there was pain in him Oh Lord now there was pain.

Moses was gasping ever more quickly yet ever more faintly. Haskell held his head up with both hands, trying to keep eye contact. He could feel Smith's muscles beginning to unclench; could see his eyes losing focus.

"I thought . . . I thought it . . . the clap was bad . . . boys . . ." Smith's eyes were closing. Greg had begun to rip the outrider's jacket and shirt open but he stopped, rocking back until he sat Indian-style; there was nothing to do. "I . . . I'll tell you . . ." Smith went on, "someone gives you the choice between . . . . 'tween gonorrhea and getting . . . shot . . . you boys get the VD, y'hear?"

His last breath came out as a pathetic sigh, somewhere between a gasp and a shrill laugh. Haskell pushed his eyelids closed.

The two men talked it over quickly and came to the bitter but rational conclusion that with two horses and three bodies, the dead body would have to be left behind. Greg took Moses Smith's horse and Haskell vaulted up onto the little chestnut colt. They would come back for their comrade by daylight and with numbers.

As C. J. Haskell set his spurs into the horse, he found himself thinking: *If and when I go, I sure as hell hope my last words are something a bit more noble than moaning about the clap.*

# 20

The nighttime landscape rumbled by, a saw-tooth of distant hills silhouetted against the purple sky and, closer, shadowy dunes and outcroppings. The sky was clear but moonless. Scofield could feel the crisp, fresh air of the late fall evening on the left side of his face as it blew through the open window; his right cheek and his right arm and leg were warm with the heat of the coal-fired boiler. When the two-car train had first set out, the outrider had been overwhelmed by the cacophony of grinding gears, belching steam, and the clatter of the heavy iron treads turning on their steel wheels. Now he barely noticed the din; his ears were accustomed, his mind near numb.

Only one drainer was with him in the conductor's cabin. He was a short man with wide shoulders and a vaguely ugly face smeared with grease. Nothing about him was quite in proportion—his nose was too long with nostrils too large; his hands were too big for his arms—and he stood, rocking back and forth as the locomotive dipped and swayed, always with his knees bent, never rising to his full height, diminutive though it was. Scofield figured him for fifty. A single kerosene lantern hung in the room. It danced about, painting the space with an undulating mix of shadow and flickering yellow haze.

The man had not given his name. But he was friendly enough, even trying to start a conversation or two. He would tuck his stringy gray-black hairs up into a shabby knit cap and turn to Scofield, explaining how some part or other of the engine worked, speaking in arcane detail for a minute or two before again falling silent. Scofield hadn't responded with more than a grunt each time.

He was not afraid. He was not resigned. He was not even angry. Rather Scofield found himself profoundly impatient. When the drainers had first taken him in, a few hours before, they had stripped his weapons, blindfolded him and he had been manhandled into the locomotive.

Shortly thereafter the cramped engine room grew hot, the clamor began, and soon the train was moving.

As soon as they'd been under way Scofield's blindfold had been removed and the three other men in the locomotive, including this nameless engineer, had begun to chat casually, as if he weren't even there. The outrider had tried to keep track of time as the sun approached and then dipped behind the horizon—he figured it to be around midnight now, maybe as much as a half hour either side. That meant they had been chugging along for a good six hours in a seemingly aimless series of slow turns and rapid straight-aways. Once, about two hours back, the train had stopped for a while and there had been some shouting and clatters and clanking out behind the trailing car but Scofield could not see what was happening. The other two drainers had left the compartment during the stop and not returned when the journey continued.

So now, hours into his mobile captivity, neither tired nor alert, not particularly hungry or thirsty and not even worried save in an academic way, Scofield just wanted to get on with it. Whatever it was. He dug in his vest pocket for a smoke, noting that the sweating engineer quickly looked askance at him as he reached into his garment and watched until he could see the cigarette. *He's watching me good and close,* Scofield affirmed to himself as he fished for his matches. He struck one but it blew out.

"Here, let me," the engineer said above the noise, a wry smile on his cracked lips. He held out a hand, pointing at the cigarette and then opening his palm. After a moment's hesitation, Scofield took the smoke from his lips and dropped it into the outstretched hand. The drainer turned and held the tip of the cigarette against the grate over the coal fire for a mere second, then handed it back to the outrider. Its tip glowed brightly.

Scofield nodded his thanks and looked away.

"You learn little tricks when you've been driving these old girls long enough."

"Oh yeah?" Scofield replied, not looking over. "How long you been driving this thing?"

"This one? A few years. About three. But I've . . ." the man stopped short, letting the next words die on his tongue.

"How long have you been working with trains overall?" Now the outrider looked over at the engineer, staring into his eyes. The man held his gaze for a moment, eyes dark in the lantern's glow, then he turned away.

"Long enough."

Scofield looked out the window again, his gaze drifting up to the stars. He'd get no information from the engineer, who now hunched over a series of levers and gauges. *Where'n the hell does a man learn how to drive a goddamn steam engine, anyway?* he mused. The tip of the cigarette shone brightly against the background of night, and every now and then little orange embers danced away from it, briefly mingling with the speckling of starlight above. It took the outrider a few minutes to realize that now and again patches of the sky were starless. Something else was different, too. The din of the engine room had dropped in pitch and the train seemed to be shaking less. It was slowing down. Then he could finally see a QV pillar as it passed close by and he realized the darker patches of sky were arrays overhead.

There was a small door to the right of the coal grate next to the bench where the engineer sat when he wasn't fiddling with gauges or peering out his window. The drainers who had left the engine room hours ago had used it and it had been so long now that Scofield scarcely remembered the door's existence when suddenly it swung open. A tall man wearing a long beige cloak with its hood pulled low over his face stooped to enter through the low, narrow door. The train was nearly at a stop.

"You got about ten. Coal us up and check the boiler, OK?" the tall man said barely above a whisper, leaning in close to the engineer, who nodded and then slipped through the open door after lowering a large lever set in the floor. Within seconds, the train was still, the clank and grind of gears gone. Now the only sound was the low crackle of the coal fire and an occasional puff of steam.

"You need water or anything?" the man asked quietly, turning to face Scofield. The lantern now hung still and the engine room was relatively bright. The outrider kept his left eye all but closed to preserve night vision, just in case he found himself able to make a break for it. With his right eye, he peered into the darkness beneath the beige hood. He could see eyes and a nose and a mouth but the face was too shadowed to perceive anything other than generic man features. When next he spoke his voice was louder, his tone oddly warm.

"Quite a night you've had, huh?"

Scofield said nothing. He allowed his left eye to unsquint and rose from the little bench where he had been perched these many hours. His legs were stiff and he almost stumbled; his body had become accustomed to the rocking motion. The outrider steadied himself with one hand on the window frame and leaned closer to the hooded figure.

As if anticipating Scofield's thoughts, the man raised his hands and took hold of the cloth of his hood, pausing briefly, his eyes looking out from shadow at the other's eyes staring back into the shadow, and then he cast back the cowl.

"Sebastian." Scofield spoke the name as calmly as one identifies an item in a grocery store. He held the even gaze of the man he had last seen huddled behind iron bars. "Y'know, I thought that voice was familiar."

"Yeah. Well, here I am."

"Here I am too. Tables got a bit turned, seems."

Neither man said anything for a while. They avoided each other's gazes, both looking about the cramped engine room for something to let their eyes fall upon other than eyes. In the steady light of the hanging lamp Scofield could now see the many gauges and toggles and handles that ran the train. It was like something out of a children's book come to life, right down to the acrid stench of burning coal a young boy might imagine as he dreamt of steam trains conquering the long-gone frontier. Here, in fact, was the very essence of the epoch Scofield had often wished he'd been born into, but it was a tainted dream; nearer to a nightmare.

The boiler let out a particularly loud belch of steam and both outrider and drainer balked involuntarily.

"You never get used to some things," Sebastian said quietly. Scofield looked up at his face then. He didn't remember the man being so tall— back when he was just a leech and not a drainer; back almost a week ago before everything had changed. The pattern of fine veins was still there on his forehead and by his eyes, and his face was still drawn and gaunt but in the warm light of the flickering lantern Sebastian's skin was not so pale. Not so sickly.

"Where are we going?" Scofield asked through clenched teeth.

"I can't tell you. Yet."

"That bad, huh?"

"You're not headed to the gallows, Scofield. There's no need for you to presume the worst."

"I figured that—you bastards wanted me dead, I'd be cold by now."

"So why the grave look?"

Scofield turned away, staring out through the little window into the black night. He dug in his vest pocket for his pack of smokes as he whispered, scarcely loud enough for Sebastian to hear: "My horse."

The drainer nodded solemnly, though Scofield wasn't looking, then took a step closer, saying "Don't worry about Reese. We know how much she means to you. She's safe."

Scofield spun on his heels at hearing his horse's name, hissing loudly "How do you know she's safe? You made me leave her in the middle of nowhere!"

Sebastian raised his hands in a motion of deference. "By now, she's back in the stable. Your stable. Her stable." He turned away, drawing a pocket watch from the folds of his robe.

"I'm sure of it," he said, looking down at the watch. He clicked it shut and looked up, his eyes losing focus as he thought. The watch slipped from his fingers, swaying on its silver chain. His lips were moving and he slowly cocked his head to one side, as if talking himself through some calculation. Suddenly Sebastian wheeled about and thrust his head out the window beside him.

"What's our timing?" He bellowed out into the night. Scofield could not make out the response. "We have seven minutes until a flyover!" Sebastian called back. "Can you get it rigged in that time?"

The night air was suddenly filled with a chorus of voices, men shouting over one another. A slight tremor rocked the locomotive, accompanied by a loud bang and the clatter of falling metal. Someone just outside the window by Scofield cursed and as the outrider turned to peer out into the night he heard several pairs of feet running toward the back of the train. He stuck his head out the window. In the starlight, his night vision weakened by the lantern, Scofield could barely make out the silhouettes of a dozen men hurrying to and fro, some carrying heavy loads, two dragging a long cable, another seeming to direct them.

The locomotive had come to a stop beside a QV pillar. Judging by the stars and the land and the intuition from years spent riding under the arrays, Scofield reckoned they were near the southwestern edge of the sunfield. There was a post not too far away. If he had figured the location correctly, it was one of the buildings equipped with a siren. Scofield was trying to figure the size of the window frame relative to his shoulder width when Sebastian's words brought him back into the moment.

"You read much history, Scofield?"

The outrider turned around slowly. Sebastian was looking down, studying the coarse fingernails of his right hand.

"More than some, less than others, I guess."

"Well you know what Marx said, at least, yes? About history?"

Scofield nodded. Outside, a man was yelling: "Will someone get the fucking braces!"

"Do you think we can afford much more repetition? Much more of the same all-consuming scourge we've worked ourselves into?" The drainer's eyes were afire when he raised them, fixed them on Scofield.

"*Gotta get that cable . . . locked . . . the rig will . . .!*" More shouting.

"I guess you gotta to be conscious of the past but there ain't a roadmap it painted us. Nothing's categorical. Seems you people feel that way. It's OK to fuck with people if it's working toward some end you see fit. OK to kill, even."

"You couldn't be more wrong."

"*Five minutes! Can . . . fuckin' lock it down in that time? We . . .*"

"Enlighten me."

"I'm going to. Or rather we are. She is, I should say, really."

"Who's 'she?'"

"*More hands! All of you get . . . drop this goddamn thing we're . . .!*"

"You keep asking questions you'll have answered soon. Patience. By sunrise I promise there will be many answers."

"How long has this been going on? Can you tell me that?"

"Yes, I think I can."

"*Secure that shit! Who . . . wrangle that cable . . .*"

"It's been going on for years, ever since the motives of the 'Haves' truly changed."

"Well that's fucking illuminating, Sebastian. Thanks for the clarity."

"If you hadn't been out here for so many years . . ."

" *. . .of time, boys. Flat out. We . . . .*"

" *. . .had you been paying any attention to those you served . . .*"

"*No good! We're out of time! Tarps and hoses!*"

"*We goin' dark?*"

"*Tarp it up! Soak the burner!*"

Sebastian cursed under his breath and turned away, leaning out the window again. "No way to lock it down? The last goddamn one? Eighty seven goddamn rigs and we can't do this last—"

"No time left, man. We'd never get far enough." Scofield recognized the engineer's voice as he interrupted. "We gotta douse the boiler and cover up."

Sebastian nodded, then drew back from the window. He swore again, this time aloud, checking his watch. A new sound now came from outside. It was a mix of rustling and cracking, as a loose sail makes in the breeze. Men's voices still murmured in the night but the urgent shouts of a minute before were gone. In their place, Scofield heard a low rhythmic chant: "*Pull one two three pull one two three . . .*"

Suddenly the voices were just outside and Scofield turned as a heavy cloth was dragged across the window, blotting out the stars and dampening all sound. Sebastian was lowering the flame of the kerosene lantern. Then he stepped before the fire grate, his head lowered, eyes again on the watch. The glow of the burning coal painted his face a flickering canvas of orange highlights and deep shadowed valleys. Finally, Sebastian put the pocket watch away and looked up. He took hold of a heavy iron handle and pulled it downward roughly. A sheet of steel slammed home behind the grate, sealing the engine room off from the fire and boiler.

"You may want to cover your ears," Sebastian said over his shoulder. Then he leaned out the window beside him, pushing the heavy canvas tarp out a bit.

"Burner's closed up. Go ahead and douse it." The drainer leaned back into the engine room and slid his hood halfway over his head. He glanced over at Scofield, then slid the cloth down farther until his face was lost in shadow. "Let me say it once more: cover your ears. And let's stand over here."

"What's going on?"

"Flyover in a few minutes. We're going dark and cold, as they say; we don't want any of your friends to drop in on the party. We have a quantum refraction tarp over the top of us, and now it's time to soak the engine. Last chance to move." Sebastian moved away from the sealed boiler and leaned against the instrument panel on the opposing wall. Not fully comprehending why, Scofield followed suit, loosely cupping his hands over his ears and turning his back to the boiler. Just as his palms met his head, a deafening roar filled the tiny space. In a matter of seconds the engine room was choked with steam and an angry, seething hiss filled iron chamber. Scofield crumpled to his knees, gasping and coughing in the searing heat, blinded, both ears popping as the breath was sucked from his chest.

As soon as it had come the onslaught ended. The engine room was suddenly silent but for the fading whisper of a dying fire. It was oppressively hot and humid, though. Sebastian stood back up to his full height and untied the lanyard around his neck, letting the beige robe fall to the floor. Scofield slowly rose, half-expecting another rush of heat and sound and pressure. Once a few seconds had passed and he returned to a state capable of rational assessment, he noted first that Sebastian wore beneath his robes a casual outfit of blue jeans and a white long-john shirt. Second he realized that there was no longer any noise at all coming from the train: no crackle of burning coal, no belch of steam, and no grinding of gears or clicks from the gauges.

The last thing the outrider noticed before Sebastian began speaking was that, as in the engine room, the world at large seemed totally silent.

"Well, it looks like we have some time to talk suddenly," Sebastian said as he folded his robe over one arm then sat down on the little bench beside him.

"Well by Golly, that's great news," Scofield replied just above a whisper. "I sure didn't get enough of talking to you last week."

"Jesus, was that just a week ago?" Sebastian said, casually dismissing the outrider's sarcasm. "It was, wasn't it? A week less one day, maybe."

"How's your arm healing up? Scarred yet or still scabs?"

"Don't be an asshole, Scofield. Don't try to be some tough guy asshole. It suits you wrong. Hell, if it suited you right, there's no way you'd be here. Listen, man: I know you think right now you're in a bad spot, but if you can keep yourself as objective as I know you're capable, if you can ready your mind for something new . . . you may just have a . . . let's call it a sunrise on your horizon. Something vague now, but brighter soon."

"Am I even supposed to respond to that?" Scofield snorted out a little laugh, looking down as he drew the pack of smokes from his vest. He put a cigarette between his lips and took matches from his pocket, pausing briefly before striking one, his gaze unfocused as he thought.

"So much for all that shit about doing you one last favor, huh?"

Sebastian looked askance at him, confusion on his face.

"About wanting to die so badly. Back there in the desert. You begged me to kill you. I guess you thought you were just calling a bluff."

"No, actually. I didn't think that. At all. I didn't know a thing about you then. I know now that you'd never taken a life until yesterday, but I didn't know that then."

"How—what makes you think that?" Scofield's face flushed hot as he pictured the dying Australian; as he remembered the blood spattered all about the other man. When the drainer made no reply, he shook his head, taking a long drag off the cigarette. He eased himself down onto the iron bench. It was growing colder in the engine room. The hiss of the dying fire was gone, replaced by the occasional rustle of the canvas tarp stirred by evening breeze.

"How much of what you said was true?"

"All of it."

"Bullshit."

"It was all true. I was an accountant. I have cancer and it's going to kill me. It's spreading and I'm dying. 'Metastasizing' is the word. Every day I feel new aches, find new scabs. I get migraines. I can't sleep some nights; can't keep food down some mornings."

Scofield looked away. "And yet here you are. You appear to be a man of some regard among these boys. A man of some esteem, no?"

"I've . . . I worked my way up, I guess you could say."

"Yet you were ready to toss it all."

"Instead of dying a pathetic death, yes, I think. Better to die fast. I'm fully devoted. That's why they listen—people respect devotion here. As they do in all places."

"What's here, Sebastian? Why? You've got me, dammit. Why'd you bastards hang Tripp? The fuck ain't you shot me yet? I got nothing to offer you and nothing to gain. You already got me so why don't you just fucking explain!" The outrider shouted these last words so loudly even he was surprised by his vitriol. He had half risen from the bench, but let himself slump back down onto it.

"You'll know everything soon. You can't imagine how much you have to learn." Sebastian sat and pulled out the pocket watch again. He looked down at the watch for a moment, counting the seconds under his breath. "I'm sorry about your friend. I wasn't there for that and I . . . it will be dealt with." He raised his head.

"Here it comes . . ." Sebastian whispered to himself.

The outrider had just drawn a breath to ask what "it" was when a new sound crept through the heavy tarps. Quiet at first, deep, bass and distant, the rumble grew. In a matter of seconds it was a throaty engine roar, suddenly deafening and just as quickly lower pitched and receding. Sebastian's eyes were raised, locked onto the ceiling as if he could see through it to the sky above. His mouth hung slightly open.

"Those were jets. Imaging. Now for thermal, I'm sure." The drainer looked down at Scofield and nodded, his thin lips drawing into a tight line.

Sure enough, not a half minute later another noise was audible and growing steadily. This time it was the staccato chop of rotor blades, the din reverberating off the desert floor as the unseen helicopters drew near. *Son of a bitch did his homework,* Scofield thought. The night thundered as a trio of heavy aircraft made their way down the sunfield's perimeter, lumbering along just above their safe operating height of sixteen thousand feet. It seemed like they hovered above the train for ages.

Then, slowly, the echo of the choppers began to diminish. Within minutes the night was quiet again.

"Thought they had us for a second," Sebastian said through a forced smile. Just as he began to rise, the narrow door beside him clicked open. The engineer stuck his head into the compartment, a broad grin turning up his ruddy cheeks.

"That was close, huh?"

"Far too much so, yes." Sebastian stood, stretching his legs. "I'll go see to the rig. How long until you can get us moving again?"

"Ten minutes. Maybe fifteen."

Sebastian nodded and put his robe back on, raising the hood back over his head. He stepped past the engineer and was just bending to leave when Scofield's voice stopped him.

"Not everything you said was true, Sebastian."

"No? Where did I err?"

"You said you always worked alone."

"You're right. I did say that and it was a lie." He paused, stooped to exit the chamber. Then, slowly, he turned his head to look at the outrider. His face was lost in the shadow of his cowl. "I'm sorry. I hate dishonesty and I lied."

"And you said you wanted to die. Then and there."

"I did want to die then and there. With all my heart. Now I don't."

"What changed?"

"The terms."

"You men wait here," said Mayor Dreg, his voice grave. "I think it best I enter the command center alone," he added in an explanatory tone as if anyone in the security detail had made any sort of protest. Dreg turned away from the three officers wearing matching black uniforms and squinted to get a look at his surroundings, shielding his eyes from the garish halogen glow of the pod station.

It was shortly after one a.m. and there was not another soul in sight. Dreg had not been to the Outpost—to the end of the line—in many years. The few buildings all looked as he remembered them, and the tavern, he noted, seemed to be open, its sign and windows aglow. But he had the sensation of surveying a scene he knew only from a movie or photographs. True, he had never been to the Outpost at night, but there was something more than that. It took The Mayor a while to put his finger on it.

Silence.

That was it. Or near silence, anyway—the only sounds were an occasional breeze and the electric hum of the lights above. Mayor Dreg shivered involuntarily, wrapping a fist around the lapels of his heavy gray overcoat. He stepped off the cement of the platform and balked as his loafers sank into the dusty soil. *Dreary goddamn place if I've ever seen one,* he thought, shaking his head with a rueful smile. Dreg pulled a leather case from his pocket and drew out a slender Dominican cigar while walking toward the large meeting hall some two hundred yards away.

While he knew he had several armed men watching over him, and while he knew that there were several thousand troops fanning out across the surrounding desert, Dreg was nonetheless gripped by a chilling fear as he left the pod station's pool of light. He quickened his pace. It was not that some unseen predator lurked out of sight; it wasn't that the enormity of the situation descended into his conscience. It was just so dark. So dark and quiet out here. *Ghastly fucking place.*

The Mayor meant several times to pause and light the cigar, but found his legs carrying him ever more quickly. The matchbox was in his hands but the hands and the legs were not working together. Only once within the glow of the Meeting Hall's light, which spilled out of a bank of windows and from bright bulbs above the doors, did Franklin Dreg feel his confidence and swagger return. Here, after all, was Ground Zero. Here was the very nexus of his virility; the concentrated martial might of New Las Vegas, and he the man atop it all.

Dreg lingered outside the pressboard doors. From within came the hum of many voices, machines, and motion. He nodded to himself. It was all happening. So a challenge had been made? Well, let it be answered. If he was to be provoked, let him roar. They were not thoughts that came to The Mayor, exactly; rather ideas fully formed and unshakable appeared as if always present, only waiting to be tapped.

He lit the cigar.

The Meeting Hall was awash in light. Bright rows of fluorescent tubes hung above, scores of lamps were scattered about on desks and countless monitors, screens, and a thousand little bulbs blinked red, green, and blue and every color in between. No specific sound could be singled out amid the electric hum, the whispering static, and the murmur and mumble of a hundred men's voices.

Dreg lingered in the open doorway. It took his eyes the better part of a minute to isolate details among the bustle of uniformed men, the serpentine coil of cables, the mountains of stacked equipment, and all those numberless lights. The space was positively alive, a writhing mass of machine and man. He had never seen anything quite like it. At first the sight was unsettling, so unfamiliar as to be even frightening. But as his vision adjusted to the brightness and the motion, he began to nod to himself. This was his doing. This was here by his edict. He took a few great puffs off the cigar and then ran a palm across his mustache, smoothing the coarse hairs flat.

"Who thinks they're in charge here!" Mayor Dreg bellowed, unaware that he was reciting, word for word, Boss Hutton's entrance from hours before. This time, however, the room fell silent. Scores of eyes rose from their computer screens and graphs or broke from conversations to look at Dreg, standing there with his feet wide, his chin out, and his chest puffed up beneath a heavy gray overcoat.

"Come on now, one of you must remember how to speak!" With a twinkle in his eye, The Mayor slammed the double doors shut behind him and made his way into the room. He clapped the two men sitting nearest the doorway on their backs, not bothering to glance over at what they were working on. A young fellow with high cheekbones and narrow eyes forced a smile as Franklin reached out and clutched his hand, shaking it vigorously.

Dreg sauntered about the cavernous room uttering "attaboys" and "good work" and other aphorisms, entirely unconcerned for the moment with the grave nature of the work being done. It failed to occur to The Mayor that this room was usually filled with nothing but folding chairs and a few dozen horsemen. The enormity and complexity of the operation and the threat such an apparatus's construction necessitated were outside his realm of thought. Rather here were his men in need of a good dose of encouragement.

Strayer had been talking to three of his officers in the far corner when The Mayor entered. He had immediately turned his back and lowered his face when he spotted Dreg, well before The Mayor had begun his shouting and salutations. Now he drew the three men into a closer huddle.

"Listen hard: Dreg is in command so if he gives a direct order, unfortunately we have to follow it. He has something big cooking and it's a fool's errand. When he briefed me in, I told him he was goddamn fool to his face. He has known about the drainer build-up for days now. I told him we had to attack then and there. He ordered me to stand down, wanted to take them out in 'one mighty blow' rather than attacking them before they could launch their own offensive. Now we're in it deep because of one fat man's fat ego."

The officers' faces were shocked but attentive. Strayer shifted his gaze every few seconds, engaging each of his men directly. "He's got fucking Federal troops lining up. He thinks I don't know how many or what they brought with them, but I do, to some extent. He's not the only guy who hears things around this town. Mayor Dreg's got a few thousand Federals pouring into the area, and if they want to end up dead, fine. Fuck it. But not us—we're not dying so he can run for president later. Got it? So we're not going to tell him one single bit of actionable intelligence, and we're going to stall until we know exactly what we're up against and we have our own strategy in place. Anything we tell him we're only telling to Feds who'll just want to brush us aside, understand?

"The man doesn't know a goddamn thing about combat operations and that's the way we like it. So we're going to use lots of terminology, lots of obscure details and stats and we're going to tell him nothing while we do it, got it? We're going to solve this with bullshit. Or at least delay things. Clear?" All three men nodded, understanding fully.

Strayer went on: "The man's ego is surgically attached to his asshole, so kiss it as much as you can. The more he feels inflated, the less he's going to get in the way and fuck things up. Engel, for some reason he took a shine to you a while back, so it's going to fall largely to you to keep his fat ass out of any real business."

"I can handle that," Major Engel smiled, his teeth flashing bright white in his dark face. "He loves hearing about munitions, as I recall, so talk about lots of things that flash and make loud booms." Engel looked at the other two officers, both captains, who muttered their assent back to him.

Dreg's circuit of handshakes and backslaps was drawing him ever nearer to the group. Strayer whispered his last commands.

"Mayor Dreg has no idea how many men even make up the forces we have at our disposal, and I don't want him to. If he asks any specifics, direct him to someone else, someone who's not here—make up a name if you have to. If he learns we have no effective Civil Defense reserves, he may send the Federal troops right in on top of us. If that happens, we're no longer in command. You boys want a chance for us to gain some ground . . . to gain some clout and control, well, it's here for the first time any of us have ever seen—let's not let the fucking politician score off this."

"Ah, Mr. Strayer!"

Colonel Ridley Strayer straightened up, let his face go blank, then slowly turned toward his elected commander. "Ah. Mayor Dreg."

"So how's my town doing, Captain?"

"Colonel." Strayer waited just long enough to let the pause linger awkwardly. "The town will be fine. Sir. But I have my work cut out for me. We do, rather. The sunfield is strategically sound but tactically under active encroachment with sporadic engagement. So far the insurgency has used low-tech and non-collateral divergence but without full leverage of both our rapid response and ranged force factors, we'll have a potentially—"

"English, man! Goddammit!"

Strayer threw an arm around The Mayor congenially, turning him to face the room. "Walk with me. Major Engel, you have a solid grasp of our tactical vernacular—come with me and The Boss here."

As Strayer and Engel led Dreg into the sea of monitors and maps and graphs and antennae, the two captains left behind turned to face each other.

"Non-collateral divergence?" the shorter of the two said through teeth clenched to ward off a grin.

"I guess we just need to leverage our ranged force factors until he leaves us the fuck alone," the other man said as he turned away with a wry smile. "I gotta wonder, though, if that son of a bitch is really as clueless as Colonel Strayer thinks . . . who's actually in charge here?"

C. J. Haskell had taken a half step into the Meeting Hall when he froze. His left boot hung in the air and his grip on the door knob tightened involuntarily. *What the fuck is going on here?* Slowly, not breathing, eyes not focusing, he eased back out of the room into the frigid night. After a long look around the Hall, he shut the door behind him and turned around, leaning against the concrete wall.

Haskell's hat fell to the ground as he let his head slump back against the building. He barely noticed. *Well this is the last goddamn thing I need right now.* He was not sure if he had thought or said these words. He was exhausted. He was cold and sore and hungry. *Christ I'm so wore down. I'm so damn wore down.*

The young man's hand was trembling from a mix of cold and nerves as he worked open the buttons of his duster and dug within the jacket for his pouch of tobacco. He spilled finely cut leaves all over the cement landing as he struggled to steady his fingers enough to get tobacco and paper into the rough semblance of a cigarette, eventually cobbling together a tube-shaped mess.

The smoke was warm and rich and relaxing, though, when finally he felt it flow across his tongue. C. J. had been a smoker for ony three years but one would never have guessed it from his affinity for the pastime. Unconsciously, he blew a perfect ring out into the cold, still air, followed by two slow plumes from his nostrils. The smoke drifted up toward the moonless starry night, fading into nothing, unwatched.

Haskell had killed another man a few hours before. He hoped the last ever—he hated it. He couldn't level with it. *Two in one fucking day.* Three in his short life. The first man he'd killed had at least been shooting back and that was over a year ago when things made sense. The second was during honest combat.

This one had been running. Neither for him nor away from him; he had been running toward where the half-brothers Joe and Eric Bay were dug in behind a QV pillar and Haskell didn't know if the drainer was making for them or was just running that way but he knew he wasn't any friend and he had led him a few feet with his rifle and then damn if he wasn't a good shot.

He sucked deeply on the cigarette which crackled and folded as the cherry hit a pocket that was more paper than tobacco. Haskell dropped the smoke as it burned his fingers, stomping it out angrily. The Bay brothers had told him they'd seen a group of some forty men jog past their hideout less than fifteen minutes before he made contact. It was a safe bet that someone had heard his shot and C. J. wondered now if rather than protecting his comrades he'd brought the Dark Angel down upon them.

Eric, the younger of the two, had told him to keep moving; he'd said the Bay boys were going to keep watch over a pass between the dunes where the group of drainers came from. Haskell pleaded with them to pull out; reasoned with them that the two brothers alone out there against dozens were as good as cold bodies, while alive back with the team they could fight on. One of them whispered something about someone "at the bridge." *Bullshit romance nonsense talk. Dead man's bullshit talk,* C. J. had raged to himself as left the brothers, feeling a strange mix of sorrow and impotence.

This had been near the very eastern tip of the sunfield and C. J. had been riding west, back toward the Outpost, ever since. The trip had taken him from midnight until now. He'd arrived minutes ago, unsaddled and watered the little colt he'd ridden to damn near breaking, and made a quick check in vain to see if Duncan had made it back to the stable. There was no sign of his horse. And not another man in sight, at that. Moses Smith's horse was in its pen, so that meant Greg White must have gotten back OK. The two men had split up hours before, Greg returning to the Outpost to report their comrade's death; Haskell going on to complete his initial reconnaissance assignment.

Reese, Scofield's girl, was in her stable. C. J. Haskell took great comfort in that. Somehow, knowing Scofield was close by made things seem more sensible, more tolerable. He respected and trusted that man as much as any other alive.

He'd left the stable at a sprint heading toward the Meeting Hall—its bright lights a beacon of security in the darkness—only to find it infested with these faceless, uniformed city bastards.

Haskell knelt slowly, picking up his hat from where it had fallen. He did not put it back on his head. Still crouching, numb, the young man wondered how much blood would spill this day. He wondered why the PV arrays had all shifted in the darkness those hours ago. Back when Moses had breath in him. He wondered so many things.

Haskell hadn't had the stomach to tell the Bay brothers of Moses's death—he had yet to deal with it himself. They knew about Tripp Hernandez's hanging. And they had been delivered supplemental ammunition and chow. Boss Hutton had the five most junior riders (Haskell was in fact younger than two of them but never counted among their ranks; he had been riding the fields for years longer and could outperform even most of the seasoned men) on a constant loop now, checking in on the dozen odd outriders dug in, delivering news and supplies, and acting as messengers and scouts while moving between these static positions and the horsemen on patrol routes.

Haskell tried to swallow Boss Hutton's admonitions, delivered by one of the young riders who had hailed him to a stop an hour before, that everything was stable and that the response was in full gear. *Goddamn fool,* Haskell shook his head, thinking back on how close he'd come to shooting the young outrider who had stopped him. *Shouting like a fuckin' banshee in the dark.* The youth, scarcely two years younger but a manchild nonetheless, had cut him off and then, never realizing Haskell had a pistol on him and was ready to shoot until the very second his face became visible in the starlight, had said that orders were to: "Stick to routes, engage only in defense, and to assume every stranger was a combatant."

These were the same basic orders C. J. had been given two days earlier and he knew well that it was just lip service horseshit to keep the men from panicking. But the young rider had given him one new piece of information: the Civil Defense Forces were slated to move into the field shortly after noon. What was that, seven, maybe eight more hours?

And that man in there. That huge, lumbering man—he knew it though he hadn't seen his face. It was Mayor Dreg. No doubt. The epitome of the city world, the other world, the world C. J. Haskell had rejected years before, now here and he had brought all the faceless nameless soulless black-clad rank-and-file city soldiers out to save the day, and none of them even understanding what a goddamn day was worth. None of them knowing what it was like to spend sunup to sundown away from the bullshit constructs of broken-down people abiding by transportation schedules and using the right fork for the right dish and blushing rather than speaking out or standing up and not knowing the smell and touch of horseflesh or the wonderful sting of windburned cheeks or worn out thighs and *I just thought it would go on and on I guess. I ain't so wise and old souled as I got em' all believing. You aren't. I'm not. Jesus Christ your horse is gone and here you are and there he is and all them. There you are. Here we are.*

Haskell reached into his pocket and clutched the tobacco pouch, then slowly withdrew his hand again, empty. He was entirely unaware of the action. *It doesn't mean shit in the end,* he thought. But it was not a thought. He did not mean anything by "it" or "the end" and as soon as the words had formed in his mind they were gone, not remembered, as fleeting as a distant breeze.

He felt very light, suddenly. He stretched, reaching his arms above him and rising onto his tiptoes and all in matter of seconds he was calm and collected and unconcerned with the greater, now focused on the moment. It was very clear what he needed to do. He had to go into that place—that hall he counted as a room in his home—and find out what was happening and he had to become a part of it. No specific thoughts or emotions stirred his thinking; rather he had acquired convicted. This thing that was happening, this threat that had now taken from him two friends at least, that had drawn him close enough to death that he had tasted its bile, that had taken over the very life he had chosen and cherished, it demanded of the young man action—it demanded his concerted action and he would rise to it and give all.

The first step would not be pleasant. Haskell had only seen The Mayor in person one time. As an almost-man of eighteen, he had attended a rally for Dreg's second re-election. Dreg had been over a hundred yards away and all the outrider could recall was a stripe of dark hair below his nose, a thatch of dark hair atop his head and those massive shoulders lumbering about the stage. Now he would have to see the eyes beneath that mane and hear the words coming from beneath that mustache. It was his goddamn sunfield, after all. *I'll be damned if I let these city boys run this show into the ground.*

"Hot damn I bet that gets those sonsabitches running!" Dreg bellowed, clapping Major Engel on the back.

The officer forced a smile, nodding. "Yeah, it—I mean yes, sir, the Falcon III is just about the best of our munitions. It packs nearly the equivalent of a traditional five hundred pounder into a missile we can load onto our remote craft. And it's guided by satellite to within five feet of the designated target. We have about ten drones in the air currently—maybe a dozen by now—and we'll have over fifty by the afternoon. Plus the manned fighter bombers and choppers."

"What else? Surely there must be more soldiers, tanks and trucks and . . . and the like! When can we have the boots on the ground move in?"

Engel leaned back in his chair, reaching for a cup of coffee. He took a sip and winced at the tepid swill. Looking askance across the large room he could see Colonel Strayer pacing back and forth in a corner, gesticulating wildly, phone pressed to his ear. Strayer's left hand wrapped itself into a fist which he held against clenched teeth. Major Engel desperately wanted to know what had his superior so worked up, but for now it was his duty to keep Dreg occupied.

Engel set the mug down and turned his attention back to The Mayor. "There are brigades fanning out in both directions along the axis of the sunfield as we speak. We have half-tracks and ATCs depositing squads every few miles. The plan is to have the area surrounded by twelve hundred hours, so by the time close air is fully in place in the early afternoon, troops will be able to overwhelm the interior." Engel tapped a few keys, pulling up a map of the area of operation. "It's going to take a while to get communication channels in place, though, or we'd be able to move earlier, but what with the frequency displacement in the field—" he looked over his shoulder and found Dreg paying no attention. The Mayor was punching away at his mobile. After a moment Franklin looked up.

"These bastards don't know who they messed with! Play that video back for me again!" Dreg was giddy. He had chewed the unlit cigar hanging from his mouth into a sloppy pulp. His suit jacket was draped over a folding chair against the wall of the Meeting Hall and his sleeves were rolled up past his elbows, the fabric of the cuffs straining against his ample arms. Beads of sweat rolled down The Mayor's neck and forehead, dampening his collar and pooling in his thick eyebrows, but he noticed none of it.

Major Engel stifled a sigh and typed away at his console. The monitor was a blur of rushing frames as he located the footage Dreg wanted to watch for the third time. Engel found the proper starting point and pressed one more button, leaning back as Franklin stepped closer to the screen. Initially the image was a hazy patchwork of blues and grays, then the camera zoomed in and refocused. On the left of the screen there was a single dot pulsating orange-yellow; to the far right were a dozen larger splotches of the same color.

"So that's our boy . . ." Dreg muttered to himself.

"Yes, that's an outrider there," Engel pointed to the smaller blotch of color, "and these larger areas of heat signatures are each four or five men. There were thirty to forty of them."

Occasional blooms of bright white popped up from the larger clusters of color. Gunfire. The scene was rotating in a slow counterclockwise pattern as the remote vehicle circled above the men.

"OK . . . here it comes . . ." Engel whispered as he watched the numbers roll on the bottom left of the monitor.

Suddenly the entire screen was white.

"Bam!" The Mayor shouted so loudly that a handful of the Civil Defense soldiers near him jumped in their seats. Slowly, the blue and gray hues slipped back onto the monitor, but now there were three bright orange circles undulating in the middle of the scene, and the larger patches of color were broken up and strewn about.

"Those are the bodies of the drainers," Engel said after a long pause. "They'll be showing up as cold blue outlines soon enough."

"And there's our man," Franklin nodded proudly as the orange dot on the left of the screen slowly began to move.

"That's me."

Mayor Dreg wheeled about in surprise. He came face to face with a young man wearing a soiled gray shirt and dusty blue jeans. He held a white Stetson in his hand and a pistol hung from a bandolier around his waist.

"What's that you say?"

"That was me you were pointing to." C. J. looked away from The Mayor and shook his head incredulously, eyes on the monitor.

"Are you Mr. Haskell?" Major Engel asked, rising from his chair.

"Yeah. Call me C. J."

"A pleasure, young man!" Dreg rumbled, reaching out and taking the tired outrider's hand in both of his fleshy palms. "Glad you got out of that one, hm?"

"Yeah. I uh . . ." Haskell withdrew his hand from The Mayor's persistent grasp and let his eyes drift around the room. "I didn't . . . know if . . ." his mind flashed back to the moments before the air strike, to his thoughts as he readied his mind for death. He closed his mouth, letting the sentence hang unfinished.

"It's a goddamn lucky thing your friend Smith told us where you'd be riding," Engel said gravely.

"Moses?"

"Yeah. He was helping me chart you and your boys' patrol paths. Until he went out to grab you with that big piece of work. Greg White, if I recall. How'd the rest of the night wind up? I heard White came back in alone."

Haskell nodded, closing his eyes and pressing a thumb and forefinger against their lids.

"Sorry to hear that." Engel placed a hand on C. J.'s shoulder, then turned and sat back down.

Dreg assumed a solemn look as Haskell opened his eyes again. "Never easy to lose a comrade."

*The fuck would you know about it?* C. J. raised his face and met The Mayor's gaze, his eyes saying what his mouth had not.

"So listen, my man," The Mayor persisted, disregarding the anguish and bitterness etched across the outrider's face. "We need to talk to that Boss of yours. So far he hasn't reported in—as long as I've been here overseeing things, anyway—and I've been waiting for a rider to show up and help me find him. Any idea where he would be?"

Haskell glanced about the meeting hall again. The scores of men, the computers and antennas, the blinking lights and cables and all of it were gut-wrenching to take in. This was nothing like the Hall he knew. The life he knew. And while C. J. understood that the Civil Defense men and the outriders and even this goddamn blowhard Mayor were all in it together, he just couldn't bring himself to cooperate until he'd been given the go-ahead right from Hutton's mouth.

"He's probably at his shack. If not there, out patrolling in that old jeep of his. My place ain't but a few houses from his and I need to head there now anyway and get some fresh clothes and chow. I'll send him straight your way if he's home."

"Do that, OK Haskell? Immediately," Engel said over his shoulder, looking back a second after he spoke to make sure the outrider had heard him.

"Sure. Yeah. Be back real soon."

C. J. took a step backward, then turned to walk away. "How about we send some men to escort you? For safety?" Engel asked.

"This is my home. I don't need a fuckin' escort." Haskell strode away from the two men quickly, not looking back as he stepped over piles of cable and dodged tables, gear, and soldiers.

He stepped out into the cool air of the early morning. It was only a couple hours from dawn now. A few hours from the full scale assault. C. J. paused about fifty yards from the meeting hall, lingering in darkness until he was sure no one was following him. Then he turned away from his hut and began hurrying west across the Outpost. The lights were still on at Matteson's Place.

# 21

If the clock on the wall could be trusted, it was shortly after 7 a.m. The windows seemed to be a paler shade of gray, suggesting morning, but Scofield could scarcely trust the clock in a room with window panes painted over from the outside. Nor could he trust the people who had painted them. He sat upright on a queen sized bed, his bare feet flat on the thin carpet. The outrider had hung his long jacket and vest in the closet, removed his boots, washed and hung his socks and undershirt, and sorted through the provisions he'd found piled by the door. They were his foodstuffs—the same canned tuna, jerky, freeze-dried fruit, and wheat cakes he had loaded into Reese's saddlebags a few short days ago. The same packs of cigarettes and pouch of shake leaf and papers. His canteen was there too. He had filled it from one of the half dozen liter-seized water bottles he'd found resting atop a sink that didn't work.

*Where the fuck and what the fuck?* Scofield wondered to himself for the hundredth time in two hours. Somehow he had dozed off after the train got back underway during the small hours of the night. He awoke to a tightening blindfold and someone locking cuffs on his wrists as Sebastian's voice told him to stay calm. Hands had guided him down from the locomotive to where his boots hit sand. A few steps later he was led onto a wooden platform and then a carpet and then Sebastian had said he should clean up, eat up, and sleep. The cuffs were removed and a door slammed and when Scofield peeled off his blindfold he found himself in this goddamn motel room.

There was a floral print comforter over white linen sheets. The sink was in a little hall that led to the bathroom. The carpet was a wretched shade of rose and the drapes were olive. The lights and fan worked but the tap and shower were dry. Shocked, numb, and exhausted, the outrider had dumped a few bottles of water over himself and scrubbed at his aching body with a little bar of soap, then slept naked on top of the sheets. He had no idea how long he'd been out.

Scofield had awoken with a start and gotten his bearings as best he could. Now that he was dressed and alert and the few possessions the drainers had left him were corralled neatly, there was nothing to do but wait. Twice in the course of an hour he had stood, meaning to grab a cigarette and put his boots on, but both times he found himself standing stock still, then slowly easing back down onto the bed.

His eyes drifted around the room yet again, searching for some ceiling vent or grate in the wall. The door was bolted shut and he could see the outline of bars against the windows. Scofield had considered shattering the glass anyway using the little fridge tucked under the sink or one of the chairs or end tables, but figured there had to be a drainer closer by than any honest citizen. And where the hell was he, anyway, that still had little clapboard motels like this? Barstow? *How far did these fuckers take me?*

Finally he rose again, determined this time to have a smoke. But without any conscious change in intent, Scofield found himself instead pulling on his socks and removing his button-down shirt to work the slightly damp cotton T back over his torso. He put his shirt on again, then his vest.

Next Scofield pulled one of the pillow cases off its lumpy polyester charge and filled it with his food and two liters of water. He took a piss, then removed his duster from the closet, draping the jacket over the bed. When he eased himself into one of the wooden chairs set beside the window, the clock read 7:23. Scofield rolled himself a cigarette with surgical care.

He lit the cigarette and watched the blue-gray smoke rise through the still air in an unbroken column. The smoke reached the ceiling and curled about the mottled plaster. Scofield felt trapped enough spending nights in his own little shack, usually opting to sleep outside next to his horse. If he didn't stay calm right now, he could potentially put himself in a very dangerous place; he needed his wits about him. Scofield had fled from his east coast roots not so much to escape the broken home, but to escape the omnipresent walls: the houses and buildings and hedges and winding streets and figure-eight highways and strip malls and millions of goddamn people packed into every square foot from Maine to Miami.

A few seconds before the minute hand clicked onto half past, there came from outside a rumble like distant thunder. The ground trembled. *Quake?* Scofield grabbed his boots and pulled them on quickly as he realized what the rumbling was. Suddenly there were footsteps on the wooden planks by the door and then the lock clicked open.

The train was drawing nearer. Now the outrider could hear its stack bellowing great plumes of steam. He could hear the clatter of gears and the grating of iron treads. Then slowly the mechanical din wound down. There were fewer and fewer creaks and whines and clicks. Within a minute, the only sound from the street was the smokestack, huffing rhythmically like some giant's breath.

Scofield waited for what felt like a lifetime, then, convinced that they were waiting for his move, he gathered up the sack of provisions, donned his Stetson, and wrapped a fist around the doorknob.

Crisp morning sunlight streamed into the dimly lit motel room, blinding the outrider. He squinted and held up a hand to block the brilliant sun, working its way up into a cerulean sky. He could see the hulking black locomotive out in the street and could discern the outlines of buildings lining the dusty lane, but it took more than a minute for Scofield's eyes to adjust enough to perceive that there was a man standing just to his right.

With a slight gasp, Scofield spun to face the man. He was squat, barely over five-foot-three, with a round belly pressing out the buttons of a dusty tweed jacket. His brown eyes were smiling above ruddy cheeks covered with a two-day beard.

"All aboard!" the man said with a twinkle in his eye.

"Where are—wait a second . . ." Scofield leaned in to look more closely at the man's face. The drainer held his gaze. "Holy shit . . . Flint? David Flint?"

"Hey, Scofield. Howya been?"

"Well not too good as of late, Dave. What the fuck are you doing here? I thought you moved back east six years ago."

Flint nodded slowly, looking away. He ran a hand through his thinning brown hair. "Yeah . . . I didn't end up moving all that far east, though. Hey, how's Hutton doing? He OK? And what about ol' Ryan . . . what's it . . . Cannell! How's ol' Ry?"

Scofield's jaw clenched. He whispered through his teeth. "We were all doin' just great until your kind came along. So what happened, huh? Money? Some kind of . . . prestige?"

"Don't disparage, Scofield—you don't know—"

"I'm not takin' any words from a fucking turncoat!" Scofield shouted, advancing a step toward his former comrade, rage clouding his thoughts.

"Probably a good idea to stop there!" a new voice called out. Scofield looked over to find its source. A towering man with impossibly wide shoulders and a face cut from granite was walking toward him, a large revolver held down by his right thigh.

The large man stopped a few feet away and cast his beige robe back over his shoulders, revealing a gray jumpsuit covered with pockets and crisscrossed by a bandolier.

"That's Russ," David Flint said. "He's a great guy to know unless he doesn't like you. Listen, Scof, I get where you're coming from right now. Keep an open mind and by lunchtime today maybe you'll see where I'm coming from."

"We all calm? We all relaxed?" Russell Ascher looked from man to man, then nodded and turned away. "OK, bring him on down!" he shouted back toward the locomotive.

The engine room door swung open with a clang and a robed drainer made his way down the little ladder. He was followed a second later by a man wearing scuffed black loafers, blue jeans, and a ribbed sweater. His sandy hair was close cropped. As the drainer escorted the man toward the motel, his head hung before him, bobbing about limply in either exhaustion or utter dejection. Or both.

He didn't look up once until he reached the motel deck. Only then did Scofield recognize the man from Mayor Dreg's office. Timothy Hale in turn recognized the outrider.

"You . . . you too, huh?"

"They ran me down with that sonofabitch," Scofield pointed to the train.

"Grabbed me in my bathrobe."

David Flint cleared his throat. "Boys, I hate to interrupt, but Mr. Hale, why don't you head on into the room here and rest up. Scofield, please follow Russell."

"Enjoy the next few minutes," Timothy called from the doorway of the motel room. Scofield looked back, squinting as he made his way across the dusty street. "You can't un-see things, you know?"

C. J. Haskell awoke with a start. He wiped sleep from his eyes and drool from his chin and looked about the bar. Matteson was behind the counter, his back turned and the phone pressed to one ear. Wilton Kretch sat in the far corner, shoveling food into his mouth. A few other outriders dozed draped across tables or lolling in chairs. Greg White was snoring away on the floor of the far wall, sounding for all intents and purposes like a slumbering walrus. Haskell was glad to see Greg White safe, at least, but Boss Hutton was gone.

The Boss had been asleep, head down atop folded arms, when C. J. had arrived a few hours earlier. Matteson had advised the young man to let

Hutton sleep; said The Boss was near delirious after more than two days spent awake and on the move. C. J. had agreed and lowered himself into the chair he now rose from, stiffly, his neck and back aching. He made his way across the room slowly, trying to mute the heavy thud of his boot heels to let the sleeping men rest.

Matteson glanced over his shoulder as Haskell eased himself onto the stool. The bartender hung up the phone without a word of farewell and turned around.

"What time did he leave?"

"About a half hour back." Matteson replied.

"Dammit," C. J. swore under his breath.

"I would've woken you, but The Boss said to let any of his men who could sleep stay that way. Sounds like you fellahs are gonna have a hell of a day."

"That's how it's looking. Fuck, that's how it's been. You've been around, what's your gut? What are we really up against?"

"Not sure why you'd ask me—I'm just a humble bartender, Haskell. I serve drinks in here and you serve . . . you serve out there."

C. J. let out a short laugh. "May be a bad time for a drink, good as it sounds. You got anything to eat?" Haskell asked, tilting his head toward Kretch, who was still slopping away. "Maybe some eggs?"

"No eggs, sorry. Just got oatmeal and toast. Maybe some oranges, too."

"A bowl of oatmeal and some fruit would do me right. Thanks."

Matteson nodded and walked into the back room. C. J. heard a lighter flick and spun around on his stool. Wilton blew a thick plume of smoke into the room and looked up at his comrade.

"What was last night like for you, young buck?"

"Not much fun. You been over to the Meeting Hall lately?"

"Sure. Damn thing ain't our Hall no more. This here's our place now. That's official, too, Boss said. You come in from a ride, come to Matteson's Place."

"What else did he say? What's the news?" Haskell rose and walked over to Wilton's table, pulling back a chair to sit. Kretch smoked in silence for a moment, thinking back over the past hours and days. C. J. watched him while waiting for a response. Wilton had a few globs of oatmeal stuck in his scruffy beard. They bounced beside his lips as he spoke.

"I ain't heard nothing new today yet. Been out of the loop some since yesterday evening. My horse needed some work." Kretch avoided the young man's eyes as he said this—Shady had needed medical attention from his violent spurring and from being ridden to absolute exhaustion.

"Hut had a message he wanted spread to the boys. I'm not sure what it was but we're gonna learn soon, I think. I was asleep when he come in."

"It was about the horns," Matteson said as he approached the table with a steaming bowl of oatmeal and two oranges. He set the food down before C. J., who nodded his thanks, and continued. "The Boss wanted me to tell all you boys that he's going to be sounding the sirens early afternoon. Maybe about one. That's the sign for the Civil Defense Forces to move in and for you boys to start a fulltime circuit around the perimeter. You boys stay out of the field after the horns, got it?"

"So we're fuckin' clean-up duty, huh? Let the army men handle this—you kiddos sit back and watch for runaways?"

"Not my fight, Kretch. I'm just telling you like I said I would to Hutton."

"Appreciate it, Matt," Haskell muttered through a mouthful of food.

Matteson walked away with a sidelong glance at Wilton. Both men saw it.

"Who's he think he is, talking to me like that?" Kretch snarled, loud enough that the bartender likely heard it.

Haskell looked up. He swallowed the oatmeal he was chewing and set down his spoon. "Who the fuck do you think *you* are, Kretch? Huh? That man's been taking care of us fellahs for years. He gives you a piece of info and you go spouting off? Tells you something The Boss asked him to say and you shit on him? Who the fuck are you? You want to ride into the field in a few hours and get ripped apart by a machine gun? Have you forgotten what happened on that dune not two days back? If some Civil Defense motherfucker wants to cruise in there and fight the fight for us, I'm goddamn thrilled. Don't you go running your mouth at Matteson, Wil. Grab your rifle and charge on in, if you're so fuckin' desperate to show you got a pair."

C. J. looked away and grabbed one of the oranges, ripping a great piece of the rind off with his teeth. He spit the peel out onto the table and began working the rest of it off the fruit.

Kretch was searching for the right comeback. He was taken off guard by the young man's words, and found himself stammering. *Maybe the little shit's right . . . Matty deserves better, I guess.* Wilton almost found himself expressing contrition. Then he slowly raised his eyes; saw a dribble of juice running down Haskell's chin from the orange slice he was eating. For some reason, those little orange droplets set him off. Kretch slammed both palms flat on the table and leaned forward.

"Listen real good, kid: you think I'm gonna—"

"Aw, fuckin' save it." Haskell rose suddenly, grabbing the bowl of oatmeal, and returning to the bar. "By the way, you got some shit stuck by your lip." C. J. sat without looking back. Kretch was silent, fuming.

Matteson winked at C. J., setting a glass of water down in front of the outrider. "Got some coffee brewing too, if you want a cup."

"That'd be good. What time you got?"

"About eight. Few minutes before."

Haskell nodded as Matteson turned away to tend to the coffee pot. "Hey, Matt, you seen Scofield recently? His horse is in her pen but I ain't seen him around at all."

Matteson's shoulders seemed to tense as he continued preparing the coffee, flipping off the machine and pulling the pot from its hotplate. He filled two mugs and then turned, placing one before Haskell.

"I haven't seen him in a good while. But I'm sure he's OK. He's Scofield, y'know?"

# 22

The sergeant lowered his field glasses with a sigh, looking up at his CO. "Anything?"

"Sand, sir. Miles of fucking sand. And these huge pillar things and there are some mountains over there . . . and more that way. Sand."

The captain smiled bitterly. It was shortly after eight hundred hours and his brigade was holding fast about three miles south of the sunfield's eastern tip. They were slated to move in at thirteen hundred. But for what? There had been no sign of another human all morning, save two outriders who stopped by his jury-rigged headquarters at dawn.

"We'll just keep looking, Sarge. Just keep watch." The captain turned away from the sunfield and raised his voice, calling out to a group of soldiers milling about several paces away. "And you men! You're Federal Army soldiers! Get your helmets back on and your gear strapped tight! We didn't get dressed up for fun, boys!"

He lowered his voice again and, speaking almost to himself, added: "There's going to be blood today." The captain took in a slow breath, then walked toward the shade under a tarp attached to the side of a troop carrier. He was using the makeshift shelter as his command center. *There's definitely going to be blood out here today.* He ducked under the black plastic tenting and took a seat in one of the three folding chairs set around a pressboard table covered in maps and charts, all weighed down by rocks, a compass, and his sidearm.

The captain unfastened the straps on his helmet and pulled it off. The tarp fluttered above his head in the morning breeze. He leaned forward in his seat, which pitched down a few inches into the loose sand, to study the paperwork in front of him for the fifth time. He had not relied on paper maps or printed photos or anything of the sort since his basic training days, some two decades ago. But Civil Defense chief Colonel Strayer had marked these coordinates as the absolute closest any power could be used, so once the brigade had arrived at its assigned location, they had "gone back to Civil War days," as one private had put it.

There were dozens of trucks, tanks, and half-tracks parked a mile south of this position. The men had carried all their gear, ammunition, and chow to this forward operating post, leaving behind a skeleton crew to man the artillery and communications equipment. All word was to be relayed by runners and flares; all supplies would be moving on men's backs. Which meant a very long, slow supply chain once the soldiers moved into the field.

If the intelligence was to be believed—which was dubious based on the total lack of activity visible within the field—as many as one hundred drainers had moved into his area of operation during the small hours of the morning. It would have taken that many men to tend to all the fresh rigs set up, *but they must have moved on through . . . if they were here at all* the captain thought, brooding over the data in front of him.

The captain raised his pale blue eyes from the table and looked out across the desert again, wondering which piece of the equation was off. Surely there was a miscalculation: there was no way four different heat-sensing drones and several manned observation flights had been wrong about that many men on the move. And the outriders who had stopped by that morning—brothers, they had said, though they looked nothing alike and were separated by no fewer than ten years—spoke of opening fire on scores of drainers.

*Be nice if I had a fucking radio to use out here.* The captain leaned back again, scratching at his clean-shaven face and then placing his helmet back over his buzz-cut gray hair. He had been a military man for all of his adult life. He'd seen action in Egypt, Colombia, and the Arabian Peninsula. He had taught a lecture series on Light Mechanized Infantry Assault at the War College. What the fuck did all of it help now? As far as he could tell, they were up against an army of ghosts in the barren middle of nowhere.

A commotion outside brought the officer back to the present and he rose, grabbing his pistol off the command center table and holstering it. A runner had just arrived.

The corporal was out of breath and drenched in sweat despite the morning chill. He leaned over, hands on his knees, chest rising and falling rapidly.

"Jesus, Captain . . . I . . . man, I didn't train with Mobile Artillery for . . . eighteen months to . . . fuckin' sprint around the desert."

"A bit of exercise never hurts, son." The captain clapped the young trooper on the shoulder. White salt stains lined his black fatigues where he had sweat clean through the fabric. "What do you have for me?"

"It's from the Civil Defense unit north of us. They sent a piece of paper, sir." The corporal rose to his full height and pulled off his helmet. The captain opened his mouth to tell the man to put it back on but let the notion go. "A goddamn handwritten piece of paper. What year is this, huh? Here."

The captain accepted a crumpled note from the soldier and turned to walk back to his headquarters. "Follow me, corporal," he called over his shoulder.

The captain sat, beckoning for the non-com to do the same. He unfolded the paper and scanned it, then placed it in a breast pocket. "What did you see?"

"Nothing, sir."

"Can you be more specific?"

"Yes, sir. Of course, sir. I jogged all the way to CDF squad nine-oh-eight—they're about three clicks, maybe four north, almost in the field—to get the report you asked for. They're dug in pretty well; sand bags and all and they have their fifty cals locked and loaded. But they haven't seen a goddamn person, sir. No sounds, so sightings . . . nothing. The lieutenant there handed me the paper I gave you. He said it came from Civil Defense command by way of one of the horsemen."

The captain took a sip of cold coffee from the mug he'd filled hours before. "That's it?"

"Yes, sir. There were some tracks, though."

"Go on."

"Some wide tracks. Like a tank would make, almost. But . . . y'know, there couldn't be a tank." The corporal shifted in his seat and wiped sweat from his brow. "Right?"

"Right. No, there certainly could not be." He pulled the folded report from his pocket again, whispering to himself: "And I certainly wonder why we're being ordered to move in earlier." Then he continued in a louder voice, "Listen, I need you to spread word to all the men—get a few privates to run the lines if you need. We're going to advance at approximately eleven hundred hours. They're going to sound horns—like a klaxon or siren, I guess. When that goes, we go. Tell the troops and then report back to me."

"Yes, sir." The corporal rose with a groan, still exhausted from his run.

"And son, put your helmet back on. We're at war here, you know."

The train lumbered to a stop; its third of the morning. Scofield sat still, watching as ancient Candice Wilbee worked her way to her feet. The elderly drainer had spoken fewer than twenty words to the outrider since introducing herself earlier that morning. There were three other men in the cabin, which consisted of a row of benches along each wall and various bins and shelves against the back side of the long car. The windows were covered by sheets of iron and only a few kerosene lanterns flickered above. They swung beneath short chains, casting a dim pall about the space. The scent of the burning fuel permeated the air.

"This . . . this stop will be a bit different than the earlier ones, I'm afraid, Mr. Scofield," Wilbee rasped, her voice low. She coughed and shook her head. "Someone bring my damn IV tower down." With that the old woman shuffled toward the door set near the front of the cabin. Hiking up her crimson skirt and muttering about getting old under her breath.

Scofield remained sitting for a minute longer, wondering what he'd see when he stepped outside. The first place the drainers had taken him that morning was a ghost town. Empty houses—hundreds of them—and old gas stations and a strip mall full of windowless stores and fading signs; a half-burned church and an elementary school with the roof collapsed and the flagpole toppled.

The second stop of the morning was nothing but acres of flatland. But it had not always been flat: Wilbee showed the outrider the foundations of dozens of homes, businesses, and what was once a public pool. A town hall. A bank run by three generations of the same family. All bulldozed flat. The roads had been broken apart and trucked away. One could have walked to within a hundred yards of the outskirts of the ruined town and never known it had stood there for over a hundred years.

Finally Scofield stood, an unlit cigarette hanging from his lips. He pulled on his hat and walked toward the two drainers who had not followed Candice. Their conversation dropped off as he passed. Scofield hopped down from the train and let his eyes adjust to the bright sunlight. Wilbee was inserting an IV needle into a port in her left forearm. The IV tower was in the hand of a young man wearing sunglasses and the distinct beige robe of his cohort.

There was nothing to see but rolling hills dotted by low scrub and Joshua trees. Scofield knew immediately, then, that whatever they were here to behold was on the other side of the train. As if on cue, Wilbee began to walk toward the front of the locomotive. Scofield followed, taking small measured to steps as he trailed the elderly woman. A pocket of warm, dense air drifted down from the engine as it groaned and huffed. The back of the outrider's neck grew damp—steam or sweat, he wasn't sure.

Then they were rounding the savage black scoop and then he could see it all. In the valley below lay a broken city. Hundreds of buildings, some dozens of stories high. A massive parking garage with sagging concrete beams and endless feet of rebar hanging twisted in the breeze like bones revealed by rotted flesh. Rusting cars and broken train tracks. Overpasses fallen down onto roads grown thick with weeds.

"Where the hell are we?" Scofield whispered.

"Only about thirty minutes from downtown Vegas, actually. Maybe a bit more on horseback." She smiled ruefully. "Never heard of Barrisford, have you?"

"No."

"Then they've done well. Your people. Those people who run that place you protect. You see that big building there? The one that used to be all covered in gleaming white paint?" Wilbee pointed a gnarled finger. "That, my friend, is a hospital. Or it was. Still has plenty of its occupants, too. Mayor Dreg simply cut off the power one day. That meant no more water, too, of course, when the pumps all died. No power, no water . . . no warning. No pity. Nothing. Barrisford refused to incorporate itself into the New Las Vegas federation, see, so after some failed backroom dealings, Dreg just . . . killed the city. Killed thousands of its occupants. Not just those left hooked up to respirators and dialysis machines, mind you."

Wilbee turned to face Scofield, staring up directly into the outrider's eyes. Her glare was hard and even frightening despite wrinkles that pointed to a life of smiles. "It was worse than that. A lot of the residents had already left, enticed by incentives. Cash, property, so on. The rest got the message when the Civil Defense Forces moved in and started evictions. Started torching houses and apartment buildings. The prison? They left that alone. Many, many men had life sentences changed to death. Slow death. This all happened in about a week, Mr. Scofield. And it happened to a lot more places than here at Barrisford. Have you ever heard of Monroe? Grayson City?"

"No," Scofield answered quietly.

"Of course not. Make no mistake, sir. This is not limited to this desert here. This type of 'consolidation,'—as the bastards like to call it—is happening in Ohio and Montana, across the Gulf states, and beyond. It is coordinated. It is the future as preordained by the few. The mighty few. To this," Wilbee swept a hand across the vista of a shattered land, "We say 'no.'"

The old woman lowered her arm and whispered something to the young drainer beside her. The young man raised Wilbee's IV tower and the pair walked away from the outrider who stood still, staring ahead with his face a blank mask. His eyes drifted from the hospital with its peeling paint and shattered windows to a block of buildings that once held offices or apartments. A half dozen roads led out of the city, each simply disappearing a few hundred yards into the desert.

When finally Scofield moved again, pulling off his hat to run a hand through his hair, Candice called out to him.

"Come over here, Scofield."

Scofield fished a lighter out of his pocket to light the cigarette still hanging from his mouth. His hand trembled as he held the flame to the cigarette's tip. Then the outrider turned and walked the thirty-odd paces to where the drainers stood. "Just a couple more stops to make, then you'll be free to go."

"What?"

Wilbee nodded. "We're going to release you. What you do with the freedom is up to you. But again, a few more things to see first. Take a look down at your feet."

Scofield looked down. Sand and rocks and dried out grasses—there was nothing remarkable at all to see. He raised his head again, a quizzical look on his face.

"Now take a look just a few feet over there. See how there's nothing growing there? Not even dead grass? This soil was turned a few years back. I know how Dreg likes to present himself. This, however, is how he conducts himself.

"You're standing on the grave of over five thousand people."

# 23

Beneath the feet of other men, Russell Ascher was very much alive and moving fast. His wide shoulders scraped the sides of the tunnel, sending dust billowing behind him in the pools of greenish light cast by chemical lanterns hung along the ceiling. Dozens of feet overhead, three regiments of Federal soldiers were advancing into the center of the sunfield, ready to begin their sweep when the sirens sounded.

*Why the fuck did they move up the schedule!* Ascher raged to himself as he tried to keep up the pace. He had to get to the capacitor bank, still nearly two miles away, before the klaxons sounded and the assault began. It was his duty to connect the wiring of the capacitors to the flux compression generator and then get that massive assembly—a hulking network of wires, pipes, and convection plates that all together was larger than a city bus—tapped to a QV pillar. That would require not only the sprint still ahead of him, not only the frenzied work to ready the equipment, but also climbing up a hundred foot ladder while carrying a massive coil of wire.

There had been no one else to do the job. Russell had both the technical knowledge and the sheer brawn to accomplish the task; now if only he were a better goddamn runner. His lungs ached but he pressed ahead unflagging, a lone man lumbering along in a dark, narrow tunnel.

Greg White rode west at a full gallop. It was mid-morning and the sun was still at his back. A quarter mile ahead he could see C. J. Haskell breaking off to head south, down into the field. Behind him he knew a dozen-odd outriders were doing the same. A few hundred yards more and Greg wheeled his horse, the late Moses Smith's bay, to the left and charged toward the towering QV pillars.

Haskell reached the field and slowed his mount—a hardly-broken colt he'd pulled from the pen—to a trot. He pulled his rifle from the saddle holster and ratcheted back the bolt, chambering a round. "Slow down, boy," he called as the colt pulled at its bit, nervously tossing his mane and speeding up without a command.

"Calm down, goddammit—horse! Christ, I don't even know your name."

Wilbee turned to walk back to the train. She stopped when Scofield asked: "How long ago was this knocked down?"

"This field? About a decade. Stopped working years before that but I guess Dreg thought maybe someone could come along and reinstate it. There's been nothing connected to it for ... long as I can recall, anyway."

Again the old woman turned and walked away, leaving little puffs of dust where her heels dragged across the ground. Scofield scanned the expanse of toppled QV pillars and shattered arrays. The sunfield had likely stood about two miles long by a quarter of that deep. Maybe a bit less. It would have been enough to run a few small towns or many hundreds of acres of farmland. The outrider had not known there was another sunfield within four hundred miles. Everything within that radius was entirely dependent on New Las Vegas. *Makes a bit more sense,* he fumed as he pressed his eyes closed tightly. Scofield was unmoving for a long time, feeling the cool breeze on his cheeks; hearing it drift across the land and whistle gently as it blew among the shattered arrays and columns.

Then there were feet crunching on the sand behind him, approaching more quickly than the elderly Wilbee could muster. Scofield recognized the voice, and turned, opening his eyes.

"I just wanted to shake your hand, if you're willing," Sebastian said earnestly, stopping a few feet from the outrider. "Then we're taking you back to your outpost. You'll be dropped within a few miles from it."

"Think I should trust that?"

"I won't deign to think for you, Scofield. Will you shake my hand?" He stepped closer and tossed his robe behind his shoulders, extending his right hand.

The outrider was still for a minute, then, slowly, he reached out and clasped the drainer's hand.

"Don't take that as anything more'n it is, get me? Ain't like we're friends now. I ain't on your team. I just ..."

"No need to explain." Sebastian released the outrider's hand. "You decide for yourself if it's the devil you know or the devil you don't."

Timothy Hale sat in the corner of the motel room sulking. He was leaning back in a chair, his eyes on the water-stained ceiling. The toilet flushed and David Flint walked out of the commode, stopping at the sink to wash his hands.

"Again, sorry to impose, Tim. Next nearest head is all the way at the Town Hall." The drainer poured a bottle of water over his hands, then scrubbed at them with soap.

"The toilet works but not the sink?"

"Yup. This toilet and only two others in town. There's a cistern on the roof. You get used to it."

Flint dried his hands and walked toward the door, stopping to lean against the wall. "You sure you don't want a book or something? You're going to be waiting around here for a loooong time."

"Don't you worry about me, Flint. If I were you, I'd be counting my own time as precious." A bright smile lifted Flint's reddish cheeks. He shook his head, looking down as Hale went on. "So you were an outrider, huh? Then I guess you know something about the resources the city has on hand."

"I know lots. Which helped out in planning, believe me. You still sound so righteous, man. I don't know how you maintain the delusion."

"Delusion!" Hale let the front legs of the chair slam down onto the thin carpet. He leaned forward, hands clasped and elbows resting on his knees. "Is a gunship delusion? Are regiments of soldiers delusion? The Defense Forces may be run by a bunch of assholes but they're goddamn good. I've seen the plans for an assault of the field, Mr. Flint—it's a strategic Royal Flush. That sonofabitch Strayer will drive his men until every one of you bastards is killed or rotting in jail."

"Yeah, well . . ." Flint pulled back a jacket sleeve to check his wristwatch. "That may be a bit hard for him to do now that he's dead."

Hale's face went ashen, his throat dry. "Strayer's dead?"

"By now . . . yes." Flint looked up again.

"We . . . it doesn't matter . . . he's one man . . ."

"Just a second ago you seemed to think he was *the* one man. Delusion, Tim. I'll go find you some books and magazines."

The capacitor bank, built into plates along the dirt floor, was locked and ready; all its wires were threaded together and attached to the massive copper spool. The spool, fifteen feet high and more than half that around, perched between two large cones of steel mesh, each a dozen feet long. Russell Ascher was literally jumping from place to place, connecting lines and tightening bolts.

*So many goddamn cables! I need ten hands!* Then, aloud, he swore to himself, "There's not enough fucking time!" Under his breath, again he cursed whoever had slipped up, revealing that the drainers had access to Civil Defense's schedules, thus causing them to move their assault earlier.

A long aluminum rod ran through the tall copper spool, its ends extending well into each of the mesh cones. The last step below ground was to connect dozens of thin filaments from the steel mesh to the aluminum pole. Ascher worked as quickly as his thick fingers could to secure the delicate wiring.

He had three glow rods tucked into his jacket pocket and the heavy coil of cable he'd carry to the surface was waiting by the ladder.

Ascher finished attaching the final filament and let out a little victory whoop. He dragged a sleeve across his brow, wiping off a mixture of sweat and dust. He looked down at his pocket watch as he hurried toward the ladder. 10:46 a.m. It was going to be goddamn close. Russell hefted the heavy length of wire up and worked it over his neck and one shoulder to hang across his broad torso.

He glanced once more around the small room, making sure there were no errant scraps of metal or loose wires, then cracked a glow rod, shaking it to brighten the ethereal green light. Russell took hold of the rickety wooden ladder and began his ascent. The rungs groaned under his weight.

Mayor Dreg's eyes darted about the room. He was working hard to keep his cool. No one had seen Ridley Strayer in two hours and now that Major Engel had found the colonel's mobile phone and sidearm, an undercurrent of alarm was drifting through the Meeting Hall.

"Probably got a case of the runs or something," Franklin said, forcing a little laugh. "That'll lead a man to drop everything for a while, ey?" When Engel responded only with furrowed brows, Dreg abandoned any further attempts at levity. He scratched roughly at an itch on the side of his nose. As much as he loathed the bastard personally, Dreg had not appointed Strayer the head of his martial forces for conversation, but because he was damn good at affairs of defense. And attack. It was unclear just what this operation would be.

"Colonel Strayer is the last man in the world who would lose his pistol, Mayor. The gun was just lying in the sand. And his mobile . . . this isn't good at all."

"Well, check the security cameras again! Ask the men again!"

"What would change, sir?"

Major Engel had already ordered a full review of every Outpost camera log and had personally questioned or sent his top captains to question every single Civil Defense Force soldier and outrider not dispatched to the field. The soldiers knew nothing, all of them merely following the orders of their designated roles; most of the Civil Defense men left around the Meeting Hall were glued to computer screens tracking flight patterns, heat and infrared monitors, and communications from the field.

And as far as Engel knew, there were only two outriders left within miles of home base: a doddering old timer named Ryan Cannell and a cold-eyed man who gave his name only as Scofield.

Dreg paced back and forth behind Engel, who was typing away at his console, feigning work as he let his mind run through the possibilities. Or probabilities, to be more accurate: he had to operate under the assumption that Colonel Strayer was at best compromised, likely dead. How, the Major scrambled to understand. No one had seen anything unusual, there had been no signs of struggle—Strayer had simply walked out of the Meeting Hall to place a call and disappeared.

Engel's thinking was jarringly interrupted when Dreg suddenly boomed: "Mr. Scofield! My friend!"

The outrider stood in the doorway of the Meeting Hall. The Mayor was rushing to meet him. He took up Scofield's right hand in both of his, shaking it vigorously. Scofield's flesh was limp and cold.

"Tell me what's what out there, old man!" Dreg exclaimed loudly enough that most men in the room could hear despite the constant drone of gear and murmuring voices.

"We already debriefed him, Mr. Mayor," Engel said, coming up behind Dreg. "He just got back from running horsefeed. I need to show you something on—"

"In a minute, Engel!" Dreg waved a dismissive hand over one shoulder. The Major's dark lips flattened out, his eyes narrowed. He didn't care to be taken so lightly. Especially when he had just come up with something very odd. There were strange dark patches emerging all around the sunfield, picked up by heat sensing drones. The officer had no clue what could be causing areas of cooler signature. Shaking his head, Engel turned to walk away and consult with his team.

"So? What's happening in my field?" Dreg asked.

"I got nothing to tell you as of now, Frank. I gotta go see about my horse." Scofield's eyes were ablaze, fixing The Mayor with a gaze so intent Dreg blanched. "I need to go see my horse right now."

"But surely—"

"It was all quiet where I saw, Mayor. Quiet as the grave."

Engel heard the door shut and glanced back over his shoulder to see Dreg standing alone. The Major hid a little smile, happy someone had slammed a door in The Mayor's face. As he sat back down to continue tracking the heat sensors, he wondered why the outrider was so intent on seeing his horse. Hadn't he just come in from a route?

Scofield had already gone to check on Reese—he'd jogged three miles straight to the stable after the train stopped to let him out. He had spent almost five full minutes with his arms around her neck, whispering to her and caressing her smooth, firm flesh, savoring the familiar smell of the one thing still steady in his world. The horse, for her part, had whinnied and neighed and tossed her mane, stamping with excitement at his arrival. She was every bit as thrilled by the reunion.

*What the hell do we do now, girl?* Scofield had whispered to her over and over again in his mind. Never before in all his life had he felt so totally unsure what was righteous and what was wrong. If there had been a way to disappear that very moment, to leave New Las Vegas and the sunfield and all of it behind, he would have done it, if only he could bring his horse.

When he left the stable, heading toward his little home—where else to go?—three Civil Defense soldiers had stopped him. He had lied through his teeth to the men, a rarity for Scofield. He loathed deceit. But in the face of all he now knew, he had to keep himself as his only council for the time being. Later there would be time to . . . *to decide, I guess,* he thought with heavy heart.

For now, though, what Scofield needed was information—no time even to grab a shower and fresh set of drawers. And with the Outpost overrun with city boys and apparently devoid of riders, there was only one place to go. Scofield pushed open the door to Matteson's Place and stepped inside.

It was cool within the bar; several degrees cooler than the warming late morning air outside. Only a few lamps shined, and Scofield made his way across the room slowly to let his eyes adjust. There was no one in sight and no sounds save the trickle from a brewing coffee pot and the quiet hum of the ventilation system. Scofield stopped at the bar, curling his thumbs under the smooth wooden lip and pressing his fingers down on the bar top. He stood there, holding on, for a few long breaths, letting his hands drop only as the backroom door opened.

"Hey, Scof."

"Hey Matteson."

Matteson checked the coffee pot and flipped a switch on its side. His back turned to the outrider, he rubbed at both eyes with the sides of his index fingers, then ran his palms across his white shirt to smooth wrinkles from the fabric.

"You seen Boss Hutton?"

"No," the bartender replied, turning to face Scofield. "Not since early this morning. Ain't seen any of you boys in hours."

"Yeah—I guess we're all at the office."

"Seems that way. You heard about the plans? For eleven or so? Won't be long now."

"No, I wasn't . . . I haven't heard."

"Figured. Hutton's gonna sound the sirens early. Start everything at eleven, not wait until one. May still be a few aircraft en route but I guess Dreg got impatient. Or someone got wind of something."

Scofield scratched his chin. "Did Hut tell you all that?"

"People talk. I know all sorts of things, Scofield." Matteson picked up a tumbler and set it before the outrider. He looked down at the empty glass. "You want a bourbon? Or maybe you're ready for something different."

Matteson's eyes were intense—glowing—when he lifted his gaze to meet Scofield's. His face took on an aspect the outrider had never seen on it before; gone was the standard half-smile, the lifted brows. After a pause, Matteson tilted his head to one side as if to prompt a response.

"I don't know what I want, Matt." Scofield eased down onto a stool, breaking eye contact. "Not the usual. Not . . . I don't know. I guess you tried another drink, huh?" Getting no response but a softer though inscrutable face, Scofield whispered: "I guess I'll just have some of that coffee. For now."

# 24

Buss Hutton hung up the ancient phone with a sigh. No answer from Colonel Strayer and no one picking up at the Meeting Hall. No answer at Matteson's Place. He'd tried a few random calls to city numbers and gotten people on the line, so it wasn't a problem with the cracked and rusting handset attached to the concrete wall of the sirenhouse. Which was unsettling—an old broken phone would have made plenty of sense.

Hutton checked his wristwatch. 10:51 a.m. Just minutes to go, *and no going back. Time to draw these bastards into the open. Time to fight.* He pulled off his hat and glanced up at the sky. It was pure blue and cloudless. The sun was bright and the day would be warmer than any in the weeks preceding it. A light breeze stirred the loose top layer of sand. The Boss pulled a pack of cigarettes from his jacket—he had given up the dream of ever quitting them again—and lit a smoke, leaning against the sirenhouse, still hatless.

Little pings and clanks sounded beneath the hood of the jeep parked nearby. The drive all the way around the eastern tip of the sunfield to this station had taken him the better part of two hours. Hutton had not stopped once, but he had slowed down to a crawl each time he passed a Civil Defense squad or a group of vehicles or one of the many forward operating posts the soldiers had established. It all looked neat and tidy— men in matching uniforms with matching weapons and dozens of menacing assault vehicles and overhead the near-constant whine of engines.

Helicopters and unmanned drones and a few large surveillance craft were flying dozens of patterns over the field. This was the first time all day Hutton had not been able to hear any mechanical noise. He savored the moment, taking slow drags from the cigarette and trying to let his mind go blank. *How many years did you think it would go on like that? Ain't you lucky, really? What were you gonna do when these knees gave out? When this brain started going sour? Shuffle around at night and read the papers in the morning? They still even print the paper? You got a pretty lucky run, ol boy.*

The sound of a horse fast approaching shook Hutton back into the present. The rider was coming from the west, obscured by the sirenhouse. Hutton dropped the smoke and jammed his hat back on, drawing his pistol. He eased around the southern corner of the little building, keeping his body tight to the cinderblock walls. When The Boss reached the southwest edge of the sirenhouse, he cocked his six-shooter and stepped into the clear, keeping the gun down by his thigh.

A smile turned up Hutton's lips and he immediately eased the hammer back down and returned his pistol to its holster. The outrider rode to within a few feet of The Boss and then reined his horse to a halt.

Joseph Bay dismounted and walked over to Hutton. He was not smiling. Hutton's grin melted back into his gray whiskers.

"How're the Bay Brothers holdin' up, Joe?"

"Ain't no Bay Brothers left." His face was hard as marble. "There's just Joe B." Joseph lowered his head, looking down at the desert. His shoulders rose and fell heavily, obviously surging with emotion though the face above them betrayed no hint of feeling.

Hutton took in a breath and began to speak, but only succeeded in stammering "Christ, man . . . I—damn Joe . . . damn . . . I got no idea what to say."

Joseph raised a hand, palm out, to stop any further attempt at consolation. Slowly, he turned his hand around until he was looking down at its palm. His fingers curled into a fist. Finally he raised his eyes. They fell on Hutton but saw nothing—his gaze was endless.

"I aim to join my kin soon. With enough blood on my hands to squeeze the Devil a glass when I meet him."

"Joe, I know it hurts bad, believe me I know, but what you—"

"It's done, Hut. It's already finished. I just gotta go through the motions. I heard your ol' jeep and wanted to come by and shake your hand one more time. That's it. It's already done."

Bay extended his hand and immediately Boss Hutton took it in his own, squeezing hard. Joseph's eyes finally seemed to focus and Hutton held them with his own for a second, then nodded. The handshake ended and Joseph stepped back, turning his head in a slow pan across the horizon. Then he wheeled and walked back toward his horse with quick, long strides.

As Bay settled into his saddle and gathered the reins in his hands, he looked back at The Boss one more time.

"Ride hard, Joe," Hutton raised an index finger to his hat brim, then pointed at the outrider. Bay nodded, a strange smile on his face. Then he spun the horse about and set his spurs into the colt.

Hutton watched Joseph Bay for several minutes as he galloped toward the field. When the horse and rider were no more than a distant object, no longer audible, The Boss walked toward the sirenhouse door. 10:59. Time to get on with it.

He worked his key into the plural locks then kicked open the iron door. All of the bulbs in this station worked, and Hutton twisted the massive dial to power up the system while bathed in a stark halogen glow. The flesh of his hands was pale and thin, almost translucent in the artificial light. A low rumble had begun, slowly growing into a whine as the charge grew stronger and stronger. Hairs began to rise all over the old outrider's body. The noise rose in pitch and intensity, beseeching Hutton to hit the button.

*Not a bad goddamn run. Pretty lucky, overall.*

He slammed a fist down on the large black button and the klaxons wailed across the desert sands.

"Go! Go! Go!" the bearded man screamed, waving his arm at the fourteen men clinging to the ladder above him. Sunlight poured down into the shaft. Though they had opened the hatch ten minutes prior, still the light of day was blinding as the drainers spilled out onto the desert, forming a defensive circle around the tunnel's mouth.

The squad leader came out last, screaming commands, spittle flying and catching in his thick brown beard. "Five right, rifles drawn, three right with charges! Four left, weapons, two left, charges! I'm with the left group! Move now, we have less than a minute!"

The group fanned out to tackle their assignments with precision—they had been rehearsing for weeks. Some of the drainers raised assault rifles to their shoulders; the rest were connecting primer charges to explosive satchels; all worked while running.

Scofield stopped walking and looked toward the sunfield, towering above the distant horizon. The echoing moan of the horns thundered through the air. *OK . . . time to head in. It's time.* Scofield began moving again. He was jogging, then running. He reached the stable and sprinted down the rows of stalls to find Reese tossing her head and shifting about nervously.

The outrider set to preparing his horse at a frenzied pace. Once she was saddled and ready, he led her out of the stall and toward the stable door, whispering encouragement to her. And to himself. Outside, he mounted up and took off riding toward the field. Scofield was still unsure what he would do once he got there.

"This is it boys! If it moves and it's not wearing black, shoot at it!" the captain barked as he leaped up from the folding table, jostling it and spilling maps and charts onto the sandy ground. He grabbed his assault rifle from where it leaned against the armored troop carrier and jogged a few yards north toward the sunfield, his eyes taking in the giant columns, a passing helicopter, the cloudless sky.

Turning around to survey his men, the captain felt a twinge of near-paternal pride. The soldiers were lined up in parade ground precision: each of the four squads was three feet apart, each soldier separated by twelve inches, all arms presented. The training would pay off today, the officer felt. He nodded to his boys, confidence rising.

"Make sure the reflectors on your shoulders are never covered. That's what separates us from dead men as far as our aircraft are concerned. We're moving in at a fast step. Ready! And . . ." the captain wheeled about, again facing the massive solar stacks a three mile trek from their position, "Move!"

Haskell pulled back the bolt on his 30.06 rifle and let it slam home. "So you been under us all this time," he muttered aloud over the persistent wail of the horns. His eyes on were a dozen drainers who had just emerged from an opening in the desert floor some eighty yards distant. *OK, Hasky,* he sighed, *get to work.*

C. J. took in a deep breath and let it out slowly as he steadied his hands. His trigger finger slowly curled inward. The sand was warm on his chest and thighs, the sun hot on his back. He figured he could get off six, maybe seven shots before the drainers zeroed in on him and returned fire. If two of those bullets found homes in flesh, he figured he'd have done his job for the moment and would take cover behind the QV pillar a few feet to his right.

The first shot was a bull's-eye. The third caught a drainer in the hip, taking him out of the fight. The sixth and seventh shot ripped a man's stomach apart. Then a hail of machine gun fire crackled through the air and shredded the sands around Haskell and he was rolling and then he was behind the column. Scores of bullets caromed off the metal pillar with loud thuds and angry whines.

*Your turn, Greg. Get shootin',* Haskell leaned a few inches away from the pillar to look east toward where Gregory White should have been positioned some two hundred yards away. The young man could not see anyone by either of the columns where he expected his comrade. The drainers were closing in. He flinched as a round skittered off the sand by his foot. *I got about ten more seconds until I'm hand-to-hand here, Greg.* Haskell's heart was beating out of his chest. He tasted bile as he drew his pistol.

Then suddenly the gunfire had shifted away—no more rounds were bouncing off the pillar or the nearby earth. Haskell chanced a glimpse around the column, thinking he'd spot Greg White engaging, but shocked instead to see Joseph Bay. And all the more amazing, the Bay was on horseback charging at a full gallop directly toward the remaining nine drainers. Bay had pistols in both hands, and through the exchange of fire Haskell could hear his wild howl.

Russell Ascher's boots landed at the bottom of the ladder with a heavy thud. The horns were still wailing above. But they were sure to stop any second. He had to throw the switch before that happened; before the surge of power from the klaxons dissipated.

The drainer practically leapt across the cavernous room, searching in the dim green light of the chemical lanterns for the little iron box topped by an innocuous looking gray switch.

He found the metal cube, scarcely eight inches on a side, and, falling to his knees, lifted the precious box a few inches off the ground, cradling it between both hands. Ascher shut his eyes, closing the tips of a thumb and forefinger on the gray switch protruding from the top of the cube.

In the next second, millions and millions of the amperes drained from the Greater New Las Vegas region during the preceding weeks would be released in one single, terrible wave.

"Get ready to see some serious firepower, Mr. Mayor."

Dreg clapped his hands, rubbing them together like a child anticipating a coveted gift. His black eyes blazed behind narrow slits of flesh; his teeth were bared in a savage smile.

He and Major Engel, along with a dozen other soldiers jostling for a view from behind the rotund Mayor, were fixated on a bank of three monitors, each displaying real-time thermal imagery from aircraft mere seconds from unleashing an apocalyptic barrage upon the clusters of drainers that had suddenly appeared on the desert floor.

*Fuck with my city, eh? Fuck with Franklin Dreg? Poor decision, lads.* The Mayor's smile broadened. He glanced behind him and then turned halfway around to face a random corporal.

"Time to wake those bastards up, huh young man!" He clapped the soldier on the shoulder so soundly the young man staggered, forcing a smile.

"Yes, sir."

"And about time indeed, boys!" Dreg bellowed, his eyes flashing as he looked at the assembled group. The Mayor took in a deep breath, ready to launch into a rousing monologue.

All at once, the lights overhead went dark. Monitors around the room flickered and then went black. The mechanical hum and countless beeps and crackling radios fell silent, replaced by the dying whine of numerous cooling fans winding down.

The Meeting Hall was plunged into an eerie silence. Only the diffuse sunlight from the windows set high in the walls lit the space, casting a pale gray light about the room.

"What the hell just happened?" Dreg whispered. A moment later, the first thunderous crash was heard from outside.


Noah Fischer had been hobbling up the dune to get a better look at who was exchanging fire. He cursed his broken hip, sweating both with pain and exertion. Something stopped him in his tracks—it took him a second to isolate the change. There was still the echo of shots from just over the sandy ridge, but there was no other noise. No engines sounded above.

Fischer cupped his hands around his eyes and raised them to the sky. It took a second for his vision and then his mind to focus on the plummeting helicopter. Down it fell, silently, rolling slowly onto one side, hanging for what seemed like ages, then it was out of sight on the other side of the dune. A booming explosion sounded as the massive craft impacted on the desert floor.

Then Fischer was hobbling again, faster than before, bounding ahead with his good left leg and dragging the braced right leg behind. He crested the dune, his head jerking back and forth as now dozens of aircraft came tumbling from the sky: a little gray drone, whirling about in a flat spin; a twin-engine surveillance craft, nose down and shrieking to earth. In the distance, plumes of dust and smoke and flashes of explosions peppered the sunfield.

Noah stood atop the dune, oblivious to the firefight taking place between three of his comrades and a squad of drainers, though the combat was a mere hundred yards away. *Oh sweet Mary Mother what the fuck is happening?*

\* \* \*

The lights above Timothy Hale flickered, then went out. He rose and made his way through the sudden gloom toward the wall switch, which he toggled up and down. Nothing happened.

Hale tried the door and found it unlocked. He stepped out of the motel room onto the wooden deck. David Flint was sitting in a chair a few feet from the doorway, flipping through the stack of magazines Hale had rejected earlier that morning.

"Hey, Tim. What's the word?" Flint asked with an affable grin.

"The lights went out."

Flint was on his feet in a heartbeat, his smile gone. "Get back inside," he ordered, pushing his coat open to reveal a holstered pistol. "Now."

Shocked by the sudden change in the man's disposition, Hale stumbled quickly back into the motel room. Flint slammed the door shut behind him and Hale could hear him working the lock.

"What's going on, Flint?" Hale shouted through the door.

"Everything!" The drainer's pounding footfalls receded down the wooden planks.

Greg White broke cover to return fire.

"What the fuck!" he exclaimed aloud. One drainer lay dead on the ground; the remaining five had turned and were running full speed away from him. Never one to look a gift horse in the mouth, White dropped to one knee and tucked his rifle butt tight against his shoulder.

He drew a steady bead on the slowest of the group, who was lagging behind by a good fifty feet, and squeezed three well aimed shots into the man's back. Crimson blooms splashed out through the drainer's beige cloak and he dropped like a stone.

Immediately the outrider shifted a few degrees up and took aim at the next drainer. Just as he was about to fire, something caught his eye: the fastest runner of the squad had just disappeared down into the sands. Suddenly another leapt and then dropped out of sight. White was just lowering his cheek back down to the rifle's stock when he heard the crashing above. He threw back his head in time to see the fighter jet plunging through two photovoltaic arrays. The massive plane seemed to catch for a second, tangled in the mass of equipment, and then plummeted the last two hundred feet to the ground streaming flames and smoke. It landed less than fifty yards from Greg, who was thrown onto his chest by the concussive blast.

With a wretched groan, the damaged QV pillar began listing. A series of loud pops sounded as thick bolts sheared along the pillar's length and then it was falling. His mind blank, instinct in total control, White found his feet under him and was running headlong away from the path of the falling column.

It landed with a deafening boom, sending up a mighty cloud of dust and flinging debris through the air. White was aware of nothing. He ran until his lungs ached; ran faster than his large carriage had ever mustered before. Around him now the desert was alive with falling columns and the fires of downed aircraft. Distant automatic weapons rattled murderously. He paid none of it any heed, surging ahead, shifting to the right to avoid a falling drone then veering left as an array broke free above.

Finally White began to flag, eventually stumbling and finding himself unable to regain his feet. He was exhausted. After a minute sucking in ragged breaths, as his mind slowly regained some semblance of thought, he realized he had been pierced in countless places by flying shrapnel. His jeans were sticky with blood. His face stung and a dull pain pulsated from his lower back.

The outrider had lost both his guns during his flight. He vaguely remembered tossing the rifle aside. The pistol had simply disappeared. Greg managed to crawl toward a fallen pillar, crossing the hundred feet of open land as quickly as his weary, damaged body would allow. At least he could take refuge under the column and get some of his strength back. Assuming he still had enough blood.

As he drew near the base of the toppled pillar, a depression in the sand caught the outrider's trained eye. *Gotta be a burrow,* he reasoned, changing course to crawl toward the relative shelter the hideaway would afford.

But when he brushed back a thin layer of sand, White found not a leech's burrow, but a hatch covering the entrance to a tunnel.

"We're holding fast a while, boys!" the drainer hissed through his thick brown beard. "Any of you hit?"

"They got Osborne and Jacob," one of the men a few feet down the ladder called back.

"And Dawson is hit, but I think he's alive," added another from above. "He took it in the legs."

"OK, we'll drag him back down as soon as we can. Hold fast. Did anyone get a hit into that fucking cowboy?"

A few of the men shook their heads; a few called out in the negative. *Goddamn madman,* the squad leader seethed to himself, wrapping his burly arms more tightly around the ladder.

"When we go back above ground, I want second team on security. Take that bastard out first if he's up there. He's got a death wish. We'll hook the drag lines to the arrays once we have the area secured. I don't want to be above ground for more than five minutes, maximum. Whoever is lowest," he looked down the shaft, fighting his acrophobia and straining to see in the pale light cast by a half dozen glow rods, "start climbing down now and get those cables."

The faces that looked up at him were barely discernible in the soft green glow, but every set of eyes was alert, ready, and hardened.

The captain rose from his belly into a low crouch. He looked around to conduct a quick assessment; all of his men were accounted for and unhurt. No more aircraft were falling and the damage seemed to be over in the field. For now.

The soldiers had been less than a quarter mile from the towering pillars when all hell broke loose from above. A cloud of ash and dust hung above the earth and trails of smoke rose from dozens of downed vehicles, but silence had returned to the sunfield, save for the crackling flames of a nearby crash site.

"What the fuck happened, sir?" called out a nearby sergeant.

"EMP I think." The captain pulled a pair of binoculars from a pouch on his belt and, after wiping sand and sweat from his brow, raised them to his eyes. "We may be in this fight without much back up."

# 25

Joseph Bay sighed as he let his horse nuzzle against his palm a few seconds longer. Its breaths were growing labored. The colt had been his partner for more than five years. Now it was another thing he would lose.

"Sorry, boy. Should have been me got hit. I'll see you soon." He took a step back from the horse and placed the barrel of his pistol between its eyes, squeezing the trigger three times without a moment's hesitation.

Cold as his heart had grown, Bay couldn't watch the horse fall. He turned away and was already pulling fresh shells from his belt when the animal pitched sideways, landing with a dull thud. Joe reloaded his six shooter, then knelt to gather up the supplies he'd taken from the saddle bags a minute before. These consisted only of ammunition and tobacco.

Bay took one long look around at the shattered landscape, the fallen arrays and smoke rising from downed vehicles, the haze of dust drifting over the earth, and then he slung his rifle over one shoulder and lit a cigarette. The hatch the drainers disappeared into was only a few dozen paces away and they were sure to have heard the shots. No matter.

The outrider walked with slow, measured steps toward the shallow depression in the sand. The cigarette hung loosely from his lips, the pistol was gripped tightly in his right hand. He found the fingers of his left clutching two crosses hanging from his neck. Bay wondered how many times he had approached similar looking holes in this desert. *All those years . . ..* More thoughts began to form but Joe banished them as he came to a stop three paces from the hatch. He blew smoke through his nose and trained the pistol with both hands.

C. J. wandered in aimless circles. Blood trickled from both ears and he could only see out of one eye. His head pounded and he struggled to form complete thoughts. *Gotta find that horse . . . gotta ride . . . should be moving . . .* He tripped over a sage bush, falling roughly to the ground after a few stumbling steps. *Gotta get up on my feet. Get up on your feet.* In his mind, the outrider rose and was walking again, but he had not moved. He lay crumpled on his right side, limply clawing at the sand before him with both hands. His mouth was bone dry.

Both of Haskell's eardrums had burst as the plane exploded on impact a stone's throw behind him. The massive four-engine charger plane had been circling at high altitude, awaiting aircraft with depleted batteries. It was the last vehicle to come falling down to earth that day; the pilots had almost managed to get the plane gliding under backup manual controls, but the flight systems were simply too dependent on power. Haskell had no idea what had happened. After Joseph Bay had gone charging into the fray, driving the surviving drainers back under ground, Haskell had sprinted to join him, then he remembered hearing explosions and then a QV pillar toppling across his path and he had turned to run the other way and then he was on the ground, deaf and half blind.

The young man finally regained his feet and began shuffling northeast, vaguely aware that he was headed in the direction of the Outpost. He had gotten it into his mind to go home to his little shack and take a shower. Haskell was scarcely aware of himself as he drew his pistol and aimed it at the drainer crawling out of a burrow not fifteen feet ahead of him. He fired two rounds into the man's back. The pistol jumped in his hand but Haskell heard only a distant ringing. He pulled the trigger several more times but found the gun empty.

The drainer slumped over to one side, then slid slowly back down into his hideaway. He had taken shelter in an old leech burrow and was alone. No sooner had the man fallen, C. J. slid his pistol back into its holster and continued walking with no further thoughts of the incident. He let his legs do the work; his mind was somewhere far away.

Wilton Kretch would have stayed put in the dry streambed for the whole fight if he'd been able. He would have holed up for days if need be. Shady had bucked him when the planes began falling and he had stumbled into the ditch while running blindly. Had not a drainer clambered in beside him to escape the maelstrom crashing down upon the sunfield, he would surely not have expended a single round that day. But when Kretch fired three shots into the back of the drainer's skull, he had revealed his position to nearly a dozen enemies, hunkered down within a stone's throw.

It was his keen eyes that were keeping Kretch alive. The drainers were spread out before him in a rough crescent, the nearest about fifty yards away, the farthest twice that distance. A series of dry washes—most scarcely three feet deep—and countless ditches crisscrossed this western portion of the sunfield. The network of streambeds had been cut more deeply into the desert by the recent rains. There were still patches of darker, moist earth in some places. And in just the few days of rainfall followed by a few days of sun, already some of the dormant plants had grown larger, lusher, and were flowering.

But though the plants could grow quickly, Kretch knew they could not move. Thus when a handful of sage bushes seemed to have drawn nearer after the outrider had briefly turned away from his assailants to check his back, he caught on to the drainers immediately. The camouflaged men had only moved a few feet closer, but Wilton spotted the change, raised his rifle and squeezed two rounds into the base of each displaced bush.

One wail of agony confirmed his assumption and took a drainer out of the fight. Maybe he'd killed another outright. Or maybe two. Wilton began to run through his options, the exhilaration of his confirmed casualty and the process of working out a plan keeping his fear at bay for the moment.

He fired another shot at nothing in particular then quickly dug a pack of cigarettes from his pocket. Kretch placed three cigarettes in his mouth and lit them all, then set two on the sand and pulled a few drags off the last. He slid down out of sight and jammed the butts of the cigarettes into the crumbling soil just below the crest of the streambed's wall.

Kretch pulled open the breech of his rifle and quickly loaded it back up to full complement, then set off crawling as fast as he could. When he figured he'd moved about twenty yards, he pulled off his hat and wiped moist soil across his brow to cut the glare of his sweaty forehead. Wilton slowly raised his head out of the dry wash, coming up behind a tall patch of desert grass. He flinched at the sound of gunfire but quickly realized it was distant. He gripped his rifle tightly and waited.

The wait was a short one. *Oh you dumb fuckers*, Wilton sneered. Two men had just broken cover and were charging his previous position. The outrider rose out of the streambed, one foot on the ground, the other stabilizing him against the sloping earth, and drew a bead on the nearest runner. Too late the man saw his adversary, and was cut down by a single shot through the neck.

Kretch took calm, deliberate aim at the second man and got off three rounds before the other drainers could return fire. Wilton took cover, then set off back the way he had come, running as fast as he could while keeping his head out of the field of fire. *That's four of you bastards. Maybe five. Come and get it. Ol' Kretch is ready to serve it up hot.* He sucked breaths and tried to force a smile; tried to keep his nerve up. But in the back of his mind, the outrider knew the odds were still soundly against him.

"I need to get back to the city. I need to get in touch with Federal Central Command." Dreg's voice was barely audible. His mustache quivered and his fists were clenched so tightly his thick, yellowed nails drew blood from his palms.

"Then you'd better start walking," Engel said, not looking up from the map he was studying.

"Excuse me, Major?"

"If you want to get back to Vegas, sir, you'll need to walk. Or take a horse from the stable. I doubt there's anything functioning within a hundred miles."

"Well, can't you get something functioning, goddammit!" The Mayor bellowed with such ferocity that his voice cracked on the curse.

Engel looked up, neatly folding the map and tucking it under one arm. He glanced back through the open doors of the Meeting Hall to make sure none of his men were listening, then took a few steps away from the building, off the concrete platform and onto the sand.

"No, Mr. Mayor. I can't. We can't. A pulse like that doesn't just turn things off, it destroys them. It will take months if not years to repair the damage to the infrastructure. Here, join me if you will." Engel turned away from The Mayor and strolled toward the distant sunfield, glancing back to make sure Dreg was following.

The two men walked about fifty paces wordlessly before Engel came to a halt and turned to face Dreg.

"Take a good listen, Mayor Dreg." He paused, his brown eyes staring directly into the beady black dots looking back at him. "Hear it? It's silence. Breeze and nothing more."

"So what can we do?" There was a plaintive edge to Dreg's voice.

"I don't know. Nothing works . . . we're at square one."

Just then the staccato crack of distant gunfire echoed across the miles of sand between the men and the field.

"Guns still work," Dreg said quietly, looking south toward the horizon of pillars. His mind was beginning to churn. "Wait . . . shells. We have shells, right? The kind that . . . that you fire out of a tube and they go like this," The Mayor described an arc with a one hand, then mimicked an explosion, pressing both palms together, then flinging his hands apart, fingers spread wide.

"Mortars?"

"Yes! That's it! Mortars!"

"Yes, sir. We have those. But we don't have the scopes or aerial coverage to tell us where we need to lay down rounds. We'd be firing blind."

"We have maps, right? Coordinates of all the arrays and columns? You just need to avoid those!" Dreg was suddenly elated, back in control.

"Mayor, our men are all over the field. And the Feds you ordered in and the horsemen. We'd risk killing as many of them as we would drainers."

"Some things can't be replaced, Major, and some things can. You learn about life's hard choices sometimes. Heavy sits the crown." Already Dreg was walking back toward the Meeting Hall with swift steps. Engel looked back at the sunfield, biting down hard on his bottom lip.

There was a soft knock at the door. Hale rose from the bed where he had been lying and staring up at the ceiling for the better part of an hour. Out of habit, he glanced at himself in the mirror, though he could see little in the diffuse light coming through the gray paint over the window panes. He looked tired and worn, that much was plainly evident.

Bags hung under each eye, eyes which seemed to have receded back into his skull. His hair, usually preened and parted into military precision, looked like a windblown field of wheat. Timothy had given up any plot of escape. He had ceased trying to understand all that had happened or figure out what was coming next. He had merely been waiting, and now, perhaps, here was an answer at the door.

"Well, I'm the one locked in. Go ahead and enter if you want." He called out, standing in the middle of the room. The lock clicked and the knob turned. Though he could not make out features in the glare of sunlight that rushed in, Hale easily recognized the silhouette of Maria Rodrigues.

"Hi, Tim."

He paused, then said in a casual voice: "Hey, Maria."

She stepped inside and looked around, then went to the counter beside the sink and helped herself to a bottle of water. A vaguely salty-sweet scent followed her across the room, like perfume applied hours ago and recent sweat. It was a pleasurable smell, and one Hale would forever remember.

"It's so gloomy in here," Maria said as she recapped the bottle. Again he was caught off guard by her Portuguese accent. "Let's go outside, OK?"

"Sure. Why not." *What choice do I have,* Hale went on in his head. He sat down on the bed to put his shoes on, glancing up and realizing that Maria had picked up two more bottles of water. *Aha. Nice long trip, then.*

It was warm outside for late November. Hale shivered awkwardly as his body adjusted to the sun on his bare arms and head and neck, leaving the cool, stale air of the motel behind. He wore a dark t-shirt and had his gray sweater cast over one shoulder. He stopped in the middle of the dusty street and, turning to face Maria, he was pleasantly surprised to find she was not wearing a beige cloak. She wore high, brown boots with tight gray slacks tucked into them at the knee. A loose black sweater, almost formless, hung low around her neck, revealing a snug white shirt with a plunging neckline. Forgetting himself for a moment, Timothy's eyes flitted between Maria's cleavage, her smooth, dark hair, the cherry colored lips, and finally to her coffee-colored eyes, which seemed to regard him with a hint of amusement.

"Did Candice explain any of it to you? Of what's next?"

"Not really. She just took me on the grand tour, as it were."

"Do you . . ." she looked at him severely, taking in a breath and starting over. "Do you understand now?"

"I understand less now than I did yesterday. Less now than two days ago. Two weeks ago. On and on. I don't know what I think anymore."

"It can take time." She turned and began to walk slowly up the street, away from the Town Hall, on the steps of which a few men were locked in a tense conversation. One was waving his arms in the air as if in frustration, another clearly trying to calm him. Hale watched the group for a moment, then took a few quick steps after Maria, falling in beside her.

"I thought I could hear explosions not long ago? They were distant. It was maybe an hour—right when the lights went out. What was that?"

"The sky was falling," she replied, barely above a whisper.

"What?"

Maria shook her head gently, dismissing the question. Then she asked "If we let you go right now, Tim, what would you do? Honestly."

"I guess I'd . . . just go to the office to check in, providing the goddamn Mayor hasn't officially fired me and would let me back in the building. Or no—honestly? I'd go home and take a shower. Maybe then—"

"No one's taking a hot shower in that city for a long time, Tim," she interrupted. "No power left. No water pumps. No nice cool air piped down the streets in summer or warm air in winter or endless power for the rich and connected and steep rates for the ragged. Going back to New Las Vegas is pointless. The city will be a mess for years to come, Tim. It will take millions of man-hours just to get the power back on. Then to clear the trash and rubble that will have collected. Then rebuild what's fallen apart. In some ways, maybe we did to your city what your city has done to so many others . . . but at least now it's been stopped."

Maria sighed, avoiding Hale's sidelong glances. "It was the hardest choice I've ever made, Tim, joining up. Now they're my people—now I know it was right, but it wasn't easy. You need to know that." Finally she looked over and met his gaze. "I was in Madrid when the field there was destroyed a decade ago. I was a student. I was as shocked and horrified and angry as everyone else. Until I learned why. It was worse there than here. Towns and cities bombed, burned, and paved over. And all in the name of what? Consolidation and fucking *progress!*" She spat the last words out as though they burned her tongue.

Hale made no reply—he had no idea what to say—and simply walked beside her with his head slightly bowed. The silence lasted for several minutes, before Timothy suddenly raised his head and looked around. They had passed the last building of the little town and were now entering the first foothills of the desert beyond.

"Where are we going, Maria?" When she did not immediately answer, he repeated her name, his voice involuntarily rising an octave. "Maria?"

Hearing the touch of fear mounting in Hale's voice, Maria smiled warmly, looking over at him. "Far away. I won't tell you where, just yet, but I'll tell you that the first leg of the journey will be by train, and the second by boat. You'll have a nice view out the windows this time, at least."

"Why are you taking me? Am . . . am I a hostage?"

"For now, yes, I suppose we have to use that word. Someday soon maybe one of us. If not, you'll have a story to tell when you're an old man. We won't hurt you. I won't let them." She stepped closer to him and reached out, gently placing a hand on his right elbow. "I promise. I always knew you were a good man, Tim. You just fell onto the wrong side of history."

"Almost got it! Keep going, young man!" The elderly lady shouted, smiling at the twenty-something as he landed another powerful kick against the window of the commuter pod.

"I can take it back over a while, if you're tired," called out a middle-aged businessman, down to his shirtsleeves and still dripping with sweat. The handful of able bodied men aboard the train had been working to break the dozen-odd passengers free for an hour now.

The pod had been cruising along as usual, carrying travelers from a suburb into New Las Vegas proper for shopping, meetings or early lunches, when suddenly it had shuddered and then come to an abrupt halt. The lights were dark, the ventilation system dead, and the doors utterly impossible to pry. Now finally, after thousands of heels smashed against it, one of the thick windows was starting to give.

"No, I got this," the young man coughed out, sucking in a huge breath. He peeled off his damp t-shirt and, bare-chested, exhausted but determined, took three running steps and pounded a sidekick into the corner of the window. The thick four by six foot sheet of Plexiglas finally gave, popping out of its frame along the bottom. One more kick and the entire sheet fell free from the car.

A cheer went up within the pod, all the men shaking hands and blushing at praise from the women. The young man leaped out first and began assisting others down to the tracks.

As he helped a heavy-set, middle aged woman clutching a large cloth satchel get to the ground, something occurred to the youth.

"You OK?" he asked the woman once she was on her feet. She nodded and he jogged a few feet away from the tracks. Sure enough, there was an eerie silence over all the land. No sounds of the city, though it was scarcely two miles distant; no noise from the factories just across the tracks. Nothing. A half mile away, the young man could see another commuter pod dead on the tracks.

He turned in a slow circle, incredulous and confused, and was just about to walk back to the pod to confer with his fellow passengers, when he did hear a sound, a most unusual one. From the distance came the sound of pounding hooves. Sure enough, seconds later some twenty galloping horses came into view, riding roughly parallel to the tracks. They were lashed into two longs trains and led by a few riders clad in the black uniforms of the Civil Defense Forces.

The strange caravan, like something out of an old movie to the young man's mind, was pulling several carts, atop which were lashed several bulky objects hidden beneath gray tarps. The horses sped past the stranded travelers heading due west.

# 26

"You know what, I'll be seventy before you're twenty-five, why the fuck am I crankin' this thing?" Boss Hutton straightened up then leaned backward, fists pressed against his aching lower back. "Come on down here, young man."

Hutton leaned against the hood of his jeep as the young soldier, twenty-one if he was a day, by Hutton's reckoning, climbed out of the ancient vehicle and joined The Boss. Hutton had left the sirenhouse, hopped in his jeep, and keyed the ignition. The old engine had turned over once, then locked up. Seconds later all hell had broken loose, every aircraft for miles dropping like flies and taking a good bit of the sunfield with them. The Boss had sheltered back in the squat concrete building until it let up.

As soon as he'd realized what must have happened, he set off walking toward the Civil Defense outpost he had passed earlier. The two mile walk had been rough on the old man, the return journey doubly so. But he'd found this young soldier to help him.

"So you just grab this part here," Hutton pointed to the short section of the L-shaped rod inserted into the engine through the jeep's grill, "and you . . . wait, what was your name again, son?"

"Corporal Alterman, sir."

"Don't call me sir and I ain't gonna call you corporal. What's your first name?"

"Um it's . . ." the young man seemed flummoxed by the question. "It's Marc."

"OK, Marc. Call me Hut." He clapped the soldier on the shoulder. There was fear in his eyes, so Hutton dropped the business at hand for a second. "Listen, this here is a real bad situation, got it? I'm not gonna sugar it up. We don't know their numbers, their plans, none of it. And I sure as shit didn't think these fuckers would have had the capabilities they clearly got. But you know what we got? We got guns and men. We got a damn sight more guns and men than they got, and we're gonna win this thing, planes and helos or no, OK?"

"Yes sir—er . . . Hut. Yeah, I'm sure we will."

"OK then. You just grab that crank and turn it like hell. Once we get this ol' girl's engine turned over I'm gonna have to set off right quick and not stop or she'll die on me. So don't take it for lack of gratitude when I race away and leave you here." Hutton extended his hand and the young man shook it.

The Boss pulled himself up into the driver's seat with a groan. He lit a cigarette and pulled off his hat. "OK, start spinning it, Marc!"

The corporal began turning the crank as fast as he could. Hutton waited a moment, then popped the clutch out halfway, fed gas into the engine and jammed the key clockwise as hard as he could. Almost immediately the motor caught, coming to life with a sputtering cough but soon settling into its old rhythmic rumble. Hutton waved the young man aside and began to roll away.

"Good job, son! Keep your chin up and barrel clear! Give 'em *fuckin'* hell!"

The Boss glanced back over his shoulder once as he eased into third gear. The soldier was already trekking back toward his outpost at a jog. *Good to have men like that,* Hutton nodded to himself, sticking the cigarette in the corner of his mouth and pulling his old weathered sunglasses from the glove compartment. *We're gonna need 'em all if we got even a snowball's chance in hell.*

It was nearing one o'clock according to the outrider's wristwatch. He checked the fuel gauge: a little over half. He could get two hours of constant driving out of that if needed, maybe three hours if he idled some and was careful with his speed. Then the jeep would be dead, likely forever. He had no reserves left in his jerry cans.

Nor did Boss Hutton have a plan. He had let himself focus entirely on the problem at hand—the jeep—and delayed consideration of the situation, but now alone and rolling across the sands he felt the weight of reality bare down on him. The distant hills were bright beige in the sunshine and beyond them the brown mountains cut vivid patterns into the clear blue sky. Miles to the north, likely just outside the shade of the arrays, he spotted three horsemen and thought to turn and intercept them, but quickly dismissed the thought. *What can I tell 'em? My boys know what to do as well as me. Shoot and ride and keep your fingers crossed.*

He tossed the cigarette butt over the side of the door and drove on. Suddenly, it occurred to Hutton that if indeed his assumption was correct and the sunfield was dead, he could turn and drive right through it, saving himself a precious hour as he headed back to the Outpost. The Boss slowed down to twenty miles an hour and eased the vehicle due north. He waited for the telltale warnings: the little hairs rising and the taste he got in the back of his throat. Nothing came as he drew to within two miles of the field.

By the time Hutton was less than a mile away from the first line of QV pillars, he was convinced that it was safe to drive through. Or rather not safe, exactly, as the area was swarming with drainers, but not suicide as it would have been a mere two hours before. With mixed feelings, he jammed the stick into fourth and sped up.

Something caught his eye and he glanced up and to the left. Maybe just a swooping bird or a bit of dust on his glasses. Whatever it was he had lost it. He drove on. Then, over the rumble of the engine, Hutton heard a strange whistling. In a heartbeat, the sunfield was alive with exploding fire.

Greg White had been stumbling through dim corridors for what felt like hours. Maybe it was minutes, maybe it was tomorrow—there was no sense of time in this labyrinth of earthen walls and pale green haze. He had managed to stanch the bleeding from his worst wound, a gash right above his left hip, but he had lost much blood. His thoughts swam now and then and he was slowing down.

Another intersection loomed before him through the gloom. He stepped into the new section of tunnel, looking left then right. The paths were identical: glowing chemical lanterns at evenly spaced intervals led off as far as he could see. White picked a direction at random and set off again, moving as quickly as he could. He gripped a long bladed knife in his right hand. It was his only weapon.

The outrider came to a sudden halt as dust filled the narrow tunnel. It was shaking loose from the walls and ceiling and at first the haggard outrider was utterly confounded. A series of dull thuds echoed through the subterranean maze and more earth shook free, billowing into the air. *Not again . . .* Gregory sighed to himself, feeling more weary than upset at the certain carnage above.

He began walking again. The thought did not completely form before Greg's attention was grabbed by a ladder a dozen paces ahead, but he was vaguely aware that there was nothing left in the sky to fall to earth. He slowed down a few feet from the roughhewn wooden ladder and waited for a lull in the thundering bombardment above, louder now that he was near a shaft to the surface.

As he caught his breath, he realized that through the din he could hear another sound: men's voices. They were coming from above him.

"I don't know what it is! I don't know!" The bearded drainer called from his position third down on the ladder. "It's fucking impossible," he said to himself, then raised his voice again, continuing, "Whoever is up top, stick your head out and take a look but be ready to get back down the hatch quick as hell!"

*How the fuck could they still have aircraft bombing us up there?* he fumed. *Something went wrong . . . something went badly fucking wrong.* Above him, sunlight poured into the shaft as one of his men pushed the trapdoor open.

"Afternoon, motherfucker," Joseph Bay hissed as he wrapped an arm around the neck of the drainer emerging from the tunnel. He pressed his gun barrel into the hapless man's ribs and fired two shots. The body was already limp as he wrenched it from the hole and then stood over the opening, peering down into the darkness.

Wide eyes stared up from the shaft and Bay opened fire, emptying his .45. The man fell away. Alive with fire, the desert thundered and heaved around him as Joe unslung his rifle and began shooting blind into the tunnel, the veins in his neck threatening to burst forth as he howled like a rabid beast.

At the sound of gunshots from above, Greg White wheeled to run from the surface shaft. Too late he realized a man had been sneaking up from behind him, a pistol leveled. The drainer pumped two rounds into White, one through the left shoulder, one low in his abdomen. Greg fell onto his assailant, driving his slender, long-bladed knife down into the drainer's neck. Cold steel slid between clavicle and spine. The drainer was weighed down by a heavy spool of cable draped across his chest and immediately toppled to the ground beneath the added weight of the wounded outrider.

White tore the knife from the drainer's torso and lifted it to stab again, but already the man was coughing blood. Already his eyes were rolling back. Greg pulled the pistol from the hands of a man already dead. He began to rise, but crumpled as he put weight on his left leg. Looking down to figure out why he could no longer stand, he saw a pool of blood spreading near his waist. And another from his left shoulder. Dumbfounded, he tried to move his arm, finding it useless. There was not much pain. But he knew this meant nothing. *I'm on the goddamn clock,* he sighed, shaking his head.

From up the tunnel shaft came more gunfire. White managed to roll onto his stomach. A dead drainer lay at the foot of the ladder, fallen from above. His robe was stained with patches of blood. They were black in the green glow of the chemical lights. Greg pulled himself toward the base of the ladder using his right arm and right leg. When he was only a few yards from reaching the bottom rung, a second body fell from the unseen murk above, landing in a twisted pile beside his fallen companion. The outrider stopped crawling beneath the ladder and looked up. Far above, a bright disc of sunlight shown down. There were robed men above him on the ladder. With a groan, he raised the pistol and began firing.

Haskell had just regained his feet after being knocked to the ground by a sudden blast. All around the sunfield, blooms of fire burst to life, tearing craters into the desert floor and sending sand and shrapnel flying.

"Not my day . . . exactly," C. J. managed to stammer aloud. His head had just been clearing and logical thought—along with a bit of his hearing—returning when an inferno had again rained down on the land. There had been a strange whistling, and then he was in the air and then on the ground, the breath sucked from his lungs by the concussive blasts.

*Not my week, exactly.*

The outrider got to his knees and wiped dust from the eye not swollen shut, squinting to take stock of his surroundings and ready at any second to be blown apart. He was again rendered deaf. Through the patchwork of black smoke and living fire, he spotted a squad of Civil Defense soldiers running due west a few hundred yards from him. They were firing sporadically at something but the shattered hulk of a downed helicopter and a toppled QV pillar blocked most of the engagement.

Haskell stood shakily. The sun beat down on his forehead and cheeks. The cord of his hat cut into his flesh and he slid bloodstained fingers under it, pulling the Stetson back onto his sweaty, sandy head. It was hot for this close to winter. And still. No breeze stirred the land. Through the columns of rising smoke, distant mirages rippled above the beige loam. Haskell stood still, staring ahead, filled with both awe and sorrow by the ruined field surrounding him. His body ached everywhere, from throbbing toes to cracked ribs to a pounding headache. There were patches of crimson on his jeans and torn gray jacket. His five-day beard was singed.

C. J. rested his hand on the grip of his pistol, trying in vain to focus; to weigh his few options. He could hear nothing but a constant ringing, and could see only half of the world he was used to through his one good eye. Thus he did not see the two robed men who had crept from behind a fallen array; who had thrown back their beige cowls and were working quickly to load a fifty caliber machine gun pointed at the young outrider's back.

But Scofield did.

Scofield gripped Reese tightly between his thighs and wrapped the lead rope of the colt galloping beside them around the saddle horn. He raised his rifle and sighted down the barrel, wincing as another shell landed nearby, sending a shockwave and debris through the air. The outrider drew in a deep breath, keeping firm hold of the rifle and setting his finger gently on its trigger. He would be able to get off only a few shots before the drainers would hear the reports and the horses through the echoing explosions. Or before they shot C. J. Haskell dead.

Haskell still stood unmoving, staring out across the sands, hearing nothing but a constant ring and the faint pulsing of blood in his ears, though now a familiar sensation stirred the air about him. The air seemed to be vibrating; alive, even.

Scofield had only planned to see; he had not planned to fight when he rode into the field that morning. He had not planned to kill. He was no longer sure who out here, if anyone, even, deserved to die. But there was no doubt that young C. J. Haskell deserved to live.

All the years Scofield had given to the field, every single sight, every memory of every experience, from the cold night air to the sunrises and sunsets and every time he had felt his horse under him and felt the trigger beneath his finger collapsed into one moment: he fired true.

The first drainer fell, shot dead through the back of the skull. Scofield's next shot winged the second man, who spun to face him, spraying bullets wildly from the huge, unwieldy machine gun. Scofield returned fire as fast as he could, emptying his rifle. He tossed it aside just as the drainer abandoned the heavy .50 cal and reached for the sidearm at his waist. Scofield rode hard, not bothering to draw his revolver, knowing a pistol was near useless at a gallop. The drainer got his weapon out and cocked in a matter of seconds, but it was too late. He lifted his eyes to find a mighty horse, deep brown with wild eyes and a foaming mouth, mere inches away. The last thing he saw was a calm-faced man with a gray hat looking down at him, and then he was crushed beneath charging hooves.

Scofield reined Reese to the left, toward Haskell. The young man had just turned around when Scofield was upon him, leaning down off his mare to wrap a powerful arm around his comrade. Scarcely aware of what was happening, Haskell found himself wrenched over double and flying off the ground, and then just as suddenly he was draped across a saddle. The familiar scent of horseflesh filled his nostrils.

He craned his neck to the right, looking up to find Scofield looking back down at him. Scof was shouting something.

"I can't hear, Scof! I can't hear!" C. J. yelled over and over again until he could tell Scofield had understood. The older outrider was mouthing something. He repeated it slowly, several times, and finally Haskell understood: *Can you ride?*

C. J. nodded, shouting: "I think so!"

Scofield tapped Reese twice with his right heel and shouted a command to the black colt beside him. The horses slowed to a trot, and Scofield drew the trailing mount close beside his girl. He wrapped both arms around C. J.'s waist, and helped the young man lunge onto the colt. Haskell slumped over the front of the horse, but wrapped his arms around the mount's neck and held on.

Still more shells were falling on the field, but they had shifted to the east and were growing more distant. Scofield watched the flashes over his shoulder, then checked to make sure he had the colt's lead secured tightly to Reese's bridle. He glanced back once more, taking a long look at the sunfield, then set his eyes on the rolling desert ahead. The outrider directed his horse northwest at a gallop.

"That's two shells on every quadrant. Every fucking bit of the grid. Are you quite satisfied yet, Mayor? Are you impressed with yourself yet?" Major Engel glared at The Mayor, hardly flinching as mortars fired behind him with loud, dull thumps.

"I'm not sure I like your tone, major." Dreg replied calmly.

"Who the fuck cares about my tone! You're ripping my men apart, goddammit!"

Dreg shook his large head slowly from side to side. "Insubordination bothers me, Engel. I've had men sacked for milder speech than you just used."

"Mayor Dreg . . . we have to stop the firing. Now."

Still fixated on the soldier's perceived impudence, but aware that he needed his martial expertise, Dreg decided to exact revenge on the rest of the troops. So some may fall, yes, but his enemies too would be cut down by the onslaught. A righteous trade. A thin smile formed beneath Franklin's thick mustache, and his great brows dipped lower over his eyes. He could feel the gaze of the dozen Civil Defense men on him. The whole firing base, a makeshift affair of mortar tubes, a tarp held up by a slender posts, a few nervous horses, and the soldiers Engel had found in hailing distance, seemed to be hanging off the tip of The Mayor's next words. He savored the moment; savagely savored the bass report of the shells as they fired off into the air and the awful rumbling from afar as they landed.

"We'll stop soon, Mr. Engel." Dreg raised the binoculars he had taken from a sergeant earlier that day, scanning the sunfield, neither looking for nor seeing anything in particular. He took a few steps across the now defunct glowline—they had established the makeshift post here solely because there was a concrete slab on which to position weaponry—and glanced down, brushing sand from his lapel peevishly.

"Just drop a few more rounds over on the eastern perimeter. Say . . . twenty shells. I seem to recall Strayer saying something about a build up there, poor fellow. Who's to take that man's place?" Dreg turned away from the field and glanced back at Major Engel. "You know, I keep meaning to ask you: what kind of name is Engel for a . . . um . . ."

"A black man," Engel finished his thought for him, incredulous that The Mayor could be asking such a thing at such a time. He shook his head slowly, looking back out over the smoky field. "I'm a quarter German," Engel finished, speaking scarcely above a whisper.

Dreg laughed aloud, nodding and looking away. "Well, that figures. Just a few more rounds, Major."

# 27

Kretch was screaming, sobbing. He wrapped his arms around his head, rolling back and forth in fetal position, praying for the onslaught to end. It took more than two minutes of pathetic moans and shrieks for him to realize that it had.

Wilton was back on his feet in an instant, his right hand wrapped around the grip of his rifle, his left reaching across his body for the pistol. He crouched low beneath the rim of the streambed, fearful that at any second another shell would land. But though the desert was still alive with the awful roar of exploding rounds, the blasts were undeniably moving away from him.

He chanced a look out of the dry wash and found himself surrounded by a veritable moonscape. The sands were blackened all around, pocked with deep craters, and smoke and dust hung heavy in the air. He counted three fresh corpses in the handful of seconds he spent upright. Just before Kretch dropped back down into the ditch, he spotted a horseman leading two mounts. They were distant but riding toward him.

Greg White reached the top of the ladder after an agonizing climb. His left leg and arm were both useless, and he had hauled his large, ruined body up one rung at a time, leaving bloody fingerprints on every bit of wood he touched. Now he was just inches beneath the narrow mouth of the shaft, bathed in sunlight and close to fainting.

White got himself halfway out of the shaft and collapsed, his legs dangling below. Through swimming vision he took stock of the field: it seemed like half the pillars had toppled or were sagging, sure to collapse eventually. Shattered arrays and ruined aircraft littered the sands and countless craters were carved into the desert floor, many of which were still sending smoke up into the cerulean sky.

With a groan, Greg pulled himself free of the tunnel, wearily rolling onto his back. It was then that he saw the burly, bearded man leaning over Joseph Bay. The drainer had stripped off his beige robe and wore a simple cotton shirt, stained with blood. Spittle flew from his dark beard as he raged, his voice low, his hands wrapped around fistfuls of the fallen Bay's vest, his face held less than a foot from the prone outrider. Bay looked dead, but for his blinking eyes. There were three beige-robed corpses lying within a few feet of the men, and others still farther out in the field.

The drainer had not seen Greg White, so intent was he on the man lying beneath him. Greg sucked in a long breath, let it out as a sigh, and set his jaw. *One last thing to do, you ol' bastard. Get it done and then get on with it.*

Mustering every ounce of strength he had left, White managed to slither across the fifteen feet of sand between him and the drainer in seconds. The man heard him coming, of course, and rose, pulling a .45 from his holster. He fired just as Greg reached him. The bullet tore through White's liver but still he raised his blade and jammed it home into the drainer's thigh.

The large man wailed in pain and staggered, firing two more rounds into Greg's back. With single-minded determination, Greg reached out and latched onto the drainer's belt, wrenching him to the ground. The pistol went flying as the drainer landed on the handle of the knife, twisting it in his wound. Again he howled, flopping onto his chest spasmodically.

Greg grabbed the hilt of the blade and pulled it free of the man's leg, pushing himself forward with his right leg and sinking the knife between the drainer's shoulders. The body heaved and convulsed and White held on, held the blade down, wrenched it from side to side, and soon the drainer lay still, bleeding out through the severed arteries in his thigh and chest.

White let go of the knife and fell onto his side, sucking in a few last breaths.

"You . . . alive Joe?" he managed to whisper.

"Not for long, bud. The—" Bay was wracked by coughs that brought blood and bile to his lips. After a moment he continued, his voice strangely calm. "The hour is here."

"I'll . . . see you . . . on the flip side . . ." White's eyes were closing.

"Off to hell with us. See you there." Bay coughed again. "Greg . . . hold on a second longer . . . I want to . . . share one more . . . ." He trailed off but was moving.

White tried to keep the darkness from closing in; to keep his eyes open. He heard Bay hacking and sucking in ragged breaths, and then Greg heard the flick of a lighter. Rich, sweet tobacco smoke drifted into his nose and then there was a hand before him, pressing a cigarette into his lips. White drew in a long, deep breath of smoke. He would never exhale it.

Joseph Bay sat propped up on one elbow, watching the life leave his comrade. He nodded and took the cigarette from Gregory White's mouth, sucking back a few drags himself. Joe Bay had seven bullets in him.

As he sank back down to the earth, the cigarette fell from his lips. Bay coughed once more, and raised his right hand before his face. It was covered in other men's blood. He smiled and then promptly died.

Boss Hutton pulled up outside Matteson's Place and threw the clutch into neutral. His hand was shaking so badly he could hardly get it closed around the keys. He paused, his left hand still gripping the wheel tightly, and looked around at the his old jeep. There were countless holes ripped into the doors and sidewalls. The windshield was a shattered wreck, half of it hanging out over the hood. Both rear tires were flat.

Still the ancient engine rumbled beneath the hood. Hutton listened to it for a good long while, knowing it was the last time he would hear it. "You done me real good, baby," he said aloud. "You done me good all these years. Saved my old ass today. I . . . thanks for that. For all that."

He turned the key and the jeep fell silent with a gentle shudder. Hutton sighed and found himself wiping a tear from the corner of one eye. Not so much for the loss of his beloved jeep—it was an object, after all, and though a cherished one, he was too old and had seen too much for maudlin whimpering over a lost vehicle—but rather because this was the first time The Boss had had a second of true quiet all day, and the enormity of the day now spread out before his mind's eye.

The pillars he had spent so many years protecting had been hard to see toppled and ruined. Harder still was the knowledge that those still standing were defunct, lifeless. The falling aircraft and the later bombardment had been terrifying, and it was with horror that Hutton thought of the many men dead in or under those crashing planes and choppers, or killed by exploding shells. But actually seeing the bodies was the worst. He had driven past scores of deceased Feds and Civil Defense soldiers, dozens of drainers, and he had seen at least ten of his boys lying dead on the sand. Some were missing limbs, hands, feet. Two were headless. Still others looked to have casually laid down to rest.

Hutton stepped down from the jeep with a loud groan. His aged body ached all over, not to mention the myriad cuts and scratches he had gotten from flying bits of shrapnel and debris. Again he marveled that the jeep had kept going as he surveyed the damage all over the vehicle. *Goddamn good piece of junk you were.*

He was not surprised to find Matteson's Place dark and empty. Enough sunlight drifted in through the smoke stained windows to cast a pale glow about the room, but against the far wall the bar was all but lost in darkness. Hutton shuffled across the floor, his boot heels dragging along the creaking floorboards. His limp was worse.

The Boss made straight for the gap between bar and wall and flicked his lighter, holding the flame close the jumble of bottles along the mirror. He knew this random assortment of liquor well, and it did not take long before the dancing flame glinted off the bottle he sought. Hutton grabbed his favorite rye from among the many bottles, then found a glass and walked back around into the barroom proper.

Sidling up to his usual stool, Hutton whispered a greeting under his breath. He paused as if receiving a reply, then lowered himself onto the stool. He poured three fingers of liquor into the glass, then carefully put the cork back into the bottle of rye.

"To all you boys," Hut said aloud, glass raised. "Goddamn I hope it's not all you boys." He swallowed the liquor down in two gulps then lit a cigarette and pulled the cork back out of the bottle.

Wilton Kretch rose from the dry wash with his rifle trained. Had he not immediately recognized Scofield and Reese, he would have fired with no regard for who the rider may or may not have been. Kretch lowered the weapon and pulled off his hat to show his face to the approaching horseman. Or horsemen—someone was draped across the saddle of the second horse, a black colt Wilton did not recognize.

Scofield had raised his rifle but realized it was Kretch even before Wilton removed his Stetson. He slowed Reese to a trot and directed her toward the outrider, who was clambering out of a streambed.

Once in hailing distance, Scofield called out: "Looks like you've had a lovely goddamn day, Wil!" There were at least ten bodies strewn about the area.

"Ain't seen much worse," Wilton replied, forcing a smile in which his eyes did not participate. Kretch recognized Haskell as the wounded man as he walked up to Reese, who Scofield had stopped a few feet away, and laid a hand on the mare's neck. She bristled and snorted.

"How about you? Good day for you two?" He inclined his head to the side toward C. J., semi-conscious and moaning, barely holding onto his mount.

"Not so much for me," Scofield said quietly. "Him either."

"Yeah. Guessed that," Wilton whispered. Then he raised his voice, addressing the young outrider. "How you doin' there, Hasky? Banged up a piece, huh?"

Scofield kicked free of his stirrups and slid off Reese, stepping close to Kretch. "He can't hear."

"Huh?"

"He can't hear anything. I think his eardrums got blown."

"That a fact? Sad story there. He looks pretty bloodied up overall, Scof. Think he's on the clock?" Kretch was studying the young man, his eyes moving from patches of dried blood on his jacket to lacerations covering his neck and exposed forearms.

Scofield waited until Wilton looked back over at him to reply. "No. He ain't on the clock. But he ain't in a good way, either."

"Yeah, lots of us ain't." Kretch glanced over at Haskell again, then craned his neck from side to side. His spine popped audibly. "Hey, you got any smokes on you? And water?"

"I got some tobacco," Scofield said, turning to his saddle bags. "But no water left. Sorry chief."

This was a lie. He had plenty left in his canteen and in Reese's water sacks, but the canteen was for him and the sacks for her.

"Here, take a few," Scofield said, tossing a pack of cigarettes to Wilton and turning away to adjust some straps on the saddle. Kretch caught the pack and fixed the side of Scofield's face in an icy glare. The implication of taking more than one cigarette was not lost on him. Kretch pulled five cigarettes from the pack and jammed them into a vest pocket, then drew out one more and lit it with a match.

"So how was it where you were, Scofy? What'd you see?"

"Bodies. Fires." Scofield did not look over.

"Yeah? Me too. I saw plenty of that too." Kretch came up behind Scofield and stood still. After a pause, Scofield looked over his shoulder. Wilton was holding the cigarette pack open toward him.

"You gonna have a smoke?" he asked quietly.

"Sure." Scofield turned and reached out, taking hold of the pack and placing a cigarette in his mouth. He left it unlit and again focused on his saddle.

Wilton walked around the horses. After a few moments, Scofield bent at the waist and looked under Reese. Kretch was standing close to the other horse and whispering something. Then he said aloud: "I don't know, Scof. I think our young buck here may be done for."

Scofield re-threaded a strip of leather through its buckle then stepped around the horses, stopping beside the colt to stand face to face with Kretch.

"He'll be fine. Lots of scratches and he got his bell rung. That's all."

"I don't know about that. I don't think so." Wilton turned his back on Scofield and leaned in close toward Haskell, whose arms were draped loosely around the colt's neck, his head lolling to one side. One of the young man's eyes was bruised and swollen shut; the other was open but staring at the ground, glazed over.

"I'm taking this horse."

"No. You're not, Wil."

"Don't get in my way, ya sonofabitch!" Kretch whirled about and leveled his pistol at Scofield. But Scofield had already noted Wilton's empty holster and held his own revolver down by his waist, the barrel trained on Kretch.

"I see how it is. Gonna shoot me in the back, were you Scofy?"

"I was gonna shoot you in the face if you tried what I figured you would."

Both men were silent for a few painstaking seconds, their eyes locked. Kretch sneered, chewing at the cigarette. His pupils were tiny dots in the bright sun, just now beginning to slide toward its western resting place.

Beneath the shade of his hat brim, Scofield's eyes were calm and un-blinking. His face was placid; friendly, even.

"This can go two ways, Wil. Holster that piece, shake my hand, and start walking."

"That's one way."

"That's the right way. Come on, man. Ease down on that iron."

"Why don't you tuck yours away first."

Scofield shook his head slowly. "You drew. You holster."

Kretch shifted his weight to stand evenly on both feet, drawing himself up as much as he could. It had always bothered him how much taller Scofield was. And that goddamn look of serenity he seemed to meet every little thing with. Wilton took a long drag off the cigarette, then slowly raised his left hand and pulled it from his dry lips. Smoke drifted from his mouth as he spoke.

"You know why I never liked you, Scofield?"

"No idea. But I'll give you a reason."

Scofield fired three shots before he was done enunciating the last syllable.

Kretch crumpled immediately, a sucking gasp torn from his pierced lungs. He pitched forward onto his chest and Scofield put a bullet through the back of his skull. No reason to let him suffer. Or to give him a chance.

Haskell dropped his head as Scofield turned away from Wilton's body. He had seen everything and understood, but figured it better to let his friend deal with the moment alone.

Scofield lit the smoke still dangling from his lips, then walked around the horses and pulled his canteen from a saddle bag. He took a long drink then cupped his hand, trickling water into it for his horse. He came back again and tapped C. J.'s shoulder, offering the canteen to the young man. Haskell wearily shook his head, then closed his eyes, again fading into semi-consciousness.

A few seconds later, C. J. felt the colt begin to trot.

Dusk was fast approaching. The eastern sky was melting from blue to purple, darker every minute, and the western horizon was just beginning to swirl with color. A handful of intrepid stars pierced the evening canopy. They had no competition from below on this night.

Major Engel had been able to find only one other officer among the exhausted soldiers who stumbled back to the Outpost that afternoon. He had ordered a haggard captain to assemble the remaining soldiers as best he could. The captain had listened and nodded and then set to his task, speaking only five words to Engel: "To a man, except me."

As the weary entourage—a patch-work assembly of three squads of Civil Defense soldiers, about fifty Federal troops, a handful of outriders, some civilians, and Mayor Dreg—plodded slowly along the pod tracks, it was toward a dark, cold city. A broken city. The beacon of spectacular electric haze shined no more.

It was just now occurring to Franklin that he would have no way to get into his home or his office—there were no staircases. And why bother thinking of the office? Over what did he govern? No thoughts of rebuilding, of helping those in peril—Dreg silently bemoaned all he had lost. He, Dreg, the fallen king, now panting and wheezing above aching feet as he stumbled the many miles back to his shattered kingdom. Only once did a darker line of thought creep in: *What have I done? My god, what have I done? I could have stopped this had I not ... waited ... no! No, this was bigger than me, I caused none of it, and we all did our damnedest!*

Engel walked beside The Mayor, his steps even and breaths coming easy. No staff or personal security force could be summoned, and Engel doubted anyone from the city would head out looking for Dreg on their own recognizance, so out of a sense of duty to the office, not the man, the major had committed to returning Dreg safely to New Las Vegas. Then he was considering turning in his commission and resigning forever.

"Wait . . . wait stop a second," Dreg suddenly whispered. They were his first words in almost an hour. "Did you hear that?"

"What did you hear, sir?" Engel asked.

"I'm not sure . . . I can hardly believe my ears if . . ." he paused, tilting his head to one side to raise an ear. "It sounded like a train."

"No chance, Mayor. All of our pods are—"

Dreg interrupted him, his voice quiet. "Not one of ours, no . . . it sounded like an old steam engine."

Scofield only looked back once to make sure C. J. Haskell wasn't following him. The young man looked over his shoulder more frequently, but kept the colt headed northwest. He had gotten back some of his strength and could hear a faint ringing, which brought hope that his ears would eventually heal. But it brought him little comfort. It was hard to watch Scofield riding away.

He pulled the note Scofield had scrawled and handed him a few minutes before. On the outside of the folded paper, the outrider had written:

> Don't read this until we've gone our ways. The city is located exactly where I'll point first, not thirty minutes ride. If there's anything there for you, head for it. If you want to see something different, ride the second way I show you. Ride a half hour and some, through the lower of two passes in the high hills. I've written some more about that way folded up in here. Get your ears back and keep your ass safe, Haskell. You may be the last of a breed.

Haskell had looked up from these words and immediately Scofield pointed southeast, his index finger and the sweep of a palm indicating a ride around a series of foothills. Then he pointed northwest, his arm held straight out for an extended moment.

Still not fully comprehending, Haskell had spoken, his unheard voice coming out too loud: "Where are you going, Scof?"

The outrider had shrugged, mouthing the words: "I don't know. Away from here. Alone." Scofield had pointed to the paper, fixed his young friend in a long, warm gaze, then reached out. After the handshake, the outriders parted ways.

Now as the sun slid slowly behind the distant mountains, Scofield lost Haskell among the shadows as he looked toward the horizon. Based on his course, C. J. had taken the second route and would soon behold the ruins of Barrisford. Scofield had written as much of what he knew as he could fit on the scrap of paper.

The last rays of light caught the distant sunfield. From so many miles away, it looked just as he had always known it; how he would remember it. He turned back east to face the coming night and prodded Reese up to a fast trot.

# EPILOGUE

Scofield had heard the billowing smokestack and the grinding gears long before he finally spotted the black train rolling across the evening sands, framed by the sunset's lingering afterglow. And evidently those on board had spotted him—it was coming his way. He clucked Reese into a standstill to wait.

The horse sidestepped and began to toss her mane and whinny, remembering well the last time this hulking beast had come for them.

"It's OK, girl. It's OK, honey," the outrider patted his mare on the neck. *I think it's OK* . . .

The locomotive drew up alongside the horse and rider, coming to a rumbling, clanking stop about thirty yards off. In the gloaming, Scofield counted four long cars trailing behind it. With an air of resignation, he reined Reese into a slow walk and rode toward the train. The windows of the cars glowed a warm yellow from kerosene lanterns and Scofield saw many passengers—all faceless, backlit silhouettes—pressed against the windows.

Scofield dismounted and covered the last few paces to the locomotive on foot. He stopped beneath the little side door, looking up, and was not surprised when Sebastian's head popped out of the open window.

"You made it through, mate. I'm glad for that."

"All luck."

"Maybe fate, no?"

"Never believed in it. Where are you boys headed?"

Sebastian looked back toward the west, then up at the sky, where more new stars were constantly emerging. "This was just the start for us, Scofield."

Scofield took in a breath to ask the logical next question, but before he could speak, another familiar voice called out.

"Mr. Scofield! So happy to see you in one piece!"

Old Candice Wilbee was making her way down from the second car, assisted by the large man Scofield recalled from the desert town.

"Thank you, Russell," Wilbee said, dismissing her associate, who climbed back aboard the train.

Scofield walked to meet Wilbee, stopping just far enough away that the old woman would not offer her hand. He glanced up at the passenger car, and could see in the lamplight the face of a pretty woman with dark brown hair sitting beside a blond-haired man. After a moment, Scofield recognized the man as Hale, Dreg's executive secretary.

"An awful day, Mr. Scofield. But a necessary one. An awful success, I suppose one could call it."

"Depending on your alignment."

"Yes, as always. Where's yours, if I may ask?"

"Right here." Scofield tapped his chest.

Wilbee nodded slowly, a kind smile on her face. "I thought as much. But I'm still going to make you an offer to come with us."

"Can't do it."

"It's not worth my trying to convince you, is it?"

Scofield shook his head, repeating "Can't do it."

Candice nodded, then shuffled over toward the open door. "I thought not, but just the same, give us a minute more of your time." She called into the car, "Ryan, Matt. Come out now if you'd like to."

Scofield was hardly surprised when old Ryan Cannell eased himself out of the doorway and climbed down to the ground, followed by Matteson, the bartender.

"Shake my hand, Scof?" Ryan asked, fixing his former comrade with an earnest look.

"Sure, Ry." They shook. "I don't begrudge you or anyone much anymore. I got no idea who to be against, at any rate." He shifted his attention to Matteson, who wore a beige robe cast back behind his shoulders. "And you kept me full of bourbon, so I'll shake your hand too."

"Still time for that new drink, buddy."

"No thanks, Matt. Can't do it."

Wilbee cleared her throat. "Mr. Matteson, would you indulge me?" Matteson nodded, and Candice turned to Scofield. "You may not know this, but your erstwhile bartender is a student of poetry. He has this one memorized that I've asked him to recite a hundred times if it's one. What year is it from again?"

"1906 or 7. Can't recall right now. It was by an Italian named *Castelnuovo*."

"Please, if you wouldn't mind."

Matteson looked over at Scofield. The outrider's face was an inscrutable mask in the dim light of the interior lamps. But he nodded once. Matteson returned the gesture and took in a long breath, then threw back his head and closed his eyes, beginning to recite the poem with a strong, deep voice.

Once countless men were filled with awe when first they saw
the Ishtar Gate.

When mighty, blue, the king unveiled,
How teeth were gnashed; how women wailed.

When shackled foe from Nineveh
or Chaldean (or many lands)
Laid eyes upon the mighty gate,
he knew the might of Babylon.
He felt the endless might and will;
he drank in timeless Babylon.
Immortal land now dead and gone.

When hooves like thunder shook the land,
When from his pleasure home he rode,

All hearts too shook like wilted leaves disturbed by gentle evening breeze.

And with his ruthless rugged men,
Did he lay waste, the savage Kahn.
And though the kingdom spanned the known,
All that was has long been gone.
(Twice ten miles of fallow awn.)

The vast and trunkless legs have crumbled.
The lighthouse shines no more.

The helots with their shouldered spears and zealots with their righteous tears and prayers for rain across the years . . .

Oh cold and sylvan (as it were), black and red the story went.

The countless walls and endless flanks and
All the grain grown in between.

The tribesman with his talisman,
Or alchemist who sought to glean . . .

Not built nor fallen in a day,
But fallen still.
And fallen still.

As all things will.

Matteson stood still, head back with eyes closed, for a long moment. Then he opened his eyes, looked at Scofield, and climbed back into the train without another word.

After a second, Ryan Cannell moved to joined him, calling over his shoulder: "You said you can't come with us. Not that you wouldn't. Is that right?"

"That's right."

"Would that have anything to do with that beautiful horse of yours?" Cannell asked, pointing at the mare where she stood a few paces distant.

Scofield glanced over his shoulder. Still looking at his horse he answered: "Everything to do."

"It may surprise you to know that the last car on our little train is all horse pens. I couldn't stand to leave without my ol' girl, either."

There was no more light from the west. The black canopy of night, studded with countless heavenly specks, spread out above Scofield, the sky as dark and the stars as bright as the outrider had ever seen. The kerosene lights had all been doused for the long journey ahead, and the outrider's ears had grown numb to the cacophony of the steam engine five cars ahead. He gripped the wall with one hand to stabilize himself, the other scratching his nervous horse's neck. His head hung out the small window of the pen, the back of his neck resting on its cool iron sill. He rode like that for most of the night, his eyes ever on the impossibly dark sky.

# ACKNOWLEDGMENTS

Were it not for a conversation I had with my brother, this book would not exist. It was he who planted in my brain the idea for a setting which grew into the novel you are holding. However, had Dave and I never had that conversation, the book would have been dedicated to him nonetheless (albeit a different book, of course). So thanks for the idea, and for being an effortless role model and constant friend.

Thanks go next to my wife, Kristin, who offered nothing but support and once again had more confidence than I that this book would eventually find its way to publication. And thanks to Ben, our son who joined us in October of 2013, for being a pretty amazing source of inspiration and motivation (and charming as all hell, too).

Once again my agent Russell Galen found the perfect editor for one of my books in Jeremy Lassen. Russ, thanks for hanging in there. Jeremy, thanks for believing in this book and for your astute and creative notes, which have made it all the better of a story. Jason Katzman, thanks for helping to sail the ship home—your help and guidance have been immensely valued.

Kevin Berresford, thanks for your early notes and enthusiasm; I'll keep writing books if you keep reading them. Mom and dad, thanks for your many readings of the manuscript and your constant support. My mother in particular deserves special recognition for her truly astute and excellent editorial faculties—all writers should be so lucky to have so careful a reader in there [sic] nuclear families.

Family, fellow climbers, friends in general—especially those of you who might see a little of yourselves turn up in this book—thanks for being part of our lives; Kristin, Ben, and I are all the richer for you. Especially if you buy ten copies.

Glendale, California—2014